MICHAEL SIEMSEN

RETVRΠ

ALSO BY MICHAEL SIEMSEN

MATT TURNER SERIES
The Dig (Book One)
The Opal (Book Two)
Matty (short)

A DEMON S STORY SERIES
A Warm Place to Call Home (Book One)
The Many Lives of Samuel Beauchamp (Book Two)
A Demon's Story Omnibus (Books 1-2)

Exigency

The Smiths (short)

RETURN

RETURN

BOOK THREE OF THE MATT TURNER SERIES

Michael Siemsen

Fantome
Publishing

Fantome Publishing, LLC
CALIFORNIA

FANTOME

FANTOME and logo are trademarks of Fantome Publishing, LLC.
Editing services provided by Red Road Editing/Kristina Circelli

ISBN 978-1-940757-17-9   (Trade Paperback)
ISBN 978-1-940757-16-2   (epub)
ISBN 978-1-940757-15-5   (Kindle)

Manufactured in the United States of America
10 9 8 7 6 5 4 3 2 1

Connect with the author:
*facebook.com/mcsiemsen * michaelsiemsen.com*
*twitter: @michaelsiemsen * mail@michaelsiemsen.com*

This book is dedicated to

ERIK V SIEMSEN

I have found power in the mysteries of thought,
exaltation in the changing of the Muses;
I have been versed in the reasonings of men;
but Fate is stronger than anything I have known.

-Euripides, Alcestis, 438 BCE

ONE

Abu Qir Bay, Egypt – Six weeks ago

Mushroom-colored sand gathered and disappeared into the vacuum tube, reappearing in the water forty feet away as a ghostly cloud. Soon, the sand would settle back to the sea floor, but it wouldn't help the ever-poor visibility at the bottom of Abu Qir Bay, the recently discovered underwater home of the ancient Egyptian port city, Heracleion. Leonardo Dunch shifted the mouth of the tube closer to the massive statue of the Nile god, Hapi, as a bright flash reflected off the chiseled red granite. Leonardo glanced to his right and saw the site's photographer give him a thumbs up.

Leonardo thought, *Why exactly are we taking pictures in three-foot visibility?* But then observed the murky water had cleared up quite a bit. Clarity like this was rare here, so he expected the better part of the afternoon would entail posing for photos next to finds. More likely, though, he'd be frequently asked to move out of the way.

Beyond the photographer's column of tiny rising bubbles, Leonardo spotted Étienne Laprise, lead archaeologist (and Leonardo's boss), in his blue-striped wetsuit thirty feet away, floating in front of the jutting sculpture of Cleopatra VII, and apparently tweezing its dark stone shoulder.

Étienne's working on Cleo again?

The Cleopatra statue had been coral clean for weeks and was just touched up the day before. And hadn't Étienne said he'd be on the palace ruins today?

Leonardo continued sucking sand away from his Hapi statue, reaching its naval after ten minutes. Scans had shown the stone went deep—possibly more than fifty percent intact—but he'd begun wondering if this thing might just be in one piece. Either way, he'd now reached a point where structural suspension would need to be affixed.

After a slew of cable-free photos, no doubt.

Étienne's vision of the site for the rest of the world was a turquoise-hued landscape with ghostly, carved stalagmites rising from an otherwise pristine sea floor. The fluorescent orange mapping grid and segment tags would have to be removed once again.

An extended beeeep and vibration from his dive computer reminded Leonardo it was time to surface for a decompression break. The forearm-mounted device was flashing a two-minute countdown to begin his ascent. Maybe a good time for lunch, too. The new cook—Josh something—had made those insane grilled cheeses the other day. It was nice to finally have another twentyish-year-old American on a boat mostly full of Frenchies, but nicer still that the dude would be making their food for the foreseeable future.

With the taste of assorted cheeses in his mouth, Leonardo turned his back to the statue, shut down the suction, unclipped the extra weight belt, attaching it to the large vacuum unit, and then bled air from his BC vest until his buoyancy stabilized.

Just as he prepared to ascend, something caught his eye at the far end of the vacuum's discharge tube. Revealed beyond the dissipating sand cloud, a figure was coming toward him. A black wetsuit with blue stripes down the arms. Étienne waved to Leonardo and gave him the "OK" sign before cutting left toward the palace.

Étienne? How—?

Leonardo spun around to face the Cleopatra statue again, baffled at how the lead diver could've moved past him so quickly. But still there, squarely focused on the shoulder, floated the person in the matching wetsuit.

Well, then who the hell is that?

Leonardo kicked his fins behind him, passing in front of the photographer as he snapped more shots of Hapi, and swam toward the mystery diver. A moment later, Leonardo reached the curious figure and steered around beside him.

The man had found something—some sort of hidden stone prism, like a thick, triangular carrot stick—and was carefully sliding it from an orifice in Cleopatra VII's shoulder. Leonardo shifted his weight to bring his legs back under him, then tapped the man's arm. The stranger's head snapped toward him. Through the facemask, surprised eyes and a pale-skinned, unfamiliar face greeted Leonardo. This man was *not* from the team. Leonardo glared, pulled the man's wrist away from the statue, and stabbed a finger upward, ordering the thief to surface.

Without warning, the man grabbed Leonardo's mask and yanked it off his face, sending stinging saltwater into his eyes. Leonardo raised his feet before him and blindly kicked outward. His fins struck what was presumably the thief's chest, propelling Leonardo away while grasping at the water in search of his mask. Inhaling air from his regulator, a small amount of sea water slipped up his nose and burnt down his throat. He snorted out and pinched his nose shut, opening his eyes a crack to find the mask. Nothing but a blurry green glare.

Surfacing too quickly would be dangerous—likely nearing twenty-five minutes at this depth. The computer would alert him to do his safety stops. But where was the thief? Was he coming after him, or making a getaway?

Slow down … Slow breaths.

It'd been a few years since diving school, where he'd drilled for this precise scenario, and he could only recall there was an acronym created to remember the steps. Was it C.A.L.M.? R.E.L.A.X.?

Where were Étienne and the photographer? Had they seen what happened? Was the thief getting away? And if so, with or without what he'd found hidden in the statue?

Leonardo staved off panic and paid attention to his bubbles to reorient himself. He tilted his head slightly downward, pressed the side of a cupped hand against his brow as if shielding sunlight, and waited for his trapped exhaled air to fill the space. A couple breaths later, his eyes sat in their new virtual facemask, and he was able to see again. He was floating about fifteen feet from the Cleo statue, ten feet above the sea floor, and slowly drifting south with the current. No sign of the thief. No sign of his mask.

His dive computer began its more urgent beep, accompanied by pulsing vibrations.

Outrage aside, his *life* was more important than an artifact. Ideally, with a few safety stops he'd reach the surface in ten-to-fifteen minutes, but he hoped that, in the meantime, Étienne and/or the photographer would see what had transpired, and stop the thief.

After three brief safety pauses, and the extended stop fifteen feet below the surface, his head was finally above water, Leonardo scanned about with stinging eyes, spotting the bobbing research vessel, *Pharos*, about two hundred feet away. He spat out his regulator and blew his diver's whistle, waving his arms in the air. Alarmed crewmembers spotted him and scrambled into action, jumping into an inflatable dinghy, and zipping to him in less than two minutes. The driver swung around him, curling the dragged tow rope around him.

"What's happened?" the ship's medic called out to him as the dinghy slowed beside him, and Leonardo grabbed hold of the rope. "Are you okay?"

"I'm fine," Leonardo called back. "Diver in the site down there! Taking a piece off the Cleo statue! A thief!"

The crewmembers peered around as they took Leonardo's heavy double-tank rig, heaving it into the small craft, and then pulled him up from the water.

"I see a fisherman over there," the driver said. "Looks like he's by himself."

Leonardo peeled off his neoprene hood, and wiped his eyes on the medic's shirt sleeve. "Get us back to the boat, fast. Any others besides the fisherman?"

"Not that I can see," the driver said as he restarted the small engine, and steered them back toward Pharos.

Ten minutes later, Leonardo and three others plunged back into the water as their liaison from Egypt's Supreme Council of Antiquities spoke on the satellite phone with his contacts. Security forces had already been dispatched to the beaches and harbors.

Below the surface, they found Étienne posing for photos. Leonardo's expression was all Étienne needed to see. Confusion morphed to dread, and he joined the group as they rushed back toward the statue of Cleopatra VII.

The divers gathered around Leonardo as he pointed at the triangular hole in the statue's creamy black shoulder. Étienne nudged his underlings aside and shone his flashlight into the cavity, peering in. He grasped at the bundle of tools strapped to his vest and found a thin ruler, dipping it into the opening until it stopped. Just under 12cm deep.

Leonardo shifted his focus to the opposite shoulder, and the identical triangle carving in the relative position. He used a hardened rubber pick to probe the outline while studying it through a magnifying glass. As far as he could tell, the groove had been etched in, as with all the other decorative lines. But the piece he'd seen the diver extracting had been of a different material than the statue's dark stone—perhaps red granite, like the vast majority of Ptolemaic sculptures from the area. Two months ago, he'd cleaned that very shoulder. He couldn't believe he'd overlook such a disparity in color and texture.

Leonardo turned back to the others as they continued studying the cavity. His eyes shifted to their feet and the sand beneath them. He tapped Étienne and gestured for them to back away before he shifted his weight and allowed his body to sink to the sea floor. And then he saw what he suspected, surrounded by tiny fragments of mortar: a black, triangular wafer. He plucked it from the sand and brought it up for the rest of the group to see.

Étienne's eyes widened, and Leonardo imagined the lead archaeologist was thinking the same thing as him: *How would anyone in modern times know about a hidden artifact inside the shoulder of a submerged, just-discovered, two thousand-year-old statue?*

Étienne took the piece from him, pinching two points between thumb and forefinger, and placed it over the hole in Cleo's shoulder. The surrounding stone's grain lined up with the triangle—a cap that had concealed the secret compartment beneath it. Unless someone had decided to x-ray the statue, they'd have never found the now-missing piece hidden within.

* * *

Étienne jabbed a finger toward the small black triangle on the table as his eyes moved from person to person inside the ship's cabin. The slim, habitually calm Frenchman was incensed. "Somebody say to me how this man knows to look for this? And someone tell me, why *now?*"

Their Ministry liaison hung up his phone and joined the group. "None of the security personnel at the ports have seen anyone come in with a small boat."

"Tell them not only small boat!" Étienne yelled, and the crew flinched. They had never heard him shout in anger. "It could be anybody! Merde. He could swim up to any shore from here to Alexandria."

"Étienne—" The ship's medic put a hand on his shoulder.

"Don't try to calm me, okay? I don't need to be calm right now. Whatever that thing was, I want to know! With all our work …" Étienne's voice faded to a whisper. "Why … why now?"

"I have an idea," one of the interns interjected. Heads turned to face the usually silent young man. "Maybe it was this."

He dropped a magazine onto the table beside the black triangle. Leonardo leaned in with the rest of the group. It was January's issue of National Geographic, with its enticing, bold-font headline:

DISCOVER THE REAL ATLANTIS…

The crew knew the issue well, each having pored over it, front to back, in search of photos or references to themselves and their finds. All eyes locked on the cover image of the submerged Cleopatra VII, her left shoulder in perfect focus, the triangular groove now seeming to pulse and glow on the page. As Leonardo had suspected, the milky black triangle had blended perfectly with the rest of the statue's thin decorative lines, carved shapes, and hieroglyphs. He scratched his beard nervously, glancing at Étienne, and their eyes met.

Étienne scrunched his nose, closed his eyes, and shook his head subtly. Leonardo got his message: *I don't blame you for missing it.*

"I am so pissed off, mes amis," Étienne said to the group. "Whatever that damned thing was, I want it back."

TWO

Philadelphia, PA, USA – Present day

UPenn's main auditorium could seat 1,259 people, according to the event coordinator, and though Cameron Langley's seminar hadn't quite sold out, it sure as hell looked like it had. Standing behind a cherry-wood lectern on the right side of the stage, wearing his second favorite suit, Cameron felt goddamned distinguished. And the audience? Goddamned rapt, if he said so himself.

"… or as Hardy referred to it, 'object-aided telepathy.' This rubber band on my wrist—you folks in the back can't see this, but trust me, there's a rubber band." Cameron snapped the band against his skin a few times, close to the lapel mic. "Ouch." Sporadic chuckles from the audience. "All right, so a few minutes from now, or a week from now, or even a century or more, a skilled psychometrist holding this rubber band could see all of *you* through *my* eyes—like a head-mounted camera—but *more* …" He tapped his temple with an index finger. "In my head, I was thinking about my notes, and the slide after this one, and the next items I plan to share with you; I felt a churn in my stomach, wondered what's good around here for lunch; felt the rubber band between my fingertips, and, of course, the sting of it snapping against my wrist." Cameron paused for effect. "Psychometry."

He waited for the applause he'd received in Tucson at that point in the presentation, but the audience simply nodded, wide-eyed.

Oh well. Moving on.

He clicked the remote to switch to the next slide, glancing back at the expansive screen where the illustrated profile of Dr. Buchanan now shone from the projector. A bit pixelated at such a size, but it was the only picture Cameron could find with Google.

He went on, "Now, as I earlier illustrated, such powers have been reported and observed all throughout human history, but the term 'psychometry' was not actually coined until the nineteenth century by this man, Dr. Joseph Rodes Buchanan."

Another click. A sepia-toned photo of Mrs. Buchanan painted the screen. "Dr. Buchanan's wife, seen here in this photograph, is who I'd consider the modern era's very first *documented* psychometrist, and was the subject of decades of research performed with her husband, and outlined in his 1885 treatise, THE MANUAL OF PSYCHOMETRY: THE DAWN OF A NEW CIVILIZATION."

Cameron once again gauged the audience's interest level. Still riveted, but they were surely waiting for him to move on to the 'star' subject of the show.

Not just yet.

Glaring sunlight burst from the back of the auditorium—a late arrival entering from the lobby, and the goddamned ushers didn't hold him until the break. Squinting, Cameron folded his arms across his chest, his gaze chastising the back of the room. The door swung shut, revealing a bearded man in shorts, waving his blundering apologies before slipping into the back row.

Cameron forced a forgiving smile and returned his focus to his notes.

Right. Buchanan.

He glanced back at the towering visage of Mrs. Buchanan, then regarded the room.

A hand beside his mouth signified a confidential admission. "Dr. Buchanan was a bit of a grumpy old fart." The audience chuckled on cue. "In most of his speeches—delivered to fascinated, rapt audiences, not unlike you wonderful people—he'd digress into ranting diatribes against the 'ignorant medical establishment,' skeptical editorialists, and pretty much anyone that questioned his research. Given a modern publicist and a skilled team of handlers, Dr. Buchanan might have, in his time, made 'psychometry' the household word it is today. Said handlers would've most certainly had Buchanan bring his wife and other test subjects onto the stage with him." Cameron pointed to the screen. "Why? Because thirty years into his research, Buchanan and his assistants had confirmed over *one hundred* psychometrists of varying skill levels."

He paused for effect. The sparse academics in the audience scrawled notes. Casual spectators merely gawked as they always gawked.

"Demonstrations are always more impactful than talking heads on a stage, right? Perhaps Dr. Buchanan enjoyed the sound of his own ranting voice. However, in his writing, we find a much more elegant, acutely focused scientist, and one more than capable of expressing a compelling case to those with the open mind required in his day."

The house lights dimmed as Cameron activated the video: a dramatic, music-backed, sixty-second slideshow of Buchanan-related images. Recorded back when he was still pinching pennies, Cameron had paid the aging narrator twenty bucks to do the voiceover.

He stepped back from the lectern and watched from the shadows.

"The past is entombed in the present, the world is its own enduring monument; and that which is true of its physical is likewise true of its mental career. The discoveries of psychometry will enable us to explore the history of man, as those of geology enable us to explore

11

the history of the Earth. There are mental fossils for psychologists as well as mineral fossils for the geologists, and I believe that hereafter the psychologist and the geologist will go hand in hand—the one investigating the earth, its animals, and its vegetation, while the other explores the human beings who have roamed over its surface in the shadows. Aye, the mental telescope is now discovered which may pierce the depths of the past and bring us in full view of the grand and tragic passages of ancient history. ... Joseph Rodes Buchanan."

The lights brightened as Cameron returned to the lectern with an earnest air. "I only wish he could be here today to witness firsthand the world he foresaw. You see, Dr. Buchanan believed as I do, that psychometry is not some supernatural gift bestowed upon a lucky few. The human mind is a magnificent computer, and the same wondrous gray matter that has given us quantum mechanics, the worlds of Tolkien, the great pyramids, and antibiotics is more than capable of *learning* a new sense. Without taking away from some of the greats discussed here today—in essence, that's all we're talking about: a sense."

Cameron glanced down to his script and read the penciled reminder added in Minneapolis: ***PACE HERE***. With hands clasped loosely behind his back, he began a slow stroll across the stage.

"Imagine with me for a moment a thirteen-year-old boy in a cave. This cave is deep below ground and has no light source whatsoever. Perfect pitch black. The young man was born in this cave and has lived there his whole life, never having used his eyes." A few *awwws* arose from the audience. Cameron flashed a smile. "None of that, now! Caveboy is purely hypothetical." Laughs. He resumed, "Living there alone, he isn't even aware of the *concept* of sight. He uses his other senses to get around, and this is perfectly acceptable to him. He knows no other way. One day, a miner breaks down a wall and daylight streams into the cave. Now, doctors know from a few sad cases that patients who've lived entirely in darkness for great lengths of time do not simply *see* when exposed to light. Some, in fact, are never able to see more than faint blobs of color or shades, if that. But for others—those who are able to *train* their inert sensory organs—well, what they see is nothing short of *magical.*"

He advanced through the series of beautiful landscape photographs, allowing several seconds for each to marinate. The onlookers loved him; they loved everything he had to say or show them. He clicked to the blank spacer slide and returned to the lectern. Sated exhales and murmurs of approval.

"Let's talk about Matthew Turner."

Postures stiffened and eyes widened. Sporadic applause. Even a gasp or two. They'd all come for this segment—the legendary name Cameron plastered across every brochure, ad, webpage, or event listing—a name that magically loosed the minimum sixty-five-dollar entry fee from each of their bank accounts. But after watching the last forty-five minutes of fascinating material, the Turner portion would now be mere gravy to the attendees. Expectations had been far exceeded. He'd sell and sign *many* books after the show.

Cameron revealed the next slide, the iconic photo of Matthew Turner on the deck of a treasure hunting ship, with tousled hair and a toothy grin. In front of Matthew and the crowd of men and women at his overdressed sides, the archetypal wooden treasure chest of gleaming silver coins sat open—the silver that had made Turner a multimillionaire at twenty-four.

"We've all seen this photograph," Cameron said. "One of very few images of Matthew, and a snapshot of particular importance, in terms of life events, right?" Next slide. "Equally familiar, we have the shot of a surely sweltering Matthew in Kenya, alongside a few archaeologists, holding the shovel he'd only moments before used to unearth the first of hundreds of metal domes—unequivocal evidence of a pre-human civilization of intelligent beings dubbed 'Narok People.' For those who've read A FIELD OF DOMES by Matthew and his late friend and mentor, Dr. Jon Meier, you may know this society by their real name: *Pwin-T* People."

He cycled through photos of the fully excavated sites and visitors' center, the woven metal armor on a giant-eyed Pwin-T man statue, an unopened metal sarcophagus, a model of a glass light tube filled with blue liquid, and case after case of weapons, tools, and other artifacts.

"Certainly hundreds of dedicated individuals have contributed to the knowledge we now enjoy of our humanoid predecessors, but everyone knows who deserves all the credit. Without Matthew, this fantastic past—and many others now added to the history books—would've remained forever buried."

Cameron reached another note penciled on his script. He continued to the next slide and turned with **DEEP SORROW** to observe the slowly zooming image.

"But not without a cost."

The audience buzzed quietly at the dramatic telephoto-captured image of a gaunt, ruined Matthew Turner outside his North Carolina home. A navy-blue turtleneck does little to hide his pointy frame, nor do the jeans that presumably fit him sometime long ago. Caught taking a bag of trash to his garbage bins, Matthew glares at the photographer with exhausted eyes. The dark circles, the sunken cheeks and wrinkles—all would seem better suited on a homeless, forty-something meth addict.

"This is the last known photo of Matthew Turner, snapped outside his home nearly three years ago. Since then, he's presumed to have continued living a hermitic life, cut off from the world. The clothing which protected his skin from unwanted psychometric energies eventually proved ineffective. Matthew has never been able to *turn off* his sense—a tragic consequence of unusually high sensitivity to imprints. Ever since the death of his father in Cuba, a devastated Matthew has avoided using his ability at all. He has groceries delivered weekly by a private service, and when they're asked how he's doing, or if a message could be delivered, the couriers always reply with the same rehearsed line: 'Our client values his privacy.'

"During this most recent phase of his life, and prior to the death of coauthor Dr. Meier, Matthew released two books: first SOUTHLAND, about the New World Viking colonies, and then DOMES, both of which will be available in the lobby after the presentation.

"Sadly ..." Cameron cleared his throat, as if choked up. "... the rumors of Matthew's death have increased this past year, and not only because no one's caught a glimpse of him. Frequent visits from relatives ended some time ago, and while the grocery delivery service continues, not a single piece of trash has entered the garbage bins. One of the remaining Turner devotees that still watches the house recently posted a note to her popular blog."

The excerpt from the blog appeared on the big screen.

> Grocery man #2 dropped one of the bags on way into side door. A string of those inflated packing pouch things fell out. Guys ... Food may not have entered the house in MONTHS. I don't want to believe this.

"I'm the last one who'd give up on Matthew, but I've had to accept the reality that his body was giving up on him."

Cameron clicked to the next slide—the same shot of emaciated Matthew with a trash bag in hand—and cast a doleful gaze on it. He began counting in his head, allowing the audience their time to grieve. It felt uncomfortably long. He thought five seconds was more than enough, but *somebody* insisted otherwise.

... 8 ... 9 ... 10.

He *"snapped"* out of it, and spun back round. "But we're not here to mourn a great loss to the world! We should celebrate what he was able to accomplish in such limited time, and we should look forward to the future he illuminated for us ... because while Matthew may have been the most famous psychometrist to date, I can say with some certainty that he is not the last!"

Applause. They needed that.

"But before we get there, let me share with you the parts of Matthew's life that aren't already known to the public, not accessible via a simple Google search, and actually," he mock whispered, "not even found in *my* book, PSYCHOMETRY AND MATTHEW TURNER, also available later. Autographed, if so desired. After we share our secrets, I'll introduce you to today's special guest, someone from Mr. Turner's past. And finally, I'll bring one of *you* up onto *this* stage to psychometrically *read* an object!"

More applause, whistles. If there were a thrill meter in the crowd, the needle would be pointed to max.

* * *

Cameron strode back onto the stage after the final break, and stepped behind the lectern. As the house lights slowly dimmed, the last few returning attendees re-found their seats. The din hushed to silence, and Cameron began.

"More than two decades ago, a young girl of only eight years, named Joss Lynn, was walking home from her New Jersey daycare. She carried her backpack and her favorite lunchbox, and was humming a summer camp song she'd learned a few weeks earlier. A car pulled up, someone she knew but hadn't seen in a while—a family friend. 'Don't talk to strangers' didn't seem to apply here, and she got into the car. An hour later, instead of being in her home, she sat on the side of this person's bed and watched with confusion as they packed for what appeared to be a long journey. Fifteen minutes later, the kidnapper was dead, police were talking to Joss Lynn's traumatized parents, and she was holding hands outside with a kid her age—a strange boy named Matty Turner. Ladies and gentlemen, please give a warm welcome to Joss Lynn Leland."

Joss's childhood photos played on the big screen as she strode from side-stage, waving and smiling at the applauding audience. She wore one of her nice conservative dresses with short heels, her bleach-blonde hair ironed and curved into a bob. Cameron handed her a microphone.

"Thank you for taking the time to be with us today."

"Thank you," she said, squinting and shielding the stage lights with one hand to see the audience. A charming, humanizing display, Cameron thought. "It's an honor."

"The honor is ours. Am I right, people?"

Joss shrunk and smiled bashfully at the ovation.

Cameron knit his brow into solemn mode, and lowered his voice. "How're you holding up these days?" He touched her shoulder.

"Oh, I'm good, real good!" she said. "I just feel so lucky to be here, and I think about Matthew Turner every day. He gave me the gift of a normal life."

"Or perhaps simply 'life.' Great to hear you're doing so well. If it's not too traumatic, would you mind taking us through that day?"

Joss nodded, and looked toward the audience, somber. "Of course."

So brave, Cameron snickered inside.

As Joss Lynn spoke, Cameron watched her from the side, gazing from her ankles, slowly past her well-toned calves, and up. So utterly engrossed was he with her pleasing form, Cameron failed to notice the theater's back door swing open as an attendee walked out.

* * *

The final cluster of guests left through the lobby's glass doors, each carrying at least one autographed book. Cameron sighed and slid his last carton of books out from under the table. He counted six empty boxes, and began tallying sales in his head. Not the strongest day of the tour, but far from the slowest. Still, quite low for these Saturday attendance numbers. Maybe weekdays were better for the on-campus events.

He gathered his pens and mailing list clipboard, depositing them into his laptop bag along with the tablet he used for credit card processing. One of these days he'd get a merch person to handle the transactions. He wondered if it came off unprofessional or down-to-earth, him running the table solo. The idea of having to *pay* someone, though: shudder. Perhaps he could—

"Are you able to sign one more?" A man's voice startled Cameron.

Cameron looked up to see a fit, bearded man in cargo shorts and a thin, button-down flannel with the sleeves rolled up. He was flipping through a paperback copy of PSYCHOMETRY AND MATTHEW TURNER.

"Didn't see you there," Cameron said. *Or hear you*, he thought. He resumed packing up his things. "Thought everyone had gone. I closed out my register, but if you have cash—"

The man cut him off. "Yes, I have cash. Do you sign the other books, too?" He gestured at the stacks of Meier/Turner books at the edge of the table.

Cameron thought, *Hmm, four more books would be a nice finish to the day.*

"Generally not—I mean, I obviously didn't write them—but if you want to bundle all the books together, I suppose I could sign them, if you wish. I may even have a couple more of my two in hardcover."

"Perfect. I'll take them all." The man dropped a crisp hundred-dollar bill on the table.

"Great. There's actually sales tax on top of that. I think it works out to one-eleven and change, but let me start getting these signed for you. I do have to get out of here. Would you like these dedicated, or only signed?"

"Dedicated would be great," the man said as he placed the rest of the cash on the table. "Just put 'Dear Matt,' and then whatever you'd care to say."

Cameron snorted and began to write the salutation, trying to think of some clever line about the name. He paused after the *r* in *Dear.*

Staring at the tip of his pen, the ink dot slowly expanding, he began writhing in his chair. His neck and back felt as though a heating lamp had just switched on behind him. His eyes rolled upward until they found the man's face, a small smile behind the light-brown beard.

Turner. Alive. Oh God, oh God—

"Whatever you want to say there," Turner said. "Doesn't have to be fancy. Or remorseful. Or pleading. Or a longwinded explanation. Really, anything."

Cameron closed the book and slid his chair back to put some distance between them. He could see it now, even with the beard and shorter hair. The bright eyes, the shape of his ears, the facial structure. Matthew Turner was actually standing a few feet away from him. And he was goddamned *huge*—not remotely the withering skeleton from the photo. "You're—"

"Doing much better, yes. Listen, while you're signing my books, could you answer some questions for me?"

Cameron peered around for another soul, but they were the only two in the echoing lobby. Through the glass doors he could see a lone student walking across the grassy court, and no sign of campus security. What would he do if he were attacked? Was that a possibility? If Turner wanted him hurt, couldn't he just pay someone else to handle it? Actually, would that be preferable?

"Questions?" was all Cameron could spit out as he reopened the book cover. He needed water. His mouth felt like left-out bread. He mindlessly stacked the books in front of him, as if building a wall of protection. Was Turner truly buying these books? Did he really want him to write in them? Surely a lawsuit was in the works.

"Yes. In the book with my name emblazoned across the cover in such a way as to suggest that I wrote a book called PSYCHOMETRY, you mentioned communicating with the First Lady of Kenya, my ex-girlfriend, Tuni. Was that true?"

Cameron's mouth and hand stuttered in sync as he tried to draw a comma after *Dear Matt* inside a copy of the book in question. He lifted the pen, observing that he'd actually written *Dear Dear.* "Well, the wording … It doesn't … *precisely* state that an *exchange of words* took place … so much as *express* what must be her feelings on–"

"Okay, so it wasn't true. A simple yes or no will suffice for the rest of these questions."

"Cam?" Joss called from the ticket office door at the far end of the lobby. "Can I come out?"

Cameron exhaled. Had he been holding his breath?

"Yes, of course!" Cameron blurted. "You can help me pack all this up." Joss began walking toward them. "And look who's here, Joss! Mr. Turner, you remember Joss Lynn Leland, right?"

A skeptical snort, then a stunned Joss's face lit up. "Are you kidding me?" She rushed toward Turner. "Are you flippin' kidding me? Holy shit … Is it really—Are you really … *you?*"

Turner appeared pleased to see her, but thrown off, awkward. She moved to embrace him, but stopped herself, recalling his vulnerability. "Oh, sorry! It's just so … Wow, right? It's so great to see you! How the hell are you? Other than *alive?*"

Turner smiled, shrugged, and stretched out his arms. "It's fine, actually. And I'm doing well."

They hugged and Cameron's transfixed eyes caught Joss's sleeve graze Turner's bare forearm. Her hoop earring bounced and then pressed against his cheek. No reaction. They separated and just smiled at each other, searching for more words.

"I like the beard," Joss offered, her eyes trying to take in all of him at once. "And you're so … healthy."

"Could we talk a minute?" Turner took her gently by the arm. As they headed toward the exit doors, he peered back and set cold eyes on Cameron. "You can keep signing all those books. Remember, 'Dear Matt,' okay? I look forward to reading whatever strikes you."

* * *

It was a particularly hot day for early June in Pennsylvania. Matt and Joss moved off the wide concrete path and into the shade of a red maple. Matt gazed past her shoulder to the auditorium lobby. Her con artist boss was watching them, then caught Matt's eyes on him, and shot his focus down to the books on the table.

"You *work* for that guy." Matt rubbed his head.

Joss cocked her head and squinted, a tiny smirk. "Eh … yeah. It's fine. I do have to work for a living you know, Matthew."

Bad opener on Matt's part. She was right (and merciful in her response, thankfully). Who was Matt to question her choices? Despite their brief childhood interactions, in her mind, Matt would rank only a hair higher than a stranger.

"Please, call me Matt. And sorry. When I saw you up there I was shocked. I assumed he'd conned you into being a guest at this seminar. I had no idea you'd be here at all."

"Appreciate the concern, but no, no one's conning me. And people not knowing about me being the special guest? That's the idea." She beamed. "Throw them some surprises. Exceed expectations. The 'today's special guest' concept was my idea. As if he gets a different one everywhere he goes. Adds to credibility."

"Wow, you're really into this gig, huh? Are you planning to do another?"

"I'm doing all of them. This is our fourth stop. We're actually partners in this, he and I, in case you're still thinking he's taking advantage of me. After he contacted me and we worked out some details, I reorganized the tour from the mess he'd begun, sourced much of the material … Hell, I wrote half of what he said today. I coach him on gestures and timing and such, too. He listens to me. Are you going to sue?" She slid the question in there without so much as a breath. Not even a shift in facial expression.

Matt's gears turned as he studied her. "No … No interest in a lawsuit." He glanced into the lobby where Cameron continued watching them through his eyebrows, pretending to be engrossed with signing the books. An idea struck Matt.

"What's he paying you?"

Joss frowned. "Well, that's not really any of your business—"

"I'll double it. Plus benefits. I have a health plan in place already, it covers everything. I think there's a thing like a 401k, too. Come work for me."

"Work? You … You don't even know me. If we're being honest, we didn't even know each other twenty *years* ago. What, you just want to ruin Cam? Punish him for using your name and slinging bullshit to sell-out crowds?"

Matt softened his face and set his focus on her eyes. No more glances toward the lobby. "No, I don't care about him."

Joss crossed her arms. "I guess I just don't understand why you would … *care* … about me. I'm a random stranger. Or worse, even. I shouldn't be any different to you than him."

Matt offered a small smile. "You are, though. You know you are." Joss's eyes wavered at this. Matt turned to go back inside. "Well, it was great to see you either way, and if you happen to change your mind—"

"About working in North Carolina? Thanks, but I don't think so."

Matt stopped just before the door. "In Jersey. I don't live in Raleigh anymore. I was only there because it's where my sister went to school. You still around Newark?" He gripped the door handle.

"Kearny, yeah, right next door." She strolled after him. "You know, when I first got my license I used to cruise past your parents' house every now and then. Never saw you, but I spotted your dad taking out the trash one night." She paused, remembering in a flash all of the news reports about Cuba, and Matt, and how Detective Turner was murdered. "Sorry about your dad, by the way. How's your mom doing?"

"She's good. Thanks." He left it at that, mentally swatting away the *"Dad"* thing. He waited, watching her face. She obviously wanted to say yes to his offer. He released the door and slid his hands into his shorts' pockets.

Joss pinched at her dress, rolling the material between her fingers. "So ... You said you'd *double* my salary? Like in movies: 'Whatever they're payin' you, I'll double it!'"

Amused by the voice, Matt said, "I don't know if I said it like *that ...*"

"Which, by the way, you still don't know. My pay, that is. Guess it's not a concern. What kind of work are we talking about, exactly?"

"Assistant type stuff. Organization. What you said you do for him." Faced with the reality of her about to accept his hasty job offer, Matt became aware of his own poor timing. The coming weeks would require all of his focus. And full independence. "Look, I really do have to take off. It sounds like you've got a great thing going here, and I didn't come to throw a wrench in that. Why don't I give you my number and if you're ever looking for a change, just reach out—"

"Where are you parked?" She grabbed his arm.

Crap.

"You're accepting? I mean, that's great and everything, but—"

"Yup!" Joss dragged him onto the path. "So let's get the hell out of here."

There was no backing out now. He'd done it to himself.

Matt pointed a thumb toward the lobby and the books he'd bought. "Okay, well ... I have to go back in for a second—"

"Do you?" Joss's mouth opened and continued rambling for at least twenty seconds: "I'll wait out here then. I don't wanna talk to Cam right now. I'm a chicken. I'll call him when I'm ready, so don't *you* say anything, okay? And hurry, if you can. Just grab your book and scoot. Or were you planning to talk to him more? I mean, if you were planning to talk to him, of course, do what you're gonna do, you know? Maybe just ix-nay on the oss-Jay talk, you know? If he asks. Obviously, you don't need my permission, if that's what it sounded like I was saying. You're the boss, right?"

Matt blinked at her.

Joss shook her head and inhaled. A flit of fingers signified either an apology, embarrassment, or perhaps a final, simple *"hurry."*

As Matt's hand returned to the door handle, Joss added, "We'll need to stop by my hotel so I can change and get my luggage."

* * *

Matthew merged onto Interstate 76. The highway bent rightward along the course of a dark green river. As Matthew negotiated the traffic, Joss observed a thin strip of a park across the river—a fleeting patch of green below a backdrop of grayish buildings, large and small. Joggers and bicycle riders followed a bike path flanked by bands of nature. Cam was probably still at the UPenn campus, outside the auditorium, sitting on one of the benches beside the main path, dazed and helpless.

Impulsivity wasn't some new, unexpected characteristic for her, but Joss was surprised by the magnitude of this particular whim. As far as decisions went, one would probably want to take more than a couple minutes thinking through this sort of *life*-level thing. It wasn't as though there'd been a ticking-clock-style "now or never" ultimatum dropped in her lap.

Oddly enough, though, sitting in the passenger seat, her purse and a bundle of books in her lap, Joss found her thoughts shifting to Matthew Turner's car—some generic Ford sedan—as her unforgiveable desertion of Cam withdrew into subconscious shadows. She'd expect a gazillionaire like Matthew to drive some exotic Italian machine.

It was quiet in the car, only the subtle rhythm of an indiscernible rock song spared Joss from the dreadful, nightmarish scenario of an utterly silent drive. New car scent and Matthew's deodorant or aftershave flavored the cool, air-conditioned space.

Awkward and unsure how or if to break the silence, she directed her attention to the books Matthew had actually bought from Cam. She flipped to the first page of PSYCHOMETRY AND

MATTHEW TURNER, reading the dedication Cameron's shaky hand had scrawled.

> *Dear Matthew,*
> *Real discovery doesn't come from new landscapes, but*
> *seeing with new eyes. We ALL envy you your eyes.*
> *–C. Langley.*

Joss felt a stare and caught Matthew sneaking a peek at the book.

His gaze returned to the road. "That's a pretty atrocious paraphrasing of Proust." He put on his blinker, checked the blind spots, and changed lanes, all in a peculiar fluid motion.

"Hm." Unaware that Cam was quoting someone, Joss had thought it a smart, impressive note. "What did he say when you went back in to pick up the books?"

"He just stammered an almost-apology before trying to spit out what I interpreted as an offer to someday collaborate on a book."

"Ha! No shortage of balls on that man, right? And what did you say?"

"I told him that, despite what would surely grow into an irresistible desire to somehow publicize and profit from our encounter today, that if he kept quiet, I wouldn't put him out of business and bankrupt him."

Joss observed Matthew's profile, his expression unexpectedly neutral. There was no irony in his words. No apparent boasting or self-satisfaction. "That's it?"

"And that I'd consider giving him a blurb quote he could put on a book cover."

"Oh, you've got him then. He won't make a peep. On the other hand, expect weekly 'reminder' emails for a while, then dailies: 'Hello good sir! Just checking in …'"

Matthew took the exit ramp for Trenton. "That's fine."

Joss aimed her chin ahead, though her eyes remained glued to this man's face. She didn't know him personally, but like with many celebrities, she'd assembled from what little she knew of him, a character—timid mannerisms, drifting gaze, whiny speech pattern, a victim—and he exhibited none of these. On the contrary, his demeanor bordered on zenlike, even with the Grand Central Station of thoughts she suspected was buzzing through that head.

Silence lingered as Matthew entered the New Jersey Turnpike.

She couldn't help but suspect he had second thoughts about bringing her along. She hadn't exactly given him a choice. The guy had generously offered her a job at a ridiculously high salary, probably expecting her to think it over, and then to either pass on it, or call him in a couple weeks. And now he was stuck in a car with her for at least an hour and a half. That had to be it—he was wondering just what the hell he'd gotten himself into. It'd explain his disconcerting immunity to her quips and energy. He wasn't even throwing her sympathy smiles. Or maybe she just wasn't as hilarious as she liked to think.

Joss's curiosity veered back to the earlier exchange beyond the lobby's glass doors. Was there no mention of her from either of them? Had Cam been so petrified that he'd been afraid to ask Matthew about her? Or perhaps he thought she and Matthew were simply heading off to grab some coffee and do some catching-up.

She decided to wait for Matthew to speak. If he preferred a quiet car (as all evidence appeared to suggest!), then she'd control herself. Deal with it. Not be annoying. Reject the compulsion to fill the air. Yes, *he* would need to initiate a conversation.

Nope. Can't do it.

"Cam's probably crapping his pants imagining what I'm revealing to you."

"Possibly," Matthew replied without pause. "May I see that first book there for a moment?"

She passed it to him and he set it on his lap, laying his free hand atop the dust-jacketed cover. He continued driving in silence.

"Are you—" Joss began, gripping the passenger door handle. "Are you *reading* it? While *driving?*"

"Yes. It's okay though. Just needed to see something." He handed it back to her.

"See something? Um, was it what I look like when I'm *flipping out?*" She smacked him playfully on the arm. "Is that what you needed to see?"

"Sorry if that worried you," he said.

She shrugged it off with a *what, me, worry?* smile. "Yeah, no … I mean, it's not a big deal. I was kidding. You know, just being dramatic."

He nodded understanding. Blank, humorless. Comprehension achieved. He glanced at the clock on the dashboard, as if to place a time stamp on this new data.

This was a broken man. This was where the kind of trauma he'd gone through eventually led.

Matthew continued, "Langley wasn't thinking about you, but that was then. You should probably fill him in. Best to not leave him hanging."

"Sure. Right."

Joss realized an instant too late that her sly side-stare had shifted to a full-facing stare. He felt the look or spotted her peripherally, and glanced her way. Busted, she shot her attention through the passenger side window, where a blur of guardrails and trees offered a less-than-riveting view. Not true. A tiny, warped version of him vibrated in the side mirror. No details, but she could at least see his eyes were on the road ahead.

Now she felt stupid. Why the hell was she acting like this? Was she actually starstruck, or was it just a natural response to the guy acting like a robot?

Matthew broke the silence again. "You can ask me almost anything, you know."

Is that so?

"Reading minds in real-time these days, huh?"

His focus held on the highway.

Joss couldn't let the invitation linger. He'd opened the door. "Anything, eh—?"

The quiet music muted and a ringtone replaced it in the speakers. Matthew glanced at the screen on the dashboard and Joss followed his eyes.

Incoming Call: Unknown Number

He mulled through a second ring, scratching the steering wheel with his thumbs as his eyes alternated between the road and display. A third ring, and he finally pressed a button on the steering wheel. "Hello?"

A man's voice filled the car; a faint accent—perhaps Russian—spoke through every speaker. "Mr. Turner?"

Matthew grimaced and mouthed a silent obscenity. He bounced the back of his head against his seat's headrest.

Shaking his head, he spoke with casual curiosity. "Who's calling, please?"

He turned to Joss and mouthed, *"Markus."*

"This is Markus, Matthew. Do you have a moment?"

Matthew decelerated, pulling behind a tractor-trailer in the slow lane. "Markus? Oh … wow, um … No idea how you got this number, but go ahead, Markus."

"Is this a speakerphone, Matthew?"

Joss instinctively pointed her eyes to the passing Pennsylvania trees, as if this ensured privacy.

"It is," Matthew said, now with shades of defiance. "I'm driving. Go ahead."

"It's good to hear that you're well enough to drive, Matthew. Mr. Ostrovsky will be delighted to receive this news, and perhaps my call will therefore not be in vain. Mr. Ostrovsky doesn't know what occupies or motivates you these days, but I've been authorized to offer three forms of imbursement in exchange for your time and efforts."

Joss could see in the side mirror that he was thinking.

Matthew's voice remained even, untroubled. "Tell me what he wants before getting to your 'imbursements.'"

"Confidentiality is of course implied—"

"Of course."

Joss turned to Matthew, and he gave her an exasperated look. He wasn't happy, but she relished this apparent collusion. With no clue what was annoying her team, Joss rolled her eyes.

Matthew mouthed *"library"* to her an instant before the caller, Markus, said it.

"The Library of Alexandria."

Matthew uncurled his fingers, and then rewrapped them around the steering wheel. "More specifics, please."

"The next large-scale Dead Sea Scrolls-level discovery," Markus said with confident punctuation.

Joss hadn't heard of this library, but she vaguely knew of the Dead Sea Scrolls.

Matthew glanced at the dashboard. "It's after three here. Where are you, exactly?"

"Ukraine. It's ten thirty here."

"Really? Are you in a bomb shelter?"

"No, but thank you for your concern. Shall I go on?"

"No. Call me back at midnight, your time."

"Very well," Markus said.

Matthew pressed the button on the steering wheel and music returned to the speakers. He tugged at his beard—in deep thought for a moment—then checked the mirrors, and merged back into faster traffic.

Snapping out of it, he peeked her way. "Sorry, you were saying?"

"Um ... I think you had said that I could ask you anything."

"Ah, right. Yeah. Offer open."

Joss regarded her sunset-painted fingernails. "Just so I'm clear ... We're pretending that call didn't just happen, right?"

He popped a piece of gum into his mouth and sent a conspiratorial smirk her way. There it was! A personality! Humanity! And, really, the perfect answer to her question: no answer.

Moving on then ...

"So, Matthew Turner, whatcha been up to the past twenty years?" He smiled again. Phew, she *could* make him smile. "Maybe start with the present, work your way backward."

He nodded. "Sure. But you have to call me Matt. 'Matthew' is for Mr. Langley, and the press, and people like the man that just called." Joss signaled agreement and *Matt* went on. "At present I'm only working on three things. My sister, Iris, and I have been working through missing persons cases. Confidentially, of course. It's not easy work ... bad news more often than not, but my family and I agree it's the most important thing I can do with what I've got. I also teach a self-defense class one day a week at a dojo near my house, mainly to women and kids."

"Wow, that's cool. Do your students or whatever know who you are?"

"No, I use a different name. Only a couple of the people that run the place know who I am and they're family friends from way back."

"So you're like a karate master? I don't think I knew that."

Matt turned the radio even lower. "Not karate. It's a very old technique called *sin arma*—essentially weaponless, or hand-to-hand combat—that was taught and practiced by a small group based in Spain. It hasn't been used for a while. Well, until recently."

"'A while.'"

"Yeah." He observed Joss strumming fingers on her knee. "Nearly a thousand years."

"And you learned it from a ..."

"Yes. An individual I've spent many years with." He tapped his temple. "Once you're all settled, if you're interested, you can come to a class and see what it's all about. All else aside, it's great exercise."

"It sounds like you're really passionate about it."

Matt shrugged. "I guess I am. Insomuch as I'd like to see it spread. I'm teaching it to the folks that run the place so they can eventually take over. There's no better modern, weaponless tactic for a person to decisively defeat a much larger opponent."

"Decisively defeat. Sounds painful. For the defeated."

Matt's phone buzzed and then chirped like a cricket. He picked it up from a cup holder and glanced at the screen. He held it out for Joss to take.

"That's my sister asking when I'll be home. You mind texting her back for me? Tell her six, and that I'll bring dinner. The unlock password is eight-six-five-three."

Joss looked at the phone in his hand, remembering that Matt had made Cameron sign those books. He'd wanted Cam to imprint his thoughts into them for later reading. If she held his phone, wouldn't she be putting *herself* into it? What if he could access everything she'd ever thought about him? See and hear the way she and Cam had spoken of Matt so cavalierly—so cruelly, if she was to be honest—when they'd still thought him dead, or at least a withering hermit? Early on, she'd said something like, "If *he's* not profiting off that goldmine of a name, *someone* should," and she laughed the time Cam said, "Why wait until his rotting corpse is found curled up in a corner?" They'd guiltlessly plotted to defraud conference attendees. And, godammit, now she was actively thinking about all of those horrible things! Placing them fresh in her memory, ripe for the psychic plucking! Oh God, there was no way all that would remain a secret forever. What would be worse: him finding out everything now, or some time down the road? And would she *ever* have privacy around him?

"It's okay," Matt said. "You don't have to worry about imprinting on it. I have control over my ability now ... as you can see." He gestured with the phone at his summer attire and hairy legs.

Joss sat paralyzed, cleared her throat, her hovering hand moving not an inch closer to take the phone from him. She tried to formulate an excuse, some rational explanation for not just grabbing the damned thing and texting his sister back. Every passing second he held the phone in the air between them heaped suspicion and guilt onto her shoulders.

After what seemed like forever, Matt let her off the hook and dropped the phone back into the cup holder. "No worries. It's fine. I'll just call her. Probably better anyway, in case she texts something back."

"Yeah, I just … It's sort of weird to—"

"You don't have to explain, Joss." He gave her a kind look, his skin glowing again with that aura of serenity.

His warmth made her feel even crappier.

"But," he continued, and she looked at his face—now that of a school principal letting a student off with a warning this time, "working with me, there are obviously special conditions. Honesty and trust is essential. In both directions. I don't care what you did or said when you were with Langley. I'm certain you'll find the work you do with us to be much more rewarding."

Joss inhaled a cleansing breath. "Both directions, eh?"

"It's the only way, given my advantages."

"Okay. So you just said you don't care what I said or did with Cam. Does that mean I don't have to do a big confessional thing?"

"No way." Matt frowned. "Please, spare me. Clean slate."

Joss sighed relief. "Wonderful. So now tell me: have you read me? Just now or before? Like how you read Cam with the book?"

"*You're* in that book, too, you know. As well as the door handle there, your seat, the seatbelt, and so on. It's like happening upon someone's open diary or unlocked phone. You can choose to leave them alone, or pick them up and peruse. I choose to leave them alone."

Matt held his earnest gaze on her for a beat.

Joss nodded. "I'd pick up both and tear through that shit without a second thought."

Matt laughed. "I appreciate your honesty. Hopefully you believe and accept my assurances that I would not. And I'll be sure to change my phone's password as soon as possible."

They both laughed, and as Joss relaxed deeper into her seat, it felt as though Matt had done the same.

"All right then," Joss said. "What's the third thing?" He shot her a confused glance. "That you're working on? You said, at present you're only working on three things. The missing people cases was one, the fighting thing was two."

He stiffened his chin and took a deep breath. "Let me get back to you on thing three. It's a bit complicated, and a large wrench was just thrown into it. I need to work it all out."

"Am I the wrench?"

Matt frowned. "What? Oh, no."

"The call then? Markus?"

"Yup. And we'll leave it there on thing three for now."

THREE

Nairobi, Kenya – Presidential Palace – Three weeks ago

Ngina rolled the candle back and forth between her palms and prayed in silence. Conscious of the sweat beading on her head and upper lip, her smock sticking to her clammy neck, she moved her face closer to the water closet's window. The breeze cooled both skin and tension as it pushed in through the thin sliver—the window open as wide as security would allow for the first floor, despite the bars.

Ngina inhaled a final whiff of the fresh air, shook out her limbs, and turned the candle upside down. She stuck her finger into the freshly-carved hole in the bottom and did a final sweep to remove any remaining wax flakes from the inside or bottom, then picked up the gold sticker from the counter. After covering the hole with the label sticker and smoothing the edges to be sure it appeared brand new, she deposited the candle into her apron's right side pocket. A final peek into the left side pocket where she'd placed the shavings and small chunks she'd carved out. One more look at herself in the mirror above the sink. Her dark skin shone again with the glaze of new sweat. She dabbed her sleeves about her face.

Finally, a quick rinse of the flathead screwdriver she'd used to carve out the candle, a brisk hand washing, and she was out the door. Seven minutes was far too long to be in the water closet, but a glance down both directions of the hall found the area clear of other staff.

She headed to the mansion's south wing.

As she passed the hallway to the main kitchen, a deep voice said, "Ngina, a favor," in Swahili.

Ngina recognized the voice of Masil, the Chief of Staff, which meant that His Excellency, President Jivu Absko, had returned early from the South.

She stopped just past the hall, backed up, and turned to face Masil.

"Did you require me, sir?"

"Yes. If you're not busy, please inform the First Lady that she will be hosting a small dinner party at seven this evening, and send the President's apologies for the short notice."

Ngina dipped and nodded, waited for Masil to go, and then she continued down the corridor.

Good and bad, she thought.

Good because she now had a better excuse for another visit to Mrs. Absko; bad because His Excellency had this keen sense—an unnerving awareness of any matters aslant. Even those few wholly scrupulous members of the staff with nothing to hide breathed sighs of relief when he was away. And Ngina, normally a member of the latter group, prayed and promised to God that this would be the last time she'd dance outside those boundaries. No more. If she completed the task without being caught, there wouldn't be another foolish violation like this.

But is that what God would want? she thought. *To abandon the Lady and little Alexander? God doesn't want you killed, so yes.*

She rounded the last corner to the master suite and found the Lady's immense guard, Thabiti, sitting on his stool outside the door. He regarded Ngina with a sideways look, his eyes tracking her without any head movement, as if that trunk of a neck could no longer twist.

"Ngina," he greeted.

She stopped and stood before him. What business did she have here, if not to drop off or pick up Alexander for school? Masil's request had been a blessing. His Excellency's early return was not.

"Thabiti. Per Masil, the Lady has an unscheduled dinner party to prepare for."

He pressed his lips together in annoyance and unclipped the radio from his belt. "Thabiti to Andra."

The head housekeeper's frazzled, nasally voice, "Yes, Thabiti?"

He pressed the talk button again, his irritation slathered atop every syllable. "A dinner party?"

"Yes, a dinner party. Get over it."

Thabiti rolled his eyes and presented an elaborate sigh. Ngina knew Thabiti hadn't suspected a lie—he had no cause to distrust her—and was clearly less concerned with a nursery maid, so much as another night of impromptu overtime. He waved her on.

"Wait," he said, and she stopped. "What's in your apron?"

She turned with what she hoped looked like a genuine *oops, how silly of me!* flail, and pulled out the candle for him to examine.

"A replacement for the Lady's lavatory. She prefers the jasmine from the nursery water closet over the cherry blossom scent the chambermaids have been using of late. Should I have Samy replace it? I should have Samy do it—"

He cut her off with a dismissive, slo-mo wave: *Candles? Go.*

She smiled apologies and opened the door to the President's suite, closing it behind her.

Beyond the dimly lit hall and elaborately decorated antechamber, Ngina found Mrs. Absko sitting cross-legged on the floor beside Alexander, nearly four years old.

"My Lady," she said with a nervous curtsy.

Mrs. Absko, beautiful despite her tired eyes, replied in her unique, foreign brand of Swahili, "I know it defies your tongue's every muscle, Ngina, but it would make a world of difference to me if you would call me Tuni now and then."

Ngina closed her eyes and wished herself transported to her old bed in her mother's house in Narok. To roll back the clock ten years—an innocent thirteen-year-old with only school and acne burdening her thoughts. "I ... I can't, my Lady."

Mrs. Absko's head sunk, her eyes returning to the little cars on the floor, Alexander smashing them into each other and simulating massive explosions. "Were you able to do it?"

"Yes, my Lady." Ngina produced the candle from her pocket, handing it to Mrs. Absko. "I'll place the rest in the cabinet, behind the rolls, like you wanted."

"Thank you. Please, don't misunderstand. I do appreciate—"

The main door to the suite opened and the President's voice streamed in. The footsteps of several others marched after him. The group halted, their voices echoing around the corner from the antechamber. The President sounded upset.

Mrs. Absko quickly returned the candle to Ngina and frantically pointed her to the lavatory. Ngina complied and hastened down the hallway, replacing the candle on top of the toilet. She peered behind her, saw the Lady rotating a hand in the air for her to hurry. Ngina dropped to her knees, opened the cabinet beneath the sink, and scooped the flakes and chunks of wax from her other pocket into the cabinet, behind a neat stack of tissue boxes. Little flakes dropped, littering the carpet and the cabinet bottom. Feeling the rise of panic, she picked and swiped and scooped as much as she could into her palm, throwing it behind the boxes. Was he coming? Was he behind her? What was she doing there at this hour? And a nursery maid tending to lavatory affairs? A lie wouldn't work. She couldn't claim to be filling in. Lavatory hands would never touch the President's son.

She closed the cabinet as she rose to her feet, spun, and strode out of the lavatory. Returning to the bedroom, she heard His Excellency still around the corner.

"Yes," he said. "Your job is to advise and you have advised. Now leave, all of you." The President appeared from the antechamber just as Ngina reentered the room. "Ah, my loves!" he said in English, then switched back to Swahili, "Oh, hello, Ngina." His eyes cut to the lavatory hall and back to her. "What were you ...? Where were you just now?"

Staff would never use a lavatory in the President's suite, even if the Lady insisted. Ngina stumbled, still unprepared. Could she mention the candle? It's what she'd told Thabiti, but the President had more cause for suspicion than Thabiti. "I ... I was ..."

His gaze moved to the Lady, on the floor, playing with Alexander as if nothing at all was happening.

The President took a step toward Ngina. "You were ... what?" He towered over her small frame.

"Very sorry, Your Excellency," Ngina finally said, her eyes fixed on the buttons of his pale silver suit jacket. "I had to ..." she brushed the tip of her nose, "... blow."

"Huh. No time to handle that in the staff facilities, eh?" He took a step back and Ngina relaxed a degree. "And why were you here in the first place?"

The party!

"So very sorry, Your Excellency. I'm escorting Alexander to the nursery so the Lady can prepare for the dinner party."

The Lady's head tilted. Apparently, she hadn't yet been informed of the imminent guests. Ever watchful, the President caught the Lady's movement, as well.

In English, he said, "I hope you received my advance apologies for the short notice, my dear. I had no warning of their visit."

Mrs. Absko, with her regal poise, smiled and nodded and helped Alexander to his feet, straightening his shirt and cradling his cherubic cheeks in her palms. "I'll see you later, Bubu." She kissed his nose, gazed dotingly, and gestured for Ngina to take him.

Ngina curtsied, and on her way toward the hall, glanced through the baroque mirror on the wall. In the instant the couple's reflection appeared in the mirror, she saw the President extend his hand to help the Lady up, but she disregarded it, opting for the bedpost. Ngina didn't know what happened behind closed doors between those two, but she knew that in another house, a husband would feel justified to strike a wife so disrespectful.

As the suite door closed behind her, and Thabiti greeted Alexander, Ngina couldn't imagine *anyone* laying a finger on Mrs. Absko. The idea was absurd. Mrs. Absko was no mere wife. She was a queen! The Jackie O of Kenya! The Cleopatra of modern Africa!

Despite her unique window into the First Couple's private life, Ngina still revered their majesty. In Kenya—and much of the continent, too—rarely could a genuinely charismatic, iconic figure rise to the top. In Mr. Absko's case, he was predestined to ascend, just like his beloved ancestors, but not just over Kenya.

During Mr. Absko's campaign for the presidency, buzz spread from Egypt to South Africa that a new dawn lay just beyond the horizon, with citizens clamoring for unification under a single, worthy ruler. With His Excellency's roots in both Islam and Christianity, his charitable work across the region, and of course, his royal lineage, what other candidate in a thousand years could bring this dream to reality? Africa, at least the western half, could be like the United States, or how the Romans used to be, not just this African Union with its meetings and arguing leaders.

As his supporters grew, a noisy few popped up, questioning his royal heritage, but no one wanted to hear this, and Ngina was certain that some sort of proof was brought to light. President Jivu Absko was a direct descendent of Cleopatra and Marc Antony. The posters and murals of His Excellency and the *"new Cleopatra,"* Mrs. Absko— their flawless faces like Greek statues, gazing off to a bright future— helped advance a national pride unfelt in as long as anyone could remember.

The Lady may not have the President's royal blood in her veins, but she was easily as beloved as her husband. And this child beside Ngina, his little hand balled in hers, did he not elevate his mother even higher?

Ngina entered the nursery, and watched Alexander run off to the TV. The boy loved being here during non-school hours when he could watch his super heroes and turtle ninjas.

Ngina went to the sink to wash her hands. Inspecting her face in the mirror, she thanked God for protecting her, and she apologized to Him. She'd have to help the Lady just one more time after all, despite the risks to her own life.

* * *

Tuni slid herself into a charcoal and aqua gown she'd never seen before, let alone worn. Perusing her ever-changing wardrobe was like shopping for free on a personal Rodeo Drive. Prada, Versace, Valentino—outfits, shoes, even undergarments—all simply appeared and disappeared. Often she'd search her racks for a top she particularly liked only to find that it had been "cycled out" of her closet. Hired stylists deemed she'd worn it too many times. Returning from a trip, she'd find a selection of new designer pieces or jewelry, often one-of-a-kind items. If they weren't put on after some indeterminable period of time, they too would vanish to wherever her clothes went.

At the back of the vast closet, Tuni kept an eye on the doorway as she grazed her fingertips across the row of hanging scarves, lowering her hand when she reached the winter coats, and slipped the ring from the overcoat pocket where she'd hidden it. Into her cleavage it disappeared.

Hello, Matthew, she thought. *I hope this message finds you well* ...

She sat down at the vanity.

Jivu leaned against the doorframe and watched her work on her hair in the mirror. "Would you like me to get Samy to help you with that?"

Tuni inserted a bobby pin and grabbed another from between her teeth. "No, thank you."

"Are you upset about the Minister and Ambassador coming?"

"Not really."

Jivu plucked his presidential standard pin from the cushion and set it in his lapel. "Are you upset about *anything*? If so, just say so."

"I'm fine. Do I sound upset?"

He wagged a finger at her. "No, no, no, of course not. You don't work with such unambiguity. That would be too obvious, too perceivable. Instead, there's a flat smile, a lingering look, polite blinking." He snapped his fingers *a-ha* and pointed at her. "Polite! That's what you are! That's the infuriating game! Quiet, polite, gracious."

Tuni thought to challenge him. *You wish me impolite? Is that what you're asking for?* But what he really wanted was for her to *engage*, and she wouldn't fall into yet another trap. She pressed her lipstick against her lower lip and regarded him through the mirror.

"I'm sorry, dear." An even more infuriating response, though she needed to stop. There was nothing she could gain from prolonging the conversation in its current direction. She had hoped he'd grumble about his trip or foolish advisors, perhaps drop a bit about money, something incriminating. Unfortunately, she could never ask, and didn't know what, if any, illicit material his ring currently held.

Jivu crossed his arms. "I'll not call you names, no matter how you bait me to do so. I won't say it."

Tuni stood and turned, allowed him a second to inspect her outfit and statuesque form, then walked to him and placed her hand delicately on his abdomen. "I know you never would. Let me find some shoes so we can get to the foyer before they arrive."

She returned to the closet, a silent Jivu behind her. Her words seemed to calm him and she'd be able to salvage an evening of peace. A pair of mid-height heels called to her and she grabbed them from the rack. She turned to go.

Jivu stood in the doorway, arms out to his sides, blocking the way. "And you call *me* manipulative. What are you up to? What is it you *think* you're going to get away with?"

Tuni put up a hand. "Jivu, I—"

"Why can't you be that lady from New York? What have you become? Nothing but a lifeless mannequin in an imaginary prison. I should have you stuffed and mounted—what would be the difference?" He looked at her with subdued disgust, as though she wasn't worth his anger. "Who *are* you?"

Tuni's internal filter dissolved in an instant. "Who am *I*? Is that some sick, ironic joke? Who are *you*? Abel? The Gray? Actually, you don't have to answer that. I know now *exactly* who and *what* you are—probably better than you do yourself—and it's certainly not the person I met, however meticulously you strove to *ease* me from that persona to *this*." She spat the last word and pushed her way past him, pausing on the bed a second to put on her shoes.

She glanced up. His eyes had changed the way they sometimes could, to those that saw an enemy before them. Fear dropped into her belly like a cement football. Fear and *embarrassment*, because Matthew would see all of this, and feel what she felt: a frightened, diminished speck of the person she once was—the person she *hoped* she used to be, and not just clinging to some false memory of a confident, intelligent woman who never existed. Now, reduced to impeccably outfitted arm candy, or worse, a high-priced whore paid in excessive lifestyle, the only happiness she could find on a given day was in her little boy, Alexander. And though guilt beat her brow for ever thinking it, he too was just another cog in the control machine, the heaviest link in her chains.

"I find it interesting," Jivu said, leaning back against the wall and crossing his arms, "all this brewing scandal. High eighties approval polls just a month ago. Now we have no-name dissidents demanding a new investigation into Hali."

Hali Ma Wenza, Jivu's original political opponent, missing since a year before the election. "I don't know anything about it. How could I?" She motioned around the room, her opulent prison.

"No, of course not. Nor could you know of these new accusations about the pipeline. Or *other* business partners—lifelong rivals, these families—suddenly talking to each other, comparing notes, demanding explanations."

Without the first clue about any of it, Tuni brushed aside whatever he was insinuating. "Jivu—"

"Universally beloved one day, *questioned* the next. After all I've done for this country. It's disgusting." He held up his index finger, wagging it toward her, shaking his head with a twisted smile. "It's just so *curious*, how this all follows in your wake."

Tuni shrugged. "It doesn't seem so bloody curious to me. Only the ultimate megalomaniac would think it so. Seems the natural evolution to me. Those closest to you grasp it first, then your acquaintances, and on in this manner to everyone else."

Jivu's smirk deflated to a straight line. He slid his hands into his pockets. "Grasp what, exactly?"

He knew the answer, but she'd never said it aloud. It would sting for him to hear, but to make her say it would uphold his control over her—clearly his utmost concern at this point, as he knew there'd be no winning back her heart.

Tuni regarded him with a warm smile. "That you're the fucking devil, dear."

He blinked. His Adam's apple rose and fell. Any hint of that acerbic smile had disappeared.

Tuni didn't know what he'd expected, but it was *not* these words. Dread returned, punching deep into her gut. She ached for a rewind, an *undo*—to pluck those words right out of his ears, and replace them with *anything* else.

Jivu cast his eyes downward.

"You know," he began quietly, buffing his wristwatch's face. "I told you before that you may leave whenever you wish."

Tuni shook her head. "Later, Jivu. Your guests are waiting."

She wouldn't say Alexander's name, wouldn't invite the threat he was so eager to repeat. Now he'd say it anyway.

"You *choose* to stay. We both know it. You stay because you've grown accustomed to a certain standard of living. A standard you wish to maintain for both you, and our beautiful son."

Tuni grabbed the small clutch purse from the table. "Yes. You're right. I'm sorry. Shall we go?"

"We both know, *dear* ... Alexander could *never* live without you."

FOUR

Newark, NJ, USA – Present day

Seated at her desk in the dining room-turned-office, Iris Turner peered up from her computer as the hum and whir of the opening garage door signaled her brother's return. She glanced at the clock; he was only about fifteen minutes later than he'd earlier estimated. A reasonable degree of lateness, but she was starving, so crap must still be given. Oh, and driving to another state without telling her was pretty messed up, too. Yes, Matt would soon behold the ol' mom-hands-on-the-hips.

The access door from the garage swung open and an unexpected female voice streamed in. Iris straightened her posture before her mind flashed to a panicked assessment of her appearance: yoga pants, ribbed tank top with no bra, no makeup, hair lazily tied back, probably something in her teeth from when she'd snacked, and who-knew-what else.

As Matt stepped in, the unannounced guest's arm appeared just behind him, and Iris made a snap decision, spinning round in place, and facing, inexplicably, the potted *Dracaena* palm tree in the corner.

"Uh ... Iris?" Matt said, justifiably baffled.

Iris squeezed her eyes shut, smiling uncontrollably at the ridiculousness, knowing she had no choice but to turn around, and all-too-aware that the guest would see in an instant exactly why Iris had turned her back to them. She sighed, her shoulders burdened by weighty defeat, and faced them with a welcoming smile.

"Well hello there!" Iris enthused, arms crossed high, covering her chest.

Matt took in the sight, smirked, and swallowed—amused and apologetic, but mostly amused. He cleared his throat. "Joss, this is my sister, Iris … I.T., I don't believe you ever met Joss Lynn Leland."

Iris knew the name, but couldn't place it. "Nice to meet you."

The guest stood half-hidden behind Matt, with perfect makeup and hair, dressed in tight jeans, boots, and a dangly V-neck. This "Joss" was pretty to be sure, but more like a hot comedienne than cover girl. Iris guessed she was around the same age—late twenties to early thirties—though how would this visitor assess the *drain clog* standing before her? Pushing forty? And exactly who was she to Matt? He'd never been the sort to just bring someone home, and after his recent trainwreck relationship, Iris knew he'd be happily single for another year before opening himself up like that again. Especially while Little Miss Bonkers was still calling every day.

As Joss smiled and greeted her, her eyes remained sympathetically affixed to Iris's. Joss said, "Hi," but Iris heard, *"Sorry."*

Well, that's a small relief, Iris thought. A less gracious woman might've given her a visible once-over before reaching out to make her shake hands.

"Sorry I didn't call ahead," Matt said, and Iris turned to him with a static, closed-lip smile and unblinking eyes.

"Mm-hm." She glanced down at the paper bags of takeout food. "Why don't you get all that going in the kitchen? I'm going to go *freshen up.*" She turned briskly and went down the hall to her bedroom to change.

She stripped off her top, grabbed a bra from the dresser, and went to the closet for a proper shirt. Matt was in for an ass kicking.

* * *

Joss ambled along the edges of Matt's living room, eyes drifting from paintings to book spines to seemingly random trinkets dispersed throughout the recessed shelves: a monocle, presumably ancient oblong coins, engraved tiles, wood pieces, a dagger. She was confused and intrigued. She glanced Matt's way—visible over the bar dividing the living room from the kitchen. He was busy opening food containers and fetching utensils.

She continued along the shelves, peering at and touching various items. "You have a lot of really old stuff." She picked up a shiny black sculpture of a human female, with seemingly exaggerated hips, backside, and breasts. "Look at this sexy mama."

"Fertility idol," he said without looking up.

She set the figurine back on the shelf and picked up the inscribed wooden block beside it, tracing the engravings with a fingertip.

"Not much of these are *really* old." Matt was suddenly right beside her. She flinched a little. "The two shadow box cases on the wall there …" He gently took the wooden piece from her, returning it to its spot, and pointed her toward the end of the shelves.

"Sorry." Joss shrank beneath him. "Guess I probably shouldn't be touching—"

"Nah." He brushed it off with a shrug, as if she could touch whatever she wanted, but she felt more than a little herded away from anything she could put her hands on. He guided her to a big, wall-mounted, wooden case, and pointed through the glass. "This one's a flint hand axe. About half a million years old." Joss nodded, impressed. Matt motioned her on to the second case: a smooth, metallic frame projecting a few inches out from the wall. "And *this* is from Kenya. A *bit* older … About a hundred and fifty million years."

Stunned, unable to wrap her head around such a length of time, Joss looked closely at the dull metal object suspended behind the glass. A little less than a foot long, and maybe two inches wide, it looked like a pipe, cut lengthwise in half to reveal the interior. Fused to the inside, every couple inches, were angled half-discs that led to small holes in the pipe. Joss couldn't imagine what such a thing would be used for.

She peered up at him. "What is it?"

Matt's gaze hung on the artifact for a couple seconds before he responded. "It's part of a pipe." He turned and headed back to the kitchen, continuing from the counter. "They used tools like that to separate certain types of molten metal. They refined everything they mined and found uses for each material."

"The dome people, right?"

"Yes. You ready to eat? I.T. should be back out any minute."

Joss was supposed to view his interest in these objects as detached—purely academic—but her barometer was better than that. When she was growing up, her bipolar father (they called it "manic-depressive" at the time) had inadvertently taught her to catch the slightest shifts in mood, to predict when one of his dark periods was on an upswing or—more frequently—when the light was bleeding out of him. Sometimes, she or her mother could head off the plunge with distractions and exaggerated reminiscing. *"Remember that amazing idea you had one time, Daddy? When we just drove, like out of nowhere, and ended up at a carnival in Maine? It blew our minds!"* But more often, for all three of them it was like being tied to a sinking boulder, fighting to swim upward. Matt wasn't necessarily hiding some deep, dome-people-related sorrow, but his indifference was an act. Joss wondered just how much time he'd spent with them.

"I'm ready," she said, and joined him in the kitchen. "So after we eat, you want to sit down, the three of us, and talk about this whole ..." she fluttered a hand in the air toward the cluttered makeshift office area down the hall "... *project,* before you take me home?"

"Definitely." Matt pulled fruit juice cartons from the refrigerator.

"Good. 'Cause I hate when something's hanging out there, like when someone says 'we need to talk,' but that talk's supposed to happen at some unspecified future time. Screw that. We're talking now, *I* say." She grinned, but he didn't look. That could've come off bitchy without the associated smile. Hopefully he got her snark by now.

Joss turned to the sound of approaching footsteps on the hardwood floor. Iris was back. Still casual, but she'd put on a bra and new shirt, some subtle lipstick, and brushed her hair into a tighter ponytail. She was cute, Joss thought, with features so similar to her brother's that Joss automatically snapped a look at Matt's face for comparison. They shared that lighter skin tone, the same shade of light-brown hair, and their eyes, both in shape and sage color.

"I know," Iris said, catching Joss's alternating gaze. "Practically twins, right?" She extended one hand to Joss while pointing her other thumb behind her. "Sorry about that ... before ... If I'd known he was bringing a guest—"

Joss took her hand and shook it. "Oh please, don't even! You have nothing to worry about. *Trust* me."

A ringtone sounded behind Joss.

"Damn, that's right," Matt said as he looked at the screen. "I have to take this. You guys go ahead and eat." He rushed past them, down the hall toward the side of the house Joss had yet to see. "Hello? ... Yes, go ahead, Markus."

Joss and Iris shared an awkward smile, silent for a beat.

"Sorry," Iris said, brushing past her. "But I'm fricken starving." She grabbed a plate, handed it to Joss, and then picked up one for herself. "Here, so I don't feel like a pig."

"Oh, no," Joss said with a smile. "We're on the same page. I think we'll be getting along *just* fine, you and me."

Iris froze, then shot Joss a quizzical look, surely wondering about the nature of this apparently *ongoing* relationship. Had Matt begun dating someone without telling his sister?

Joss hadn't intended ambiguity when she'd said it, but she let this teaser hang out there for a moment, guiltily enjoying the sight of gears cranking in Iris's head.

"I'm your employee now!" Joss revealed with a grin.

Iris's reaction wasn't exactly relief, or recognition, or even acceptance. She just smiled politely, said, "Hm, well, welcome," and began serving herself.

Had Joss been too familiar? Overly friendly? Maybe Iris's jury was still out on whether there was something more to this surprise visit. Or perhaps her stomach was as incorrigible as Joss's, and digesting anything other than food would have to wait.

* * *

Matt passed Iris's bedroom and turned into his own. "Sorry, but before you get to all that, tell me if you're looking for me to travel somewhere."

"Yes, Matthew," Markus said in his ever-cordial, butleresque tone. "You'd be required to come here, to Ukraine. Naturally, Mr. Ostrovsky would never allow the artifacts of interest to leave the property."

Matt envisioned Markus wearing a sleek white suit, reclining in a high-backed leather chair in his office at the Ostrovsky estate, a room where Matt and Markus had exchanged a few words several years ago, just days before everything went to hell in Cuba.

"I figured as much." Matt hadn't yet worked out how he'd tweak his plans around this Ostrovsky involvement. For now, he'd focus on legitimate concerns and feigned curiosity. "Now, aside from the shenanigans going down in your country right now, tell me why in a million years I'd agree to go anywhere near Mr. Ostrovsky or his property. How could I possibly trust him?"

"Well, I'm not sure what this *shinan* word—"

"Shenanigans. Military movements. Political upheaval. Invasion—"

"Yes, I inferred this is what you meant, and I can assure you there's no cause for concern in the area here. As in business, Mr. Ostrovsky always aligns himself with the appropriate team. Travel would be coordinated outside the traditional systems, and absolutely safe. As for trust … Mr. Ostrovsky, would you care to answer this one?"

Vitaliy Ostrovsky's thick Ukrainian accent joined the conversation—jubilant, and with a bit less of the husky smoker's croak Matt recalled. "Of course! If there is one thing I appreciate, it is distrust. In business, if person not questions me, I think this man is weak. I maybe look for how I make terms more favorable for me, okay? So yes, this is good. Matthew, first let me start by saying this thing with you and Gray: not personal, and not me."

Thing with you and Gray? Could Ostrovsky know what I'm doing? No, no way. He's talking about Cuba.

Ostrovsky went on, "This was favor for *business*. Territory one of my company needed in Africa. He's nobody then, but connected. First saying give me this, give me that. I tell him 'Fuck you, I go elsewhere with my money.' Some people die, but not relevant." The sound of ice in a glass, a deep gulp and breath. "What I was saying? Yes, a couple months later, he phones me, saying he knows you're on way with this professor, tells me if I say 'fuck off' to professor, I get my land deal. Well, small part of deal. He breaks balls to this day for what I still need, but this is other story. Now you understand."

Matt was quiet a moment, recalling again, through a burst of images, the eventual consequences of Ostrovsky's rejection of Dr. Rheese: the disintegrated opal, the loss of Tuni, the deaths of numerous innocents, Matt's father among them. "I'm not sure I do."

"It wasn't me! This is what I'm saying. You have no reason to distrust. We never ourselves met for business together, you and me. This is new. We are same, you and me. How do I tell this so he gets? Markus?"

"Yes," Markus rejoined. "What Mr. Ostrovsky is trying to convey, Matthew, is that he's asking for your forgiveness, and to put the past behind you both as it has no connection to the proposed meeting and arrangement. Further, Mr. Ostrovsky would like you to see him as an equal in this transaction, on level ground. There are, of course, certain concrete assurances he will provide to allay any remaining fears you may harbor. Now, if I may proceed."

"Right," Matt said, and sat down on the side of his bed. Neither could say anything to convince him that Ostrovsky was even marginally trustworthy, but The Gray was indeed the responsible party—the sole puller of strings leading to every tragedy—and would soon be held responsible. "Go ahead."

Matt's phone vibrated against his ear.

Markus said, "You should receive a photograph any moment." Matt pulled the phone away and opened the image. Markus's voice was small and tinny through the minute speaker. "Matthew? Are you there? Did you receive it?"

"I got it. Just a moment."

Matt zoomed into the photo and rotated his phone sideways. He knew this artifact from another picture, but he'd never seen this side of it.

On a black surface, beside a coin placed for scale, sat the craggy length of carved granite, like a gamepiece from Jenga, but with three long sides instead of four. A deteriorated row of engraved symbols covered most of the camera-facing side, and they were not the characters Matt had expected.

He said aloud, "That's odd."

"Yes, yes!" Ostrovsky cheered. "Odd indeed!"

Matt forwarded the image to his personal email address. He put the phone back to his ear just as Markus asked again if Matt was still there. Time to turn on the poorly restrained interest. "I'm here. So what exactly do you think this thing is? What's the significance? I see it's inscribed in different languages. Markus mentioned the Library of Alexandria earlier."

"That's correct, Matthew," Markus said. "It's believed that, prior to one of the many disasters befalling the great library, a group of patrons evacuated some or all of its treasured scrolls to a secret location. In the face of a prolonged invasion, this artifact was intended to guide a later generation of Alexandrians to the hidden site."

Matt glanced again at the image on his phone. Ostrovsky had surely had it translated by now. "Assuming this group and evacuation are a real thing, what led you to believe a recovery didn't occur as planned? The Museum and Library were rebuilt multiple times, existing for several hundred years."

Ostrovsky cut in, his tone swollen with pride. "Because, Matthew, a piece has been sealed tight, exactly where it was originally hidden, for nearly two thousand years. It's never been seen, except by those who hided it, myself, and a few others in past two weeks."

Matt lay back on his bed and slid his free hand under his head. "I doubt that."

"Why?" Ostrovsky demanded. "Why do you doubt?"

Because I found this thing on eBay. Because you bought it off eBay. Because the person who alerted you to its existence only did so because I pointed them to it. Evidently, you and The Gray share certain sources, and, unfortunately, they didn't first seek their finder's fee from The Gray. But let's just go with the visual evidence in the photo ...

"The wear on the object. Some of the characters are almost completely rubbed away. That doesn't happen to granite that's been sealed inside some protective casing. I don't know ... maybe if there were chemicals—"

Markus interrupted, "You're surely correct, Matthew. But Mr. Ostrovsky is referring to the second artifact. A sister piece to the one I sent you. It's in pristine condition, appearing today as perfect as when it was made."

Both keystones ...

Matt deliberated, half-hearing Markus as he went on about the objects, details Matt had known for a few years, such as the three engraved languages: Greek, Demotic, and Hieratic—dialects as accessible to Matt as English. But the symbols in this photo were different from those Matt had known. He'd accepted the information he'd read in imprints—that all three keystones had been engraved with the same messages. The pic on eBay had happened to be of a side that matched the others. This new side in the photo—new to him, anyway—read: *song hymn Thonis.*

"Regardless," Matt continued the skeptic act. "These 'patrons' of yours could've simply fetched their hidden treasure two, five, even twenty years later, and they'd have no need to use these stone pieces as guides. They'd know exactly where they hid these scrolls. Or their children, or grandchildren. You get what I'm saying? You're assuming too much from very little information."

A slurp from the other end of the line. Ostrovsky chuckled. "He is such the wise one, no?"

"Matthew," Markus said. "The piece I speak of—the one sealed away, the perfect one—was moved from some prior hideaway to the one where it was recovered, two centuries after it was made. The keepers of this secret were still keeping it, generations later."

Yes, they were. Crap ... Just how much do you know?

Matt began, "Well, then ... maybe you've got something there. But look, if all you need is a translation—"

"I'm afraid that's not all," Markus interrupted. He sounded even more self-satisfied. "They've been translated, but the *code* is the problem. There are ... contextual issues. I'm afraid we're at a standstill without your help. Now, as I mentioned, Mr. Ostrovsky is prepared to offer multiple forms of compensation." Markus paused. Matt said nothing. "Shall I proceed?"

Matt remained silent as he counted down from thirty, though he was more than a little curious about these *"multiple forms of compensation"* or *"imbursements."* Ostrovsky must've known that money wasn't a driving motivator for Matt these days. Hopefully, some creative threat wasn't part of their plan to compel him.

... three ... two ... one ...

Matt inhaled deep, exhaled into the mic, and said, "Go ahead."

* * *

Iris and Joss had just sat down at the small kitchen table, take-out Cuban food arranged on their plates almost identically. Matt moseyed back into the room, his stride a bit off, his expression too cool. Iris saw through it in an instant. Big things were rattling around in that head.

"What's up?" Iris asked, predicting his response.

"Oh, nothing. How's the food?"

Denial and redirection. Typical plotting Matt.

Iris touched Joss's arm. "Look at my brother right now," she said, and Joss frowned, confused, before turning to observe Matt. Iris went on, "That's his secret face. Call him on it when you see it."

Matt harrumphed and served himself dinner. "Look at my sister. That's her intrusive face."

Iris persisted. It usually required three attempts to make him talk. "Who was that on the phone?"

"I'm going to Ukraine. I'll be back in a couple days."

Two attempts, Iris observed. *Vitaliy Ostrovsky. The Ukrainian billionaire.*

"Is it—?"

"Don't try to talk me out of it. It's happening. This is my *resolute* face, if you recall." He smiled, and pinched one of Iris's shoulders as he sat down at the table. They'd discuss it later, after Joss was gone. He was irritated, but keeping it jovial for the sake of their guest.

Iris caught Joss's averted eyes. She wore the perfect *Mom and Dad are fighting again* expression—clearly seeing through the feigned light banter.

Joss said, "Sooo …" to fill the air.

Matt swallowed a bite and set down his fork. "Sorry. Let's talk about the work—our mission here at Subzero Ventures."

"Get it?" Iris asked Joss, receiving only puzzlement in return. "The name? My idea. Get it? Cold cases?"

Joss nodded, enthusiastic. "Oh, nice. Very clever."

"I.T.'s been congratulating herself on that for two years," Matt said. "Moving on ..."

* * *

In the living room, as 11:00pm approached, Matt and Iris were still sharing stories about missing persons cases they'd investigated. Matt's clinical approach to this subject wasn't fooling Joss any more than his earlier attempt. Pain wilted his face the longer they spoke, aging him another ten years in a mere two hours. Only a small fraction of their cases could be closed with what anyone would consider a happy ending, but Joss didn't sense that he planned to quit anytime soon. No, this was simply his cross to bear.

As their stories went on, Joss felt no less appreciation for the uncanny nature of her situation. She was in the home of *the* Matthew Turner, had earlier shared a bottle of wine with the man's sister, and for the past couple hours had sat listening to firsthand accounts of their amazing work.

A newborn taken from a hospital's maternity ward, now seventeen, reunited with his birth parents. An elusive serial killer of runaways caught and imprisoned. The six-year-old girl taken by her mother's dangerous ex-boyfriend, safely recovered, two states over. Matt's initially rocky relationships with local law enforcement, the Department of Justice, and the FBI had reached a stable, professional groove, and those few individuals familiar with his involvement in cases continued to protect the secret. They certainly didn't want to alienate the greatest, irreplaceable resource at their disposal, nor would their objectives be aided if even a single leak slipped through the cracks.

It'd been a long day, and Joss was exhausted. However, she didn't detect the same fatigue from the siblings seated across from her, and she refused to be the one who called it a night. One of them had to give her a ride, after all.

"You look tired," Iris said to Joss, interrupting Matt. "You about ready to wrap it up, continue the discussion tomorrow?"

"Not tomorrow," Matt corrected. "I'll be back maybe Wednesday or Thursday."

Iris sneered at him. "Oh, yeah. So you're leaving *tomorrow*? Guessing I need to figure out flights and such? You know tomorrow's Sunday, right?"

Matt nodded to her and stood up. "Yep. And yes, please, to Belgorod."

"Ukraine?"

"Russia. I've got a ride from there. Thanks. You're the best." He turned back to Joss. "C'mon, I'll give you a ride. You have a car at your house?"

Joss stood. "Sure do."

"No, no, no," Iris said to Matt. "You need to pack. I'll take her home. And check your messages on the cork board. Pete Sharma's been relentless since last night. Would you call him back, please?"

Matt ignored his sister, instead holding out a hand to Joss. "Again, it's great to have you onboard." She shook his hand. "We'll get into details or whatever when I get back. Enjoy a week to yourself. I.T. will backdate your payroll to today, so it'll be like a paid vacation."

A few minutes later, in Iris's car, Joss listened as Iris revealed why she was so eager to give her the ride.

Joss said, "And you want me to …"

"Just another set of eyes, you know? Look out for him. He doesn't take care of himself by himself. I mean, I don't expect you to go in his room when he's gone to sleep and check him for artifacts."

"Is that what *you* do?"

Iris glanced at her, maybe a little embarrassed. "Sometimes … Okay, yeah, every night. He doesn't get real sleep when he's reading! It's not like dreaming, you know? His brain is as active as the person he's experiencing. It's why he was so deteriorated after Cuba."

"And you pulled him out of that?"

"No, he did that himself. I mean, I was taking care of him as best I could—groceries and bills and whatnot—but one day something clicked in him and everything just stopped. It turned out he could turn it off, after all. Great, right? *Phew!* But, no, instead of rejoicing at this, he only twisted it to fit into his depression. Instead of thinking, 'Wow, now I can live a normal life,' he thought, 'Wow, if I'd realized this sooner, so many things would be different.' Like our dad, and Matt's old ex, for instance, maybe would've worked out different if he hadn't been at the mercy of his ability."

"And you disagree?" Joss wondered aloud.

"No, but it doesn't matter." Iris turned onto Joss's street, pulling in front of the unlit house Joss pointed toward. "Who says he could've turned it off way back when? If he'd just tried harder? No reason to believe that. Anyway, I hope you don't feel like I'm piling all this crazy responsibility on you."

"No, no. Not at all."

"Good. 'Cause I need to pile some heavy responsibility on you." Iris smiled.

Joss tried to match Iris's face as she stifled an *uh-oh*.

Iris looked at her earnestly and said, "I know we don't know each other … You can absolutely say no. It's just—there's only me, you know? I can only do so much. All these trips he's been going on, I have to stay back and manage the work. He knows it. Half of me thinks he's not on some big mission, but just going places to escape from *me*—the one yanking the damned needles out of his arm."

Big mission?

Joss waited for her to go on, but quickly realized Iris was awaiting a go-ahead. "What do you need me to do?"

* * *

Matt stood over the open duffle bag at the foot of his bed, eyes fluttering through a visual inventory. He'd packed all the clothes and personal items he needed, but something was missing. He walked to the wall, pulled a few artifacts from the shelf, and zipped them in his backpack. A thin bar of sunlight shot between the curtain panels, and Matt glanced at the clock on his nightstand: 5:54.

He poked his head in I.T.'s door, finding her still asleep, as expected. At her desk in the office area, Matt scrawled on a sticky note, *Pete info in the key file. Luvya.* and stuck it to her monitor screen. Outside on the front porch, he set down his duffle, locked the door behind him, and turned to his car.

"Morning," Joss said. She was sitting on his trunk, dressed in dark blue jeans and a gray pullover hoodie emblazoned with a bold red **R**. At her feet stood a lime-green suitcase.

Godammit, Iris.

"Can we stop for coffee on the way?" she asked. "My body's upright and here, but my head's still buried in a pillow."

This was not the trip for I.T. to assign him a babysitter. He tried to think through the cloud of grogginess in his head, but this early, and with everything weighing on him since yesterday, the only thing he could think to do was tell her to go home. Whatever Iris had told her, just cancel it.

Say "I'm in a rush, can you please move?" and leave it at that.

"Rush," he said as he walked down the steps.

Joss scrunched her face, confused. It hadn't come out right. Matt stopped at the back of his car, and observed the "R" on her sweatshirt.

"Rutgers?" he said as he motioned her to move off of the car.

She slid down. "Not me. An ex. I went to NYU. This is just the warmest sweatshirt I have."

Matt popped the trunk open and placed his bags inside. Joss bent to pick up her suitcase just as the trunk clicked shut. He brushed past her to the driver's side door and got in, ignoring her stunned "Uh …"

As he stepped on the gas, he caught a glimpse of her dazed face in the side mirror, palm upturned at her side.

Thirty minutes later, Matt stepped into his airline's short, first-class check-in line. He felt bad ditching Joss like that, but he wasn't going to stand there and argue. Besides, I.T. had surely prepped her on how to counter any of his objections. The reality was, he simply couldn't be responsible for her. And he couldn't have her slowing him down, or saying the wrong thing to the wrong person. And he needed to be agile, free to pivot on a whim.

With Ostrovsky involved now, Matt's complex new plan had many more moving parts, and having never read a single imprint from the man, Matt had little basis for predicting behaviors. It's why he agreed to risk a trip to Ukraine at all. He needed to get in Ostrovsky's head. Though he was certainly curious, the artifacts they wanted him to read were unlikely to contain anything surprising.

That reminded him. He needed I.T. to block any calls, texts, or emails from Peter Sharma while Matt was gone. His archaeologist friend could screw up everything with a single excited message.

A voice behind him said, "I'm still gonna need coffee."

Matt closed his eyes. "Shit." He turned around to see an unruffled Joss standing beside her bright green suitcase. "Look, I'm sorry about earlier—that was incredibly rude of me—but you just can't come with me."

"I understand. I'm not trying to cramp your style or anything, and Iris gave me a bunch of things to memorize so I could argue with you on her behalf, but in all honesty, for someone who's never been out of the country, I'm actually super stoked about the free tickets waiting for me at that counter."

The woman in line behind Joss pointed. "Sir, they're calling for next in line. That's you."

Matt grabbed his duffle and Joss followed him as he walked backward toward the counter. "I get it, Joss, I do—"

"I could hardly sleep last night thinking about the fact that I'd be in Russia tomorrow."

Matt sighed.

"I won't even talk to you," Joss went on as Matt gave his passport to the ticket agent. "You can read, watch movies, stare mindlessly at the back of the seat in front of you … whatever you want. Pretend I'm not there. We're just a couple of travelers who happen to be going to the same place."

"Did you bring your passport?" he asked her.

"See, that's the thing. I don't even have to go with you to your meeting thing. Wait, what? Oh, yeah, I have it!" She grinned, elated as she dug in purse.

He'd do exactly that: leave her in Belgorod, Russia while he carried on to Ostrovsky's private airstrip.

"How many bags?" the ticket agent asked.

"Just one more." Matt grabbed Joss's suitcase and set it on the big scale, noticing the lime green was patterned with tiny pink flowers. "This is hideous, by the way."

"Mean," Joss said.

Matt took the tickets, handing Joss hers. "Let's go get that coffee. Starbucks or Dunkin'?"

FIVE

Belgorod, Russia – Present day

The jet touched down and taxied off the runway. Outside, Belgorod, Russia's small international airport appeared practically deserted, save for the cluster of cargo planes near the outlying hangars. When the jet turned to cruise alongside the row of gates, Matt observed forklifts unloading full, shrink-wrapped pallets. Humanitarian aid for the thousands of Ukrainian refugees streaming into the small city.

A passenger behind Matt asked their neighbor about the red cross-emblazoned cargo.

"Ukrayinski," the man replied with resentment. Not all the locals were thrilled about their new guests from across the border.

The jet continued along the terminal, passing plane after parked plane at roughly 20mph, and then abruptly *stopped*. Passengers bowed in unison, clutching purses and loose items before they fell. The engines whirred down. Confused heads popped up between seats like groundhogs, peering forward for an explanation. Alas, the flight attendants appeared equally puzzled.

Matt glanced through his window again, spotting a black private jet idling in the jet's path. Something told him this roadblock was no accident.

The overhead speaker clacked and a pilot spoke in Russian.

"What'd he say?" Joss asked.

"Just a moment." Matt pressed his cheek to his window. "There's a little jet blocking our path. Some guy in a suit now talking to ground crew … Hang on … Ground guy talking on his radio. Just signaled to the cockpit. I think they want to open the door."

"They're bringing the rolling stairs," said a woman up the opposite row.

The cockpit door opened. An irritated pilot eyed the rows of passengers, then leaned to the flight attendant's ear. She nodded, unbuckled her belt, and stepped to the aisle as the pilot returned to the cockpit, shutting the door behind him.

The flight attendant spoke in English, "Mr. and Mrs. Porter from United States?"

Rubbernecking travelers scanned the cabin for the condemned. Matt sighed. Joss had used her real passport, but Matt had traveled under his Todd Porter alias.

Great. They know Joss came with me.

He felt Joss's anxious, awaiting stare. Without turning to her, he subtly lifted a finger from his lap. She took the hint and settled back in her seat.

"Need I consult the rosters?" the irritated flight attendant continued. "Please come to front, Porters. Your private aircraft will take you from here."

Markus had said Ostrovsky's plane would be waiting here, but failed to mention it'd stop his flight on the way to the gate, if that was part of the plan. They were probably worried about security in the airport, or Customs.

A soft thud resounded from outside the forward door—stairs now ready for steppers.

There was no use prolonging the inevitable. Matt opened his backpack, extracted his thin black turtleneck, and pulled it on. He fished around beneath half-eaten snack bags and device chargers, finding his beanie and gloves nestled at the bottom. Brushing crumbs from his hat, he nodded to Joss, and then stood.

Transfixed gawkers followed their short walk to the front.

Matt paused beside the flight attendant as she unlocked the hatch. He pulled on his hat and gloves, asking her in Russian, "Is this legal?"

Her face shrugged. "No concern for you. You're American. This will save you hours bypassing Customs."

"Take me with you!" a man in the front row joked.

Scents of fuel and freshly laid asphalt streamed in as the door swung wide. Matt glanced back at Joss. "It'll be fine. Really."

She smiled, unconvinced, and followed him outside.

At the bottom of the stairs, the suited man stood with his arms crossed before him. Airport security and ground crew stood back, waiting. The man was pale, bald on top, and wore a silver suit that stretched tight around his pot belly, but draped loosely everywhere else.

He gestured for them to hurry, calling out in Ukrainian, "Come now. We are blocking the plane."

Matt stepped onto the tarmac, replying in the man's dialect. "Ah, yes. That must be why it suddenly stopped."

"Yes, that is why." The man reached for Matt's backpack. Matt pulled it out of reach, receiving a disgruntled mug in return. "Come now. Get in." He pointed to the private jet's steps.

"Nope," Matt said. He kept his gaze fixed on the man's furious eyes. Joss clutched and twisted a wad of shirt in the small of Matt's back. She was scared. It was a mistake to let her come at all. He'd been right to ditch her at the house, and should've stuck to his convictions.

"What is this 'nope'? We must move the jet!"

"*You* must move jet," Matt said flatly. "Not my problem. I don't even know who you are."

"*Ach!*" He threw up his hands. "I am Yevheniy! Mr. Ostrovsky's personal driver! You want back on that plane? Lose five hour in

Customs? You know I'm here to pick up you and the lady." Yevheniy surveyed the ground crew and other onlookers' faces. Clearly, no one wished to say anything to an Ostrovsky man, but their patience would soon expire.

"The lady is not here for picking up." Matt glanced back at Joss. "She's staying at a hotel in town."

Yevheniy flailed a hand in the air. "I don't care! Send her to the hotel! You come on the plane, she stays here!"

"Are you talking about me?" Joss said. "What's he saying?"

"I'm trying to explain about you staying in town here. I'm not thrilled at the idea of leaving you here on the runway to figure it out by yourself."

"Well good!" She gulped. "I wouldn't exactly be 'thrilled' either."

"Come or stay if I care!" Yevheniy in broken English.

"Listen, Yevheniy, I have to get her to a hotel. Can you just park that thing somewhere for an hour?"

A sudden *clap* behind them. Matt spun and saw a luggage handler set Joss's suitcase down, while another stood in the big jet's open cargo hatch, Matt's bag in hand. He tossed it down to the first handler, who proceeded to drag the bags to them as he scowled and murmured.

Yevheniy balled his hands into upturned fists of frustration. "There is no hour to spare! We've a set window to enter and leave airspace! Now we go, so we're not shot down on way, yes?" He pointed to the small jet again. A young, suit-clad pilot popped his head out the door, outstretching his arms in a *"What's the hold-up?"* gesture.

An instant later, a lanky official on a stairway shouted "Ay!" and strode toward them from the terminal, walkie-talkie in hand, trailed by a security team. The big jet's pilot revved up his engines to a piercing whine.

There was no way around it. Joss was coming with him to Ukraine, and it was entirely his fault. Defeated, he motioned Yevheniy on. "Let's go."

Grumbling, Yevheniy grabbed both of their bags from the luggage handler and quickly shuffled to the private jet.

Security and the hollering airport official had broken into a jog—seconds away.

Matt spun to Joss. "I'm awfully sorry, but—"

"Well, I'm not!" She grabbed his wrist and marched after Yevheniy. "Let's get the hell out of here!"

* * *

The drive from Ostrovsky's private airstrip to his property's front gate lasted only a couple minutes, but revealed plenty about the billionaire's power and political status. Though Ukraine's conflicts flared no less than 100 miles east—separatist and Russian forces having yet to drive the battle this far west—the airstrip, road, and perimeter of the Ostrovsky estate were lined with Russian armor and troops. The T-90 tanks, personnel carriers, and anti-aircraft vehicles had all been painted black, and the soldiers all wore unofficial black uniforms. What had Markus said? *"Mr. Ostrovsky always aligns himself with the appropriate team."*

Entering the front gate, they left behind the army of bored, gawking troops, and now set eyes on an uninhabited palette of greens speckled with pink, yellow, and red flowers—nothing like the flat, snow-covered fields from Matt's previous visit. As Yevheniy cruised along the lengthy driveway to the main house, Matt noticed a wall, perhaps fifteen feet high, hidden just beyond the bordering tree hedge. Subtle anomalies among the shadows—untreelike movement—revealed a sampling of Ostrovsky's own perimeter guards acting as *"bee-watcher-watchers."* Though he could only make out a few of them among the foliage, Matt knew he'd entered the lion's den, now completely surrounded.

If three are visible, expect three hundred.

The war math of Haeming Grimsson, an eleventh century Icelander with whom Matt had become more than a little acquainted. The opal. A thousand years ago, its faceted surface adorned the pommel of the Norseman's exquisite sword. Now it existed as dust and memories—shot into countless tiny pieces by a madman in Cuba—an indeterminate number of its microscopic particles forever entombed within Matt's body.

"Wow," Joss breathed. "You weren't kidding about this place."

"Yeah," Matt replied.

Joss motioned to Matt's bare hands as she went on. "I think I could deal with living here … You know, minus the tanks, guns, and such."

Matt looked down, realizing his gloves lay on his knee. He mouthed "thanks" as he slid them on.

Yevheniy pulled beneath the massive carport jutting out from the house, and parked at the end of a row of luxury vehicles. He remained in the driver's seat, regarding the rearview mirror. "See you later," he said bitterly. He wouldn't be opening any doors for them.

Matt and Joss exited the vehicle. Automatic doors slid open at the house's guest entrance, and a suited attendant stepped out, stopping just outside the lobby with a welcoming smile.

As they walked across the carport's cobblestone surface, Matt pulled his beanie down over his ears and neck, overlapping the black turtleneck's collar. It felt both comforting and unnerving to be back in his trademark "uniform"—fully covered to protect his skin from accidental imprint reads. He'd dressed this way for so long that he'd grown used to the heat. Though no longer worried about his skin grazing imprinted objects, it'd taken a while to reprogram his instincts and lose that exposed feeling when outside his home.

"Welcome," the attendant said.

The glass doors slid open behind him. Out walked Markus, Ostrovsky's thirty-something affairs manager, as always, adorned in a stylish suit—this one beige, all sheen, sharp lines, and tapers—his black hair arranged in a perfect coiffure, polished shoes clacking onto the marble tiles.

"Almost beat me to the door this time," Markus said, placing his hands behind his back and offering a subtle bow in place of a handshake. "Welcome, Matthew. And to you as well, Miss. I am Markus, the house manager."

"Nice to meet you," Joss said as she stepped into place beside Matt.

"Shall we?" Markus said, extending a hand toward the door. "In case Matthew did not tell you, Miss, we have a brief check-in process."

"I'm aware, thank you."

Matt appreciated how she presented herself—matching Markus's manner, his brevity.

Inside the check-in office, Markus handed them off to security clerks. "I'll see you momentarily."

Matt and Joss passed through the security scanners without a hitch, and were led by a clerk through the "interview" room. Matt was curious why they didn't require a polygraph test like last time, at least for a new visitor like Joss.

The final door opened to reveal Markus once again, standing at-ease with his genial, if plastic, smile. "Thank you, Gustav. Matthew and Miss, right this way, please." He indicated the left fork of the great hall, a different path than the one Matt had previously walked. "Mr. Ostrovsky awaits you on the terrace."

Matt and Joss followed behind him, taking in the hall's marble floor, vaulted ceilings draped with what were surely ancient tapestries, wide-spaced display cases on pedestals, and a few seemingly unprotected paintings spaced out along the walls.

"It's like a museum," Joss whispered to Matt.

Markus replied without slowing or turning. "That was the steering wheel from a rather famous sunken cruise ship. The case here on the right contains the famed bust of Zenobia ... And finally, in the recess coming up on the left, we have Cézanne's *Card Players*, currently the most valuable artwork in the world."

The hall ended at a T where floor-to-ceiling windows revealed a vast landscape one would hesitate to call a back-yard. Markus paused, allowing them a moment to take it all in.

Outside, each stepped level boasted its own showpiece. The terrace just outside the windows evoked a Tuscan château, edged with marble statues and potted cypress. A lavish seating area surrounded a fire pit. The next tier down housed an impressive, boulder-encircled swimming pool seemingly transplanted from a tropical resort. Beyond stood a pool house, followed by gardens, stables, and riding fields. In the distance, someone had their horse cantering around a riding ring.

"The pool house actually has two levels," Markus confided. "One below ground that connects to the main house via tunnel. You can see the tunnel's glass ceiling there, in the pool floor."

"It's all quite impressive," Joss said.

Markus guided them to the right where they came upon a vaulted ballroom, its mahogany floor empty of furniture, and then they finally came to a break in the wall of windows. Beyond an opening through which one could drive a bus, Vitaliy Ostrovsky sat at an umbrella-shaded table. He spotted Markus and stood, smiling wide, practically charging at Matt for a handshake.

Matt was surprised by Ostrovsky's garb: brown loafers, slacks, argyle sweater vest over a cream polo.

Ostrovsky seized Matt's gloved hand and squeezed it too hard. "Matthew, Matthew! I have been as eager like a little boy all morning! I am overjoyed you decided to come." He released Matt's hand and turned to Joss. "And you, Ms. Leland! Look at you." He regarded her from head to toe, though sans any detectable creepiness, remarkably. More like a father appreciating his daughter's prom dress. He set his hands on her shoulders and planted a light kiss on each cheek.

"Pleased to meet you, Mr. Ostrovsky," she said.

"Come, sit," he said, turning and walking to the table.

Matt and Joss shared a look, Joss's face expressing surprise and approval. This wasn't the crude, ever-naked eccentric Matt had described on the first leg of their journey.

Just wait, Matt thought, and followed Ostrovsky's lead to the table, taking a seat across from him. Gilded plates lay adorned with grapes, cheeses, caviar, crackers, and what looked like cubed Spam.

"Please, help yourself to a tasty snack," Ostrovsky said. "And tell Markus what you would like for drink. I recommend the Golden Shower. Delicious."

Matt cleared his throat, shifted in his chair, and heard Joss inhale sharply at the beverage name, as well. Glancing casually around, he observed her nodding, with a polite smile and furrowed brow.

Ostrovsky misinterpreted their reserve and faces as mere curiosity. "You know what this is, Golden Shower?"

Matt put up a hand. "I'm sure it's a wonderful drink."

"Yes, of course! It is delicious, so I say—especially with this weather, my God … Vodka with citrus and ginger ale. Some sort of fruits muddled up in there—pineapple … orange pulps, maybe. But it is also when man pisses on woman, like for sex. I mean, it is possible other way, though I think mostly man on woman thing …" Ostrovsky mulled this, as if making a mental note to add the topic onto his list of research tasks, then quickly added, "But believe me, drink is scrumptious, truly! Nothing like urine, if you will have trust. Markus, bring three, please."

Matt didn't look again, but felt Joss's stiff energy, heard her breathe slow and deep. She seemed the type to be amused rather than offended by this sort of thing, or at least he hoped this was the case.

Ostrovsky laced his fingers behind his head as he leaned back in the chair. "That is my first born, Veronika." He nodded toward the riding ring in the distance. "Only ten, but highly skilled with the animals." He smiled for a moment, gazing out, his thoughts a mile away. The girl stopped the horse and an adult on the ground took hold of the reins. Ostrovsky's attention returned to his guests. "She was getting fat. Real Honey Boo Boo, you know? This is downside of spoiling. But now is okay because they find her something she want to do all day, and disgusting belly is shrinking." Joss must've made a face at this because Ostrovsky's eyes shot her way. "You don't like this? You think I should let her get bloated and sweaty like American child?"

Joss flailed. "No, no … not at all. Exercise is wonderful."

"Mr. Ostrovsky," Matt intervened before he could go on. "How about we discuss your project? Your recent acquisitions."

Markus returned with a servant holding a tray of three sparkling, electric-yellow drinks. The man set the glasses atop quark coasters on the table.

"You see? Like glass of iced piss!" Ostrovsky turned to Markus. "Bring the cases now."

Markus returned a sharp nod and zipped away. While they waited, the sounds of small birds and a light breeze filled the silence.

Ostrovsky's eyes alternated between Joss and Matt, studying them. He finally said to Joss, "You are assistant? Like *personal* assistant? For Matthew?"

"Yes," Joss said, her expression pleasant yet absent of warmth, like Markus.

"And what does this involve?" He always struggled with Vs, pronouncing it *een-WOLW*.

Joss hesitated, either unclear on what he'd said, or unsure how to answer.

Matt knew where Ostrovsky was going. "Strictly professional," he said, hoping to end it there, and then glanced back through the hangar-sized opening in search of Markus.

This only encouraged Ostrovsky. "Because those lips! Matthew! How long can you go without knowing—"

"Please," Matt interrupted, "Ms. Leland is only recently hired, and I insist we—"

Joss leaned forward, crossed her arms on the table before her, and cut Matthew off. "I have yet to get him drunk enough, Vitaliy, but don't you worry. He'll know soon enough."

Ostrovsky's eyes bugged out. His face, mouth agape, turned comically from Matt to Joss, and back. He laughed heartily, pounding the table. "Holy shit, this one! … Matthew!" He shook his head, leaned back in his chair, and lifted his glass in toast. "Za tvoyo zdorovye!"

The pair picked up their drinks and returned the toast. Matt knew his face had flushed, and his leg had begun shaking. He pressed his heel against the ground to stop it.

Markus reappeared from the house with two metal cases, one stacked on the other, and a shoulder bag. He placed the cases on the table side by side, and rested an index finger on the one closer to Ostrovsky. "A," he said as he touched the first case, "and B." He opened the leather bag, extracting a can of compressed air, and a box of disposable gloves.

"Good," Ostrovsky said. "You can go." He pulled on a pair of the gloves, slid the "A" box in front of him, twisted and released a latch, then swung the top open.

Matt and Joss's necks extended in unison to glimpse the contents. Ostrovsky's hands disappeared inside, then—gingerly, eyes slowly widening—his hands emerged with a prismatic length of red granite pressed lengthwise between. He glanced up at his audience, satiated by their fascination. He maneuvered the artifact onto one palm, freeing his other hand to fetch a square of thick cloth from inside the box. As if it were some ultra-delicate glass piece, Ostrovsky set the relic down on the cloth and pulled his hands away, finally able to breathe.

Eyebrows high on his head, goofy smile, and constant nod, Ostrovsky said, "Anh? The *Taria* … Are you ready?"

Matt's hands remained folded before him on the table. "What does that mean? 'Taria.' Where was it found?"

Ostrovsky snorted, "You don't know what this means? I thought you know everything."

"Off the top of my head, I can think of twelve different definitions. 'Strength' in Romanian, 'wait' in Maori, 'stripe' in Portuguese, 'mushy' in Arabic … There's also Basque, Spanish, Maltese—"

"Yes, yes, Einstein," Ostrovsky said with a flutter of fingers. "This could be Greek, Egyptian … some dialect, who knows? You do *your* thing now. Why ask me?"

Matt continued, "So it was found in Greece or Egypt?"

"Could be Latin," Ostrovsky demurred.

"May I ask who called it that?"

A vein swelled in Ostrovsky's forehead. "Are you going to touch it or not?"

"No," Matt said flatly. "Not here, and not until my questions are answered. As I'm sure you're aware, the vulnerabilities caused by my ability require me to set certain conditions. And I make no exceptions to these rules."

Ostrovsky, bewildered, looked to Joss for help. "What is this?" He glared at Matt. "Why come here? I know you don't trust me, despite our assurance. You call goddamn embassy in Kiev, tell them you're coming to see me, as if you disappear they know where to look! Come on!" He leaned forward, elbows on table, pleading. "This is deal between comrades, Matthew. You don't make me *feel* this. Why you bring this one here, if not to safeguard you while you do the thing?"

"You *really* don't want to tell me where you got it," Matt said calmly. He wanted to hear Ostrovsky say eBay—not to humiliate him, but to bring him down to Matt's level, or at least a bit closer to it. "I can only assume you're ashamed, as you clearly have no concerns about legality. Half the pieces we passed in your hall were either looted, smuggled out of their source countries, or flat-out stolen from an existing collection, and yet there they are, proudly displayed. What could be so embarrassing? I'll know as soon as I read it, anyway."

Ostrovsky smirked with pursed lips and sipped his drink. He sighed and finally said, "eBay. Markus get for me on eBay."

Matt smirked, feigning amused surprise. "Seriously?"

"Serious," Ostrovsky said, and gave him a *calm down* gesture. "Woman in Athens. She say it was in family for generations, pass down since before they move from home … Egypt. *She* call it Taria." He rotated his head an inch and called out, "Markus."

Markus appeared a few seconds later. "Yes, sir."

Ostrovsky gestured for Matt and Joss to drink their now-sweaty beverages, and both complied. "Markus went to pick up the Taria from seller."

"How much did you get it for?" Joss asked, but then caught Matt's face. "Sorry. Just curious."

Markus answered, "By their previous living standards, the family was very well compensated. And the seller had only asked for the equivalent of one thousand dollars."

"Tell them the story," Ostrovsky said, and focused on his fields.

Markus put his hands behind his back. "Very well. The family lived in a rather impoverished neighborhood. The seller, a widow in her early forties, thought little of the artifact, but was fearful of her mother finding out it was being sold. We met in a neighboring apartment building where she brought the item—which she called *The Taria*—loose in a purse with other items … keys and such. As you can see, the inscriptions in the middle of each long side are worn down, some of them rendered illegible. This is due to a family tradition involving the object. Typically mother to daughter, a song is taught to the next generation. One line of the song per side, and the surfaces are rubbed with a thumb while singing."

"Did she sing it for you?" Matt asked.

"Yes, by my request." Markus replied. "She and her young daughter sang it quietly as I recorded. There's a bit of background noise, but it's fairly clear if you'd like me to retrieve it."

"No, that's okay for now," Matt said. "Was the song in Greek, though?"

"I don't believe so," Markus said. "The woman doesn't know what any of the words mean. She says they're just sounds, a tune, like singing along to a song in a language you don't speak, even to her elderly mother who taught it to her. The meaning is presumed to have been lost many generations ago, but the ritual remained. Sing the song, rub the stone, turn to the next side, so on. Like a ..." Matt saw for the first time Markus searching for an English word. "... A lucky thing."

"Superstition," Matt said as he settled back in his chair, pondering.

Ostrovsky, impatient, threw up his arms. "Okay, enough? You will look at thing now?"

"No," Matt said. "I'm sorry, but it's just like I said. Not here. Let me take it to a hotel in Belgorod for a couple days."

"Impossible," Ostrovsky said, shaking his head and sliding the cloth back to his side of the table. "They will not leave my property."

"Okay," Matt sighed, and eyed the second box. "The second one you mentioned. Is it from the same woman?"

"No," Markus replied as Ostrovsky returned the Taria to its case. "And it might be of particular interest to you, Matthew. Sir, may I?" Ostrovsky nodded dismissively, and Markus put on a fresh pair of gloves.

Beneath the table, Matt pinched one of his gloves between his knees and slowly slid his hand out. In the corner of his eye he caught a subtle head movement from Joss as she noticed what he was doing. Wisely, she immediately returned her attention to Markus as he opened the second box.

"And why would it be of particular interest?" Matt said as Markus dipped his hands into the container.

"Because ..." Markus began, and brought the second artifact into view. It was the exact same shape—a triangular prism of apparently identical dimensions to the first—but in such pristine condition that it could be mistaken for a recently created fake.

Matt frowned. "A reproduction isn't going to help me learn the history of the authentic one."

Ostrovsky laughed.

Markus spread a new cloth on the table and gently set down the object. "It's no reproduction, Matthew," he assured. "It's absolutely genuine, and possibly a superior sample as it pertains to your talent. You see, Taria B has not been touched by human skin in nearly two thousand years. Since being recovered, it has only been handled with gloves or other barriers. You will find no—*imprints*, is it?—from modern-day persons. As to its remarkable preservation, this is due to the airtight encasement in which it's survived, untouched and unseen, shielded from light and all manner of wear, since the third century."

Matt and Joss leaned forward, heads floating around the object like snakes. The inscriptions were absolutely pristine, and, once more, were not what he'd expected.

Matt opened his mouth to ask another question, but Markus interrupted. "Don't bother asking where it was acquired."

"Okay … Well, have you been able to translate this yet?" Matt said, his face alight with thrill. He mumbled to himself as he read the inscriptions on one face. The first in Demotic, a Hieratic script the Egyptians used for documents. *"The people,"* it said, and then switched to Ancient Greek: *"With life."* He was about to reach for it to flip it over and read another side, but paused and asked, "Would you mind?" He glanced at Markus.

Markus reached for the artifact, but Ostrovsky grabbed his wrist. "No! If you wish to read, you read. You want to be first person to touch my most precious piece, you do it *here … my* property. There is no safer place in country, I assure you." He released Markus's wrist.

Markus scooped up the second Taria and returned it to its metal box.

Knowing he was only *playing* the defenseless psychometrist of yesteryear, Matt considered a quick change of plans. While it had no bearing on his plans, he *needed* to read that Taria. He felt like a drug addict sitting in front of the purest, highest-quality substance he would ever encounter, and it appeared Ostrovsky wouldn't soon bend on the thing leaving the grounds.

Both artifacts resealed in their cases, Matt, Joss, and Ostrovsky sat mute for several minutes, Ostrovsky playing with his empty glass, spinning it in tiny turns on the coaster, his expression resolute. Joss engaged herself in a solo thumb war. Beneath the table, Matt's bare hand remained firmly planted on the table's underside, funneling Ostrovsky's real-time thoughts into Matt's head. The imprints rushed in as brief spurts, as the side of Ostrovsky's hand intermittently grazed the wood tabletop.

Arrogant piece of dung useless American ... wasting my goddamned time ... whore mother can suck me ... Matt had been reading long enough to know that Ostrovsky wouldn't relent any time soon. And then Ostrovsky thought, *He gets one more goddamned minute to change mind before I kick him out. Him and ...* his eyes moved to Joss—her face and then her chest. Ostrovsky's thoughts instantly switched to things Matt didn't wish to see and so he popped his hand off the table. Though Ostrovsky's current distraction might delay their ejection for a moment, Matt readied his words of acquiescence. It simply couldn't end here—not after everything it'd taken to reach this chair.

Matt inhaled a deep breath and said, "Well ..."

But Markus, as if on cue, spoke over Matt, leaning to Ostrovsky. "Sir, may I offer a suggestion?"

Ostrovsky growled, snapping out of his daze, and flipped a hasty hand in the air for Markus to proceed. Matt returned his fingertips to the table's underside.

"Philippos," Markus said, and Ostrovsky chewed on this. "Staffed, but currently no guests."

Matt watched the side of Ostrovsky's bare hand resting on the table as scattered thoughts about Markus's suggestion bounced around Ostrovsky's head. It seemed a good idea—frustrating because it was a compromise, bullshit because he'd have to wait—but a logical choice. But Rostik should meet them there; he was still in Alexandria …

Rostik. A dangerous contractor. He stole Taria B from its hiding place …

Matt tried to drill deeper on this Rostik character, but Ostrovsky's focus shifted back to this island.

Philippos, a private Greek island in the Aegean Sea, owned entirely by Ostrovsky, with turquoise beaches and an epic main house Matt observed in the billionaire's thoughts. Ostrovsky particularly liked that this would solidify and prolong Matt's stay, enabling much lengthier readings. And the longer he spent reading the Tarias, the better the chances of finding the scrolls … *if Turner agrees …*

Oh, I'll agree, Matt thought, and Ostrovsky, as if hearing him, made his decision. He picked up his empty drink and tilted it to his mouth to catch the dregs of alcohol in the ice melt.

"Let's do it," Ostrovsky said, his sharpened eyes turning and landing on Matt's. "You agree, Matthew?"

He knows! Matt thought, reflexively yanking his hand from the table as if Ostrovsky somehow sensed it there, and had been reading Matt in reverse. It was Ostrovsky's pretense: the simple, predictable man—unobservant, face-value. Even while reading him, Matt didn't catch it, but now it was clear. Ostrovsky had earlier observed Matt's hand beneath the table, noted it, put it together, *used* it. THE ART OF WAR. Have the enemy believe they're winning up until they've lost.

Joss turned to Matt, confused. "Agree to what? Did I miss something?"

Matt swallowed—a child caught sneaking cookies. "Yes, it seems a sensible solution."

"What 'it'?" Joss said, frustrated. "What's happening?"

"I'll tell you later," Matt replied. "Everything's fine."

Ostrovsky smiled, gratified, as after a prolonged massage, and reclined slowly in his chair. He nodded to his glass.

"More, Markus."

SIX

ALT 41,000 feet – Black Sea – Present day

Three days ago, Joss Lynn Leland was in Pennsylvania doing her spiel on stage with Cameron, knot cinching her gut, knowing the odds he'd press her for post-conference drinks again. It'd always been a transparent scheme, beginning after their second seminar.

"Let me buy you dinner," he'd said. "We've much to celebrate."

He'd flagged down a server for another round before Joss was halfway through her first. After gallantly offering to walk her to her hotel room, Cameron was sloshed and stumbling, believing himself ten times more charming and attractive than usual. In the hotel hall, he'd passed his room, following Joss to hers. He waited, leaning with one hand against the wall, as Joss slid the key card into her door.

"F'we keep this up," he'd slurred, "we minuswell save the cash an' get one room ferm'ow on."

She'd stopped him with a finger jab to the chest. "Not happening, Cam. Now or ever. Night."

Either by alcohol-induced amnesia, or obnoxious, misguided persistence, Cam had given it another go in Boston (even leaning in with half-open mouth, and copping a feel) on their walk back to the hotel. She'd elbowed him off, punched him in the throat, and told him that kind of crap couldn't happen again. He'd sulked for the rest of the walk—hacking and gagging—and *she* felt like the ass.

But it wasn't until Matt showed up that she'd even considered ditching Cam. It simply hadn't been an option. Why not? Howsabout a little self-respect?

Now she found herself halfway around the world, 40,000 feet in the air in a multimillion-dollar private jet, seated facing the world-famous Matthew Turner, on her way to some luxurious personal island. As she gazed at Matt—off in space again as he peered out his window, one ungloved hand in his pocket—she tried to keep all of it in perspective. This kind of thing didn't happen in real life. And while she'd pondered ulterior motives on Matt's part, perhaps hiring her with similar eyes to Cameron's (her trust in men may be a bit dented) she now perceived Matt's outlook on her as somewhat paternal. It jived with his initial job offer to her, what she'd interpreted as some conviction that he must *rescue* her from this charlatan. She'd initially scoffed at Matt's judgment, truly believing that he had it all wrong. She and Cam were *business partners*, you see (notwithstanding the occasional harassment, but she could handle Cam's malarkey herself).

Now, getting to know Matt better, her hindsight sharpening, and with enough distance from Cam, Joss found more truth in the "rescued" notion than she'd previously cared to admit. Because that's what Matt did, right? Rescue people?

Is that all this is? Weaning me off Cameron? We both know Matt could've put his foot down on me coming. What purpose have I served, exactly, as his tagalong?

Maybe, despite the location or company, he considered her safest under his supervision. She was one of his successes, after all. He'd forever have a vested interest in her wellbeing.

She leaned over and peered around her seat back. Markus, still buttoned up tight in one of his sharp suits, already had those wide-spaced, steel-blue eyes on her, Mona Lisa smile firmly in place.

She faced forward and sat upright. Though he was quiet—usually only speaking when spoken to—Joss imagined Markus's brain was this high-speed blender of observations, analysis, and calculations, always busy in there, and eternally loyal to his employer. Did he ever get time off? Would he even want it? It was a funny idea, this old concept of the devoted butler, like Alfred and Batman. Had Alfred ever said, *"Apologies, Master Wayne, but I'm taking off a couple days to take a shower, do laundry, and clean my own damned house."* Oh, but why would they *want* to do anything but work for their master, right? Serving is their life.

Does Alfred even have his own house?

She wanted to stand up, sit down across from Markus, and say, *"So, Markie, where ya from?"*

Just imagine the look on his face! Or maybe not … He could respond as smooth as ever—who knew?

"Pardon me, Matthew." Markus's voice, right over Joss's shoulder. She and Matt looked up. Markus had both metal cases in hand. "We have another ninety minutes before Athens. I trust you're eager to pre-examine the Tarias?"

* * *

As if being presented their favorite meal, Matt and Joss watched intently as Markus set the second Taria—the faultless one—onto the cloth-covered table between them.

The flight attendant who had brought the table emerged from behind a curtain with a tray of beverages.

Markus sat down in the seat beside Joss, and waved off the flight attendant. "Later, Eta."

She nodded, returning to the galley.

Markus tugged his gloves tight at the wrist, and edged closer. "There were originally four," he began, sliding the two artifacts together to line them up lengthwise, careful to keep them from touching. "As evidenced by the inscribed ellipses at one end of each. See?" He lifted each and held them close to each other so Matt could see the semicircle created by the two quarter circles. "When all four are joined together with the correct sides facing out, presumably, a full circle is displayed at this end."

Matt nodded, knowing this was incorrect. The ellipses were carved precisely so people would *think* there were four keystones. "What's at the other ends?"

Markus turned them around and Matt observed the unique engravings on each. The triangular end of the older—well, more worn—Taria had a cluster of Hieroglyphs, a group of characters generally used in a city's name. In this case, he saw a snake, water, sunrise, and others.

"Djanet," Matt said. "Tanis to the Greeks."

"Yes," Markus agreed. "But what of this one? Mr. Ostrovsky's people have been unable to translate it thus far."

"It's Demotic script … Would you mind?" Matt twirled a finger, and Markus rotated it. "Yeah, right there. You read it from right to left. The *off* thing about it, and probably the reason your person couldn't figure it out, is that you don't often see an inscription like this. Sort of a formal Demotic. Looks a lot like modern-day Arabic, but shares more in common with the hieroglyphs Demotic was based on. The whole point of the script was to be able to *write* it, and quickly, with ink. If you were making something more permanent, decorating a wall or something, you'd have still used Hieroglyphics."

"Sorry if it's a dumb question, but if they always used the Hieroglyphs, why do you think they put that other language on this thing?" Joss asked. "And can you read it?"

"The pieces were inscribed in three different languages as a code," Matt explained. "Combined, they're essentially a treasure map, and the people who made them wanted to ensure that only an intellectual like them could decipher the text. Very few people at that time would've been able to perfectly translate all three, and I'm assuming there's key information in each language that doesn't exist on the other two pieces. This here," he pointed at the Demotic inscription, "says 'spouse,' possessive, and 'relative,' so I'd translate that as 'in-law.'"

Markus smiled. "Very good, Matthew. This is very, very good."

Matt reached out, hovering a hand near the Tarias. "May I?" What he really wanted was to yank his gloves off and get inside those things, but one thing at a time. The translations would likely sharpen Ostrovsky's focus on the scroll hunt, and that's exactly what Matt needed.

Markus nodded, *proceed*.

"Joss," Matt said. "Could you take some notes, please?"

Flustered for an instant, she dug around in her bag, withdrew a yellow notepad, then found a pen at the bottom of her purse. "I'm ready."

Matt spent the next few minutes dictating his translations of the inscriptions, flipping the stones with his gloved hands. Joss separated the translations onto different lines, and marked them with Markus's designations of Taria A and Taria B, followed by a number indicating the side. When finished translating, Matt peered across the table at her pad.

"Oh, I like this," Matt said, indicating her notes.

"I defined side one the same for both stones," she explained, pointing with the back of her pen. "You started reading 'B' on a different side than 'A,' but they're both in order here. I used the curved lines on the ends as the reference point. So this line is side one, the curve is side two ... like that. I can change it if—"

"No, no," Matt said. "That's perfect."

Matt observed Joss striving to remain nonchalant, but she clearly appreciated the opportunity to contribute.

"This is how we catalogued as well," Markus commented. While he had yet to share the translations completed by Ostrovsky's people—likely to keep from influencing Matt's translations—Markus had a clipboard with printouts at the ready. "Go ahead, Ms. Leland. Begin with your A-one, if you would."

Joss cleared her throat ceremoniously. "'Return, protect, wisdom, tomb, remember, The Great, meet at,' and then the side inscription: 'Tanis.' Did I spell that right?"

"Spot-on," Matt said, then, curious, turned to Markus, who was scribbling little notes on his clipboard. "Are we in sync so far?"

Markus shrugged. "In essence. I've made notes."

Matt sighed. "Okay, read the next one, please, Joss."

"'Of all time, heretic, the people, with life, song, him, Tanis' again, and then the side symbol, 'in-law.'"

"Two things." Matt pointed at her sheet. "Him is actually *hymn*—like a song—and it's not Tanis again, it's Thonis, with a t-h. Different city all together."

Markus leaned forward. "May I borrow that a moment?"

Joss handed him the notepad, and Markus compared the two, scrawling more notes for himself.

"Markus," Matt began. "Obviously, I'll be able to offer some more clarity once I've read them, but out of curiosity, did your people have any theories on the inscriptions' meanings?"

Markus tapped the pencil against his chin. "Some common themes: hymn and song, family, plus the two locations. The problem is that we must assume the inscriptions on the *inside*, that is, the sides that are hidden when all four Tarias are joined into a box, are irrelevant to discovering the location. 'Tomb' is tempting, but it's on an inner side, and therefore misdirection. Further, without the other two, deciphering the meaning began to feel exceedingly futile."

Matt nodded slowly, admiring the Taria creators' ability to fool their secret's pursuers—even now, nearly two thousand years later. They understood human nature. Give someone two pieces of a puzzle with ostensibly obvious final shapes—triangles, a square, a circle—and their minds can't see past them. He marveled at the fact that the circle misdirection had been an afterthought, a final layer of protection on top of all the others.

"You disagree?" Markus probed.

"Oh, no, not at all. I was just wondering what gave anyone the idea that the Tarias had something to do with the Library of Alexandria."

Markus's rigid smile and unblinking eyes, the slight hesitation—he was considering whether to share more undisclosed information.

"So," Joss interjected, "when's the *real* party going to start? What're we waiting for, exactly?"

No one responded.

Markus set his clipboard down on his lap. "Taria B was found sealed in a location inscribed with a particular date. This date is shortly after the only truly recorded destruction of the Library." Matt raised a finger, but Markus cut him off. "That's the only information I can share at this time."

Matt scoffed at the absurdity. He'd know everything Markus was hiding after reading the Tarias. "But I can just—"

"Yes, of course," Markus interrupted, "and whatever you learn while experiencing the artifacts are protected by the confidentiality and recompense agreement you signed in my office. It's quite plainly illogical, but here we are."

A hint of independent thought from Markus, Matt observed. A first.

"Understood," Matt said, setting his eyes on the smooth surface of Taria B.

That old familiar buzz trembled in his head—the mental equivalent of salivating over a beloved food. He'd been playing it cool since Ostrovsky's house, exuding a take-it-or-leave-it persona, and he'd grown bored, even agitated, with reading seats, utensils, the linty reservoir of paper money fibers in the bottoms of his pockets, coins, the omnipresent fragments of opal in his body. But this was no mind-filler read. Despite knowing all that had occurred in Alexandria, he had yet to personally meet any of the players.

"Well," Matt began. "I'd prefer to wait until we reach the island and I have some privacy ... but if you just want to break the ice, I guess I can quickly gather some basics, confirm your date and place. Up to you, Markus."

Markus motioned to the Tarias on the table: *Help yourself.*

Matt glanced at Joss as she shifted in her seat, eager eyes and smile. Markus sat staring as well. Matt had said "quickly," but expected to spend at least ten minutes.

"You know," Matt said, "it takes me a few minutes to get going, then to gather anything solid ... so, maybe ..."

Markus took the hint and moved to a nearby seat. Joss mumbled apologies while rifling through her bag for a magazine.

Matt pulled close the cloth bearing the shiny, perfect Taria B. He slid off a glove, glanced once more at Joss—now at least pretending to be engrossed in a magazine—and picked up the artifact, curling his fingers around it.

* * *

As far back as he could remember, the sensation of entering an imprint felt to Matt like rushing forward or backward, with a sharp sucking sound in the ears, a forced re-inventory of body parts, their positions and motion, the introduction of sights, smells, sounds, tastes, and the ubiquitous internal dialogue of some other person invading his head, overlapping with Matt's own thoughts—like wearing headphones with a different song in each ear.

With the imprints of individuals who thought in images as opposed to words, the *head* part of the transition went much more smoothly, as if Matt had just walked late into a movie. The typical image thinker, upon encountering a familiar person, tended to go through a subconscious highlight reel review: this is my older brother, Chenyun, a jerk, our last conversation was negative, I wish he'd move to Taiwan—all in a flash of visual snippets. This played out like having a friend who'd seen the movie from the beginning, whispering in Matt's ear whenever something occurred that required explanation: "They think this guy is the real killer, but the sister's husband's been acting suspiciously."

Lately, Matt's ability to move from reality to imprint and back had grown so smooth and effortless that he seldom felt an inkling of his former anxiety. Even with his caseload back home, he'd developed a technique for dealing with high-intensity objects: a tiny, bloody shirt, for instance. Reading from an object was no longer an all-or-nothing exercise, but could now be fine-tuned to Matt's preference. Evidence recovered from the scene of a murder? Matt would virtually poke his head in and take a look around before opening the door any wider, like dipping a toe in a pool of unknown temperature. He'd more than once found himself dropped into the mind of a victim, violent murder in progress, and that was back when he still needed his timer to pull him out. In those days, it'd be too late to back out of the imprint—he'd committed himself to five minutes of that sort of torture.

But wary of Iris's judgment (by way of her assigned proxy, Joss), and with the commotion of traveling, Matt had only ventured into less-than-enthralling imprints. Thus his cannonball-style plunge into the Taria with Joss right across from him, not to mention Markus seated nearby.

Lurching forward into the body, Matt bathed in the flood of input, a disorienting jumble of thoughts and senses that reminded him of the old days of reading. He even went through his former rituals—Dad's info prioritization technique.

I'm female. Thirty-nine years old. My name is Supatra. I was born and currently live in Alexandria, Egypt, third year of Augusta Septimia Zenobia, our exquisite empress, with whom I'll imminently speak.

I'm both disgusted and amused, leaning against a wall in the Serapeum, the temple of the manmade god, Serapis—a cunning unification of traditional Greek characteristics into two of Egypt's most revered gods, Osiris and Apis. As if to say, "See, Egyptians? We have the same gods, though ours are even better."

I like this Supatra already, Matt thinks, and draws himself backward and downward, deeper into her unconscious memories.

"Hello, Steward," says a voice in Patra's head. Actually, it's Patra's voice, but her internal dialog ends there.

Matt senses something peculiar about her subconscious.

*Oddly barren this deep. Superficial details only. She's known as 'Patra' to most. An advisor, philosopher, translator—one of three appointed stewards of the Musaeum of Alexandria, the vast university complex which included the library, of which she was Head Librarian. And someone with access to Queen … excuse me, **Augusta** Zenobia!*

Matt thrills at the rare, impending encounter with someone whose name had actually endured to the present day, though it remains curious this is the Taria's most prominent imprint.

Patra is eager to speak with Zenobia, but she's not particularly emotional.

The fact implies the Taria holds no imprints more interesting than this moment in the Serapeum.

The thrilling life of a librarian—no less exhilarating two thousand years ago!

He wonders where on her person she has the Taria.

Don't feel anything in her hands … Doesn't matter right now.

He allows himself to float forward again, back toward Patra's consciousness. In imprints, this was always the "look at me!" section, the parts demanding to be seen, felt, fully experienced. Back in the day, it was what trapped him inside a reading, each time his nervous system severed from his own body—only able to perceive the imprinter's senses—until Matt was physically detached from the artifact.

No more.

His fist squeezed tighter around the Taria. He willed his ears to hear the jet's hum, his nose to smell the leather. Nowadays, it was very likely he possessed the only central nervous system on Earth capable of interpreting input from four ears, two noses, four arms, four legs, and so on. Or at least, the only *human* central nervous system.

He considered sneaking a peek to see if anyone was staring at him, but thought better of it. Ostrovsky had caught him using his ability at the table, but he and Markus didn't know just how vulnerable (or not) Matt was while engaged in a reading.

Releasing his body once more, he let his mind fully immerse into Patra's, where he'd left off: *disgusted and amused ...*

I'm both disgusted and amused, leaning against a wall in the Serapeum. Obscured by a column and its flanking bushes, the small group in the courtyard cannot see me, but I can hear them. Our Empress, Zenobia—a woman who at first appraisal I'd lumped in with the myriad predictable, avaricious, foreign rulers—entertains and indulges a clutch of priests. I hope they're finished soon ... She's only in Alexandria another two days. But these priests are likely amusing her even more than they are me.

"Augusta," one of them says repeatedly, addressing Zenobia by her official title—equivalent to Empress or Queen—as he attempts to speak over his companions. "Augusta, it's not a mere rumor—"

"Is that so?" Zenobia interrupts him, and the whole flock of prattling holy men fall silent. "You have firsthand knowledge of Emperor Antonius slaying his own brother?"

"Augusta," the priest says breathlessly, his blessed ears not wishing to hear it spoken so bluntly. "I speak of tomorrow's exhibition! The one in which the venerable Emperor will be mocked before thousands! It's no rumor, but confirmed by the Governor himself. An open invitation has been circulating mouth to ear!"

"Really?" Zenobia says smoothly, her Greek tinged with a distinct Aramaic accent—a hallmark of the Palmyrene tribes from the northeast, where I first met her—her homeland. "Governor Cassius confirmed this? Is he attending?"

"Augusta?" Another priest, baffled.

I observe one of Zenobia's courtiers appear from the colonnade, striding toward the Empress, official business painted all over. He disappears beyond the column before me just as he begins his scheduled announcement. "Her Majesty must bid you all farewell."

"Let Cassius know that I hope to see him there," a merry Zenobia says, and the priests stifle their gasps. "I look forward to the performance."

She may be enjoying the priests' anguish, but this is actually troubling news. With Augusta now coming, the little show, a silly political farce intended for a small audience of friends, may ignite unintended uproar. I told Kaleb it was unwise and dangerous. One would think I'd learn. As always, he derived a challenge from my caution. Somehow, I must persuade Augusta to not come.

"Supatra of Alexandria," the courtier calls. "Daughter of Gaius of Alexandria and Avita of Meroe."

I step from behind the column, see Zenobia, seated like a true queen in a temporary throne atop a plinth fashioned from stone blocks, and draped with gilded silk. As I walk to her, I notice where the blocks came from. The olive trees in front of every other column now sit on the ground.

Zenobia is a statue from the Old Kingdom, stiff and formal and gazing ahead to nothing as she dismisses the aide. I approach and kneel onto one knee, my key sliding between my legs, and I shove it aside.

There it is—the Taria. Matt could feel it beneath her robes. *It's some kind of giant key, hanging from her waist by a cord. Feels long though, much longer than the stone in my fist.* "Keystone." Now the term made more sense.

"Rise, my beauty," Zenobia says. I look up and the aide has already taken his leave. The Augusta's face bears a warm smile, that of a friend. "Come, sit with me. Come close." She points a manicured toe to the step below her leather-strapped feet, and then slides off her throne to join me on the lower level.

I climb the stone steps to her, careful to keep my head below hers, and take a seat. I say "Augusta" as I sit, avoiding her eyes.

"Please, Patra, look at me," she says, placing a hand on my wrist. Her fingers are long, each one embellished with a gem-encrusted ring, her fingertips henna-dyed, with red wine nails filed to points. "When it's only us, nothing has changed, understand?" She lifts my chin so I meet her eyes. At thirty-seven, her beauty is more astonishing than ever, face painted up to evoke Cleopatra Philopator—who, in her day, strove to conjure the goddess Isis.

Visions of our prior meetings flash before me—the more modest accommodations of her land, Palmyra. Her husband before he was killed. The fun of teaching her back then—a Queen no one could imagine becoming Augusta of all these lands—and later, her son, my little Wahbi, only five when first we met.

"My Queen," I begin, and I can see she wishes me less formal. It hurts her. "How is Wahbi?"

She laughs. "Like a weed! You wouldn't believe how tall! He misses you. I would've sent for him, had I known we'd be here. Perhaps you'll consider … resuming? From time to time, of course, as your work allows."

"Of course, my Queen."

I wonder how else Wahbi has changed. Upon the death of his father, the King, he inherited all titles, and is therefore the true Augustus. Though, at twelve, still too young to rule, a boy his age could rapidly decay in so potent a vat. And if the rumors are true, the Augusta will soon disembark, collecting Wahbi on her way to reconquer rebelling northern lands. Surely she'd charge him—at least symbolically—with the task of bringing those renegade lands back under Roman rule. It would be a message to Rome: *"Do you see? We've stabilized the region down here. No need to consolidate under a single ruler again!"* But everyone knew that the present state—an Emperor in the North, and one in the South—would last only as long as he in the North was too busy to address it.

Zenobia reaches back and picks up a plate of fruits, setting it between us. She daintily plucks a grape from the bunch and bites it in half, chewing with her lips closed—a stark contrast to the thirty-year-old woman I tried to teach Latin. She's been practicing Roman finesse. Only six years ago, one warm night we'd both enjoyed, the Queen sat in the dirt near a fire circle, legs spread out before her in a child's manner, wholly at ease, as a servant presented a stone platter. Zenobia had torn a wing from the duck, devouring the meat, and spat gristle and bone into the fire. *"Delicious,"* she'd said with a messy grin.

"Eat," Zenobia says. "The dates are from home. They've been warming in the sun."

"Thank you," I say, and she sees me searching for the appropriate formality.

She puts up a hand. *Thank you* is enough. She craves the relative normalcy of her former life. I peek up at her hair, a dark bronze, bleached lighter in sections by the desert sun, and arranged high in elaborate coils, beaded string holding small gold plates above each ear. Combined with her face, the entire arrangement surely took an army of staff the whole morning to create.

"You like it?" she says, having caught my eyes aimed well above hers. She smiles wide. Her teeth have been scoured clean since last we met, now gleaming white as a young child's. "It took the entirety of the morning to prepare. I adore it, but it's heavy as a house. Like carrying a wheat basket. A chore I endured more than once, if you recall."

It's how she wants me to remember her. I was right. She does crave the days of simple nobility—*Palmyrene* nobility, a full rank below the merely *affluent* of Alexandria. Many of her people still live a nomadic life, organized into small tribes. If I didn't know how she'd ascended to the throne, and further, to Roman ruler of the entire region, I'd never believe it.

She's given me every indication that speaking freely is not only acceptable, but encouraged. I must broach the performance. "Augusta," I begin.

"Zenobia, Patra. You of all people, *please."* Desperation in her voice. She needs it like water.

"Zenobia," I say, and she inhales deeply, as if leaving a musty chamber and finally breathing fresh air. She nods. I continue, "I came to invite you to the Musaeum, to hear two of our esteemed guests relate their exploits from Galatia to Kashmir and back. However, I must admit that I overheard your audience with the priests."

"The performance," she says, eyes narrowing, wicked grin. "I cannot *wait*."

"Yes, Aug—Zenobia, it's sure to be entertaining, but that's not my concern. You see, the performers, some of them are friends of mine, colleagues at the Musaeum. I ... fear repercussions."

"All the better I attend!" she proclaims. "It'll appear I commissioned them, redirecting any venom to me."

"That's *beyond* kind of you, Zenobia, though I don't wish anyone to suffer because of some silly exhibition. Their intent, these friends of mine, was to put on this little performance—something they'd been musing on for a few days—for the Musaeum residents. Then word spread beyond the walls and, not grasping the consequences, they had it moved to the amphitheater to accommodate a larger audience. And now ..." I motion to her.

"With my attendance, you foresee a full amphitheater and the tale spreading beyond the city. I understand." She puts her hand on mine, soothing. "Listen to me, Patra. You know that I love you, and you can ask me for anything. It would be done. But this ... It sounds to me that the ox has already breached the pen. If you still wish me not to attend, I will not. But believe me when I say that my presence will absorb the responsibility, and even if word reached Emperor Antonius, he has his hands full in Rome for the foreseeable future. A man like that—a soldier—he won't leave the Empire to the Senate and Magistracy, and with me here, he wouldn't send a mere squadron of ships to dish out punishment. Losing them would be too much of an embarrassment." She chomps a date, continuing with her mouth full, "No, it would be all or nothing: the Emperor goes about his business, forgetting in a day this tale of distant mockery, or the alternative, marshalling his entire fleet to dethrone the usurper, the *insolent* warrior queen." She smiles warmly again. "A trivial, satirical performance, miles across the sea, frankly doesn't warrant an undertaking of that monumental scale."

SEVEN

ALT 18,000 feet – Aegean Sea – Present day

Matt set the Taria on the cloth. "Do we have internet access? Where are we? How long until we land?"

"No internet just yet," Markus replied. "Fifteen minutes before we put down in Athens. What did you see?"

That was always the question, wasn't it? What had he *seen?* As though vision were the extent of an imprint's substance. He no longer felt compelled to correct people, explaining the deep, cerebral aspects of reading, the wholly enveloping act of entering another's mind.

Joss wore a familiar expression he'd observed on countless faces: the eager, *tell me everything* look one might flash upon seeing a friend enter the room with their hair standing on end, black-smudged face of a cartoon explosion, and a dead alien slung over their shoulder. It was the face Tuni always had when he'd come out of a session in Kenya. It reminded him ...

"Markus, you brought the other item we discussed?"

Joss perked up: *other item?*

Markus snapped a nod. "As promised. Deliverable after two days' work, regardless of findings."

Matt didn't like it at all, this leverage. Whatever Tuni had sent, it'd been intended for Matt. Ostrovsky justified withholding it, offering it as compensation (or *ransom*, to the vaguely observant), contending the package would've never made it out of the Kenyan presidential property if not for his operatives. This claim alone was concerning, but Matt downplayed his interest. If Tuni had been prevented from communicating all this time, who's to say she hadn't been attempting to reach out from the very beginning?

He'd long ago purged any lingering feelings (the positive ones, anyway), but the idea of her in trouble, or in pain, or *scared*. Terror was, by far, the most unbearable of emotions. A marriage with President The Gray now suddenly seemed unlikely to resemble Matt's long-held vision of blissful opulence. But hey, maybe it was all roses for Tuni, after all. She could simply be saying *"Hi, hope you're well. Things are bloody SPLENDID in the palace. Cheers!"*

"So?" Joss demanded, patting the table impatiently. "Let's hear it!"

Matt turned to Markus. "Alexandria, late third century, and the Library still exists. The ruler is a queen from a neighboring land, Zenobia. Have you heard of her?"

"Of course, Matthew," Markus said as he returned the Tarias to their cases. "And the Tragedy of Alexandria is soon to occur."

Matt feigned surprise. "*Tragedy* of Alexandria? We talking 'tragedy' in quotes here? Never heard of it. Is that supposed to be some known thing?"

"Fairly," was all Markus replied.

Matt stared. "I've heard of a *lot* of things." He knew what information existed in the historical record. Or so he thought.

Markus rolled his fingers to move on.

Matt glanced at Joss, still waiting for a recounting. "Sorry," he said. "Here's what happened ..."

As Markus jotted notes, Matt described the building—the Serapeum—Patra, Zenobia, and the conversation he'd witnessed.

* * *

For some reason, when Markus spoke of a "private island," Joss had envisioned a cute little thing, maybe a bit larger than a sandbar, with a single wind-blown palm tree at the top, situated beside a relatively nice beach house. From the shore, Philippos looked more like a tropical resort island, with a dense thicket of trees above a pristine beach, extending out in both directions until eventually wrapping around to some unseen rest of the island.

The dock led to a charming little beach hut with the flap up window covers. Elsewhere, this looked like the building where you'd grab a burger, or maybe check out a volleyball, or grab a stack of fluffy, fresh towels.

Joss stepped off the small boat and onto the wood pier. Markus's husky bodyguard, Grisha, helped her up.

The driver opened the storage compartment where the luggage had been stowed and Joss motioned to her suitcase. "Should I—?"

"No." The only English word Joss believed Grisha knew.

Markus called from the beach, where he and Matt stood waiting on a walking path that began where the pier ended. "They'll bring all of your items, Ms. Leland. Please, come."

She made her way to them, taking in more of the Greek isle scenery. "Sorry," she said as she approached.

"Now," Markus began. "The entire island is yours to roam—no rules or restrictions, but I do ask that you inform myself or Circe, the island manager, if you plan to venture to the south end. There are cliffs and caves, all quite spectacular, but also hazardous terrain. It'd be preferable, in fact, if someone took you there in the motorboat. I only ask this for safety purposes."

The trio passed the hut, entering a shady stand of trees, a cobblestone path replacing the smooth concrete. Markus gestured toward a pair of enticing hammocks with little side tables for drinks. Beyond stood another, smaller hut—or more like a storage shed—

with its paneled doors swung wide, its only purpose to supply ready stacks of those fluffy towels Joss had envisioned.

"Footwear, headwear, and sunglasses can be found in the cabinet around the side there, as well as all manner of sun lotions. It's hottest about this time each day. And you'll rarely see a cloud in the sky, so do protect your skin. You may find as others that afternoons here are best spent in the water. Life preservers, snorkeling, and more advanced watersport gear can be found back in the beach hut we first passed."

Continuing up a weaving path bordered with what couldn't possibly be native foliage and flowers, they reaching a sprawling single-story house, all glass and dark wood, its steel I-beam structure left exposed. A short bridge over a koi pond led to the tall wood doors.

"Beautiful," Joss said.

"Pleased you like it," Markus said. "This is the staff quarters where I'm staying, and where you can fetch me or Circe at any time. Additionally, everyone has a radio, so if you don't wish to make the walk, have any staff member ring for me. And now to *your* lodgings." He extended his arm toward the continuing stone path.

As they rounded the corner of the staff building, Joss remained mute despite the desire to ask why *she* wasn't staying in the staff quarters. Recalling the initial conversation at the mansion in Ukraine—the part where Mr. Ostrovsky suggested a less-than-professional relationship between her and Matt—Joss wondered if Markus was about to lead them into some grand bedroom, declaring, *"And here is where* you *two will be staying!"* Funny to imagine it, but what if he actually did? And what if Matt didn't snap right up and protest?

"Here we are," Markus said as they exited the grape-tangled arch of an arboreal tunnel.

"Jesus," Matt said quietly.

Joss stopped beside them and took in the sight. "That's a *house?*"

The one-story structure was elegant yet primitive, built with large blocks of roughhewn stone, expansive glass, and coarse wood accents, like a refurbished, modernized, Ancient Greek ruin. It looked to Joss like the secret lair of some Bond villain.

"I've never seen anything like this," Matt admired. "Mr. Ostrovsky's architects win again."

Markus nodded, clearly proud of the property, and led them inside, touring them through room after room.

"An interesting detail observed only by those arriving via helicopter ..." Markus indicated a framed photograph on a wall near the kitchen.

Joss leaned close. Shot from an aircraft of some sort, the photo appeared to exhibit some other island, or this island, but prior to any construction. Blanketed with trees, the only signs of human presence were the pier and a set of umbrellas on one of the beaches.

"No buildings," Joss said.

Matt leaned in beside her. "Wow, I see it. That's amazing." He stepped aside.

Markus pointed to an area of the photo for Joss. "The roofs are all painted and embellished to match the surrounding trees, and all structural shadows are masked by clever landscaping. The property is nigh invisible to aircraft and satellites."

Joss followed him into a wide hallway. "Mr. Ostrovsky doesn't mess around when it comes to vacation, eh?"

"He wishes for his guests to feel safe as well," Markus said without turning. "The island had to meet the strict requirements of many government security agencies in order for Mr. Ostrovsky to host their officials here."

"Surface to air missiles?" Matt joked.

Markus stopped between a set of doors, turning to him with an earnest expression. "Philippos is fully secure." He turned to address Joss, indicating a pair of French doors. "These are your quarters, Ms. Leland."

Joss put a hand on her chest in a *"who me?"* gesture before shuffling forward and opening the doors.

"Yeah, this'll do," she said, taking in the suite. The Greek theme didn't stop at the structure—from the column-flanked fireplace to the pale linen palette, the room would appear aristocratic and cold if not offset by the abundance of rugs, brightly-colored upholstery, and dark wood accents.

Matt's room was equally impressive, and essentially the same size, though Joss noticed at once that the chandelier over *his* sitting area was far less elaborate than hers.

Haha, she thought. *I'm so ridiculously petty.*

Markus observed Matt assessing the ostentatious king-sized bed. "Your bedding is all new and unused, and the staff have been instructed to utilize gloves for everything during your stay."

Matt conveyed gratitude with a nod; however, his gears continued turning. What was his deal? Safety? Other guests who'd used the room?

On the airstrip in Ukraine, before they'd boarded Mr. Ostrovsky's jet, she'd whispered to him, "Are you sure you can trust these people?" to which he'd matter-of-factly replied, "I don't have to trust anymore."

It was such an uncanny sentence, uttered with a singular, pure intent: to reassure her that she was, indeed, safe. And it'd worked. Stepping into the plane a second later, he appeared to have moved on with a *"now that that's behind us..."* air, but she'd stood there a beat, surprised at herself for suddenly feeling warm inside, and small, and safe.

Back in the hall outside their rooms, Markus pointed out that their luggage and personal items could be found in their respective closets, and informed them that dinner would be served on the veranda at seven. In the meantime, they were encouraged to settle in, change, explore the house, or walk down to the beach. "You'll find assorted swimwear and other seasonal attire in your armoires. I trust the selection is ample, but please don't hesitate to ask for anything you require."

"Thank you, Markus," Joss said, and he turned to leave them.

Just as Matt and Joss looked at each other to confer on their plans, a radio cracked on Markus's hip.

A woman's voice spoke—Greek accent, but clear enough English for Matt and Joss to understand. Her tone was disciplinary, like a teacher. "Markus, did you tell them about the kitchen?"

At this, Matt peered up at the hall ceiling, and Joss followed his gaze. They spotted the camera at the same time.

Markus spun an about face, smiling to the pair. "In the kitchen you'll find a fully stocked pantry, refrigerator, and bar, entirely at your disposal, but you may also, at any time, ring the main kitchen to request unscheduled snacks, meals, and, of course, drinks. I encourage you to utilize the staff, despite their apparent absence. Invisibility is their standard directive." He lifted the radio to his mouth and gazed up at the camera. "But, of course, Circe."

"But, of course," Circe replied.

* * *

Matt's eyes popped opened before sunrise. He stared at the slowly turning ceiling fan, its blades of woven husks—foreign and disturbing until he recalled where he was.

Philippos. The island.

How long had he slept? It almost felt like too much, an entire day, but the wine from last night—some renowned chateau, $75,000 per bottle according to Circe—still muddled Matt's thoughts. He and Joss had made a game of estimating the cost of a sip. The chef had personally served them their meal: a surprisingly delicious rabbit Joss took to calling "Bugs." Later, the two had ambled down the beach, chitchatting about their contrasting Jersey childhoods, the insanely wealthy, and the Milky Way, glowing above them with depth and colors impossible to see near a city.

When he'd finally turned in, Matt hadn't even thought to grab something to read. He'd actually gotten real sleep—probably more than five hours. This was undoubtedly a good thing, but with his brain in its current bog, he felt unsettled, anxious.

He slid out of bed, brushed his teeth in the pale light of the brightening sky, and threw on a pair of shorts and a T-shirt. A jaw twitch guided his focus to the backpack on the sofa. Maybe something familiar, something small to bring with him.

"Just one quick fix, right?" he murmured. "A little hit to take the edge off?"

Matt shook his head, disgusted with himself and his addict tendencies. Shunning the artifacts in the backpack, he went to the wall, pulled aside the heavy curtain, and found a sliding glass door.

He stepped out onto a chilly, tree-covered path, stretching his legs and neck as he walked toward the beach. Once beneath the open sky—fresh air smelling of moist bark and sand, salt water, algae, stone—he broke into a jog.

* * *

Sipping her iced tea beneath the shade of a wide umbrella, Joss inhaled the delicious, late-morning air. The smell of hot sand. She peered down at her toes, week-old, sapphire-blue polish chipping away, and wondered if pedicures were part of the package here on zillionaire Fantasy Island.

She sensed movement in her periphery and glanced down the beach. Indeed, it was Matt, jogging toward her, bare-chested, sweaty, with a shirt flopping in his hand. She faced forward, nonchalant, her sunglasses facing the water and other islands in the distance, while she gave her body a quick review.

A minute later, Matt arrived beside the other lounge chair, breathing heavy and begging for water. "Should've brought some," he muttered as he filled a glass from the ice-filled pitcher.

"You missed breakfast," Joss said, still gazing out at the water.

"Sorry. I thought I was going to circle the island."

"But?"

Still breathing heavily, he'd swallowed too fast, and coughed.

He wiped his mouth and chin. "But it's really fricken big."

"Well, they said when you come back from your run to just ring them up and they'll bring it out here. Look." She waved the walkie-talkie. "It's like our little bell ... Well, *your* little bell. Sorry, should I be *doing* something? I feel like I should be doing something. Like *work*."

Matt plopped down onto the other chair and slurped more water. He looked intense again—that busy, distracted face. "Nah, you're fine. Did they ... Was it Markus? The Taria?" He sort of babbled, but Joss understood where he was going.

"Yes, Markus did stop by. He asked me if you were planning to read the thing out here or somewhere else."

He put his legs up and sat back in the lounge chair. "And you said?"

"I said I wasn't sure. That'd we'd let him know."

Matt considered for a moment. Joss twirled her drink into a mini-whirlpool, watching the ice swirl around the glass. From the corner of her eye, she caught Matt glance her way.

"Here's fine," he declared officially. Serious business out here in the Greek Isles. Joss wondered if wine was the only way to get him to lighten up. He went on, "Shouldn't get too hot before lunch. But if I'm into a reading, and the sun starts beating down to where it looks like I'm going to burn—"

"I should slather you with sunblock?" Joss snarked, instantly regretting saying it aloud.

Matt didn't skip a beat, letting her off the hook by pretending he didn't hear. "—just tap me, or maybe move the umbrella. Or have one of the people do it?"

"Sure, yeah, that's no problem. I'll keep an eye out."

Christ. My contributions to this trip are a single page of notes, and straight-up sexual harassment.

She picked up the walkie-talkie. "Hi, this is Joss. Matt's out here and ready for you."

Circe replied instantly. "Thank you, Ms. Leland. Please clarify: ready for meal, or ready for Markus?"

Matt shrugged and held up two fingers.

"What's that, two meals?" Joss affected dramatic confusion. She figured continuing the playful tone—sans innuendo—might defuse her last comment. "Ready for peace? Bathroom break?"

He finally smiled. Thankfully. "*Both*, please."

"Circe, he's ready for both."

EIGHT

Alexandria, Aegyptus (Roman Province of Egypt) – 271 CE

Patra sat on the stool before her mirror, brushing her waist-length hair in long, slow strokes, her gaze floating somewhere between her reflection and the mirror's silver frame. In her lap, she absentmindedly rubbed her thumb over her key's smooth handle, stoking in unison with her brush.

A light, wooden tap on the wall: Unza, her servant.

"Now?" Unza's voice queried from around the corner—one of her eleven Greek words.

"After a turn," Patra replied in Coptic.

Patra's tunic top lay bunched in her lap, her stola hung on the wall. She expected no visitors, and didn't yet wish to be dressed. Unza would return in a while.

She explored her reflection, feeling old, tired. "Hello, Steward."

The nearly forty-year-old flesh beside her mouth was beginning to sink, now keen to follow her breasts on their slow journey toward her feet. When had her passion begun this dither? She'd grown up in the Musaeum with her father, surrounded by the most brilliant thinkers in the world, learned to translate eleven languages before turning twelve, and had a knack for completing the thoughts of cogitating philosophers. She'd loved it—every moment!

Even when Father had made her study with the mathematicians, drawing diagram after diagram of cuboids, precise angles, and polyhedra, she'd found pleasure in solving the equations' mysteries. *"Mathematics,"* explained Apollonius, *"is the infinite story, encapsulating the clues and eventual answers to every mystery of the cosmos."*

Patra still believed this to be true, and if numbers were the stairway to enlightenment, she wished to decipher every digit. Though she counted as friend every prominent mathematician at the library, she hadn't been invited to a forum in over a decade. Her mind was no longer as malleable or absorbent as it once was. Or, more likely, their persistence and patience while simplifying theorems for her had dwindled as she'd grown. An unrelenting little girl hurling question after question—the endearing nature of this spectacle had gradually expired. Add to this her increasing partiality toward her own generation—perhaps a craving to belong, or to be the smartest one in the room, instead of the least.

In time, she'd escaped the trappings of being her father's daughter, establishing herself with achievement after achievement, building her own philosophy atop Plato and Plotinus, combining them with the traditional Egyptian theories of the human soul. How gratified had she been by the ovation in the Great Hall? Standing there, *moved*, celebrated by intellectuals younger and elder, as she'd concluded her lecture: "...or perhaps a guide for us all, myself especially, for attaining true happiness—perfected within *this* lifetime, relished in *this* world, and to not merely await the afterlife. Thank you all."

Given her breadth of talent, they'd elevated her to Steward less than a year later—the first woman to hold the title—and that's who she'd remained for the past four. Could she return to philosophy? Sit down with the men now building on her work? Start anew with other areas of thought? Of course she could, but she was always so busy, anxious, head muddled by an endless list of tasks. The occasional unwelcome whisper in her head: *Could it be that my greatest ideas are behind me?*

Yes, her legacy was set, and her roles as Steward would remain: facilitate *other's* best work, recruit from abroad, grow the library's archives. But what of true happiness? What of relishing life in *this* world? A cruel, self-inflicted irony.

Unza's voice, beyond the curtain to the hall, "Now?"

"Now is fine, Unza," Patra resigned.

Unza entered, her ever-present flaccid expression upon her dark brown face, droopy lower lip, apathetic left eye. She pulled Patra's blue stola from the post on the wall. Patra stood and raised her arms in a V. Unza set the stola down, then reached past Patra to the tray. A shake of a bottle, brushings of oil, sharpening the blade.

As Unza shaved under her arms, Patra bemoaned the day ahead. She wasn't looking forward to warning Kaleb and Philip about their planned performance. If Patra was—as everyone suggested—stubborn as stone, then Kaleb was the ultimate, unmovable mountain, and he'd never see as she did the potential repercussions. No, to him, the world was full of reasonable people, and he could always explain himself out of trouble. Philip, conversely, was capable of reason, but he wasn't the one she needed to worry about. Philip had a family, and he lacked *Prince* Kaleb's royal sense of entitlement. Philip, however, had no power against Kaleb's charm. For Philip, Kaleb's confidence and good cheer defeated basic logic every time. If there were any chance of stopping this, she needed to get Kaleb alone.

Unza pulled Patra's arms down forcefully, turned her sideways, and patted powder beneath her breasts. On to the perfume stick—a dip in the jar and a swipe down the breastbone, a dip and a swipe arched over one hip, then the other, circle the knees, Xs on the ankles...

Patra had long since given up arguing with Unza about her strict grooming rituals (dip and a swipe behind the ear, dip and a swipe beneath the chin, a grunted cue to lift her left foot), accepting that her servant lacked the sensibilities of even the simplest of normal persons. Though, strangely, Unza had a memory like no other. Navigating from one end of Alexandria to the other, head down—though shown the course only once—she'd make all the right turns without a single mistake. The same held true of items Patra had misplaced. *"Unza, have you seen my purple thread?"* got Unza stomping straight to some box in the study and slapping the spool into Patra's hand. Others might've thought her angry, aggressive, but it was not some *mood*, it was simply her way.

After helping her into the stola, Unza slid and twisted Patra's girdle up so the key hung outside the thigh, where she preferred.

"Perfect, thank you," Patra said, but Unza spun her around once more by the shoulders.

"No," Unza said, grunting as she tugged at and straightened the stola's orientation until satisfied.

When finally finished, Patra left her bungalow—one of eight private units situated behind the Library, while the vast majority of residents lived in the dormitories at the other end of the Musaeum property. Kaleb and his apprentices stayed in the dormitories, but were typically up and about this late in the morning, likely eating or on their way to a classroom.

In the lush courtyard between the bungalows and the rest of the complex, Patra eyed two cats lapping water from the fountain. The animals heard her approach and bolted to the vine-wrapped wall, which in turn sent a flock of tiny birds panicking into the air.

"Good morning, Steward," a pair of young Musaeum girls said as they passed, baskets and trimmers in hand. They were Philip's daughter, Theophila, and her friend, Eugenia.

"Good morning, girls," Patra replied with a smile. "Off to collect grapes?"

"Plums, Steward," Eugenia said.

"I used to perform the very same chore. Watch out for Arachne!" It was what the elders had always said to her when she was off to harvest fruit from the gardens. And indeed, she'd come face to face with spiders whose memory, after all these years, still sent shivers up her neck and behind her ears.

"Yes, Steward," the girls sang in unison.

"Theophila," Patra called after them, and the girls stopped. "Do you know where I could find your father?"

"He's in Astronomy with Steward Kaleb, Steward."

"... *special requests or prefer a list of options?*" A woman's voice.

"*Well ... I think ...*" Joss's voice, with a staff member. *"I'm not sure if he can hear us. He's, ah, taking a little nap."*

"I'm up," Matt said, leaning forward and stretching his arms. Unsure if the staff knew who he was or why he was there, he let the smooth Taria slip to his side, into the folds of the towel beneath him. "Is it lunch time already?"

He reacquainted himself to the surroundings. The lounge chairs, the beach, the freckled young woman standing over them with a patient smile, and Joss, shiny from a swim, wet hair slicked back. When she realized he was up, one knee quickly rose, her toes had pointed, and shoulders pulled back, as though preparing for a summerwear magazine photo shoot. Matt pretended he hadn't noticed, focusing on the attendant

They ordered lunch from an extraordinary selection of options, ate together inside the house at an informal dining area—Joss sharing her uneventful morning ("I went for a swim ... *alone.*") and then Markus showed up, requesting an update on Matt's reading thus far.

"Very good." If Markus was disappointed by the lack of new revelations, he hadn't shown it. "Will you be returning to the beach?"

Matt looked at Joss, receiving an indifferent shrug.

"The Tarias?" Markus said, clarifying why he'd asked.

"Ah, right," Matt said. "If you could leave B with me, to read at will, that'd be great."

Markus blinked for a moment—a well-dressed, *almost* lifelike robot processing the input and calculating every potential outcome. Most likely he was running through a *"what would Ostrovsky want?"* exercise in his head.

"Let me get back to you on that request." Indeed, Markus wished to bounce that one off the boss. "In the meantime, I'll meet you right here at …" a glance at his watch, "… one-thirty, for your afternoon session. Good?"

"Good." Matt waited for the click of Markus's shoes to fade out around the corner. He looked at Joss, who'd remained conspicuously quiet. "You all right?"

"Me? Yeah, totally! I mean, it's like I said before, I feel like I should be doing some kind of work, and you're doing work, but I'm sort of on this vacation just because of where we are. If you gave me a list of to-do's I'd be all over them, and without any *thoughts* or anything, so I hope you'll tell me as soon as you need me to do something." Her eyebrows awaited acknowledgement. He nodded, absolutely, he'd tell her. She went on, "I tried to go snorkeling earlier but that Christof guy with all the gear said he *strongly* advised I not go out alone. But don't worry about me, seriously. You've got work to do, I'm on standby, and I'm on a goddamn Greek Island … *for free*. Plus, this bikini? It's like twelve hundred bucks. Yeah. For a *bikini*. Go about your business, boss." She paused, then, "I mean, it's not like I'm your *date* and you're ignoring me. And besides, I'm not one of those high-maintenance types." A breath. She swallowed. "I'm fine … That was a lot of words."

Matt waited a few extra seconds in case she had more. He strove for a normal smile. "Good, good. Well, I was just going to say, if you're bored, I have a little mission for you. Actually, even if you're not, I sort of need you to do something for me anyway … tomorrow … if you're cool with it."

Joss leaned close, all ears, visibly relieved to be moving on, and Matt was right there with her. If she was truly hinting at being interested, he couldn't tell. Her ever-flirtatious manner reminded him of his ex, Isis Meier—a woman who thrived on male attention, toying with men for whom she bore zero actual interest—though he'd never seen an iota of awkwardness in Isis.

Whatever was going on with Joss, he didn't know how he felt about it, and there simply weren't any vacancies in his head to accommodate new occupants. Fortunately, he now had plenty with which to occupy Joss.

"Let's go for a walk," Matt said, rolling his eyes upward to indicate the cameras and who-knew-what-else.

* * *

Patra and three friends shuffled their way through the hot, stifling crowds, all vying to enter the amphitheater. Blessed with mild afternoon heat and a constant flow of scattered clouds, they'd be fine if able to reach the front rows of seats reserved for Musaeum members. Outside the amphitheater's wall, a collective jubilance energized the air, a carefree sort of spirit that seemed to permeate all classes of Alexandrians, but only on occasions such as this. Public announcements and inaugurations brought the masses, but were typically received with cautious skepticism, and varied across the social strata. Changes at the top rarely reached the bottom, so why care if the faces were new? This event, however, presented no overt agenda, and no cost to attend.

Rumor had it the show would be amusing rather than dramatic—much preferred to the often dispiriting material the players favored. It wasn't that the average citizen found no occasion to laugh, but rather, to laugh with and amongst a thousand others elevated one's joy to transcendent levels.

And it helped that Prince Kaleb, the star of the show, was famous.

Patra's group finally reached the amphitheater wall, and slid little by little, arms grazed and shoved by the throngs—all eager for good seats, or perhaps any seat at all—toward the arched central entrance.

"Pardon us," one of Patra's colleagues, Icarion, said to a row of men standing shoulder to shoulder, facing into the amphitheater, blocking the entry passage.

Two of the men glanced back, sneering. "Already full," one said bitterly, a quick eye to Icarion's affluent garb.

In any other circumstance, a peasant would not feel so emboldened to snub the wealthy, but this was a *public* event, and Patra's group may as well have walked into a tavern on the city's west side. There'd be no rank this afternoon, or so the band of men had thought.

"Step aside, you!" barked a deep, authoritative voice from above.

Patra looked up to find a city guard atop the wall in full regalia, spear in hand and finger pointed at the men. Another stood on the opposing wall, a warning eye on the group as they parted at the middle, allowing Patra's party through before once more closing ranks.

"Steward Supatra," called another commanding voice from above—a centurion. "Augusta Zenobia invites you to the podium."

He motioned beyond the wall, and Patra peeked over the clutter of heads before her. Beneath the purple tent in the distance, Zenobia—a luminous idol above assorted dim, mooted company—sat in the shade beside another radiant figure: her son, Augustus Vabalathus. But Patra thought only of her former student, Wahb Allat.

"Wahbi," she said, an uncontrollable smile splitting her cheeks as she slipped with surprising ease between people, her hand still clasped to Icarion behind her.

"Only you, Steward," the centurion called, and Patra halted, glancing back at the ruffled friends she'd been dragging through the crush.

"It's fine, truly," Thester said before Patra could apologize. "We have seats. We'll find the others."

At the end of the curving aisle, after she was allowed past a barrier, attendants helped Patra up the tall, marble steps to the cordoned podium.

"Patra!" Wahbi cheered when he saw her, standing up from the throne he shared with his mother, and rushed to Patra.

Now twelve, he stood nearly as tall as Patra, and appeared a different boy, adorned in silk robes with purple embroideries and gold threading. As they embraced, Patra caught the disapproving glares of courtiers on the podium above (public affection wasn't appropriate for their Augustus) but Zenobia simply beamed, and only she rightly mattered.

"Come, Patra," Zenobia called. "Join us!"

"I missed you so much!" Wahbi said as he pulled Patra up the last few stairs. "Come, sit with *me*."

Patra hoped he didn't mean the throne. Fortunately, as they ascended to the top of the podium, courtiers arose and facilitated, guiding the young Augustus back to his seat, and stationing Patra on a newly placed cushion at Zenobia and Wahbi's feet.

Just below her, Patra discovered a rare view, that of Governor Cassius's balding head and the gray-blonde dome of his aide, Thomas.

Thomas turned ever so slightly without actually looking at her. "Steward," he said, the word swathed in all the warmth of an iron commode seat.

"Thomas," she replied, and turned toward Cassius's shiny pate. "Always nice to see you, Governor … and, *oh my* … myself, as well!"

"Eternally droll, Patra," Cassius said without a backward glance. "I polished it earlier. Just try to avoid an accidental glimpse of that dusty old tomb between your legs."

Patra grinned. She hadn't been this close to her childhood friend in at least a year. It was too bad he brought his pet snake, Thomas.

Behind Patra, Wahbi's eager, cracking voice: "Can she come back with us after? So we may have time? I have to tell her everything about … *everything!*"

"Perhaps, my love," Zenobia said, then leaned forward and put a hand on Patra's shoulder. "It's *wonderful* to see you again."

Patra observed activity beginning on the stage below, and the musicians in the orchestra were sitting up, preparing to play. She glanced behind her. "And you as well, Augusta. Please accept my humbled gratitude for this invitation."

A triad of horns broadcasted a royal ingress, and the buzzing audience roared approval before falling quiet. Two of Kaleb's players strode out from opposite sides of the stage, outfitted as courtiers—identical to those littered about Zenobia and Wahbi's podium.

"Thank you, little people!" one of the *"courtiers"* began, and Patra recognized his voice. Kaleb had roped in Xander, one of the new young poets.

Xander and his companion strode to the edge of the stage and abandoned character for a moment to bow respectfully to Zenobia and Wahbi. The audience heeded their cue, facing and paying hushed respect to their monarchs.

Zenobia murmured to Wahbi, "Stand and return," and he complied, rising from his seat and extending his in-turned hands toward his subjects. "Good. Now, half-turn, and sit." Wahbi sat.

The players on stage re-seized the audience's attention, resuming their belittling onslaught. "Thank you, thank you! Your applause is both appreciated and required! You up there—the crushed herds of *nearly* people—if we're to hear your ovations, you must work harder than all the rest here in front ... as you do in life."

Astonishingly, the spectators—above and below—erupted with laughter, delighted by this brutal mocking from the perceived superior perspective of Roman elite. Patra feared not Zenobia's reaction. The Empress had always distanced herself from Rome and the Senate and the chaos that was the Western Empire, but Patra couldn't say the same of the courtiers around her. From their lofty standpoint, there existed a single empire, and to condemn any part was to attack the whole.

Zenobia's voice near Patra's ear: "You didn't tell me one of your friends was the Prince of Kush. Are you *close*?" A romantic tone.

Patra merely flashed a coy smile, appeasing the same old Zenobia's undying interest in Patra's marital status—though more specifically, her venereal status. While Kaleb was indisputably attractive, and rumors about him and Patra circulated the Musaeum halls, he was already married to a Cretian noble he'd twice met, having been arranged since before he was born.

"Is that him?" Zenobia whispered, and Patra returned her attention to the stage.

The courtiers had ceded the stage to Kaleb and Philip. Patra scanned the audience, her chest tightening. She prayed her friends would adhere to their promise to exclude their caricatures' most provocative acts.

"Yes, the 'Emperor,'" Patra replied. "And the brother, 'Quintus,' is played by my friend Philip, the sculptor."

"Ah yes ... *my!* Take either, really."

Philip and Kaleb tour the stage as whimsical music plays, the pair portraying an idea-hurling Quintus dismissed at each turn by an irritated Emperor Antonius. The audience chuckles at each stop on the stage: Philip's *"Quintus"* pulling a chunk of brick from one of the arched background's columns, demonstrating that the structure needs repairs, Kaleb's *"Antonius"* scoffs in return, takes the brick, spits on it, and slips it back into the space—*Fixed!*

After each of these little exchanges, Kaleb performs increasingly silly, self-congratulatory dances.

Finally, in a bout of frustration, Quintus storms off the stage as a self-absorbed Antonius faces the giggling audience, admiring himself in an imaginary mirror. He preens his hair, rubs his cheeks red like a woman, flexes his arm muscles, and then, after a sneaky peek left then right, lifts his robes to reveal his manhood.

The audience roared, weeping with laughter at the sight.

Kaleb wears a flesh-colored loincloth, wrapped tight so as to appear nude, with crudely drawn curls of pubic hair above a near-invisible bump. He pouts and flicks at the tiny phallus, as if to awaken it. With each flick, a string player plucks a single, high-pitched note.

Behind Patra, Zenobia and Wahbi were laughing—hysterical as any audience member—but the others around the tent remained cautious, reserved. Below Patra, Cassius and Thomas sat tilted toward each other, both men's shoulders bouncing whenever they couldn't help but snicker, but otherwise only sharing a hushed word after each gag.

Emperor Antonius now inspects a squad of Praetorian Guard, scrutinizing their uniforms for imperfections until it's revealed he's more interested in what hides *behind* their tunics. One by one, they're fired and sent away as he discovers each is more amply endowed than he. Desperate courtiers then carry a baby boy onto the stage, outfitted in a miniature Praetorian uniform.

The audience burst into laughter before Kaleb even took his reticent peek beneath its tunic.

Zenobia shouted to Patra over the boisterous assembly, "He's brilliant! I love him!"

Foreboding tubas trumpet the beginning of another scene.

The Emperor jumps into action, rearranging his royal robes in the invisible mirror, splashing nonexistent perfumes on himself. An old woman's voice sings a muddled, universal greeting off-stage, "Yooooohoooooo!"

Antonius uses a hand to sample his own breath, then doubles over, retching at the odor. Desperate, he searches the imaginary selection of objects, finally opting to gargle with perfume. He spits wildly, disgusted, attempting to clean his tongue on his robes as his *"mother"* appears on stage. Quintus follows behind with a tattletale's scowl, tugging Mommy's stola and pointing at Antonius.

No … oh, no. He promised he wouldn't … You promised, Kaleb!

As the oblivious mother (a large man with rosy cheeks, a red palla draped over his hair, and his face and beard powdered white) ambles about the stage, horns and strings playing her snobbish monologue, Antonius tries to discreetly eject Quintus from the room. He wants alone time with Mommy. The brothers wrestle, drag one another across the stage, pretend everything is fine when their mother glances back, and then resume their childlike spat when she looks away. The crowd enjoys each of the pair's comical, frozen positions.

With every shove, trip, and fall, Alexandrian bellies shake with merriment, mouths gasping for air, gawking eyes, slapping backs, whistling, pointing.

Patra's mind was a jumble of worry and pleasure. Joy for Kaleb and Philip—all their work practicing this ridiculous farce now rewarded with an audience elated beyond the duo's most ambitious dreams—but terrified too, for this sort of insult wouldn't merely flow through the city and stop at its borders. Certainly not with what Kaleb was *about* to do.

With the mother distracted (facing the audience and the invisible mirror as she tests the Emperor's assortment of apparently feminine perfumes), Antonius produces a dagger, hiding it behind his back as he feigns capitulation to younger Quintus. And then, with the audience suddenly silent, Antonius slings a friendly arm over Quintus's shoulder, kisses his cheek, and then slides the blade across his brother's throat.

A number of stifled gasps break the amphitheater's silence. A lighthearted tune rises once more from the orchestra.

Gratified and swollen with pride, the Emperor moseys back to Mother as Quintus—thick red stripe now painted across his throat—clutches at his neck and struggles in the background to grab her attention. Lengths of red silk dangle from between his fingers. The courtiers from earlier quietly enter, now clad in riding armor, as Quintus falls dead. His limp body is shuffled off-stage. A voice backstage whinnies like a horse, and then *clip-clop, clip-clop* ...

The audience remained quiet; only a few nervous laughs rose conspicuously from the masses. Even they hadn't taken this last scene lightly.

In actual recent news, Emperor Publius Septimius Antonius's brother, Quintus, next in line to rule, had suffered a mortal accident in Rome. Upon falling from his chariot, he was mangled in the axle and then trampled by horses. His throat was said to have been opened by a splintered wood plank. Rumors of wicked secrets and alternate theories always pervaded after such events, but to see one portrayed, and in graphic detail, was striking and disturbing. Moreover, for such a thing to be being presented by the intellectuals of the Musaeum, by Prince Kaleb of Kush, it must be *true*.

Patra sneaked a glance back, observing Zenobia's mischievous smirk and contented eyes. She'd thoroughly enjoyed the performance, relishing its brazen messages.

Suddenly, the laughter returned—the sort of delighted shock that pleased Kaleb to no end.

On the stage, Kaleb straddled the man portraying the Emperor's mother, while two musicians battled below them—a frisky horn for Antonius's eager advances, strings and a bow representing the mother's halfhearted resistance. After wrestling through layers of embellished silk robes, mother hooting and giggling and slapping at his head, Antonius finally triumphs. The pair spends the next five minutes rolling and kissing, animating a series of outrageous sexual positions, from plausible to preposterous, their tempo and absurdity growing as the orchestra rises to a blaring climax.

NINE

Nairobi, Kenya – Presidential Palace

At the right time of day, the second floor veranda offered the most stunning of views. After a solitary lunch, Tuni often came here to look out on the panorama. Nairobi couldn't compete with the splendors found in many cities—no epic coastline or riverfront, no crowd-drawing selection of landmark buildings with some signature architecture, or even a pervasive charming character—but whenever she gazed out beyond the presidential property's wall and landscaping, she sought none of these charms. Out there, between sparse treetops, the cluster of shiny skyscrapers, the rust-colored rooftops of upper class and shantytowns, modern malls and dilapidated street markets, Tuni saw the delightful freedoms and hardships of real life.

When Tuni was Alexander's age, her father had left her mother, and the two had to move into a house along one of South Africa's slums. Even in her darkest days, her mind wouldn't allow her to idealize that place. Sure, there were moments of joy, sips of carefree childhood, now-embarrassing pride at living in the neighborhood's least dilapidated house. And there'd been thirst. And hunger. And people who'd wished to take her away, watching her from cars and through school fences.

When Tuni was eight, a friend had been taken. Tuni felt ashamed no longer remembering her name. The bad people planned to sell her, Mum had said, to a rich person, far away. How searing, the irony now—Tuni had thought her friend so lucky: a poor girl's twisted fairytale dream.

Within the year, Mum had managed to get them out of Cape Town and into Tuni's aunt's house in London. Daddy still wanted no part, but his sister was more than willing to take them in. And there was state school, then prep school, on to university, and then a hop across the pond to finish in New York. It was up and up and up, and yet, here she was back in Africa, the property of a rich man, far away.

The noon sun's angle had shifted enough to cast its glare on the balcony's bulletproof shield. Now gone the illusion of an unobstructed view, Tuni rose from the lounge chair, stretched her back and neck, and went to the black-out tinted glass door. Thabiti slid it open before her hand reached the handle, chilled air whooshing out and pressing her flowy dress against her.

"A good sit, Mrs. Absko?" he said as she entered the hall.

"Yes, thank you," she replied.

"The nursery?"

She nodded as she passed his looming bulk. He waited the usual five-second count before his footsteps followed.

The main hall's glass doors parted and she stepped back into the thick midday heat. In the courtyard below, landscapers uprooted Tuni's pink and yellow sorrels from the planters, tossing them into dirty heaps on squares of burlap.

Tuni went to the balustrade, calling down to them. "I beg your pardon. What's this?"

The gardeners peered around, spotting her above. All but one turned back to their labors.

He removed his hat to answer. "Upandaji maua mengine, Mama."

"Planting *what* new flowers?" Tuni demanded.

He pointed to the crates of red bulbs beside the fountain. "Damu lily, Mama."

"Blood lilies?" Tuni murmured, then called back, "Aren't they poisonous?"

The gardener shrugged ignorance.

"Toxic?" Tuni persisted. "Sumu?"

He replaced his hat, resuming his duties without another word.

"Rude turd," said Thabiti's deep bass. He, too, stood with a hand on the balustrade, observing the courtyard below. "You want me to stop them?"

"No, never mind it. Thank you, but no. Sometimes I forget I no longer care about such things."

"But Alexander … You said the poison—"

"He's not going to run down there and start eating them. Although I'll not be the least bit shocked if, in a week, these flowers are lining every room and hall. And then, when my husband's allergies go bonkers, we'll see them removed with equal haste."

She resumed to the nursery.

Blood lilies. How clever.

Through another set of sliding doors, back into the meat-locker cold, Tuni turned down the short hallway to the nursery. She peeked in the narrow window and spotted Alexander building a brick fortress with the nursery maid, Ngina, and the teacher, Kim. Tuni rapped twice on the window, waved to all three, and opened the door.

"I'll see you in a moment, Thabiti."

He nodded and scooted onto the stool at the end of the hallway. The man hated standing.

"Come look, Mama," Alexander said in Swahili. "It's a pirate ship!"

Tuni went to the colorful carpet, treading cautiously through the minefield of plastic blocks, and nestled into a small space behind her son. "I was just going to say what a beautiful pirate ship."

"Not beautiful, Mama," he said as he turned with a frown, and then switched to English, "cool and awesome!"

"Sorry, of course." She shared a smile with the amused pair. "That's what I meant. Cool and awesome." Evidently, his ninja turtle DVDs were giving him more than just daily pizza cravings.

Alexander continued building and playing as they looked on. After a moment, Tuni glanced at Ngina, wondering if she had any news to share. A couple glances later, Tuni caught Ngina's eye, and the young lady's expression suddenly betrayed an uncharacteristic tension. Ngina stole a glimpse at the corner over Tuni's head—where Tuni well knew a camera hung. She needed a moment alone with Ngina, but not here.

"Kim," Tuni said, and the forty-plus Ugandan looked up. "I read an article the other day about women who only breastfed for a few months deciding to resume with children three, four, even five years or older."

Kim made no attempt to mask her revulsion. She said, "Yes?" as her head shook *"Please, no."*

"Well, I've always felt guilty at stopping so quickly with him—it wasn't exactly my choice—and I wondered if you had any suggestions as far as stimu—"

"I'm afraid I don't, Mrs. Absko, no ... It's not something I'd, well, I wouldn't ... have learned of these things at university. If you're *thinking* this is ... perhaps speak to ..." She motioned toward Ngina, who nodded affirmative.

"Ah, yes, of course," Tuni smiled, embarrassed, and turned to Ngina. "You know of this practice?"

"Yes, my Lady. It doesn't work for all, but warm compresses to begin, and then suction must be applied regu—"

"Ngina, please," Kim interrupted, tilting her head to Alexander's wide eyes.

"Oh," Tuni said, and eyed the exit. "Should we …?"

Kim smiled broadly, careful not to insult her. "If you wish, that would be fine, a private talk."

"Do you mind?" Tuni motioned to Alexander. Kim was a professional, not a babysitter.

Kim brushed it off, no problem, and reengaged with Alexander. "How many pirates do we have onboard now? Three fell off now, yes?"

"Three are dead," Alexander replied. "*Blasted* off, psshh!"

Tuni and Ngina walked toward the door, and Ngina's face revealed she hadn't until just now realized what Tuni was doing. Trepidation curled her brow as Tuni opened the door.

"We need to chat a sec, Thabiti. Would you mind?"

He cocked an eyebrow, regarded Ngina for a beat, and slid off the stool. "No problem, Mrs. Absko." He lumbered out of view.

"My Lady," Ngina whispered, but Tuni popped her hand between them, and mouthed *"Wait."*

A count of five before Tuni tiptoed to the edge of the wall and poked her head out, spotting Thabiti a good distance away, hands in his pockets as he studied a painting on the opposite wall. She turned back to Ngina in the narrow passage.

"You have something for me," Tuni hushed.

"I've been afraid … It's not …"

Not what? Good news?

"Do you have it?" Tuni demanded, looking down at the apron pockets. Ngina nodded, repeatedly licking her lower lip. "Well give it, quickly. *Please,* Ngina!"

Ngina lifted a quaking hand to her chest, reached into her brassiere, and produced a folded square of pale-slate cardstock. Without a thought, Tuni seized the paper and wrestled with her eager fingers to unfold it.

The white ink had been stamped into the thick stock. Like a semi-formal wedding invitation, the lacy letters leaned rightward—a single sentence in quotes, split into two lines, and centered on the now-creased page. Tuni read the sentence, then she read each word. Unable to grasp the meaning, she squeezed her eyes shut, sucked in a breath, and read it again, slowly.

> *"Light may earth's crumbling sand be laid on*
> *thee, that dogs may dig thy bones up easily."*

"Can't be … Where … Where did this come from?"

Ngina's eyes had already welled with tears, and now two drops streaked down her cheeks. The girl was no idiot. This was the most cold-hearted rejection imaginable. *"Live, die, suffer—I couldn't care less."* No, worse! It dug deeper than apathy.

"It is from him. I had to destroy it, the envelope, but it was from your friend. I am so sorry my Lady. I didn't wish to give this to you. I knew how much you'd hoped …"

Ngina knelt to pick up the sheet. Tuni hadn't realized she dropped it. Her breath whistled into her nostrils. She'd clasped her hands over her mouth at some point. The woozy swirl in her head might've explained why she was leaning against the wall. The sick wouldn't leave her throat.

"Mrs. Absko, are you all right?" It was Kim. Or maybe Thabiti. Or others.

The paper crossed her eyes once or twice, but she didn't need it to know those words, now stamped into her being. She heard them again and again in her ears.

She was moving. Hands on her sides. Someone supporting her weight.

Kind, mothering words came muffled through pillows, while cold, heartless words—her own voice, clear as day—sneered menace through her head. *No one has ever been so alone, and no one's ever been so deserving.* What had she thought? Matthew was sitting around on her old doorstep for the past five years? *It should be a shallow grave for me.* Justifiable bitterness. Please, Matthew, set aside your own inconceivable problems, and help me undo my own stupid choices.

Still some meat on these bones when the dogs dig me up. There's the love I've always craved. Yes, those dogs will absolutely adore me.

* * *

Light fingers stroked her hand. She lay in a bed—*her* bed. She knew the shape and texture of her pillow, the cool surface of her sheets, her comforter's weight. How had she arrived in the suite, and in bed? What time was it? Who was touching her hand? Jivu?

She opened her eyes. They stung. She'd fallen asleep with her contacts in. Only the entryway's table lamps were on, casting the room in a dim amber glow.

"There you are," said a familiar voice in Swahili. But it wasn't Jivu sitting on the bed beside her. It was Thabiti, and he continued caressing her hand.

"Thabiti," she croaked, jerking her hand to her and recoiling away. "What are you—?"

"Shh, Tuni," his deep voice rumbled—deeper than usual speaking quietly.

He'd never before called her by her first name. No one here would, and even Jivu used an assortment of pet names. It sounded odd hearing it aloud, like it belonged to someone else.

She continued scooting to the other side of the bed, dragging the covers with her. Someone had taken off her shoes, touched her feet, laid her down. What else had happened while she was out?

She spoke through her teeth, "Thabiti, you need to leave. Now."

He ignored her command, instead studying his upturned hand on her sheet, grazing each fingertip with his thumb. He closed his eyes, inhaled a deep breath. "I've worked for Mr. Absko a very long time. Long before you came."

"Thabiti, I'd love to hear your history some time, truly. We've never had more than a few words in all these years. I'm sorry for that. But you being here, in this room, just the two of us, you *know* it's entirely improper. Listen to me now ..." She punched each word, "You need to leave."

"Don't worry. There is no surveillance in here." He looked at her straight on—also new. He'd only ever given her the side-eye, always respectfully focusing just a bit off her face. "Hear me a moment and then I will go." He smiled bashfully, a goofy sort of grin splitting this face she'd thought incapable of expression. "It's not so easy to say."

Oh, God. Honestly?

"I think I understand, Thabiti. Now, please, for your own sake ... If the President were to come in here ... really, even ten minutes after you've gone, he'll smell you."

"He's with everyone in the meeting room, barking about the Russians this, the Russians that. I don't know more than the little pieces, but I think everything is falling apart for him."

Tuni waved this off and tried to speak, but he cut her off.

"I've loved you since the day you arrived at the old house."

Well, there it is. What's he expect me to say now? Me, too?

"It's uncomfortable for me," he went on, his football player shoulders writhing inside his black sport coat.

"Yes, for me, too."

"But all I've ever wanted was to be close to you. I wrote a poem..."

"Oh, you don't—"

"Don't worry, I didn't bring it." He chuckled, a low wheeze from deep within. "I won't make you listen to that. But it tries to explain what I mean." He twisted toward her, drawing a meaty leg onto the bed. Tuni already sat as far as she could without falling off the bed. "What I mean about only being close. See, I know I could never have someone like you. You are one in a billion—a queen, a ... *goddess*. At first I thought this makes sense, this pair, you and Mr. Absko. Of course a destined king would have such a woman. But over time, I see that you are beyond even him. He does not deserve you. I know you know this. And I know he knows this. It's why you can no longer go out in the world. He's afraid he will lose you, because he knows he shouldn't have you in the first place."

Tuni only stared at his droopy, doleful eyes.

"I wanted to say all this ... to tell you how I feel for you ... before you go. It hurts me to know I'll never see you again, even though my love for you makes conflict with this, wanting you to stay for myself. It's selfish, and not true to my love."

"What do you mean before I go? Where am I going? What have you heard? Is he sending me somewhere?"

Thabiti frowned and shook his head. "No, no. Your friend—his message."

Shit.

"Friend? I don't—"

"Shh-shh, it's okay. You don't have to worry about me. This is my point. It's my love." He grinned and shook out his hands. "It's crazy how easy to say now!"

"Thabiti."

"Yes, your friend. Your message got out. It was very smart, however you did this. Even I had no idea. But the message back, Ngina must have made a mistake, because Mr. Absko found out and got it. He had me bring Ngina to him, and he told her all the names of her family to start. She was crying already before he was done, and then he didn't even tell her what he knew. He just said 'Now you will tell me everything,' and so she did. He gave her a new message, told her just what to say to you, and he burned the real message right there."

"Do you know what it said?"

"That's why I'm here, Tuni."

It still didn't sound right, her name. And he was talking to her like a lover. She raised her eyebrows, waiting.

"It said," he switched to English, speaking with clumsy emphasis, "'Opportunities turn more when you take them. I hope your birthday was good. Matt.'"

Good God! Matthew!

She found her hands stacked over her mouth as before, in the hall. She had no clue what it meant, but it seemed to be pleasant, and real, and confident, and *Matthew*. Unconsciously, she moved closer to Thabiti.

"Are you certain those are the precise words?" she asked. "Try not to think of the English words, if it's difficult. Say it normally, as it is in your memory."

He returned to Swahili. "Yes, good. 'Opportunities multiply as they are seized. Hope you had a good birthday.'"

"Had? Your positive it was 'had,' past-tense? My birthday isn't for another week."

"Yes, it was past-tense. I guessed maybe he thought it would take longer for the message to reach you."

"And the ring? It didn't come back, then?"

"Ring?" He puckered, confused. "I don't know about ring. Ngina made no mention—"

My poor Ngina, you held out despite … Thank heavens if it's true!

"Not ring. I was thinking of something else. Okay," she said, sliding to the foot of the bed and jumping out, sheets and blankets crumpling to the floor. "Now you really must go, come on." She grabbed his arm and tried to pull him up. He acquiesced and rose, following her to the antechamber. "If he smells me on you or you in here, it's simple enough. I fainted outside the nursery and you helped me here."

"Yes, that is what happened. Ngina and Ms. Kim helped as well."

Tuni's mind was too busy to absorb much of anything. "Great, that's brilliant. And thank you, Thabiti, I mean it. You have no idea how much this means to me."

He tried to respond as she pushed him out the suite doors and shut them behind him. She marched back into the bedroom. The pungent bite of Thabiti's signature sweat seemed to fill every corner. It wouldn't be so prevalent if he'd only been in there a moment. She flipped on the ceiling fan.

Shite! The bed!

Some serious gymnastics must've taken place in that bed. Jivu would think she'd seduced Thabiti and had a go, all to spite him, or under some delusion that it'd be the final straw to let her and Alexander leave him.

She grabbed up the heap and dragged it across the bed, straightening the corners of each layer on Jivu's side, but left her own side ruffled. She'd been sleeping, after all, and it wasn't as though she'd ever be able to get it as perfect as the maids.

Next, the restroom. The air freshener from under the cabinet. She turned on the fan and filled the air inside the lavatory with the faux floral aroma. It would drift out to the main room enough to dampen Thabiti's scent. Jivu would sense if she sprayed it directly in the bedroom, and therefore know it was to cover up the only other scent present. She waved the commode door a couple times, then closed it, leaving the fan on inside.

And now a shower.

She went to the closet and slipped out of her dress, flinging it toward the corner hamper, so it would land on the floor. Her underwear joined the dress, bra dangling halfway over the basket's rim. Clearly, no attempt to hide her clothes here.

In the vast main bathroom, Tuni strode across the heated marble floor to the shower, turned the knobs outside the glass wall, and waited for the array of streams to warm up inside. She stepped in a moment later, instantly drenched in perfectly sweltering heat. This shower may be the one thing she'd miss about this bloody place. With soft water pouring from ten wall heads, and the bulbous rain drops from overhead, it was like being submerged in a stand-up bath.

Just one week until her birthday. One week until the freedom. Freedom from fear, freedom from—

"I heard of your incident today." Jivu stood a few feet away, a dim ghostly form just beyond the wall of steam.

No, she wouldn't miss the bloody shower. She wouldn't miss anything at all about this place.

TEN

Island of Philippos, Greece – Present day

Lying atop the covers of his bed, fingers laced beneath his head, staring up at his suite's textured ceiling, Matt seethed on Kaleb's recklessness. Armed with the knowledge of what would soon come of that little show, he could be perfectly satisfied by what he knew of Kaleb's eventual fate.

He closed his stinging eyes. Patra's affection for the Prince was clouding Matt's judgment, and he *wanted* to remain outraged. His secondhand knowledge of these people and events hadn't prepared him for this firsthand experience.

Yesterday, Markus had shared a brief rundown of what he knew of the Tragedy of Alexandria. Unbeknownst to Matt, the bloody invasion had been referenced in a single surviving parchment, a document unknown to historians. While coy about his source, Markus relayed the details he'd received: the dethroning (and possible beheading) of Zenobia and her son, the Musaeum's destruction, the burning of the Library, thousands dead—all due to some unspecified satire performed in Alexandria, the tale of which had reached Rome with surprising speed.

Prince Kaleb's life and death had been effectively erased, his name nowhere to be found in the history books. Markus had searched all over, and contacted his experts. The same held true of Patra and Philip. Three individuals so deeply connected to the events, overshadowed and expunged by those who mattered to historians: Emperors.

Records weren't even clear on the destruction of the Musaeum, whether it was a complete loss, if only the Library had been harmed, or perhaps the Serapeum, where many archived scrolls were stored.

Matt had now witnessed the fateful performance in person, and, like with all fateful imprints, he wished he could warn Patra that she was right to be concerned, and moreso than she knew. Kaleb's execution was an abhorrent event, only exceeded by what they did to Philip. Of everyone concerned, Matt was only certain of Kaleb's descendants' fates. If they were in Alexandria at the time, they'd somehow made it out, had children of their own, and at least one of his grandchildren, Vabalathus, bore a daughter, Aviena, whom Matt well knew from her wealth of imprints on the third keystone—Matt's keystone. But what of Philip's little ones? What were their names? What was Philip's wife's name? Aviena didn't know of any of them, let alone their fates. Patra would know. He'd dive in for this info once he had Patra's keystone back in hand.

The noon sun shifted, casting only shade on Matt's window, dimming the room and repainting the place in muted shades of blue. He wasn't yet interested in lunch—his stomach still complaining about the heavy breakfast: *"American breakfast!"* the chef had declared as his staff arrayed the table with generous portions of only the finest ingredients for coronary heart disease.

Matt turned over to face the clock on the nightstand: 12:20.

Today was the day.

Would Markus simply bring Matt the package from Tuni as agreed, or would he have to ask for it? 12:21.

By now, Paul Kleindorf at DOJ had his ducks in a row—Matt didn't need to check on that. No doubt, Iris had already checked and double-checked and triple-checked all the moving pieces. Her OCD wouldn't have it any other way. 12:22.

And Joss … Matt hadn't heard her door open or shut, and he couldn't call her without arousing suspicion, so he hoped she was on top of her portion. Would Markus deny her? Possible, of course, but he doubted it. 12:23.

* * *

Now this is what I'm talking about, Joss thought as she selected a sarong from her closet's free selection and tied it around her waist, over the bikini bottom.

In her vast marble bathroom, she brushed her hair, reapplied her makeup, and gargled mouthwash. She'd probably taken the cloak and dagger nature of her mission a bit too seriously, making contrived *vixen* faces in the mirror, and testing which walks appeared most natural.

You're an idiot, she thought. *Practicing natural. Pffft.*

Her request wouldn't be odd in the slightest—she had to keep that in mind. On her way out to the hall, she glanced at the wall clock: 12:24.

Perfect.

Finally grasping the layout of the property, Joss made her way through the house to the arboreal tunnel leading to the staff quarters. As she rounded the corner to the front of the structure, Circe appeared ahead, expectant expression already set.

"Good afternoon, Ms. Leland," she said, blocking the path.

Joss had met her in person the night before when dinner was being served. A petite brunette, perhaps a full foot shorter than Joss, Circe was all business, and dressed like the manager of a luxury resort: light, monochromatic skirt suit, medium-height heels, hair parted to the side and pulled tight into a ponytail, walkie-talkie in hand. The only thing missing was a nametag.

"Does your radio need new batteries?" Circe's eyes flicked to Joss's bare midriff.

"Oh, no," Joss said. "Markus had said we could come here if we needed anything."

"Of course," Circe said. Joss couldn't put her finger on just what made this woman so scary. "We do, of course, prefer to come to you whenever possible. What can I do for you?"

"Actually, is Markus available? I need to ask him something. I didn't want to say it over the radio ... sort of a surprise for Matt."

"You could use the hardwired telephone in your quarters."

Circe wasn't coming off outright suspicious—probably just annoyed she wasn't allowed to deliver a particular standard of service—but it had Joss discombobulated, nonetheless.

What if they *had* heard what she'd come for ... some sort of advanced listening devices on the beach eavesdropping on her conversation with Matt? Entertaining world leaders here, it wouldn't surprise her to learn of spying gear hidden in the island's remotest nooks. And on that note, what about her room? Were there cameras in her bathroom? Could people see her changing and showering and making stupid-ass faces in the mirror?

These paranoid thoughts had to go. She wasn't here to steal goddamn nuclear launch codes or the Hope Diamond.

"Not really," Joss replied, and decided to wrap her nerves in embarrassment. "See, I was hoping to bring this case ... from Markus, the case he brings ... Sort of an excuse to go to, um, Matt's room. I'm so sorry, I didn't mean to bother you." She coughed out a sheepish laugh. "It's really not that important." She turned to go.

"No, not at all, Ms. Leland." While outwardly accommodating, Circe's tone conveyed zero warmth. "I do hope I didn't give you the impression you would ever be a bother. We're here to exceed expectations. Follow me, please. Markus is in the office."

With short, quick steps Joss associated with an old-timey nurse, Circe led her across the short bridge to the staff quarters, koi fish below them splashing and piling atop each other in anticipation of food. Rounding a corner to a hallway inside, a long wall muffled the sound of a sports stadium crowd on TV, along with the bassy voices of some unseen staff members in a discussion. Suddenly, she was smacked with the enveloping scent of a garlicky soup cooking.

"Something smells good," she said as Circe stopped at a door, and knocked.

"Are you hungry, Ms. Leland? I could have a snack sent."

"Oh, no thank you. I can wait for dinner."

"Nai?" came Markus's voice through the door, with an unfamiliar tone.

"Circe. With Ms. Leland. We have a special request."

The door swung open, revealing Markus without a jacket, tie loosened, and top button undone. "Ms. Leland. What can I do for you? Is everything all right?"

Circe bowed slightly and took her leave.

Joss rubbed her neck, eyes wandering as she *"found the courage"* to speak.

"This is so embarrassing," she said, glancing up to meet Markus's gaze. His eyebrows ascended his forehead. "I'll just say it."

Markus pulled his arms behind his back. "Please."

"I was hoping you could give me the case thing to take to Matt. I was going to sort of surprise him with it, like 'Hey, Markus said to give this to you!'"

He didn't get it. He just sort of frowned and chewed on the remains of whatever he'd been eating.

She went on, "'Cause he's, um, showering right now, probably finishing up. Christ, I'm sorry. Never mind, I'm gonna go drown myself—"

"No, please, *I'm* sorry, I simply don't ..."

Her fingers wriggled at her waist. "You know ... sometimes guys can be afraid to, um, *make a move.*"

He half-smiled, half-grimaced—a pained expression—as he finally grasped what she was saying. Mercifully, he stopped her. "Yes, yes, no need to explain, Ms. Leland. Just give me a moment, please."

"And I'll be like 'whoa, hey, I didn't realize you were, um, busy,' and then, if he's in a towel or whatever, I cover my mouth a little like this and go '*ohh … l…*'"

Markus muttered as he closed the door, leaving Joss alone in the hall.

Yes!

She inhaled deep, gathered herself, and the door reopened a moment later.

Markus appeared with the metal case in a gloveless hand. "Dinner will be at seven." He handed it to her. "I'll come by at six-thirty to retrieve this."

"Thank you so much," she said. "I hope you don't think—" He stopped her with closed eyes and a hand: *Please. No more.* "Sorry … Okay … Thanks again—" The door clicked shut.

Joss led herself out of the staff building and walked back to the house—a casual stroll for the cameras, but with a triumphant brass section blasting in her head. She stood at the door to Matt's room for a moment, listening, then hovering a fist, too reticent to knock. She was certain at least Markus was watching. Finally, she rapped twice and stepped back.

"Coming," Matt said, and the door opened a few seconds later. "Oh, hey there."

Joss held up the case as she took a step forward to enter. "I thought you might want to keep reading."

He moved back, allowing her to invite herself in, and swung the door shut. "Here, let me put that over here." He mouthed a *"shh"* as she handed him the case.

* * *

Standing over his desk in the office, Markus wonders if the enamored Ms. Leland will be successful in her endeavor. His eyes flash to one of his monitors, a split screen of four cameras: the hallway outside the master guest suites, the main sitting room, dining room, and kitchen. He wishes they'd installed temporary monitoring in the suites—primarily Matthew's—but no doubt his powers would've sensed this as easily as any foreign official's security team.

Markus opens the door and relinquishes the case to hands he may soon envy. Ms. Leland likely knows this…

* * *

Matt set the case on a table and turned to Joss. "Perfect. They don't have cameras or monitoring in the rooms."

"How do you—" Joss began. "Wait, that fast? You read it?"

"Yes. Markus's imprint from just now. And—fun fact—he's gay."

"Well, yeah, no shit. You just figured that one out?"

Matt shrugged. "I hadn't thought about it. Anyway, good job. He give you any trouble? Say when he'd be by to take notes?"

Joss shook her head, uttering a vague "Hm."

He went on, "He doesn't seem to care too much about what's been happening during my sessions. Just waiting for someone to start hiding scrolls from the Library."

Something had occurred to Joss and her senses fogged. She'd stopped hearing Matt, now finding herself wondering what *she'd* just imprinted on the case. A few days ago, Matt said if he ever accidentally came across an imprint from someone he knew, he treated it like a diary, disregarding it. He'd specifically asked her to surprise Markus, hoping he'd forget to put on gloves, so Matt could gather everything Markus (or anyone else) had imprinted on the case. If he was now going to dig deep into that thing, how could he *not* stumble onto a few of Joss's thoughts while he was at it?

"Sorry, what?" she said. Matt was staring at her, waiting.

He repeated himself. "I'm going to lie down for a bit—check a couple things in the Taria, then see if I can dig up anything else from Markus. You can hang out if you like." He gestured toward the cushy sitting area.

"Yeah, sure, that's fine. I actually sort of hinted to him that I wanted the case so I could wheedle my way into your room. So, me being in here for a while kind of gives the right impression." Matt stared at her, eyebrows raised. She continued, "Like it worked, you know?"

"Right. I gathered that from him. Good thinking." He took the case to his bed, setting himself up with pillows. "If I end up taking longer, you can go back to your room if you like," Matt said as he opened the lid. "Meaning, you don't have to just sit there, bored and waiting."

"Yeah, either way," Joss said casually. "You want me to go?"

Matt didn't answer. She stood up and saw his hand resting on the Taria, eyes closed.

"Okay, well, I guess I'll just go to my room. Maybe take a little catnap of my own." She headed to the door. "Just wake me up then…"

No response.

* * *

Patra's imprints run like a fixed narrative, unwilling to yield to Matt's deeper probing. It reminds him of reading of Irin's journey through the mountains and across the plains.

In the Library's scribes' chamber, Patra has Atilius working on a tablet borrowed from Samaria, translating it from Hebrew to Greek. Matt resists the imprint's forward momentum, finally pausing as Patra huddles over Atilius.

Now, deeper…

The process advances visually, dropping through the marble tabletop into a dark room. It's Patra's bedroom, lit only by moonlight splitting the sheer drapery. Flat on her bed, she stares at the ceiling. This is an odd scene; the fact that it's a *scene* at all is unique. Subconscious and stored memories always presented themselves just as Matt's own memories and thoughts appeared when recalled, with only minor variations in format.

Patra sits up, goes to her vanity, and lights a candle. She sits down, the Library key clutched in both hands against her belly as she gazes at herself in the mirror. A shuddering chill spirals down her spine—no, Matt's spine. *He* is seated in the chair. *His* eyes are locked on Patra's in the mirror.

"Hello, Steward," she says.

What?!

She speaks directly to Matt. It isn't a dream, or misinterpretation, or anything else reasonable. It's a buried message—intentionally imprinted this deep—awaiting a capable reader.

Her face hangs with grief. "I hope your visit is timely, and your objectives in accord with our society's timeless principles..."

* * *

After an indeterminate period of time on her bed—rolling over, getting tangled in her sarong, kicking it off, pulling on covers, kicking them off—Joss eventually fell asleep. Her dreams were horrible: first, she was walking on the edge of a cliff, loose soil beneath her bare feet, teetering, but always leaning more toward the cliff, just about to fall. Then, worse, a constant, quick-cutting replay of every interaction with Matt in which she came off mortifyingly desperate, fawning, dopey, and everything she said to him came with dorky smirks and batting eyelashes. His responses became exasperation, *embarrassment* for her, and pity—how one might look on a mortally wounded friend on the battlefield as they say, *"I'm gonna make it! Don't worry about me, guys! I'll pull through!"*

But was any of that real? Besides the stupid sunblock quip, had she been flirting at all? No! This was one of those horrible fear realization nightmares. Now aware of the dream, she tried to adjust the memories to her will, and then suddenly she heard Matt's voice—close—next to her ear, a distance reserved only for the most intimate of messages. He said her name once, then again. And it was *real*, he was there in her room, sitting on the edge of her bed, the heat from his shoulder and arm close enough to feel on her own arm.

She opened her eyes.

Indeed, he was there on the bed, his eyes on her eyes, with an intensity she'd never seen from him. How long had he been there, observing her in only the bikini? She felt only the sheet on her, covering maybe half a leg.

"Hi," she said softly, and began scooting herself up, but he put a hand on her shoulder to stop her.

"*Shh.*" He bent close to her. She closed her eyes, his face drawing near, breath in her hair, goosebumps … "We have a situation," he whispered. "We need to go. Like *now.*"

Uh, what?

She pushed him back and looked at his face. He was serious. She was about to ask what had happened but he shook his head and mouthed, "Later."

He helped her out of bed, pointed to the crumpled pair of jeans she'd thrown in the corner, and for some reason that gesture, at that moment, triggered a wave of shame. She was practically naked, wearing this bikini in a big corporate conference room, pointing at a presentation screen, as baffled, suit-clad coworkers stared.

She pulled on the jeans—violently—over her bikini bottom, marched to the closet, and threw on a shirt, mumbling obscenities to herself. Turning to exit the closet, she slammed right into Matt, and he put his hands up in a *"calm down"* gesture. He nudged her back into the closet, placed his hands on her shoulders, and leaned beside her ear again. This time, though, his voice was more urgent, annoyed, perplexed.

"What are you doing?" he whispered. "Settle down and just follow my lead. Get some shoes on, get your purse, whatever you can carry, but only essentials."

And then it hit her. When he said they had to go, he meant *go*, as in leave the island, and apparently with haste … an escape! He looked at her, severe, waiting for some sort of acknowledgement. She nodded, and he turned to go.

"Are we in danger?" she whispered.

Matt paused in the closet doorway, grimacing slightly, as if to say yes, but not wanting to scare her. "No, no. Not yet. Not if we go now." He disappeared around the wall.

It was a unique sensation, that of skyrocketing dread mixed with utter humiliation. She wanted to burst out laughing like a crazy person, but the fear quickly drowned out everything else, and she did what Matt said, grabbing her things and following him.

* * *

It'd been a mistake to let Joss come on the trip with him. She was a weakness, and his own weakness had influenced the snap decision to let her come. This was no revelation. It'd been no less clear when he'd first seen her in his driveway, sitting on his car, or again, when she showed up at the airport. And now that he needed to sneak off the island early, Joss in tow? Ridiculous. It wasn't her fault, but stifling his anger at her presence proved a challenge.

Not anger, he corrected as they reached Joss's door to the hallway. *Worry.*

It killed his focus. She killed his focus. Beyond mere extra baggage, curbing his speed, she was a full-fledged handicap, fog on a windshield, an open wound on his palm.

Matt stopped at the door and motioned for her to wait. Her hand tightened around his. He closed his eyes, inhaled slowly.

Akel al-khowf.

33rd Precept: *"Consume their fear."*

The Nizari—a league of elite Spanish Muslims with whom Matt had spent years training via Haeming's imprints—observed eighty such precepts for the effective *"supernatural warrior,"* the *mohareb khareq.*

Consuming the fear of one's enemy had initially seemed to fall under the Nizari's more spiritually based concepts, such as the types of prayers required before and after killing, or like the superstitious custom of rubbing cucumber on one's armor. However, Matt later grasped the meaning, and very real phenomenon of *Akel al-khowf.* In battle, if a warrior sensed their opponents' fear, it fueled an empowering force. The same held true of innocents in need of protection. Frightened women and children could be used by the warrior as a source of inner strength and fearlessness against attackers.

In Matt's case, he'd found the precept's truth when his ex, Isis Meier, was freaking out, begging for him to kill a spider in her bathtub. Matt feared and detested spiders just as much as his girlfriend, but observing her terror prior to seeing the offending *hell-spawn* had emboldened him to handle the situation. He'd consumed her fear.

Matt turned to Joss and flashed a tranquil, confident smile. "It's going to be fine, okay? Security won't know we're leaving until we're already gone. Just be cool for this hall camera. I've come to get you to show you something in my room. Yeah?"

Joss blinked, wide-eyed, took a deep breath, and nodded. "I'm good."

"Great. I'm going to let go of your hand now, okay?"

"Oh, of course, yeah." She shook her head as she released her grip.

Matt relaxed his body, opened the door, and strolled across the hall to his suite. Joss closed her door, a little too purposefully, with two hands on the knob, but nothing anyone should've noticed. She smiled as he waved her in, and he shut the door behind him.

"This way," he said, leading her to the bathroom.

They walked to the far end of the bathroom, to the locked door beside the linen closet. The little sign above a keypad and knob read **Staff** in multiple languages. Matt punched in a six-digit code and twisted the knob. The door swung open.

"I have one of those button pads, too," Joss said. "I thought it was cleaning supplies or something."

Matt raised a *"just wait, there's more"* finger, crouched to the floor, and pulled up a flap of carpet, revealing a silvery ring. He slipped two fingers into the ring and lifted. The closet's square floor rose smoothly on two hydraulic rods. Joss arched over him, gawking at the short flight of stairs leading down to the tunnel.

"No way," she hushed. "I'm shocked! Shocked, but I guess not surprised."

Matt grabbed the small duffel he'd left by the door, slinging it across his chest, and walked down the stairs. "Please close the door behind you, and pull down that hatch until it clicks."

Joss followed him down, observing the dimly lit cement tunnel. "Where does it lead?" She ducked to close the hatch above.

"All over the house," Matt explained as he led her down the narrow passage, head crooked slightly to avoid hitting the low ceiling and sporadic lights. "Goes to most rooms, and also to the staff and security buildings."

"Security buildings? I didn't—"

"There's a lot we weren't shown on the island. What we need to do right now is stop real quick in the master suite to grab something-"

"Do we have time for that?" Joss interrupted. "If we're in a hurry—"

"We have time. We're making our exit a day earlier than I'd planned. I'll explain everything later. Anyway, besides the service staff, there are eight security officers, all former Ukrainian military, that I'd just as soon avoid on our way out."

"Well, yeah."

"Except ..." Matt turned a corner and stopped at the foot of another cement staircase. "Right now, all but one of them are eating lunch in the staff building. And guess where our second stop is?"

"The staff building. Jesus, why?"

"I have the Taria you fetched in my bag—not part of the original plan, but we're taking it with us. Now I need to get the other one. You're going to stay in the tunnels though. Got it?"

"Whatever you say," she replied, and then murmured, "Stealing from Ostrovsky seems like a super idea."

Matt ignored her as he twisted the knob on the hatch to Ostrovsky's room, turning it without resistance. He'd intentionally broken the lock while scouting the night before and, presumably, no one had yet discovered his excursions. In the closet up the stairs, Matt punched in another code on a keypad. The door eased open before him.

A backward glance to Joss at the foot of the stairs, justifiably nervous. "Peak in if you want, but don't leave the closet, okay? I'll be right back."

She nodded and whispered, "There's no alarm or anything?"

"No, these are all isolated keypads. The only alarms are on room doors and all the windows. Sit tight."

Matt strode from the bathroom, straight through Ostrovsky's bizarre bedroom—a column-filled expanse with an imposing curtained bed atop a staired pedestal; it was *Emperor Ostrovsky*, evidently, or perhaps he thought of himself as some Greek God. Matt entered Ostrovsky's study, walls lined with dead things, furs, bookshelves, and weapons. He peered up at the apparent pièce de résistance: an elephant's head, dominating the room from up high, eyes glaring black, and roaring mouth, as though it'd just crashed through the wall.

Matt went to the opposite wall, adorned with weapons ancient and new: a tommy gun, Zulu spear, .45 Beretta, feathered blowgun, long sword, short sword, katana, .44 Magnum revolver al a Dirty Harry. He grabbed what he'd come for and returned to the bathroom, where Joss's sideways head poked from the closet floor.

"A stick?" She gawped. "That's what you came for? Wait, is it a toy sword?"

He motioned her back down the stairs as he replied, "*Bokken wakizashi*—a short, wooden, practice sword. I needed a weapon."

Joss didn't further voice her skepticism, but her face was sufficient.

"Trust me," Matt said, grabbing her hand. She wouldn't understand why it was a better option than the alternatives.

A right turn, a left, and then the tunnel stretched out in the distance for as far as they could see, and with no more breaks in the walls for branching passages. Their breath and steps echoed, amplified in the corridor. After a couple hundred feet, the passage ended at a T, and Matt stopped and set down his duffle bag. He slid the short sword into a belt loop on his side. Joss maintained her grip on his other hand.

He faced her and whispered, "Two minutes, maybe three. Don't be scared, okay? We're pretty much done."

Joss's grip tightened on his fingers. "You're leaving me here?"

"Veerrry briefly," he said, once more smiling reassurance.

He left her at the T-junction, and headed down the slightly sloped passage to the staff quarters. Matt had never been this far, and wasn't positive about which room the stairs would put him in. Walking the grounds above, counting steps and paying attention to his position relative to the main house, Matt had estimated the tunnel ended somewhere in the front portion of the staff building.

The passage ended at a grate-covered drain hole and a metal ladder leading to another hatch. Matt peered up the passage to Joss— a barely-lit orange blur. He probably should've had her pick a different shirt. He waved, in case she could see him, and then pressed his fingertips to the hatch above.

My name is Circe Sarkis, female, thirty-eight, from Piraeus, Greece...

Circe's office, next door to Markus's. It made sense for the tunnel to lead there. Unfortunately, from what Matt had observed over the past few days, Circe rarely left the staff building and there was a strong possibility she was in her office at present. Matt gathered the office's full layout through a few of Circe's imprints, discovering the hatch lay in a corner, only half-concealed beside a filing cabinet, and at least six feet from Circe's desk. Fortunately, the desk faced a wall, and if Circe was in her chair, she'd have her back to the hatch.

Matt gently twisted the knob, applying light upward pressure with his free hand. It didn't feel right. Something sat on top of the door. He put his back into it and the hatch popped up suddenly, emitting a horrible, piercing scritch of metal slicing into metal. And right there, six feet from his intruding head, sat a gaping Circe, frozen in shock.

As she babbled, unsuccessfully searching for the muscles required to call for help, Matt forced the hatch out of the way and scurried up the stairs, wrapping his arms around Circe's head, and drawing her face into his abdomen.

"Wait, wait, *o-hee,* no!" Came her muffled protest as Matt dragged her from the chair.

As he pulled her to the hatch, she clawed at his sides and back, feet kicking wild-yet-noiselessly on the carpeted concrete floor. Halfway down the stairs, her teeth gnashed into his belly skin, and he let go. As he fell backward, he clapped both hands against her ears—not with enough force to burst her eardrums, but delivering sufficient pain to incapacitate. Scrabbling to his feet, the wooden sword clacking against the floor and wall, Matt climbed over Circe and pulled the hatch shut above them, hoping no one had heard the struggle or the horrible shriek of the scratching metal.

"Don't touch me!" Circe shouted before he reached her. "What is this? What are you to do with me?"

Matt pried one of her hands away from her ear as he helped her up. "Nothing, just be quiet. Go." He nudged her down the dark tunnel toward Joss.

Circe, still frightened, shambled along, blathering. "You cannot possibly think you'll get away with whatever this is. They'll kill you. You know this, yes? Security? They'll kill you."

Joss was understandably shocked. "*She's* what you had to get? I thought you said—"

"No," Matt said, unclipping the shoulder strap from his duffle bag. "Please lay down, Circe. Face down."

She dropped slowly to her knees. "You both they will kill. The two of you." Matt pulled her hands together, and her words abruptly lost their venom. "You should simply stop now, I'll not say anything. No one will have noticed me yet gone."

He extended the strap and tied Circe's wrists. "Is Markus in his office?"

"Markus? I believe so. Why?" Then, suddenly angry again, "What *is* this? Release me now!"

Matt crossed Circe's ankles and wrapped them tight with the remaining strap, leaving her hogtied at Joss's feet. "Watch her," he said to Joss. "If she gets loud, step on her face." He felt his T-shirt where Circe had bitten him. Cold and wet with saliva and blood. "And watch out. She bites."

Uncertain, Joss nodded, and Matt rushed back to the hatch.

Back in Circe's office, Matt slid the sword from his side and pressed his ear to the wall. He heard voices from a speaker in Markus's office, and a muffled snicker. Was Markus watching YouTube videos? Matt went to Circe's door, cracked it open, and peered down the hall. Men's voices around a corner. Three voices. Greek. Stationary. He poked his head out farther and scanned the rest of the hall, toward the kitchen.

The three men laughed and walked away, continuing their discussion about which of them would marry "ScarJo." Matt stepped into the hall, crept the short distance to Markus's door, and knocked with three quick taps. The sound from Markus's computer halted.

"Nai?" Markus answered, audibly annoyed.

Matt adjusted his voice down and replied "A moment, sir?" in Greek.

A chair rattled. A second later, the door opened. Markus went from irritated to dismayed in an instant. Matt lunged forward, clasped a hand over Markus's mouth, and wrapped the other arm around his neck, pressing the smooth wooden blade just beneath Markus's Adam's apple. Matt drove him back, shutting the door behind them with his heel.

"Where's Taria A?" Matt said, and the stiff Markus only glared.

Matt's wrist against Markus's collar provided the answer he sought. Matt glanced back at the corkboard over the desk, behind which hid a large combination safe. "Thanks," Matt said. "Are you going to make noise if I release you, or do I need to knock you out?"

Matt squeezed the bokken a little tighter, lifting the Adam's apple and pinching Markus's trachea enough to make breathing an effort. Markus, with cold eyes locked on Matt's, shook his head. He was telling the truth, and, interestingly enough, felt *hurt* by this assault, and not physically.

"Stay close to me," Matt said as he released him, and then stepped to the desk. "Away from the door." He slid the sword back into his jeans' belt loop.

The corkboard rose with ease, aided by springs or counterweights, and remained in place as Matt touched the thick black dial on the safe. He twisted out the combination from Markus's memory: 13 – 58 – 40. The latch handle turned and Matt pulled the heavy door. He ignored the small black cases and stacks of various foreign currencies, grabbing the metal Taria case, and setting it on the desk.

Matt glanced at Markus, standing with his usual rigid posture, hands crossed before him, and almost *eerily* calm face, flat smile, indifferent eyes.

Matt wrapped the Taria in its cloth and shoved it in his pocket. "Now, where's the package?"

Markus directed his eyes to the set of drawers in the side of his desk. Matt slid open the top drawer, finding only pens, pencils, paperclips, and other small office supplies. He closed it and opened the next drawer.

"The small box," Markus said, but Matt already recognized it from previous imprints.

He picked it up and popped it open. A man's ring, immediately recognizable as Damascus steel by the wavy patterns. Matt swiped a finger across it to check its authenticity.

Agony! Piercing! Pain! Terror! No!

Matt jerked his hand back, unsteady at the knees, one hand clutching Markus's desk. He choked down a painful gulp, wiped his singed, wet eyes on his shoulders, and labored for a clean breath. That sort of imprint burst hadn't happened in a long time.

He pulled himself together, stood upright, and stole a glance at a fascinated Markus.

Matt shut the box with a pop, shoved it into his other pocket, and placed his hands on Markus's shoulders. "That came from Tuni St. James?"

"Tuni *Absko*, by way of several couriers, but yes ... What *was* that?"

Matt ignored the question, still shaken by the imprint. He strove for composure, but a spike had just been plunged into his left wrist. The right had already been pinned to a post, ulna and radius pried apart. He was being *crucified*. Residual pain throbbed in his wrists—torn flesh and splintered bone. His nervous system couldn't tell the difference between imprint and reality.

He forced it all away, concentrating on his grip on Markus's shoulders, the incoming stream of thoughts, and asked, "Anything I need to worry about on my way out of here? ... Yes, I know about security, what else?" Markus kept trying to speak, but Matt cut him off as each thought flashed by. "Yes, we're taking the boat. Aren't you the smart one ... Helicopter? I didn't know you had one. Where? ... Wow. The awesome never stops here, does it? Who knows how to fly it? ... Oh, well a lot of good he'll do you right now. Who else? You? Really? ... Well, good for you."

Markus shook Matt's hands off, declaring, "We *won't* go after you, Matthew."

"And why's that?"

"Because our primary interest has always been in recovering the Library's contents."

"And keeping us here for as long as Ostrovsky has artifacts for me to read."

Markus smirked. "That was a secondary interest."

"Your friend Rostik arrives tomorrow."

"That …" Markus considered his words, "… may not have been the wisest decision. It wasn't my desire. And he's no friend of mine."

"Right, well we won't be here."

"Evidently," Markus said. "Have a safe journey."

Matt put a hand back on Markus's shoulder. "What does Rostik look like?"

An imaginary picture of Rostik materialized in Markus's mind. "I don't know. He doesn't do face-to-face. This is a face you'd do best to avoid knowing."

"Big help. And what are *you* going to do when I leave this office? You're not just letting us go—"

"You, too, are making an unwise decision." His eyes landed on Matt's pocket—Taria A. "Mr. Ostrovsky will obviously wish to retrieve his property. I'll have to see you in Alexandria."

Reminded of the wooden sword, Matt slid it out, raising the tip to Markus's neck. "What makes you think I'd go there? You think I actually care about some scrolls that may or may not even exist anymore?"

Markus tilted his head cynically. "I don't need your ability to deduce your intent. Just know that your other requested imbursements have yet to begin."

Matt shrugged. "Well, I really only had one, and you've already handled it, so thanks for that."

"Your note hasn't necessarily arrived at its destination yet, and if it hasn't, it will be stopped."

"Well, you seem to find that possibility unlikely. That's quite a bonus you paid the couriers for punctuality. As for the other 'imbursements,' your boss obviously has the power to make big things happen, but in Africa? No. Not to the extent I would've needed. Anyway, I'll return the Tarias and *wakizashi*. I only need to borrow them for a short time."

Markus grinned and blinked. Matt smiled back, their eyes locked.

They stood there in silence a moment until Matt lowered the sword.

"I'm flattered," Matt finally said. "Now then, would you do us a favor and stay here for ten minutes before calling anyone? ... Five? Sure, I'll take it."

Markus slid by, traded places with Matt, and busied himself with the empty Taria case and safe.

Matt opened the door, surveyed the hall, and hastened back to Circe's office. Down the hatch, he duck-jogged through the tunnel to Joss.

"That was a long goddam time," Joss growled.

He grabbed her hand and picked up the duffle bag.

"Thank you for a lovely stay, Circe," he said. "Someone should be along soon to fetch you."

Cheek smushed against the floor, she sneered and said in Greek, "You're an ill-mannered peasant."

Matt and Joss followed the tunnel uphill about fifty feet to another set of steps.

Matt put a hand on the hatch. "*Great.* This one is actually inside the security building. We don't have time for this. Stay here a second." He slid the sword from his side and twisted the knob.

The hatch glided open above him with a quiet hiss, sunlight shining from a nearby window, illuminating the baggy black cargo pants of the enormous Grisha, Markus's guard, sitting before a pair of security monitors, munching on some sort of dried dumplings.

Catching the hatch's motion in his peripheral, Grisha snapped his head toward Matt, eyes wide. He recoiled, cursing in Greek as one might swear in a haunted house when one of the "monsters" pops out from the darkness.

Matt dashed up the steps with both hands on the bokken, wielding it defensively, with the blade pointed downward across his torso. Grisha stood, tripped backward a couple steps as he fumbled for the semi-auto pistol under his arm. Too late. The sword's blunt edge struck Grisha's wrist, flinging his meaty hand at his own face, landing with a slap. Matt followed up with a light blow to the solar plexus using the bokken's tip. Fragments of popcorn and spittle flung from Grisha's mouth as he lurched over. A final nudge from Matt's hip dropped Grisha to the floor, gagging and dry heaving.

"Handcuffs!" Joss's voice from behind.

Matt spun round, put a finger to his mouth to shush her; he didn't know if any other security men had returned to the building. She mouthed sorry as she jabbed a finger toward the cabinets behind him. Sure enough, several sets of cuffs, both metal and the black plastic tactical sort, hung from little pegs. Unsure what Grisha had stashed on his person, and wishing to not waste another second by conducting a thorough search, Matt opted for a combination of restraints. Grisha groaned as Matt pulled the pinned arm out from under him, locking his wrists behind his back with metal cuffs. He then added the zipties, crisscrossing two sets over the metal cuffs.

Matt grabbed the bokken from the floor, stood, and pointed to Joss. "You have my bag?" She held it up. "Let's go."

Outside, sunlight pierced the leafy canopy, littering the ground with shiny little fragments. Matt took his bag from Joss, hooking it once more over his head, and led them away from the security building, toward the unseen dock to the west. They trudged through the soft, sandy dirt, aided now and then by more rigid, viney ground cover.

Matt slowed and glanced back at Joss. "You good? We're almost there."

She nodded, tired but resolute.

"There's one more guard in the boathouse," Matt said, "and we need the keys. Shouldn't be a problem though if he hasn't been alerted yet."

"What if he's been alerted?"

"Then we'll see a crapload of guards either on their way to, or standing around the boathouse. In which case, I'm going to very quickly learn how to fly a helicopter."

"That's not funny."

"Shh." He stuck a shushing hand out behind him as the boathouse came into view through a stand of palms' prison-like bars.

To the right, the mild Aegean waves lowered the docked speedboat, then lifted it just as easily. If the boathouse window didn't directly face the pier, Matt might have elected to go straight to the boat and hotwire it—ridiculously simple in small vessels.

"Follow me to the back," he whispered, "then stay there until I get you."

They ran across the sand between tree trunks and bushes, avoiding the crunches of dry leaves and branches. At the back of the boathouse, Matt peered toward the path leading to the staff quarters, envisioning Markus examining his watch, then sounding the alarm. Matt had Joss hide on the shady side of the boathouse, out of view of anyone coming from the staff quarters.

He mouthed, "Last one. Be right back."

Matt crept alongside the windowless, white paneled structure. A quick glance around the corner to the concrete deck and wide-open window. All clear. He stepped up onto the deck, inching foot over foot toward the window.

A metallic clatter—the sound of keys dropping on the counter beside him. Matt froze.

"There you go, Matthew."

Matt's shoulders slumped.

Markus.

Was there a gun pointed through the wall behind him? Had someone snatched Joss silently away?

Matt stepped into view of the window. On the counter lay a ring of three small keys attached to a little day-glow orange float. Beyond stood Markus, arms crossed, satisfied, close-lipped smile. And beyond Markus, surrounded by hanging life jackets, scuba gear, and wetsuits, stood a troubled, confused guard, empty hands at his sides.

Matt used the tip of the bokken to slide the keys toward him.

"Please," Markus said, indicating the sword. "Take it easy with that. It's six hundred years old."

"Seven hundred and twelve," Matt corrected, dropping the keys into his palm.

Markus popped his eyebrows. *Touché.*

Matt cocked his head sideways and yelled, "Joss!"

She appeared a few seconds later. "Jesus Christ. Guess we've given up on stealth, huh?"

"Safe travels, Ms. Leland," Markus said, and Joss snapped her head his way.

"Oh." She grimaced. "Yikes." She offered him an apologetic smile.

Markus leaned forward, resting his elbows on the counter. "If you'd remained here, Matthew, I would've been able to manage Rostik. I'll have precious little control in Egypt. Do take care."

Matt flashed Markus a peace sign, hooked his arm around Joss's, and ran down the beach to the pier. He jumped into the boat and helped Joss down.

"So he just gave you the keys? And who's *Rostik*?"

Matt stuck them in the ignition and twisted. "Yup. And I'll explain later." He pressed the ignition and the twin engines sputtered and growled to life. "Can you undo that back line?" Matt stepped between the split windshields, and untied the front cleat.

Back at the steering wheel, Matt pulled the throttle into reverse and the idling boat trembled, slowly backing away from the pier, and traversing incoming swells. On the beach, Markus stood with his hands behind his back, gazing out at them.

Once Matt had driven them a good distance away, past two other islands and well out of sight of Philippos, he figured out their course with the boat's GPS. He beckoned a reluctant-yet-intrigued Joss to man the controls.

"You see this map here?" he shouted over the wind and engines. She nodded. "Just follow the line there and watch out for other boats." He showed her the throttle. "There's no brakes. Just **Go** and **Don't go**, got it?"

She shouted back as she grabbed the wheel and rested a hand on the throttle. "I got it, but where are *you* going?"

"I need to figure out our *next* destination."

He grabbed his duffle bag and sat down on the backward-facing seat adjacent to Joss. Unable to find a long enough length of string anywhere, he unlaced one of his sneakers and fashioned himself a Taria necklace, pulling it over his head and dropping the dangling artifact inside the collar of his T-shirt. He stood up to take over driving but saw that Joss had it well in hand, so he grasped the windshield frame, planted one knee on the seat cushion, and watched the water ahead.

"So?" Joss said. "What was that about back there? Just letting us go like that … kind of makes me even more worried. Is the boat going to blow up or something?"

"Ha, no. He knows where I'm going, knows I'll take good care of the artifacts, and figures I'd refuse to read anymore if detained … Or at least not share what I learned. Hell, I could simply lie. Send them on a wild goose chase. This way, I keep reading and lead them straight to the scrolls. He's confident I'll be easily trackable."

"So that Rostik person is supposed to track us? But he won't be able to?" She glanced at his face, then back to the island-dotted waters ahead.

"I'll be trackable *enough*. I'll need him and others close when the time's right."

"Okay, cool. Ambiguity. Big fan. So, where are we going, at least? Egypt?"

Matt was about to say *"I'm going to Egypt. You're going home,"* but thought it through. He'd lost three days with travel and the island—probably another now, getting to Alexandria. Many balls would require juggling.

"Hello?" Joss prodded.

"Just a second."

Rostik was the only factor making Joss an ongoing problem. If Matt could get rid of him early on, Joss's safety wouldn't be an issue. Set her up in some random, different hotel, fill her in on everything, and have her coordinate with Iris on some of the other pieces, freeing him up to work on the primary objectives.

Crap. Iris is going to freak the hell out. Another benefit to having a Joss "buffer."

They'd need to take separate flights, stagger times, keep apart …

Then there was Patra's deep imprint. Absolutely unexpected. Bewildering.

As someone rarely surprised, those two simple words, *"Hello, Steward,"* had shaken him to the core, and her voice now echoed in his mind. He'd heard them before, those words—his first time reading the Taria, as well as the last time she'd gazed in that mirror, brushing her hair—and thinking on it now, the phrase had been oddly disembodied, and unlike normal thoughts. Had he thought to investigate either incident, perhaps she would've gone on, as with the last reading:

"Hello, Steward. I hope your visit is timely, and your objectives in accord with our society's timeless principles. Your very presence here demonstrates your training and commitment, so we must assume not only noble intent, but also familiarity with our methods and media. For your prospective efforts, you have our eternal gratitude."

But that was all! She'd returned to her bed and hung the keystone on a wall hook. Matt had tried to drill down deeper, rewinding and exploring the room in new ways, but it was useless. Perhaps fast-forwarding … Nope. As before, he wasn't able—or, he suspected, wasn't *allowed*. If more hid within, he didn't have the "training and commitment" to find it just yet. It was like trying to fold one's ears when, clearly, no connection existed through which to send such a command, or no muscle on the receiving end to obey it.

He'd given up for the moment, moving on to the case where he'd found the details on Rostik, but the Taria hanging from his neck had called for ongoing reading. If Patra didn't have Matt's ability, then she at least knew someone who did. After all those imprints— hundreds of thousands he'd read by now—not once had he found evidence of another like him.

And then the boat's hull crashed through a high peak, yanking Patra's face from his thoughts, and replacing it with Tuni's. The small box in his pocket had shifted just enough to remind of its presence, and the ring inside—something Tuni wanted him to see.

He *really* needed to brain-dump all this on I.T., but ridiculous as he felt about it, he was afraid to talk to her. His little sister. Asinine.

"I'm no time-ologist," Joss shouted over the wind and engines, "but this very well may be the longest second anyone's ever waited."

"Let me ask you this," Matt finally said. She was all ears. "Do you want to go home, or come with me to Alexandria? There's obviously dangerous stuff and dangerous people all wrapped up in this. I'm confident you'll be out of harm's way, but you know, I thought the same thing here. There're no guarantees."

"Let me ask you this," Joss replied. "Do you *need* me there, or will I still just be a burden?"

"Well, I never said—I mean, I can figure it out if—"

"You're supposed to say 'yes, I need you.' Just say 'yes.'"

"Yes."

She grinned. "Well, then, let's go see the Sphinx!"

"The Sphinx is in Giza."

"Pyramids then … Mummies … Desert. Whatever."

Joss steered the boat around a small, uninhabited island. Matt stared over the bow.

A crowded street in Ancient Alexandria bounced before him as the boat traversed the small swells. Patra's view overlapped Matt's perspective of the sea and distant mainland, both places equally present in his eyes. More dizzying were the voices around him: a shouting Alexandrian merchant twenty feet off to his left, in the water, seeming to move at the same speed as the boat; crowds walking in front of and behind Patra as she made her way to the Musaeum.

Matt began feeling seasick and closed his eyes.

ELEVEN

Alexandria, Aegyptus – 271 CE

Most pagan elders resented the presence of Christian and Jewish scrolls in the religious texts section, despite the rolls' sequestration in specific receptacles. Their very presence in the Library, in the elders' eyes, bestowed undue legitimacy to their adherents. The fact that precious hours were spent translating such things, creating even more scrolls, seemed to highlight the undeniable fact that the Jews weren't going anywhere, and that Christianity as a belief was growing in tandem with the piles of papyrus.

In the scribes' chamber, Patra had Atilius working on a tablet borrowed from Samaria, translating it from Hebrew to Greek. What Patra and her colleagues found particularly fascinating about the tablet was that it seemed to recount the familiar tale of Jesus, but in this version, the Hebrews' archangel Gabriel referred to the Messiah as "Simon."

"Have we determined how old it is?" Patra asked Atilius as she bent over his shoulder.

Atilius continued writing, his gnarly, old, ink-stained fingers as steady as a painter's. "During the rule of Octavian, same time as Jesus ... This from the original transcriber. Kaleb says the date is not unassailable, since it's only the scribe's understanding of the oral tradition."

Patra ran her fingers down the tablet's sharp edge. "Yes, I agree with Kaleb. So everything in the text is identical except the name? An interesting concurrence. Can we keep it? Send them back a papyrus copy and a fair price?"

Atilius replied without looking up from his work, "That is for you stewards to negotiate. I am but a lowly scribe."

"I was only asking your opinion, Atilius. If you think they could be swayed."

Once a steward himself, Atilius had been at the Musaeum since before Patra's father, and he'd never quite warmed to the idea of answering to a female. "As with innumerable others before them, they'll wish to know why we desire the original, though opinions are the privilege of a worthy few. I am but a—"

"Yes, yes, lowly scribe," Patra interrupted and flicked his ear. "You're intolerable. Have you …?" She faded off, abruptly walking to another table, that of Nelpus, also a Hebrew and Greek translator. "Good day, Nelpus. What are you working on today?"

"Nothing less than the word of the Hebrew God," he said, angling the papyrus for her to read. "Or at least Philo's interpretation."

"The Septuagint," she said. "Are you truly so audacious as to check the work of seventy *identical* translations produced by seventy isolated translators?" She spoke ironically, sharing her peer's skepticism about this allegedly conclusive translation of the Hebrew Bible.

"Remarkable, wasn't it?" Nelpus grumbled. "The entire Old Testament translated into Greek and not a word misread or disagreed upon … *Seventy* men, Steward."

"I know," Patra assented and sat down beside him, observing the untidy stack of sheets. "I take it you've found something of interest? Mistakes?"

"'Mistake' would imply error," he said shrewdly. "I seek to ascertain *intent*. Do you think you could acquire us more originals?"

Patra rubbed her sore eyes and prepared to deliver another futile speech on avoiding unnecessary controversy, but the echoes of running feet in the main hall drew her attention. They grew louder—multiple people—three? Four coming?

"What's happening?" Nelpus said.

As the footfalls neared the scribes' chamber doors, Patra rose to her feet, mumbling. "Children ... only passing through ... Someone will stop them, discipline—"

But the doors swung open a crack, and one of the guards appeared in the bar of sunlight. "You're needed, Steward."

A young man called out, "Steward Supatra!"

Patra stepped outside, allowing the guard to shut the doors behind her.

Three stricken faces greeted her in the colonnade—breathless young astrologers she'd seen around. Having found her, none now wished to deliver the message for which they'd been sent.

"Speak, boy!" Patra demanded. "What's happened?"

A crowd grew behind the boys, with more coming, unseen voices calling out to others, "Something's happened!"

Patra cradled one of the young men's cheeks, meeting his eyes as calmly as she could muster. "Go ahead, dear."

His breath heated her wrists.

"Ships, Steward. Beyond the lighthouse. Hundreds. The Emperor."

She verified, "The Emperor's fleet is coming?"

He swallowed and nodded.

Devastating news—the worst possible news. But true? It could be only a rumor.

She strove to maintain composure, found a familiar face in the circle. "The observatory, please. Have a look and right back to me." The woman snapped a nod and slipped out of the group. Patra returned focus to the boy. "And who sent you here? With this urgent message?"

"Thomas Egnatius, Steward," he replied.

Thomas, the Governor's aide.

So it was true, or at least more likely to be. Thomas wasn't the sort to spread misinformation. He took actualities and molded them to a serve a personal agenda. These boys hadn't been sent to *inform*. No, he'd sent them to place blame.

Remembering once more the throngs of Musaeum members around her, she raised her voice for all to hear. "Why must *we* be concerned with such a visit? Is it so unusual?"

But, of course, she underestimated her colleagues' astuteness. These were, after all, the Empire's very brightest minds. They, too, would have foreseen the repercussions of Kaleb's performance. A few weeks ago, she'd construed their free-spirited laughter in the amphitheater as a sign of naiveté, but it'd only taken an evening's reflection in their beds to imagine the aftermath. The only question remaining in any wise mind would be *scale*. And the answer appeared to be at hand.

"Find the other stewards," Patra demanded. "Have them meet me in—" She deliberated a moment. Somewhere smaller, private, quiet. "Send them to my residence. And everyone—I mean *everyone*—meet back in the main courtyard at nightfall."

She waved away the onlookers and other youths, nodded to the guard, and steered only her messenger into the chamber, arm around his shoulder. She gestured for Nelpus, Atilius, and the rest of the scribes to leave the room, and they silently obeyed.

The boy gawked at the forbidden room.

Patra directed his chin forward, back to her face. "What is your name, dear?"

"Phorus, Steward."

"How old are you, Phorus?"

"Thirteen, Steward."

"Fine. Good. Tell me more. Everything you were told or heard. First, how far away are the ships?"

"One third have blockaded Canopus and Thonis, Steward, and the rest are amassing here, a mile offshore. They say it can be nothing other than an invasion."

"And what of Augusta Zenobia and Augustus? Are they still in the city?"

"Yes, Steward. Augusta has sent out a single ship to offer gifts and greetings to the Emperor." Phorus breathed shallow, eyes on his own hands.

"What else?" Patra said. "Tell me whatever it is you're afraid to say."

He set his big brown eyes on hers—pleading, nervous. "I may have heard wrong—"

"Say it, boy, or I'll warrant your fear! Save the caveats, and speak."

"Thomas Egnatius, Steward, he … After he sent us, he … I think he might've said to the others there … that he wasn't going to let the Musaeum bring down the whole city. That he'd have the Governor send, well, *all* the stewards and performers to the docks and …"

"Yes? And?"

"… and spike them to poles—so … so they'd be the first thing the Emperor sees upon entering the bay."

The boy's face blurred as Patra's thoughts grew muddled. Everything was happening too fast. She needed to … She couldn't think of what she needed to do. She needed to think, to breathe. In an instant, the chamber had grown hot and thin of air.

"May I go find my parents, Steward?"

"What? Yes, of course, sorry. Thank you, Phorus. Tell no one else of this, understand?"

"But," he began, "my parents—"

"Yes, you may tell them, of course. I mean … just try to be discreet with this, yes? We don't need to have the entire Musaeum in an uproar over what you *may* have overheard, understand? We're only waiting for all the facts and will disseminate them in the courtyard tonight."

Phorus nodded understanding. Patra released his arms and he opened the doors, running off.

Still in a hot daze, Patra locked the Library doors.

"I can see them, Steward," said a winded voice. "The ships outside the harbor. It's true."

Patra tried to thank the woman she'd sent to the observatory, but nothing came out—only a vague gesture of acknowledgement, and she made her way back to her residence.

Unza, just inside, carrying a bundle of towels, was surprised to see Patra return so early. She frowned at her mistress.

"Why?" Unza said, and Patra saw the question was directed to her anguished face, not the unexpected return.

"Merely some busy-busy things." Patra forced a smile and Unza rolled her head around with annoyance, having been unnecessarily burdened with concern. "The stewards are coming here. Have wine ready for us."

Unza grunted recognition and plodded off toward the kitchen.

Patra went to the window, swung the shutter out to open it, and peered beyond the treetops to the distant sea. The tiny sails looked like colorful whitecaps atop impossibly large swells. The boy had said hundreds. No, there were thousands. This was an invasion force—naval masses unseen in the region for centuries.

Alexandria had had its share of conquest and turnover, but these transitions generally occurred only at the top, such as Zenobia's brief campaign only a couple years before. There was no siege on the city, but a short-lived skirmish well beyond the walls, followed by the charitable beheading of Probus, the vile prefect Rome had left in charge of Alexandria. It was the reason Augusta Zenobia, the "Warrior Queen," was viewed so warmly by the citizens: while every conqueror arrived brandishing a banner of liberation, she was the first actually received this way by the average Alexandrian. She was beloved by Egypt as a whole. Embracing Nile culture, the Ptolemys, and the Pharaohs—all these gestures were more than a little inspirational, and evocative of a long-lost national pride.

Below the horizon, ascending the stairs from the courtyard to her house, Patra spotted Kaleb on his way to her. She'd prepared for his usual carefree flippancy, but he appeared suitably grim. As he reached her little terrace, Philip jogged into view at the other end of the courtyard.

Patra had the seeds of a few ideas—what they needed to do first, how their priorities should be ordered, the initial steps—but she needed Kaleb to *own* this discussion, *own* their planning, and she needed Philip to bring all of his incredible foresight. If the three of them together couldn't strategize an optimal solution, no one could.

* * *

"I believe we know what must be done," Kaleb said, but his disposition didn't share his words' confidence. He sat at the edge of one of Patra's cushioned chairs, elbows on his knees, perpetually wringing his fingers as he stared at the floor. "It comes down to time. Time and weapons and more than only us to wield them ..."

As Kaleb went on, Patra's eyes traced the green embroidery on his gold tunic, twisting and looping from his shoulder, down to the end of his sleeve: crescent leaves, flowers, splitting vines; his almond-toned hands, smooth and hairless and immaculate as any philosopher's or royal's; the near-black beard, meticulously trimmed from his chin and back, along the jawline, disappearing up into the thick waves of his personal favorite attribute—his vanity somehow able to select just one. Her love for him had become a tainted wine, yet one she still longed to drink.

"Kaleb," she interrupted him.

His drifting gaze found its way to her for the first time since he arrived, those pale, sandy eyes brimming with remorse, desperation, pleading. It was likely the closest thing she'd ever see to an apology or admission of guilt.

"You're not picking up a weapon," she said. "None of us are. Our weapons are in here. If or when this predicament reaches the point where blades meet, what we now plan must already be completed, or it means we've failed. We needn't think further than the blades."

"Our fundamental concern," Philip said as he peered out the window to the ship-strewn sea, "I guess we three agree, is the Library. We keep speaking of our members as if they're all trapped there, but this is only because we depend upon their numbers to salvage the collection. In truth, we could have the Musaeum complex evacuated in less than an hour, our people scattered into small groups, and fleeing south to Naukratis or even Merimba. Everyone can still leave the city. But it'd have to be now."

"But the Library," Patra said.

"Precisely." Philip looked at her, despairing. "Our oaths to the Library transcend all others. None of us took on those vows blithely." His chest quaked with his next breath. Patra had never seen him so tormented. He continued, "But … I do … I have a family—"

"You do. *Go*, Philip," Patra said, and not in a way to make him stay or to rend his heart. She had only the Library, and she'd remain to protect it. "Leave now. There's a reason we're three." She turned to Kaleb, albeit less tenderly. "And you may go, too."

Kaleb rose. The three now stood in a triangle. "If *everyone* stays to evacuate the collection, the Library could be empty in a few days."

"If everyone stays," Philip countered, "we'll all be dead in two days. The children … *everyone*. What if we focus exclusively on …" His voice faded off.

Kaleb stepped to Patra, moving his neck and head to find her eyes. "Whatever we concentrate on preserving, I'm not leaving you to manage this by yourself. I know that I—" He strained to swallow. "If any of us should remain, it should be me." A thought struck him. "What if we assemble everyone—?"

Patra interrupted, "I sent out word to gather in the main courtyard at nightfall."

"Good," Kaleb said. "I propose we announce that it's left to their choice. Of course, most will flee, take their families, get the children out of the city, but many will stay and help. I know at least half of my boys would refuse to abandon us, even if ordered. We prioritize as Philip suggests, but our goal is everything. Every last scrap."

"It's a good idea," Philip said, "to let them choose. It's what we should do, absolutely. But keep in mind, even if thirty remain to help—fifty even—it'll take a *week* to save the entire collection. It isn't only the clearing of shelves, the loading of carts. The collection won't be safe until it's far from Alexandria. Presume we somehow empty the halls. Not a single orphaned scroll in a dusty corner. As soon as the Emperor's forces arrive—and there's no doubt they'll come, be it to plunder or burn—they'll report their discovery to Antonius at once. Next we have an army tearing through every district, slaughtering utterly innocent citizens, in search of every tattered remnant of papyrus. By the time the first legionary enters our halls, the entire collection must be miles away, and we simply don't have that kind of time. I say we leave the scrolls. They can be rewritten, each and every one. It's the reason we three are stewards—the reason our predecessors were."

"I know," Kaleb said. "I'm trying to be optimistic. We don't have many choices. No matter what, though, Philip, you're leaving with your family. Patra and I will handle the Library."

Philip shook his head. "No. I'll see my family to the south wall tonight, ensure they make it out, but I'll be back here before midnight. Don't try to change my mind. We don't have time for that, either."

Through the window, in the distance, Patra heard the distinct clanks and footfalls of maneuvering soldiers: Zenobia's army of Palmyrenes.

She needed to speak with Cassius, immediately. And then … *yes,* the Augusta. Patra knew now what must be done, and just then, in her mind, another piece fell into place, and another.

The room had gone silent, she realized.

Patra looked up to see her two friends staring at her.

"Listen," she began.

TWELVE

Athens, Greece – Present day

Matt knew plenty about The Gray from what the mobster had imprinted on the opal. He knew what kind of man he was, his perceptions of various people and issues, his ambitions, and what he was willing to do to obtain the things he wanted. But Jivu Absko's last contact with the opal had occurred many years ago, and his imprints on the obliterated gemstone hadn't contained everything Matt required. If they had, Matt wouldn't have needed to delve into that steel ring's long and excruciating history.

Through all the centuries since the world's most notorious crucifixion, the types of nails used in such executions had been collected by interested parties. Found by chance at construction sites or during targeted excavations, bronze or iron spikes had been extracted from lengths of buried wood, obtained from tombs, or discovered below ground, loose and without contextual artifacts. In the present day, *Holy Nails* rested atop silken pillows inside transparent cases, nestled deep within locally and internationally celebrated cathedrals. Despite Jesus of Nazareth's presumed standard limb count of four, there were at least thirty such spikes venerated as "true" *Holy Nails*, from Europe to the Middle East, and Matt had personally examined a few.

As he'd explained to the nails' eager holders, the Romans never had a factory cranking out spikes specifically for public executions, and of the millions produced under the Empire, a tiny fraction were ever utilized for crucifixions. Nor were the condemned interred in the ground still attached to their posts or crosses. With no hardware stores expected in Jerusalem for a couple thousand years, the Romans had those nails pried right out, rinsed clean, and sent off to less gruesome projects.

"If I was trying to track down real crucifixion nails," Matt had advised a crestfallen Bishop, *"I'd be looking at structures: walls, ships, fences, buildings, corrals, and such."* Didn't exactly narrow it down, but it'd seemed helpful to at least eliminate **the ground** from consideration.

In all his years, Matt had yet to come in contact with a genuine artifact from *any* crucifixion, let alone the *big one*. Until Absko's ring.

While his ability to prioritize imprint order had radically improved from the days of passive observation and only being able to fast-forward sections after he'd experienced them, there still existed an apparent pecking order within objects. A person's intense emotions following a loved one's death logically overshadowed someone else's afternoon of wheat harvesting. A broadsword blow to the chest topped a nagging papercut. And being nailed to a pillar won out over two thousand years of *everything else*.

Matt just couldn't escape it. The crucifixion scene was like a giant, ferocious dog guarding all the other imprints' secrecy, and the animal was all bite. Attempt after attempt to bypass it had failed. Eventually, they'd left the boat moored to someone's private dock, walked along a highway to a small marina, and Joss snacked on a tray of assorted fried things while Matt tried and failed and tried and failed.

In the backseat of an Athens taxi, with sunset approaching, Matt pumped himself up for a brilliant new plan: jump in long enough to gather his bearings, pluck another moment—anything else—from the background, and push away the agonizing forefront. He'd done it successfully in the past with painful objects.

"You sure?" Joss whispered as Matt stared down at the ring seated in the jewelry box between them. "Every time, it's like you're being burned."

Matt eyed the taxi driver. He was yelling at a cluster of bicyclists blocking the lane.

"Gotta drive through it," Matt quietly replied. "Jump across the fire. Just hold the box steady on the seat for me." She chewed her gum faster. He flashed her a buoyant smile. "Don't worry."

He leant his upper body over the center seat, preparing to put his weight into it. The dainty finger touches weren't doing the trick. His reflexes jerked him back with each attempt. Stupid reflexes.

He nodded a three-count, watched Joss's hands tighten around the velvety box, and pressed his whole hand down onto the jutting ring.

Agony! Searing! People yelling! Arms tied to beam on shoulders; naked, one wrist already pierced, angry Roman legionary holding second spike against other wrist, the hammer's smash, bone splintering! Throat erupts with fire. The legionary swears, tries to pull the misplaced nail from the bone, wags it, twists, and finally yanks it out. He roars at me, "Shut up! Another scream like that and I'll gouge out your cursed eyes!" He places the spike again, hammers it between the wrist bones—tearing and scraping, bones spreading—and he shoves me. "Let it go!" he yells to unseen others, and suddenly the beam's full weight is behind me, pulling me backward, slamming me to the ground, both wrists exploding anew—

* * *

Joss watched Matt's hand press down onto the ring in the box.

He winced and hunched over, stifling a cough. His hands blocked her view of the box, twisting and tugging against her grip. She clamped down even tighter. He looked like he was strangling the tiniest fairy. The side of his face screeched down the black pleather seatback between them.

What was so goddamn important in this ring that he felt the need to put himself through this? He was basically telling Joss, *"Trust me. It's critical that I jump into this venomous snake pit for a few minutes. Oh, and would you mind holding me down as they strike? Thanks."*

Suddenly, he released a piercing, inhuman scream, seizing backward and thrusting his feet into the footwell. Joss panicked and pulled the ring box away just as he fully extended his body, smashing the top of his head into the rear window.

Terrified, the driver stamped the brakes, hurling Joss forward into her seatbelt's unyielding grip, then whiplashing her back. He yelled, *"[something something] Christo!"* and slammed the brakes again. The car swerved right, and Joss grabbed hold of Matt's floppy body before his head struck anymore hard surfaces. The front tire chirped as it skidded up against the curb.

The driver flung his arm over the passenger seat, ogled Matt, then unintelligible yelling, yelling…

"I don't know what you're saying!" Joss shouted back. "He's obviously not doing this on purpose, asshole!"

She cradled Matt's head in her lap, stroking his sweaty hair as he trembled. The closed ring box lay tucked beneath her leg.

What the hell? Why isn't he out of it?

His seatbelt was wrapped around his neck, so she wedged her hand behind his back and probed around for the release. The driver was still yapping, pointing to her door.

She pointed back at him, mocking, yelling over him as she fumbled with the door lock and latch. "Yeah, yeah, get the hell out of my car! No goddamned hurt people allowed! Blah blah blah I'm an asshole …"

"*You* God damn!" he finally managed in English. "Asshole *you*! Go! Go, sneakers!"

Matt finally came to as Joss slid out of the car.

Joss laughed maniacally—more to piss off the driver than with genuine amusement. "Did you just call me *shoes*?"

Matt stumbled onto the curb, babbling. "Pack … pack."

Crap, his backpack!

She released his hand and jumped back in the car to a fresh stream of crazed Greek. Behind her, Matt's legs twisted with hers and she felt him fall. Determined, she grabbed the backpack from the far footwell.

"Yeah yeah yeah, I'm going, buddy!"

The car sped off the instant she cleared the doorway, and she helped Matt up from the curb.

"You okay?"

"Too much," he whimpered, and she saw his grimace. Tears streamed down his face.

"Come here," she cooed, and pulled his head to her shoulder. His arms curled limply around her back. "Shh, it's okay. It's all done. You're done with that damned ring."

She guided him to a bus bench halfway up the block, and they both sat. Matt rested his elbows on his knees, sighing deeply. Cars whizzed by beyond the row of parked cars. Window shoppers passed on the sidewalk behind them. On an apartment's metal balcony across the street, a couple chatted and smoked cigarettes.

Matt wiped his face on his shoulders.

"Man, I'm too screwed up to be embarrassed," he said with a snotty snort. Joss found a hardly used tissue in her purse and gave it to him. "I'm sure it'll all come bearing down on me later."

He leaned back, rolling his neck in a circle, and then hovered reticent fingers near the back of his head, inspecting the swollen area.

He murmured, "Might have a mild concussion."

"Hey, are we okay out here on the street?" The thought had suddenly struck her. "I mean is it safe? That Rostik guy you were talking about—"

"Yeah, no … one hundred percent safe." He stood up, twisting his torso each way until his back cracked. "Rostik has no idea where we are until Alexandria, and Markus has zero interest in interrupting me on my way there. Not to mention, this is a pretty random little suburb." He sat back down and hung his head low, rocking it side to side. "Think I screwed up my back in that cab, too."

Joss sat and watched her shoes. She wanted to ask what he'd experienced, but figured he'd tell her if he wished.

"Sorry," he said. "Heard that."

She popped her palms off the bench seat, turning to see his bare hands gripping the seat edge. He'd read her mind!

"Still getting a handle on my head," he began, eyes tracking each passing car. "Can't really filter out noise until I get my walls back up. But not much to share about the imprint anyway. Still unable to get past the beginning. As for what I experienced, it's hard to say who the victim was. Pain like that sort of washes out everything else. Quick flashes of a wife, nephews, the inside of a little home, but otherwise, nil. Just fear and pain and fear. The soldier's face—that's crisp. Plus his name and everything. He's holding on to the nail in the beginning, so he sorta overlaps with the condemned man."

"So is it ... Could the victim be—?"

"Jesus? No. He's just a guy. Jesus wasn't even born yet when this was happening. About another decade later. But I guarantee you that's not what Mr. President believes."

"You think he believes it was one of the actual Jesus nails?"

"Without a doubt. And consider that for a second: what it would take to get your hands on one of the Holy Nails. That is, if it wasn't stolen, but let's assume *bought*—you bought it from some other pompous gazillionaire. Those things are supposedly pieces of history, coveted for centuries, and, if you're someone who's *that* interested in having one, you'd believe the object to be a connection to God, right? A spiritual capsule, like the Holy Grail or Ark of the Covenant."

He looked at her, wide-eyed.

"Yeah, for sure," she said. "I would think so."

He was so intense, so familiar, comfortable. She liked it. A minute bit of guilt crept in, knowing the uncharacteristic engagement was likely due to his fresh trauma, though not enough guilt to kill her buzz.

"So you bought this spike," he went on. "You've got it now—a new, most-prized possession—finally in your hands. And then, you have it *melted down* and turned into a ring for yourself."

She shook her head. "That's … That's *insane*." He was right. It didn't sound like something a sane person would do.

"Right?" He looked back out toward the road. "It'd take a seriously detached mind to reconcile that act. Obviously, he's thoroughly narcissistic. I already knew that much. It doesn't take a *me*, really, to come to that conclusion, but—"

"What if it's a big eff-you?" Joss interrupted as the thought struck her. "Like he doesn't actually believe in Christianity at all, but so many people do, and so he's all 'Rrrr, I wear the thing that killed God on my finger. I'm more powerful than God.'"

Matt stared at her and tugged at his chin whiskers.

"… Rrrr … Or not." She shrugged.

"No, sorry … I think you're right. I think you're exactly right."

"Damn right I'm right! Psych one-oh-one, baby! One semester. C-plus. Boo-yeah. Gimme some, bro!" She held up her hand for a high-five. "C'mon. Up high!"

Matt cracked a little smile and gave her a feeble high-five. She was about to tease him, demand another, keep his spirits up, but his mind was already drifting off.

"You thinking about her? His wife?"

"Yeah." He absentmindedly rubbed his wrist as he zoned out on a wall of ivy across the street.

She side-eyed him, watched his mouth twitch with little micro-movements, nibbling on the insides of his lips. "I can only guess how rough that is for you. Someone you love so much … out of reach like that."

He snapped out of his daze and looked at her. "Hm? Oh …
yeah. Hey, you grabbed the ring out of the taxi, right?"

"Yup." She patted her purse on the bench beside her.

"May I see it, please? I'm pretty sure, now that I've gone as far
as I have, that I can skip through all that."

Joss nodded emphatically. "Oh, sure, absolutely. Right now?
Right here on the bench?"

He *mm-hm'd* and held out his hand.

"Hell … flippin' … no." She swatted his hand away. "You
aren't touching this thing again. Not as long as I'm around, no sir.
You almost launched yourself out the back window of that goddamn
taxi! I had to drag your convulsing body out of there while cabby
guy's screaming Greek obscenities at us!"

"Albanian," Matt said calmly. "He's from Kosovo."

"Oh, well that explains why I couldn't understand him."

"Anyway, I just wanted to make sure the ring was actually in
there. I thought it slipped out of the box in the commotion."

Uh-oh.

She hadn't checked before clapping the box closed in the
backseat. Her focus had been on a seizing Matt.

He saw her face and tilted his head forward. "Don't tell me."

Her fingers swam around her purse. "No, I got it. It's in there."

Please, God, let it be in there.

She extracted the box from her purse, pried open the top, and
sighed relief at the shiny ring inside. "See?"

"Phew," Matt said, and she pinched it shut just as his hand
zipped under hers, lightly smacking upward. The case popped up,
and Matt plucked the box from the air with his other hand. "Thank
you." He leapt from the bench and sprinted down the sidewalk,
calling behind him, "I'll be back in five, ten minutes, tops! Don't go
anywhere!"

Joss scrambled to her feet, grabbed her purse and his backpack,
and went after him. Looking up, her eyes caught him at the last

second, cutting left down a side street at the end of the row of shops. He was too damned fast.

At the block's end, she slowed to a stop and peered up the side street. It inclined sharply upward and narrowed into a tree-covered, hillside, residential neighborhood. No sign of him on either side of the street. The first few houses in view had short walls and hedges and plenty of bushes he could be hiding in, but she wasn't going to chase him down. If she happened to find him hiding: *Gotcha!* and then what? He runs off again, farther. And she was an employee, lest she forget. It'd probably been a tad improper for her to withhold the thing in the first place.

She scanned her surroundings. The corner shop, called Fiat Shop & Shop, appeared to sell women's clothes, coffee and pastries, and Fiat automobiles. A pair of 30s twin sisters flicked through shirts on the outdoors clothing racks, both women holding their cell phones out to the side as if they were carrying a pizza pan.

Joss stared until she realized she was staring, interrupted by the revelation that she might very well have cellular coverage here. She pulled out her phone and powered it on, glancing up Matt's escape route while waiting for the spinny boot-up thing to finish.

The phone beeped and toned and dinged as endless texts, voicemails, and other notifications fought for priority.

Texts first.

They displayed in oldest-first order: Cameron, of course, Mom, random number, Cam, Cam, Iris, random, Iris, Iris, Iris ...

Iris first.

> Iris Turner: Everything cool? Tell Matt to answer my texts, please.
> Iris Turner: You there? Testing ... testing ...
> Iris Turner: You still on that island? Check emails, please. Call me.
> Iris Turner: Used to bro ignoring texts. Hoping you would not. Assuming you're not getting these. Call me ASAP.

> Iris Turner: If you get this, please tell Matt that Isis
> Meier is trying to reach him. And not for
> "the usual BS" … He should know what
> that means. Emailing this, too.
> Iris Turner: Argh. Silence. Trying not to panic, you
> guys.

She hasn't gotten anything from us since leaving Ukraine. Gotta be losing it at this point.

Joss tried to remember the time difference in New Jersey. She guessed it was 10:00 or 11:00am, and Iris would definitely be awake … if she'd even been able to sleep.

She tapped out a quick message to start.

> JLL: Hey Iris, we're all good! So sorry! Haven't
> had signal.

The send status bar crept rightward, paused … almost … sent!

Relieved that at least the one went through, Joss began composing a more detailed message. They were in Athens, on way to Egypt … come to think of it, they probably needed plane tickets … Should she mention Matt and the ring? Would it worry Iris even more? Was that a betrayal of Matt's trust? And then her phone buzzed and rang.

Iris.

Oh yeah, she did say call, *didn't she …*

"Hi!" Joss answered. "You got my text, I hope?"

"Hi!" Iris echoed, cheerily pissed, and then switched to just-pissed. "Put him on the phone."

Joss peered up the residential street: skinny old guy walking poodle, poodle, bushes, no Matt. She hesitated a second and sucked in a quick breath.

"I swear to God, Joss Lynn, if you say he's not there, I will reach through this phone, strangle him, and fire you."

"But … what if he's actually not here?"

"I get it," Iris said, "he's your boss. He's Matt Turner. And I'm only the sister, and very far away. Just do me this favor. If he's standing there with you, say 'I'm not sure when he'll be back.'"

"Seriously, he's not here. I'd tell you. He … stepped away, just a few minutes ago. I'm not sure when—that is, I don't know … how *long* … before he *returns*."

"All right. I believe you. Well … so help me clean out all the paranoid theories my brain's been producing to fill the void. You guys are totally safe, normal, all that?"

"Totally."

"Are you still with Ostrovsky or his people?"

"No, it's only us. We're going to Egypt."

"Oh, really? So Matt spoke to Pete Sharma, I'm guessing?"

"Um, no, I don't think so. I don't know who that is. He hasn't spoken to anyone as far as I know. We just got cell signal. Or, I did anyway. I'm sure his phone is still off, and in his backpack … which I'm holding right now."

"Okay. I know you'll send me a nice, long, detailed email with everything that's happened and going to happen. I do still need my brother to call me though—unrelated to what you're doing out there. Tell him it's about Isis Meier. On second thought, tell him it's about Isis and the *test*."

"That's his ex-girlfriend, right?"

She find out she's dying? Pregnant?

"Yup," Iris said.

"Got it. So should he call her first, or you?"

"Me! Definitely me! I swear to God if he calls anybody in the *world* before he calls me, I'm disembrothering him. And I pay the fricken bills! I'll know. On that note, do you guys already have your flights?"

"Nope."

Joss ambled into the Shop & Shop while waiting for Iris to go to her computer and check flights. Shiny little cars were parked on one side, café in the back middle, and then there were the aisles with clothes, car seats and mirror balls, and wooden bird nests. She *had* to get a picture of this place.

"All right, you ready?" Iris asked, and they proceeded to finalize the flights while Joss ambled down the aisles, marveling at the random inventory.

As they awaited confirmation, Joss caught a figure out of the corner of her eye, outside, walking from the side street. It was Matt, and he appeared to have come from a quick, fully-clothed dive in a swimming pool.

Without informing Iris, Joss hurried back to the entrance to intercept Matt at the front door.

"Okay, you're all confirmed," Iris said. "You've got about three hours. I'll send the itinerary to both of your e-mail addresses. Did he get you setup with company email on your phone yet?"

Joss popped out in front of Matt, noticing that his hair, face, and neck were drenched, as well as the top half of his T-shirt. He stopped before her, blinked for an instant as if he didn't know who she was, and then recognition seemed to click in. His mouth opened a little, eager to tell her something. He regarded the phone against Joss's ear, and mouthed *"Who's that?"*

"Hello?" Iris sang.

Joss mouthed back, *"Iris."*

Matt frowned, nodded, and looked at Joss's breasts. No, he was just thinking—his eyes continued drifting down toward her elbow, and then back up to the phone.

Iris again, "I lose you? Joss? Can you hear me?"

Finally, he came to some conclusion, motioned for the phone, and set it against his ear.

"Hi sis," he said, and then quickly rattled off without a break, "All's well. In Athens. Going to Alexandria. Back in two weeks. Both phones going away. Let you know new info soon. Love you, miss you, sorry, bye!"

He pulled the phone away with Iris already unleashing a tinny, crackling tirade, while Matt fumbled and searched for a hang-up button. Joss reached out to end the call for him, but he suddenly stepped back and hurled the phone to the ground. Glass and plastic exploded out across the sidewalk. Matt sighed relief and brushed residual Iris anxiety from his hands like dust.

Joss glared at him. "Well that's splendid."

"We're getting new ones," he said, and gestured for his backpack. "I need to kill mine, too."

"I liked that phone. It was brand new. Anyway, what's the deal here? You okay?" She looked up at his dripping hair and wet shirt. "Someone hose you down to get you out of their back yard?"

He touched his head, hair, and shirt, apparently unaware he was wet. "Oh, no, this is sweat. I made it past the crucifixion. I'll tell you what I learned …" He peered up the street. "… on the way to that phone shop up the street."

* * *

President Absko knew that Matt was no longer holed up at home, though he wasn't certain of Matt's status ability-wise. Absko had fantasies about hurting Tuni, torturing her with both mental and physical weapons. Last month, he considered sending their son, Alexander, to a week-long archery camp for affluent children—without telling Tuni—and he'd ignore her desperate questions, refusing to acknowledge the boy's absence. He dreamt of splitting her heel bone so that each step she took would stab at her the way her words speared him, of hammering her cheekbones and nose so she'd be grotesque. *Because he loved her.* It tormented him more than anything, this sole weakness. Everyone else in the world remained entirely disposable, but the one person he'd allowed in, a woman he'd so methodically groomed—the queen with whom he'd share his kingdom—now feared and despised him.

With his new cell phone sitting on a picnic table in a darkening city park, Matt shared with Iris and Joss all he'd learned from Absko's ring. How, five years ago, Absko had orchestrated the mental breakdown of Fernando Solorzano—the mercenary who killed

185

Matt's father—beginning a month before Matt and Tuni had even arrived in Tahiti. The draining of Matt's bank accounts while they were in Cuba. Matt's secret leaked to the media. Ensnaring Tuni in a cunning seduction plot, followed by periodic lies about Matt and other friends, intercepted letters and emails, forged replies, and later, the finishing touch: replacing Tuni's birth control pills with placebos.

Now aware of both Ostrovsky and Absko's unexpectedly adept hacking capabilities, Matt had Iris set up brand new email accounts, and told her to go buy a new phone for herself. In a taxi on the way to the Athens airport, Matt feverishly typed names, dates, and places for her, as well as a lengthy list of other key information.

As Matt's thumbs hammered away at the phone, Joss quipped, "You writing a novel over there?"

"The stuff of," he replied, and remained silent for the rest of the drive, freezing periodically as he reviewed scenes from the ring wrapped around his middle finger.

During their relatively short hop over the Mediterranean Sea, Matt and Joss had the half-capacity jet's rear rows to themselves, so he used the time to update Joss on all-things-Tuni, and answered her many questions.

"So Absko had set all of that up just to get revenge on this Rheese guy in Cuba?"

"Absko wasn't simply out for revenge with Dr. Rheese," he said. "It started out that way back in Kenya, since Rheese screwed him, but that ended up being a lesser motive. Rheese was one of a handful of people who knew the other side of Absko—the gangster. Or I should say, the handful of people who Absko couldn't trust with that knowledge. And rightfully so, really. Rheese would've sold him out in a heartbeat, given the opportunity. Since Absko was prepping for his big step into the public eye, he was legitimizing all of his businesses and cleaning the skeletons from his closet."

"I get that," Joss said, "but it must've been a personal thing, too, since he didn't just send his people to handle it. Seems like he really wanted to pull the trigger himself."

"It wasn't his original intent," Matt said. "His plans changed several times after Tahiti. In the end, killing Dr. Rheese ended up a bonus on top of his real prize: Tuni, the beautiful and inspiring wife. He saw her as his final ticket to becoming Nairobi's mayor, then a senator, and finally, President. Already painting himself as a descendent of Marc Antony, he'd now acquired his very own Cleopatra. He knew it was all about the story with the voters."

"Yeah, well, I know you see your ex as this sad victim of a master manipulator, but from everything you've told me so far … no offense, but I hate her."

Matt laughed. "That's not the first time I've heard that sentiment, believe it or not."

"I believe it. For your sake, I'm withholding the derogatory terms that come to mind. But go on, tell me the rest. I want to know how a girl goes from madly in love with you, to marrying the murderous gangster who got your father and others murdered, nearly got you killed, and somehow she doesn't realize a few months later that dude's the biggest crime lord in Africa."

"Valid skepticism," Matt said, and then took Joss through the chain of events.

After convincing Tuni to resume her work at the Narok/Pwin-T archaeological site, Absko had begun taking her out on the weekends, showing her "all of this beautiful country," while secretly hiring photographers to capture their outings. Journalists were paid to publish "rumors" about the happy couple before they were even a couple. Absko would show Tuni these reports, feigning outrage at the invasion of privacy. Then came the announcement of the mayoral run, followed by opinion pieces from entertainment news outlets romanticizing a future with so beautiful a couple at City Hall, and beyond.

Absko hadn't anticipated just how well the mayoral campaign would work on both fronts: his spreading popularity, and a dazzled Tuni. Still unaware of a criminal past or questionable activities, Tuni genuinely liked this character Absko was playing, and soon after, found herself swept away by Kenya's instant love for her, with tabloids fueling the fire with premature speculation: **When Will Jivu Propose to Tuni?** accompanied by the inevitable name combo a la *Brangelina* and *Kimye*. They became *JiTu*—eventually stylized to simply *G2,* much to the delight of the Gatorade marketing team. Paparazzi just happened to be nearby when he got down on one knee.

"Okay, but five years later and she's just now crying for help." Joss shrugged, then put her hand on Matt's arm. "And if I'm out of line in the slightest bit, please tell me to shut up. You stay so cool when I'm jabbering on, and I think it encourages me to keep on with the *blerrrgh* ..." She hunched over and pantomimed violent vomiting.

"You're fine, really. I can't be offended by the opinion you develop from the given information. But remember that this is only her first *successful* communication. In reality, she's been trying to contact me and others since the very beginning."

Matt went on explaining Absko's quick rise in Kenya following the "leaked" proposal photographs. In short time, the people had demanded Absko skip the middling Mayor's Office, and run in the country's first presidential election.

Combined with his touted lineage from famed ancient royalty, his history of philanthropy, support for admirable causes, and the fact that one of his organizations singlehandedly crushed the drug trade in East Africa (by shutting down his own drug business), Absko appeared to simply ride the wave to the executive office.

But now Matt knew all the little schemes hidden beneath the surface, the bribes and staged sound bites, eliminated opponents and detractors, and where all the *literal* bodies were buried. More importantly, he'd found out who Absko was currently crossing, and as soon as Matt and Joss reached their low-profile hotel in Alexandria, Egypt, a phone call would be made.

* * *

"Well, hello," Markus answered. "Matthew, I presume?"

"How'd you know it was me?" Matt winked at Joss, sitting on the bed beside him, listening near the cell phone's earpiece.

"A number from a virtual phone pool, calling my mobile from Alexandria? Not so mystifying. I wish I could claim I was expecting your call, but alas."

"You can tell where I'm calling from? How the hell do you manage that?" Matt had already explained to Joss how the app he was using would fool Markus's phone's reverse lookup tool. It should appear they were in the Windsor Plaza at the opposite end of the city, and that Matt had made an effort to hide this fact.

Markus smugly ignored the question. "To what do I owe the pleasure?"

Matt sighed for effect. "Well … look, I'll be honest. I'm not trying to screw over Mr. Ostrovsky. I'm trying to live a normal life, do my thing quietly, and mind my own business."

"Of course. Commendable."

"I'm serious, Markus. You should know, after all I've been through, I have no interest in stirring up pots. I've got family, friends, and plenty of other people who I don't need pulled into some mess I created. I mean, I guess *I* didn't really create it—I was trying to protect myself and my employee—but I shouldn't have taken the artifacts with me. It was stupid."

Markus was quiet a moment before responding. "Go on."

"Okay, so what's done is done, right? I can't take that back. But maybe I can give you something else of value to make up for it."

"Three days, and you've found the scrolls already?"

"No," Matt scoffed. "And the more I read these things the lower my hopes fall, but we can talk about that another time. No, I'm talking about the item you were holding for me, and some very interesting information I happened upon that I think your boss would like to know."

Markus hummed an enticed little purr, "Mmm … Matthew, I enjoy you more with our every interaction."

Joss grinned and gave Matt a thumbs-up.

"Anything of immediate concern?" Markus asked.

"Absolutely *all* of it of immediate concern."

Markus dropped the playful tones. "Tell me. You know well that I, personally, wish no harm ever comes to you, and so you'll believe me when I say that if your information is of the value suggested, I'll do what is within my power to refurbish your current status."

"That's all I ask," Matt said. "I'm sure you know the name Nestor Utkin?"

"No questions, please, Matthew. Share what you called to share."

"He's been paid off to report rapidly declining returns from all of your Kenyan and Ugandan mines, has apparently been doing so for a while, and has been told to advise your board to dump them as soon as possible."

"Interesting indeed," Markus replied. "I presume the returns had not been declining?"

"Not in the slightest."

"Very well. Is there anything else?"

"Oh yeah," Matt said. "That's only the beginning."

Matt spent the next fifteen minutes sharing all of Absko's juiciest betrayals, double-dealing, bribery, "disappeared" Ostrovsky employees, as well as a sampling of sabotage against some of Ostrovsky's associates and competitors.

"… and that's about it," Matt concluded. "Sound like enough info for you to—how'd you put it? *Refurbish* me?"

"I should certainly think so. I'll obviously be working on this right away. If you discover or recall anything more, you may wish to use text messaging instead."

Matt took the opportunity to fish. "Because you've got people here looking for me?"

"You already know what's coming, Matthew. I explained what is beyond my control."

"So I should be worried?"

Markus was quiet for a beat. "Not *today*. Now, I'll bid you—"

"Just a second," Matt interrupted. "My note—would you tell me if you were able to stop it before it arrived?"

A smile seasoned Markus's voice. "Unfortunately, despite all my efforts to prevent it, your message was delivered. Good day."

* * *

Joss was sure Matt remained conflicted about her staying in Egypt, but he seemed to consider her valuable enough to keep around. After concluding his phone call with Markus, he'd chewed his cheek while regarding her, gears apparently cranking on whether or not he needed to put her on a plane. He hadn't said anything, instead proceeding to jot down the next batch of to-dos for her to handle while he was out *"taking care of some stuff."*

Now three days into their stay, they'd fallen into a good rhythm, and Joss had begun to feel like an actual asset. Before heading out for his morning who-knows-what activities, he handed her the latest list, but offered none of the usual explanations or clarification. No words at all—he simply stood and waited.

She quickly scanned the notepad, choking near the bottom. "Oh God, really?"

"Sorry," he said, turning for the door. "It's necessary. Work out the arrangements with I.T. She already knows what's up. Back in a bit."

She plopped down on her flimsy bed, greeted with a chorus of *twangs* from the pokey mattress.

Sure was nice of someone to wrap a sheet around these springs.

Though their bargain-basement hotel room offered no pyramid or sphinx views, Joss didn't mind hanging out inside. They were in a sketchy part of the city, and she'd been enjoying working with Iris. Joss had always thought herself pretty damned organized and resourceful, but I.T., as Matt called her, was a no-nonsense efficiency machine—and any name or ambiguous task Matt had given Joss, I.T. always knew exactly what he was talking about.

Lacking a desk to work on, Joss liked to steal the blanket off Matt's bed for extra butt cushioning, prop up all of the room's pillows against the headboard, and nestle in with her notepad and phone.

She always waited until after noon local time to begin her calls to Iris back in New Jersey, where it was 6:00am, and then ended up chatting with her off and on throughout the rest of the day. I.T. preferred to tackle one or two tasks at a time, instructing Joss to keep the next items on the day's list to herself until the previous job was complete.

At 12:30, Joss figured I.T. had had a chance to get some coffee in her, and made the first call. "Morning, Mizz Turner. All right, number one for the day: he wants me to track down a 'low-profile' archaeologist here."

"Other specs?" Iris replied. Regardless of the time of day, she tended to be curt, but Joss didn't mind. Matt had mentioned I.T. always spoke like their father when work lay ahead.

"Yeah. He wrote 'Not Pete, not connected to Pete, available on short notice for a full or half-day excursion.'"

"So presumably a field specialist knowledgeable about the area. Did he say why not Pete Sharma? The guy would literally drop whatever he's doing to help Matt, plus he's taken to calling me every hour on the hour. Guessing he's still avoiding him?"

"He didn't say." Joss scanned her notes again. "Oh, and I'm supposed to remind you not to even tell Pete that Matt's here."

"I think I'll get that tattooed on my hand. You know, since I can't seem to recall the other eighteen reminders."

"Sorry," Joss said.

"Pshh, don't be. Nothing to do with you. Did you give him my list yesterday of Things Pete is Desperate to Reach You About?"

Joss flipped to the previous page in the notebook. "Ehhh … yup. Translations, emcee, highlight selections, VIP list, common courtesy and manners … the whole shebang. He put little checks next to most of it, but I don't know if he gave me any of these things as tasks for today. Again, I don't get to know what any of this stuff actually means."

Iris sidestepped the not-so-subtle request for insight. "Yeah, that's my bro. Speaking of broken record requests, do you know if he's called Isis yet?"

Joss was well aware he hadn't, and she'd stopped passing on Iris's reminders.

Iris, Isis. That's gotta be confusing as hell. I wonder if that's why he calls Iris "I.T."

It was pointless. Matt had zero interest in calling this ex for whatever she wanted. "I'm not sure. He hasn't mentioned it, and I'm sorta not really—"

"No, no, you're fine. It's not your job to press him on it. He knows what it's about now, and it's his fricken job to call her."

Joss wasn't going to ask about personal business, but if Iris needed a sounding board, Joss was more than happy to listen to any juicy tidbits that might slip out. She uttered an unassuming "Mm-hm."

"And I know what it is …" Iris continued, "… without those questions—*legitimate* questions—but without excuses anymore, you know? Now he's just scared. Like he needs another weakness, you know? That's what it is."

"Mm-hm."

"I'm surprised he hasn't shipped *you* off back home yet. Can I ask you something personal? You don't have to answer. But, you know, if you don't, I guess it's pretty much an answer anyway."

"Sure," Joss said. "I love personal questions."

"You two got anything going on? Any kind of hanky panky?"

Joss snorted. "Hahah, no. No 'hanky panky' for us, but I appreciate the reminder of my grandparents. Trust me, no *mousing around* or *carrying on* here. It's all work."

"Okay. Call you back."

Fifteen minutes later, Iris had an archaeologist for Joss.

"Her name is Jo Shelsher," Iris said. "You might've read about her in the news a couple years ago? American lady that identified thirteen previously undiscovered sites in Egypt via Google Earth—pyramids and everything."

"Yeah, I think I read about that." She hadn't read anything about it.

"Well, she won some grants and has been out there off and on for the past ten months." Iris gave her Mrs. Shelsher's address, cell number, and e-mail. "And I just spoke with her. She's heard of Matt, of course, and is free for a couple days, waiting on techs for one of her digs. Sounds eager to help with whatever he needs."

"Perfect. I'll wait for him to get back and we'll give her a call."

Iris hung up.

Joss flipped the page back to the newest to-do list.

Next ... Paul Kleindorf.

Call and give list on next page...

She tapped in the phone number.

A deep voice answered. "Admissions."

Joss glanced at the number she'd dialed. "Sorry ... I was trying to reach Paul Kleindorf?"

The man replied with an aloof, "Who's this?"

"Joss Lynn Leland. I work with ... Matt?"

"You sure? That sounded like a question."

"Yeah, I—"

"A joke. You must be Californian. Inflections at the end of statements."

She laughed. "I'm from Jersey, actually. Born and ... bred?"

"Right. This is Paul. What can I do for you?"

Joss grabbed Matt's long list of numbers and banks. "I have some numbers to give you—I assume they're account numbers—and bank names."

"Well then it's great to meet you, Joss Lynn Leland. How many we talking about?"

"I don't know ... five, ten, fifteen ... a little more than thirty. It's a full page."

"Sounds delicious. So you know, as soon as you provide this info, we're going to use it. Matt's down with that, I presume?"

"He said to call and give it to you, and no note or anything saying to have you wait, so ... yes?"

"Fire away."

A few hours later, Matt was still out, and Joss had completed or delegated each line item except for one. The second-to-last task—the one she'd dreaded all day—remained on the pad, unstricken by her pencil: **Call Cameron...**

After the weird initial tone and brief delay of international calls, a single ring sounded before Cam picked up.

"Hello?" He was outside somewhere. Wind static and a passing car.

"Hey, Cam," she said cheerily.

"Who's th—wait, *Joss?*" The background noise lessened as he stepped inside somewhere.

"Yeah, how's it going?"

He grunted. "Well ... if I'm honest—"

"Ever been to Egypt?"

THIRTEEN

Nairobi, Kenya – Presidential Palace – Present day

Happy birthday to me.

Tuni blew the dollop of soap bubbles from her palm, and rinsed off the remaining suds.

Thirty-seven years.

She stepped out of the shower, shut off the tap, and grabbed a towel.

How many were good ones? Twenty-four? Combine the wasted and/or miserable, and that's what, thirteen years? No, can't say that.

She had Alexander. The past five years had been the trade-off for such a gift. If she should truly find freedom today, as she still believed, then there'd be no more lost years. Her *average*, as it were, would only improve with each passing day.

"Bubu," she called. "You still okay in there?"

She'd left Alexander coloring at the secretary desk in the bedroom.

"Yes, Mama," he replied. "Come see. I'm making all the Autobots have purple eyes."

"I'll be out in a minute. If anyone knocks, you ask them to wait, yes? I'll be right out."

"I know. You said that already."

Getting Alexander away from his father would eliminate more than the man's foulest evils. Her little angel had grown increasingly rude in recent months. During "family time" every other night, Jivu enjoyed undermining her and planting terrible ideas in his son's head.

Tuni would try correcting Alexander when smashing his toys out of frustration. Jivu would say, *"He's a perfectionist. He can smash whatever he finds too convoluted to build, or if he's dissatisfied with his own work. There's no fault in strict standards."* Or when Alexander would yell at her, *"This shirt is ugly, Mama! I don't want to wear this one!"* She'd warn him not to speak to Mama this way, followed by Jivu's interjection, *"It's his choice, Mama. He may be small, but he's still a man, and we all know it's men who rule the world."* And then he'd kneel down to Alexander's level, look him in the eye, and say something like, *"You don't ever* have *to listen to a woman, understand? You are polite, respectful, and you do what you know you're supposed to do—schoolwork and such. But* no *woman is above you, not even Mama."*

Well, no more of that rubbish. Fortunately, he was only four, so the damage could likely be corrected before truly engrained.

Tuni buttoned her khaki slacks—one of only two pairs of pants in her entire wardrobe—and brushed her hair back into a ponytail.

The internal-only phone on the wall rang.

"Yes?" Tuni answered.

It was Masil, Jivu's Chief of Staff. "Good morning, Mrs. Absko. The protestors have bypassed the cordons at the bottom of the drive and are gathering outside the front gate. There's no danger of a breach into the property, but I ask you to stay indoors."

Protesters?

She'd spent the past week sleeping next door with Alexander, in his room. Though the days had passed excruciatingly slow, she'd seen little of Jivu, nor heard much of the upheaval converging on his administration. With his attention on damage control, flying to neighboring countries to garner support and conduct press conferences with "unsullied" journalists, he'd had no time to terrorize his First Lady.

"I understand," Tuni replied to Masil. "Thank you. Did the President make it off the property safely?"

She knew he was on his way to Mombasa to "survey" a collapsed apartment building. They'd stick some work gloves and a hard hat on him, and he'd probably pull a wounded child or puppy from the debris. Cameras would flash.

"Not just yet, but there's no need for concern. The heli will arrive soon and fly direct. It's a much faster method anyhow."

"Very well. That mob can't make it around back there?"

Masil chuckled. "Mob ... this is no mob, Mrs. Absko. Just a small group of picketers. But no, there's no access to the pad or private road. And we have forces stationed, if you still worry."

"Got it. We'll stay indoors. Thanks again."

"Including the courtyard," Masil added. "In case anything is thrown over, you know? Again, nothing to worry about."

A faint knock from the bedroom.

"Whatever you say, Masil." Tuni hung up. "Just a moment," she called, though doubted anyone would hear from around two corners and through the door. She opened the drawer and grabbed a metal nail file and the small, pointed scissors, stuffing one into each back pocket.

Exiting the bathroom, her script repeated in her head. *Alexander had a rough night last night and I'm keeping him home today. No, no, he's not sick. Just some night terrors ...*

No, not terrors. Night*mares* would be better. She didn't want some nurse or shrink or anyone else to be called in.

Yes, she'd say, *he should be just fine tomorrow morning, and ready for school.*

The chair at the secretary was empty. Alexander's crayons lay strewn across his coloring book and the desk. She hurried to the antechamber, turned the corner, and halted. Beside Alexander stood a smiling Danya, the new nursery maid, swinging shut the entry door behind her. She wore her hair short, relaxed, and brushed forward and across her forehead like a too-tight helmet. Even thinner than her predecessor, Ngina, Danya's arms were tight, sinewy branches, with knobby muscles from hefting rich people's thick babies.

Through the shrinking doorway, Tuni caught a glimpse of Thabiti, gawking from his stool outside the suite, and two of the additional security personnel assigned to the suite today. She believed there were at least five out there besides Thabiti. Jivu had certainly not forgotten Matthew's note.

"Oh, hello, Danya," Tuni said as Alexander bounded past her, back into the bedroom. "I meant to call you. I'm keeping Alexander home today for his nightmares. He's not sick."

Not sick? Real smooth, Tuni!

Only four days into replacing Ngina (with whom, apparently, she traded spots at a private nursery school), Danya hopefully wouldn't be alarmed by Tuni's uncharacteristic garb and hair.

"Sure, my Lady," Danya replied, an inquisitive knit to her brow. "May we ..." She motioned to the bedroom.

Tuni huffed. "Well, no. We may *not*. He'll be ready for school again tomorrow morning. If there's anything you or Kim wish to discuss, we'll pick it up then." Tuni brushed past her and reached for the door handle to see her out.

"Miss, please," the nursery maid said in English, and blocked Tuni's path.

Had Jivu sent Danya? Had he thought of Alexander today, ensuring the two would be separated?

Tuni's eyes flashed. She was still the bloody First Lady. She replied in English, "Danya, I know you're new, but—"

"Mrs. Absko," Danya interrupted, a commanding hand thrown between them, while a pearly white smile shone from her mocha face. "I'm here to *help* you. And there's a camera pointed at the door and *us* right now, so if you could make a good show of embarrassment and good cheer, put your hand on my back, and show me into the bedroom, perhaps security will return their attention to the rumpus outside the walls."

"You're ..."

Danya's dark eyes widened with her smile as she nodded *yes, you're getting it now, dear.*

"Of course!" Tuni slapped her forehead. "I can't believe I forgot! Come, please, let me show you." She curled her arm around Danya's shoulders and guided her out of the antechamber, laughing.

Just through the wide, columned archway, Danya stepped out of Tuni's grasp and faced her. "This is far enough." She regarded Tuni, from bare feet, up to her head. "You don't normally look like this, do you?"

"Well, no," Tuni began. "Just a moment, though. Who do you work for? Please don't say 'Interpol.'"

"No, I'm with the National Unity Party." She caught Tuni's stunned flinch. The NUP were Jivu's loudest opposition, and known for violent attacks. "And no, despite what you've apparently heard, we're not the terrorists blowing up factories and abducting people. That's your husband's doing, killing two birds with one bullet, as they say. Now, you'll need to fix this." She nodded to Tuni's outfit. "What do you need for the boy? Critical items only."

"Where are we going, Mama?" Alexander asked, and tugged on her pant leg. "You look silly like this. Why you're dressed like a man?"

Tuni leaned over and pinched his chin. "We're going on a short trip, bubu. Are you ready to go have some fun?" Alexander nodded wildly, his mouth an O. "Can you pick out one small toy to bring, and fetch Rafiki from your room?" He sprang away, running off to his room. Tuni observed Danya's skeptical look. "He's a blanket. *It's* a blanket. Now, then, tell me what interest your party has in *me.* When I leave this place, I'm leaving the bloody continent. I'm not going to become some sort of political—"

Danya swatted this away. "No, certainly not. The truth is they—*we*—have no interest whatsoever. We're working with an American agency. You're one of *their* interests, not ours. Now, I've been here a bit too long. I suggest you change into something more your usual style. You'll pass many people on your way out, and our protest in front is a good distraction, but no one's been blinded." With this last line, she flit her fingers toward Tuni's makeup-less face. "And I wish you two the best of luck." She turned to go.

"Wait, that's it? Where do we go? What're we supposed to do?"

Danya paused in the archway and shrugged. "I don't know. Whatever you had planned. We assumed you'd make your way out through the employee gate in back." She glanced at her watch. "You've got just under an hour before our protest *gets out of hand*. I'd suggest you make your final run at that time. The additional security staff outside the suite and those remaining on the back walls will probably be diverted to the front at that point."

Tuni darted after her. "Final run? Hold on! If you came here to help me, I don't understand why you're suddenly leaving now. How is this helping? 'Do what you're gonna do. Best of luck.' What sort of rubbish is that?"

Danya set her hand on the door handle, smiling politely. "We're doing all in our power, Miss. I expect you'll have more help from the Americans once the President's heli takes off, but they haven't shared their plans with us. Good day." She opened the door and stepped out.

"I need a bag, Mama."

Tuni spun to see Alexander, his arms overflowing with toys.

"Oh, bubu, no. I said one toy. *One* toy, bubu. Put all of these back and choose your favorite."

"I can't take just one. I need all of 'em."

Tuni sighed. Now she was sweating. "Listen, angel. I'll make a deal with you. This time—*only* this time—I'll let you bring three instead of only one. But they have to be small, okay? You have to fit in your pockets. No bag."

He dropped the entire heap of toys on the floor and stomped back to his room.

She called after him. "And fetch some socks and trainers, too."

Back in her closet, she rolled her khakis up to her knees, and slid into a long, opaque sun dress. Her pants made the dress puff out around the hips and rear, but it'd have to do. She found some passable shoes she could probably run in, and went to the bathroom to fix her apparently grotesque face.

'*I suggest you make your final run...*' Cheeky tart. '*Security will* probably *be diverted.*'

But what had she expected? Rescue troops rappelling from black choppers? No, she'd expected precisely nothing until Danya showed up. All week, Tuni had replayed Matthew's words in her head: *Opportunities multiply as they are seized.* At first she'd thought it was some sort of code, some anagram to puzzle out. *Tinier soup pot lumpy lit ...* No, he knew she was no good at jumbles. It had to be literal. It could be as simple as telling her an opportunity for escape would arise on her birthday, and that she must seize it. That was what she'd gleaned, and that was how she'd proceeded. There'd be an opening, but it'd be up to her to seize it.

While it'd felt a tad dispiriting at first, knowing she was essentially on her own, she'd stiffened her chin and accepted her duty. It was strangely empowering, especially after years of feeling powerless. The lioness must protect herself and her cub.

She noticed her contact lens case on the counter and pulled her dress up to pocket it. Was there anything else she was forgetting? Cash! There was around 20,000 Kenyan shillings in the desk. It wouldn't take her far—it was less than $200 U.S.—but certainly enough to get out of Nairobi. She'd figure it out from there.

The wad of bills joined the scissors in her back pocket just as Alexander reemerged from his room, a big, camouflaged backpack slung over his shoulders.

"I'm ready, Mama."

"Alexander," she scolded. "Take that off right now."

His face scrunched with fury, and his nostrils flared as he filled his lungs for an outburst. She strode right to him, not about to allow this, when the suite doors opened.

Beyond her view, Thabiti said, "Yes, sir," as Jivu walked briskly into the antechamber.

His gray twill suit was still buttoned up. His tie—yellow and blue, split vertically, the colors of the Mombasa city flag—remained cinched and centered. He'd returned for a forgotten something.

He froze inside the door, eyes darting from Alexander to the backpack, to the toys scattered across the carpet, to Tuni's hair, her shoes, her oddly shaped backside, and then her eyes. His cheek twitched. He couldn't even muster a triumphant smirk for catching her.

Jivu clicked the door shut behind him.

Hands playing with his slacks pockets, he sauntered forward.

"*Jambo*, Baba," Alexander greeted his father. "Mama won't let me bring my toys."

"No?" he said as entered the room, and then slowly circled behind Tuni. A hand grazed over her buttocks, followed by a series of lewd squeezes—*probing, vulgar, control.*

Alexander pouted. "No."

"Aw," Jivu replied, one word spat with each slow step. "What a … nasty … scheming … *whore.*"

Tuni's eyes remained glued to Alexander, her lids battling away the blur of encroaching tears, as Jivu slinked around to her front. The boy had clammed up and cast his gaze on the floor. He knew these words were bad, and that Daddy was mad at something.

"Go take that to your room, Bubu," Tuni choked out with unconvincing good cheer.

"No!" Jivu roared in her face. "You will do nothing that a woman commands you!" His spittle struck her cheek and eye. Still facing her, an inch away, he lowered his voice. "I told you, Alexander, you're a *man*. And this … *this* … is the worst kind of woman! A devious, conniving *bitch*."

He turned away, disgusted, and paced alongside the fireplace.

Grab Alexander and run … grab him and run for the door. Jivu wouldn't do anything in front of Thabiti and the others. Or would he?

"As I'm sure you're aware," Jivu said, "my accounts have been hacked. They say 'hacked,' but maybe seized, I wonder? *All* of them, all but here." He sneered contempt toward his *"insignificant"* legitimate accounts. "You know what these piece of shit reporters are asking about now? Tripe from a *decade* ago. Things I've never told a *soul.*"

"Secrets, Daddy?"

"Shut your mouth, child," Jivu snapped without a glance his way.

He strolled to her, hands in his pockets. She hauled her eyes up to meet his. The mad little smile had returned. He was losing his grip. Why were her bloody feet pinned to the damned carpet? This could only get worse with each passing minute.

He spoke low, soothing. "You know what else they're asking? The bloodline question again … despite the incontrovertible proof. What did you send to Turner?"

He stroked her cheek. She felt the ring's cool surface glide across her skin. The *fake* ring she had Ngina commission. The ring Tuni had swapped on the bathroom counter while Jivu showered.

"It was only a note," she said, but in five years she hadn't been able to successfully pass a lie. Not when challenged directly. Not when his sensors were on. "I only said the days weren't always bright, and that I hoped he was doing well. Nothing more."

He nodded mock sympathy. "The palace has lost its charm. Woe is me." He suddenly barked, "You're incapable of a single truth!"

His hand shot to her neck with a pop, and tightened, fingertips feeling as though they'd breach the flesh at any second. Her body strove unsuccessfully to cough.

She'd waited too long. Why had she waited? Now she'd die for her weakness.

Alexander came running, little arms in the air. "Baba, stop!"

Tuni flailed and kneed and kicked, but in that moment Jivu seemed invulnerable to pain. He slammed her against the wall, her head striking a painting. The artwork dislodged from its mounts and tumbled onto Tuni's head, the frame hooking over her as the canvas fell to the floor. When she opened her eyes, Alexander lay in a ball near her foot, covering his ears, and Jivu was already stomping away, back toward the fireplace.

Jivu swatted the decorations off the mantle, a high *pang* as his ring struck one of the candlesticks. Cursing, another swing, more debris.

Tuni scooped up Alexander and charged for the door. She shifted the boy onto one hip to free a hand, reached for the handle, and felt her leg jerked violently back. She lost her grip on Alexander, the child crashing into one of the doors. He cried out in pain. Tuni reached out to him, tried to pull her legs back under her.

Alexander's body shrank away from her, Tuni's breasts and arms and chin burning as she was dragged from the antechamber, back into the bedroom. Her body flipped over, onto her back, the room a blur.

"What did you send to him?" he demanded, and then came the first real hit to her face—an open-handed slap that might as well have been a punch—the first actual strike after a thousand threats and intimations.

How lucky I am, she'd always thought. *At least he doesn't beat me.*

"What was it?" Another slap, the opposite cheek, harder than the first, stinging.

She screeched from the pain. Something had torn her cheek. She managed to throw her arms over her face, and pressed the dress sleeve against her eyes.

A sudden quiet. She dared a peak between her arms. He was standing over her, frowning at his palm. He drew it closer to his eyes and then pinched something off with his other hand. It was skin. A short string of Tuni's flesh, snagged by an inexplicably splintered piece of his ring. It must've been damaged when he struck the candlestick—something that wouldn't have happened to his real ring.

206

"What did you do?" he murmured. He slid off the imposter ring and peered at the inside. "Deceitful … conspiring … *bint il-ahba* … You've no idea what you've done." He tossed the ring aside.

She didn't know what he'd said, but dropping into his native Arabic wasn't a good sign. She righted herself and pressed her back against the wall, sliding up onto her feet. Alexander was still whimpering in the antechamber, calling for her. Her eyes scanned about for a weapon—anything—and then she remembered the scissors and file.

"Fortunately …" Jivu began, and crouched down by the fireplace. Tuni reached behind her and felt the file sticking halfway out of her pocket. Her fingers probed for the sharp end as Jivu rose, one of the candlesticks in hand. "… you won't live to enjoy any of it."

Her head low, watching his feet slowly approach, Tuni wrapped her fingers around the file's dull end. The candlestick was long. He wouldn't have to step right up to her. Too far for her to stab at him. She'd need to lunge forth before he could swing.

"That perfect skull," Jivu said as he neared her. "In the next era, no one will have any idea how beautifully the flesh clung to it."

"Don't move, sir," Thabiti's voice, right over Tuni, in the archway beside her. "Drop the candlestick."

Tuni looked up and saw the pistol and disembodied hand jutting from the antechamber. She turned back to Jivu. His glare appeared more stunned and betrayed than defiant. Best for her to leave now, not think, *seize the opportunity!*

Go!

Her legs complied, pressing her back against the wall, and sliding her upright.

She called, "Alexander?"

"He's outside," Thabiti said without pulling his eyes from Jivu. "He's okay."

"I shouldn't be surprised," Jivu snarled at Thabiti. "A shame your brother's already dead. Penance must now be passed down to your niece."

Tuni paused at the archway. "Do it. Shoot him."

"As long as he doesn't move, I'll not shoot him."

"You shoot him, you're a hero to your country."

"No, Tuni," he said softly. "I cannot."

Jivu stifled a choke. *"Tuni?"*

Tuni eyed Jivu. His mouth agape, lips forming questions, mind calculating and analyzing and denying.

She peered up at Thabiti, his ribbed forehead coated in its usual shiny glaze, his upper lip speckled with tiny orbs of sweat. The idea struck her and she went with it—no hesitation.

A step forward, onto her tiptoes, she curled one hand behind his thick neck, the other hand sliding up his chest. She pulled him toward her, he turned—eyes remaining fixed down his pistol's sights—and she opened her mouth, pressed her lips hard against his, a swirl of tongue, and then eased down, sucking his lower lip until it popped back against his teeth.

"Thank you, Thabiti," she said seductively.

A final glance Jivu's way. He appeared primed to explode. She flashed a smile, then *ran*.

* * *

During her first two years in the Presidential Palace, Tuni enjoyed the freedom to wander every room and hall, sharing chats and meals with the staff on the lower level, and taking unannounced trips into the city. The majority of the staff from that time remained, and so she'd decided days ago that her escape would find its highest odds of success in their domain.

Her rehearsed excuse for leaving the suite turned out unnecessary. Jivu's return and assault ended up beneficial. Before entering, Thabiti had taken out the five extra men posted outside. Tuni had only managed a fleeting glimpse, but it appeared that two lay unconscious, one moaned and writhed, while the final two stumbled and reeled, nursing their heads. The dash to the staff stairwell had felt like a blurry mile, with Tuni waiting for someone to shout, or chasing footfalls, or a gunshot.

Alexander, bless him, had pleaded for her to slow down midway through the first flight of stairs. It was a good reset. She'd caught her breath for a beat, told Alexander everything would be okay—no one was going to stop them from their great adventure.

"We still get to go on a trip?" he'd said, and poked the bump on his head. "Why Baba hit us? He wished to come, too?"

"Yes, Bubu, but he can't. Now you just have to keep quiet until I say, all right? This is *our* secret adventure. Lips sealed." She sealed his lips with a swipe and pinch and his giggle reinvigorated her.

Through the kitchens and staff halls, they were met with a constant flow of stunned faces, *"My Lady?"* and inquiries. Was everything okay? Did she need help?

Tuni kept her mouth shut, letting her cheeks' bloody cut and swelling bruises do the talking.

Now, huddled just inside the shipping and receiving entrance, she surveyed the service gate and rear wall. She didn't recognize the shipping clerk, a middle-aged man casting an icy stare her way. He *really* wanted to pick up the telephone on his work table. Tuni mouthed *"Please,"* and he chewed his cheek.

Gunshots rang out from somewhere outside, hung in the air, and echoed off the perimeter wall. Alexander grasped her leg tighter. Another burst of shots, rapid-fire, *crack, crack, crack!* The clerk knocked over a cardboard barrel of foam peanuts as he scurried to the hall.

Tuni prayed these were warning shots fired in the air, and that no one was hurt or worse.

"Is it real, Mama?" Alexander asked. "I'm scared. Can we stay home?"

She forced an enthusiastic smile. "It's all part of the adventure, my love! Of course it's not real!"

His face alit with skeptical wonder, looking out on the rear court with new eyes. If only she could truly delude him—both of them—with such a fantasy.

Two more shots in succession, but from different locations. Shouts from the wall. Running.

"Do you need a car, my Lady?" asked a woman's voice behind her.

A jingling key ring dangled from an unfamiliar maid's fingers. Tuni was speechless, her focus locked on these kind eyes before her.

The maid continued, "It's the white Subaru in the lot, second row. You know how to drive manual?"

Tuni stammered, "I ... I do."

She deposited the keys in Tuni's hand. "I'll have the gate opened. You should go now. The guards have all dispersed."

Tuni nodded. Rushing out the door into the burning sunlight, she tried to remember if she thanked the woman or if it'd only been in her head. She glanced back, but couldn't see inside the dark room, and Alexander was now pulling her hand.

The black metal gate buzzed and began rolling open as they reached the end of the wall. The staff parking lot lay just around the corner.

"Which one is *sububu*, Mama? They're *all* white."

She looked out on the three rows of cars, and indeed, the vast majority were white. The maid had said it was a Subaru ... which row?

"Which row did she say?" Tuni said aloud.

"Second row!" Alexander cheered, and dragged her on.

A whistle from the gate. Tuni spun toward the sound.

There, beyond the gate, a dark car sat parked in the tree shadows just off the service road. A man stood beside it, on the passenger side—a Caucasian man with silver hair, black five o'clock shadow, sunglasses, and wearing green slacks and a tucked-in white polo shirt, reminiscent of a park ranger.

Oh, thank God, he's white, she thought, and then immediately felt semi-ashamed of the semi-racism.

The man quickstepped to the rear passenger door, and beckoned Tuni forward with a small-yet-urgent wave.

Tuni glanced behind her to the house and roof. It appeared all clear. She tossed the kind maid's keys toward the wall, and pressed Alexander forward.

"This way, Bubu! We're going with the man out there."

He proceeded on, unsure. "Who?"

She picked him up, hugged him tight across her, and ran up the sloping driveway without another backward glance. The waiting man's face, aimed at the house, told her the coast was still clear.

As she neared the car, she spotted another man—shaggy blonde mop, younger—in the driver's seat, his bespectacled eyes tracking her through the rearview mirror.

"Come, come, come," said the older man as he swung the back door open.

The driver put the car in gear as Tuni pushed Alexander inside. She slid in after him, suddenly aware of her heart thumping. Doors shut, the car revved up the road. She dared a glance out the back. The gate was slowly rolling shut. No signs of pursuers. The wall disappeared entirely behind the road's thick tree canopy.

"Mama," Alexander whined, and she saw her hand still clamped around his wrist.

"Oh, I'm so sorry, Bubu." She rubbed out the finger marks. "Here, hand me your seatbelt over there. We don't have your car seat so you get to sit like a big boy."

She clicked in his seatbelt and pulled on her own, eyeing the silent men in the front.

"Thank you so much. You've no idea how much I appreciate your help. It's been quite a day." She peered out her window as they summited the hilltop—all downhill from here.

"S'okay, s'okay," the passenger replied. "Hide down now."

Tuni pulled Alexander's head down toward her, then slid low in the seat, bending over him. At the bottom of the private drive, she snuck a peek between the front seats. They'd reached the wide-open second gate, passed right through, and turned onto the public street. She peered out the rear window for pursuers. No one. And no guard in the security booth.

Under the overhanging trees near the booth, an old pick-up truck with a dilapidated camper shell—an offensive eyesore to the highfalutin neighborhood—sat parked in the no-parking zone. Probably the guard's truck.

"Lucky the protestors didn't come around this way, too," Tuni said.

"Hide down," the older man repeated.

Cruising through the rich neighborhood next door to the mansion, Tuni and Alexander both watched the tops of big houses flash by. Unaware neighbors pruned cacti and fetched water jugs.

Tuni liked how the driver was navigating the neighborhood. Two right turns, a left, a right, two lefts. He seemed to be following a well-planned path.

Well clear of the neighborhood, she sat up. The driver glanced at her in the mirror, but didn't object. "Thank you again," she said. "Alexander, say thank you to the men."

"Thank you," he said, and in English, even.

"S'okay, s'okay," the passenger replied, and he lifted his ringing cell phone to his ear. An inaudible voice spoke on the other end, and the man replied, *"Tak, u nas ye, shcho zhinka, i dytyna tezh."*

What the hell was that? Russian? Thabiti had said Jivu was yelling about Russians.

He listened a moment. *"Tak, dobre. Piznishe."*

He hung up as the car merged onto the highway.

"Excuse me," Tuni said with a light, *purely out of curiosity* tone. "Was that Russian? Are you Russian?"

"Nyet," the passenger said, and the driver chuckled. A few seconds later, the passenger twisted halfway around, displaying his profile. "S'okay. You will be best now, okay?" It was the thickest Russian accent she'd ever heard. "You safety, okay?"

The driver muttered something to the passenger.

"I say yes, you will be *fine* now. *Fine?*" Apparently, he was asking her. "This is right English? Black-white, here-there, bad-fine?"

"Yes, I suppose," Tuni said, and leaned back in her seat. "I hope so."

"He don't know how to talk, Mama."

She slowly slipped her right hand behind her, found the two rounded ends of the scissors, and pulled them from her pocket.

* * *

Down the hall, a self-closing door shut with a click and resounding clunk.

"May I sit?" Mr. Absko said, motioning to the bed.

Thabiti nodded, his pistol still trained on his boss's chest. "Slowly, sir."

The President smiled as he sat. "I love that. Still respectful as you threaten my life." He'd abandoned his usual, more Arabic emphasis, altering his Swahili to Thabiti's native Mombasa accent. Thabiti wondered if the President was still conscious of these shifts.

Thabiti didn't like his back to the suite entrance, and he wouldn't chance even a quick shoulder check. Mr. Absko was a remarkably fast man when compelled.

Thabiti walked across the room to the foot of the bed, rotating his aim as he moved. Mr. Absko kept his eyes in his lap, studying his fingernails. Now properly faced for any comers, Thabiti glanced through the antechamber to the suite door—still ajar, with a long view down the main hall. Had all of the guards come to? He'd been careful with his fist and telescoping baton. Those men didn't deserve cracked skulls for doing their jobs. He felt bad, though. New guy had taken a good one to the kneecap before Thabiti punched his temple.

"How long have we known each other, Thabiti?" Mr. Absko said, but he knew the answer. Nineteen years.

The President was about to get wordcrafty with him, something Thabiti had heard the man do to others on many occasions. Strange to be on this side. Strange to see The Gray with these eyes. Another man, sitting on a bed, sweating, afraid for his life, because he knew as well as Thabiti that this couldn't end with a handshake.

"Long time, sir." Another glance to the door. Still no heads poking in. Perhaps they'd all gone after Tuni. Perhaps she needed more help. He'd already done more for her than he would've ever imagined. Sacrificed everything. Had it been for nothing, though?

"Long time, indeed," Mr. Absko said. He was nodding to himself, supposedly entertained by memories of good times had. "I want you to know something. What happened, all this, means nothing to me ... as far as *you're* concerned, Thabiti." He was giving this speech to the carpet at his feet. He didn't wish to look Thabiti in the eye, because that fear and rage he hid so well from his voice would be visible in his gaze. "I say this not to trick you into lowering your gun. I say this because it's natural for you to be afraid right now, how this will all play—"

The baton's knobby end struck Mr. Absko's right shoulder bone, reflexively sending his face tilting the opposite direction, toward Thabiti. His temple met with Thabiti's thrusting elbow, and a high-pitched wheeze streamed from the President's nose as he flopped, unconscious, to the bed.

Thabiti collapsed his baton and pocketed it as he stepped around bedside. A harsh flick to Mr. Absko's cheekbone while watching his eyelids. Out.

He holstered his pistol.

On his way out of the suite, Thabiti stuck in his earpiece. "Thabiti to Mosi, what's our status in back?" The response would tell him many things.

A short delay, then, "We're a bit light. If you have anyone, send them."

No guards in sight, and all four radios remained submerged in Thabiti's water pitcher behind his stool. They'd have to seek out a hardline, but had more likely headed straight to the security office.

Thabiti clomped down the stairway to the lower level. "I've got it covered. Is the property breached?"

"Yes and no," Mosi replied. "They broke down the vehicle gate, but no one wanting to enter. We fired warning shots, so we think they're afraid to be shot."

"That would be a logical fear, man." He strode through the empty kitchen, burners still alight, pots steaming, timers beeping. "Just keep every man you've got there."

"No shit, man."

Thabiti snatched his keys from the check-in board as a new voice cracked onto the channel. "Thabiti, report to the security office." Suhuba, head of security. The suite guards had apparently called or made it back.

"I'm on my way," he replied as he breezed through receiving, and struck the gate button on the wall.

"No you're not. You're heading to the parking lot."

Thabiti yanked out the earpiece and broke into a run. His achy knees protested, but time and luck were quickly fading. The big metal gate was halfway open when he made it to his pick-up. The gate had a twelve-second delay before it'd begin closing, but Suhuba could cancel from the office, and it'd then close the second the chain reached the end of its cycle. Thabiti assumed he'd have no grace period, and there was no action-movie-crashing through *this* gate.

He fired his engine, slammed it into gear, and gunned it straight to the gate, and out.

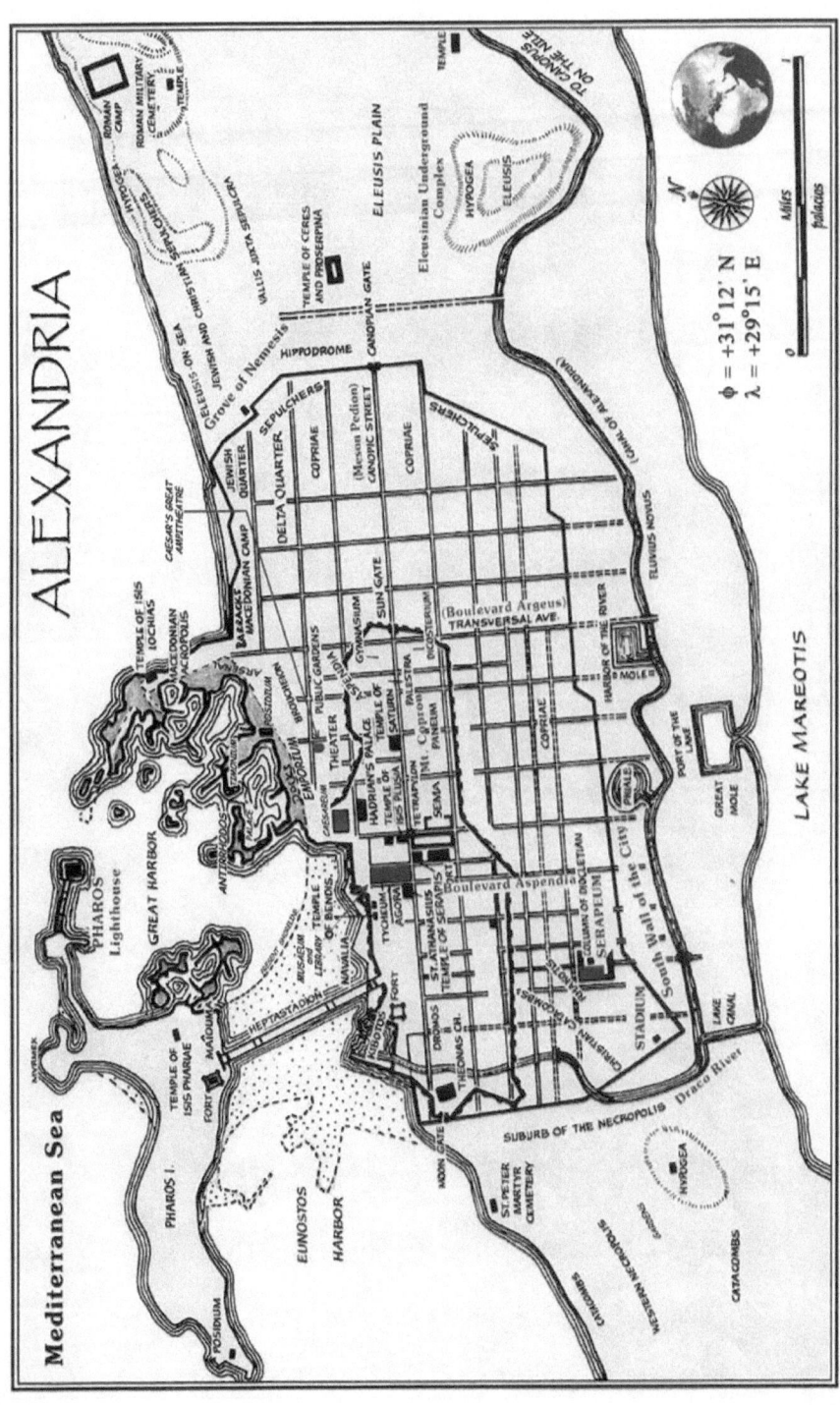

FOURTEEN

Alexandria, Aegyptus – 271 CE

Patra dismissed Unza and turned back to her mirror. "Hello, Steward. As you've observed, we are in crisis. You may or may not be aware, but the preservation of the Library's collection has been we stewards' duty since its earliest days, a mission launched by Euclid as the very first scroll slid into the stacks. But it was Zenodotus, the first librarian, who, along with Alexander Aetolus and Lychophron of Chalcis, organized our collection, and established the role of library steward to ensure knowledge's persistence. The voice conveys knowledge—"

She considered going on, studying her own eyes for trustworthiness, and opted to leave it there.

"I'm walking to the Governor house," she said as she passed Unza, polishing a silver goblet, "and then to the Serapeum."

Unza grunted without looking up from her task.

Patra made her way down each of the Musaeum complex's levels—ignoring hails from alarmed members above, and avoiding the pregnant gazes of passers-by—until she reached the main gate. The road outside the high walls bustled with distraught citizens with full arms, some leading slaves carrying their litters filled instead with valuables, or hauling loaded carts from the Palace District toward the temples. Foolishly, the moneyed populace believed Emperor Antonius would sooner respect the temples' sanctity over that of anything else in the Royal Quarter.

Heading uphill toward the Governor's residence, Patra drew her palla across her face to filter the dusty air. The busy main thoroughfare continued on to the temples, while Patra veered left up the private road.

Dense, spiraled bushes flanked a pair of marble pedestals, marking the estate's formal entry path for guests, but Patra had little interest in climbing the near-one-thousand stairs leading to the front gate. Instead, she remained on the road, a flagstone-paved route that led to the primary entrance in back.

Halfway up the incline, her lungs and feet demanded a rest, so she paused, glancing out toward the now-visible sea.

So many ships.

She looked up the curving road again, the palace's second story looming beyond the path's crest. From his verandas, Cassius would have an even better view of the cluttered waters to the north. Did he fear for his own life? What might he be planning? There was certainly more to consider than the Musaeum, if he even intended to take Thomas's purported advice to offer up the offending performers at the bay. It remained for her difficult to imagine Cassius taking such a cowardly approach. Then again, she still had trouble seeing him as governor, that rascally boy with whom she'd grown up.

She continued uphill, recalling the young Cassius in his family's orchard.

Sometime after her mother's death, Patra's father began courting Cassius's widowed mother. That summer, the two adolescents spent every day together, either exploring the vineyard, reading in the vine-shaded atrium, or playing in the small river.

Patra would never forget the day he'd pulled her behind a low wall, slid out of his tunic, and said, "Now you."

She expressed her skepticism, but obliged him nonetheless. The two sat in the high grass, touching and poking each other with equal curiosity, but she put a stop to the probing after they touched tongues.

Cassius had pouted for about a week, but their friendship resumed, and the pair remained close all the way into their twenties. After his wedding, contact between them declined. Now, they only saw each other a few times a year at large social events, but there remained an unspoken bond, reaffirmed with shared glances, knowing smiles, and brief-yet-brimful discourse.

As Patra finally crested the road, a detachment of city guards came into view outside the palace's rear gate. She caught their eyes at once.

On her final approach, one of the guards called out, "No visitors today."

Patra continued forward, stopping a few strides from the line of guards. She noted an apparent commander—armor and helmet reminiscent of a centurion—standing beside the gate's left pillar behind them. "Please have the governor informed that Steward Supatra requests an audience."

The commander's lips parted, but the voice of the first guard repeated his original declaration, this time with pointed emphasis. "No ... visitors ... today."

Patra glared at the audacious guard. "I understand you've received your orders, but—"

"Then turn around and walk away," the guard interrupted. "Unless you need assistance leaving."

The guard beside him smirked, and another somewhere down the line snorted his amusement. Patra stepped back and scanned the faces before her. Most simply stared ahead, expressionless. A few glanced her way.

Cassius would certainly see her if he knew she was here, but how to get word to him if this impudent brute wouldn't even let her complete a sentence? She turned toward the obscured commander—

a pair of seemingly benign eyes considering her from behind two guards.

"Commander," she said, stepping forward. "I only ask that my name—"

"Step back!" the first guard barked, and swung his javelin down before her, inches from her face.

She halted, recoiling at the weapon's windblast, and the shout.

"Janus," the commander said, and the scowling guard shot him a look before stepping back into rank.

Patra stood in stunned silence, consumed with equal parts fear and rage. Left to his own, this "Janus" would be more than happy to flog an old woman unconscious, or worse.

"Janus, is it?" Patra said, backing away from the men. "I shall have to remember this name for my next encounter with my *friend*, the governor." Janus seethed, poison shooting at her from his eyes, but his sandals didn't move from the line. "I am the *head librarian*, in case you were unaware, and a childhood friend of Governor Cassius. Of course he wants no visitors, but he'll absolutely wish to know what I've come to report … as well as how his closest associates are treated—"

Janus could hold his tongue no longer. "Blather and whine all you want, old hag. You're not stepping foot in this gate, and unless you want my sword shoved up that—"

"Silence, Janus!" the commander ordered. "Not one more word!" He pushed through the line, and marched a few strides toward Patra, halting smartly before her. "Please accept my apologies, Steward. Unfortunately, there are no exceptions today. I have orders from the governor's aide that the Empress herself is not permitted in, so …"

"Thomas?" Patra blurted. "Of course Thomas would order such a thing!" She cupped her hands beside her mouth and screamed, "Cassius! Cassius, it's Patra!"

The commander raised a hand. "Again, Steward, I'm sorry."

Patra sidestepped him and continued crying out to the palace.

"Please, be quiet, Steward. You *will* need to leave now."

"I'll shut her up, Marius," Janus sneered, breaking ranks once more. Three others joined him, javelins at the ready across their chests.

"Just don't hurt her," the commander, Marius, said as he turned to go.

The four guards converged on Patra, wicked smiles in their helmets' shadows.

"Of course not," Janus sang.

Patra stumbled backward. She landed on her tailbone—a sting up her spine.

A muffled shout in the distance. Heads turned.

Another, still small, distant, but now intelligible: "Marius!"

Patra scrabbled to her knees, then feet. She craned her neck to see beyond the tall men, spotting a figure on one of the verandas. Cassius!

"Step aside!" Marius called, and the remaining rank split in half.

Two of the guards went to the gate, extracted the ground stakes, and swung both sides out.

"You may enter, Steward," Marius said.

* * *

A servant led Patra upstairs to the governor's second-floor vestibule, and into the expansive atrium. Sunlight streamed in through the roof's wide, square opening, though unlike Patra's domicile, and most others, no rainwater pool lay beneath the opening. Instead, a set of lush couches formed the traditional square, surrounding the floor's allusive blue mosaic.

The servant motioned Patra to one of the couches just as someone entered the atrium from an abutting room. It was Thomas.

Heading out toward the vestibule (with an indifferent glance and slow blink vaguely sent her way), his blasé façade wasn't fooling

Patra for a second. She followed him with her eyes, glowering until the last of him disappeared around the column.

"An ill-timed visit, Patra," Cassius said. He walked from the room Thomas had left, scooped up a goblet of freshly poured wine, and sank into the opposite couch.

"Agreed," she replied, accepting her own wine from the servant. "Have you asked the Emperor to go home? 'Come back another decade?'"

"Clever." He gulped down half the cup.

"Thank you, before I forget …" Patra motioned in the main gate's direction. "… They were seconds from attacking me."

"The guards? No." A silly idea, apparently.

"Oh yes, no question. One of them swung his javelin a hair away from my nose, called me an old hag, and threatened to shove his sword into an orifice."

Cassius's air of nonchalance evaporated, replaced in an instant with outrage. "Was it only one of them? What did he look like? Don't try to protect him—"

"His name is Janus."

Surprised, Cassius nodded, peered around, and summoned a servant to his side. He whispered to the man, and the servant dipped his head before hastening from the room.

"It's handled," Cassius said. "Now, what brings you here, besides the obvious? If it's simply a plea to protect the Musaeum, please, spare me. Your friends kindled their own pyres."

"Of course. And no, I wouldn't waste either of our time with the obvious. A week from today, the Musaeum will surely be rubble. There's nothing we can do to prevent that. But the collection … that's another matter. All the knowledge and known history of the world—over five hundred years of work—it *can* be saved."

* * *

Zenobia and her generals had gathered in the Temple of Isis, east of the Great Harbor. Lookouts perched atop the temple's northernmost colonnade, monitoring Emperor Antonius's lurking fleet, and relaying their maneuvers to map scribes below. Clusters of Palmyrene soldiers sat in square formations, shaded beneath the temple's exterior colonnades, but then spilt out onto the street, continuing well into the Jewish Quarter, where armored horses and empty chariots appeared to fill every shred of open space.

Waiting to be called in, Patra sat on the steps, leaning against a column base, and observed the faces of those soldiers seated nearest the lookouts as they eavesdropped on every update. They made no attempt to mask their apprehension.

"Steward Supatra of Alexandria," called a courtier.

Patra stood. "Here! I'm here!"

"Follow me, please."

Patra hustled behind the quick-footed courtier, into the temple's vestibule. Palmyrenes, Romans, and Egyptians; Hellene, Christians, and Jews, all bustled about the halls simply as *Alexandrians*, desperate to prevent an end to their way of life.

Inside the main temple, a crowd of disgruntled Palmyrene generals and advisors flowed from between the two towering statues—Isis and Osiris—and Patra tailed the nimble courtier as he scurried out of their path. The grumbling horde looked as though it would have trampled over the pair if they hadn't moved.

When the last stragglers passed, the courtier motioned Patra into the cleared area.

Zenobia stood behind a wide table, eyes on its surface. "What happened to the light?" she said, then called, "More light."

Servants materialized from the walls and behind columns, stoking torch sconces, and dragging iron stands closer to the table. Zenobia's bespoke armor glinted at every layered tip.

"That's good. That's enough." She peered up as Patra entered the field of light. The whites of Zenobia's eyes shone bright, framed by a wide maroon bar painted from ear to ear. "There you are! Please, come to me. Refill me! I am starved of unbloody words."

The servants withdrew, disappearing once more into the shadows.

Patra exhaled a rueful sigh and hung her head. "I don't know that I've much better to offer, Augusta … Zenobia."

Zenobia sank, ever so slightly, but it was there. She closed her eyes and nodded. "Well … at least come with a hug."

"Of course!" Patra said, shuffling around the table and wrapping her arms around the cold armor.

Zenobia gently slid her long nails across Patra's scalp, kissed her head, cupped her cheeks, and raised Patra's eyes to hers. "Will you stay with me? Wahbi will be here soon."

Oh, no. Oh, no no no …

"Wahbi's coming? Coming here? I'd heard you sent him east!"

"I did. And yesterday, he turned his men around to come back."

"Oh, Zenobia … And it's too late to—"

"Yes. As a mother, I'm terrified, of course. But as a general, relieved my army will be whole. So, does this mean you'll stay?"

Patra stepped back. "I'm sorry … I wish I could. The Library … my friends …"

Zenobia's posture returned—back to business. "Absolutely. I won't keep you. It was good to see you, nonetheless."

"Actually, if I may have another moment …" Patra waited. Though still wounded, Zenobia beckoned her on. "I've just come from the Governor's Palace. I mentioned my desire to move the collection into the library at the Serapeum."

"That's wise. Antonius wouldn't harm the temple."

"Unless he's told what's there. My friends and I, we bear no optimistic illusions. The Emperor views the performance as a mutiny far more threatening than a rebelling nation. And imagine, the *personal* nature … His vanity and arrogance surely fills his mind with an insatiable bloodlust. He'll kill every person. He'll destroy every last thing Musaeum members cherish."

"No doubt. You fear he'll be notified of your actions?"

"He may be notified. We'll take measures to obscure our movements, but we've no illusions. The Serapeum's library may very well end up in ashes. You know of the galleries beneath the temple courtyard?"

"Yes, I've ventured down there. Beautiful sculptures."

"Well, I'm told the priests use a variety of secret tunnels to travel unseen between the surface structures and galleries."

An astute smile curled Zenobia's lips. "Their magic tricks … light from stone, the overflowing modius crown …"

"Possibly." Patra had no desire to besmirch the priests. "But more importantly, if real, these passages are known by precious few, and convoys from the Library to the Serapeum would be difficult to conceal. If you ordered the Temple closed for its own protection, our couriers could come and go, and, once inside the walls, would be free from onlookers. Spying eyes at the gates shouldn't presume any destination other than the Serapeum library, right?"

"Not without an alternative destination in existence. The priests are your only liability. Have you come to ask me for their deaths?"

"Oh, ah … no." Patra scanned the columns and shadows around them. She whispered, "The servants … could you …?"

Zenobia snapped, "Everyone, out!" Dark figures skittered from corners like startled cats and shuffled out of the hall. When quiet returned, Zenobia motioned Patra to wait. Suspicious, she listened a moment, then growled, "I said *everyone*, Heptus."

A courtier ambled from behind a column. "Apologies, Augusta. I failed to apprehend 'everyone' meant—"

"Everyone?" Zenobia barked. "Let us settle the definition here and now! 'Everyone' means everyone! 'Everyone but Heptus leave,' means everyone but Heptus leave!" The repentant courtier stumbled hurriedly toward the main hall. Zenobia called after him, "'Everyone may live but Heptus,' means only Heptus is executed! More? Are we settled now?" She turned back to Patra, smirking. "My head snake. I do hope that all you've shared was for the benefit of our audience?"

Patra turned to her, not shaded with artful connivery, but distraught.

FIFTEEN

Alexandria, Egypt – Present day

Joss shifted the rental van into park, but left the engine running for the A/C.

"Well that was stressful," she said, peering past Matt to the condo complex entrance.

This property and most of its neighbors offered short-term rentals to foreign workers—specifically, the archaeologist, Jo Shelsher.

"So, uh …" Joss went on, "… I appreciate the confidence, but let's switch before she comes out."

Matt's hands lay folded in his lap, and his focus drifted around his knees. "Hm? What's that?"

"I said let's switch. Half the drivers here seem to want to kill the other half. I mean, why do they even paint lanes on the roads?"

"Lanes?" He looked around as if just waking from a nap. "Where are we? Is this where we're picking her up?"

"Yes." She looked at the clock on the dash. "We're a little early."

Matt nodded and took a deep breath, blinking rapidly, his brow drawn tight with angst.

"So, what's happening right now?" Joss asked, motioning to the Taria's pointy lump under Matt's T-shirt.

"Just a sec," he replied, squeezing his eyes shut, one hand floating between them in a frozen *stand by* sign.

The thing never left his chest. Before the island, he'd been sharp and present most of the time, even when surreptitiously reading something. If he'd been doing any of this deep immersion stuff before, it would've been in bed, or when Joss wasn't around.

The hand dropped to his lap, and he faced her, now fully alert. "Sorry about that. Just needed something to finish." He glanced right, toward the condos, with a twitchy, nervous air leftover from the reading. "Should we go in, or is she supposed to come out?"

"She said she'd come out. Five more minutes. Maybe enough time to fill me in on … I don't know, everything?"

Matt frowned. "Like what? This?" He pointed to his chest. "Or *all this*?" A finger swirl in the air.

"All of the above! I know nothing! I mean, something *obviously* happened on the island—something that surprised you, that you're still tripping on. And as far as 'all this' …" She mimicked his finger swirl. He appeared genuinely dumbstruck. "… I've tried to be a good trooper and do as I'm told, no questions asked, but that's not how you sold this relationship back home. If there's stuff I don't get to know, like for my own protect—"

He motioned for her to stop. "I'm sorry, Joss. As far as this whole mission goes, I just assumed … I guess because you're pretty much setting up all the—"

"There's the problem," she grinned. "You keep thinking I'm smart."

He swatted away the modesty as he removed his seatbelt.

He shifted in the passenger seat to face her. "To put it succinctly, we're ravaging Absko's world through multiple fronts, including foreign governments who want him imprisoned, and now through Ostrovsky and furious others who were betrayed and are burdened by fewer legal constraints, with the goal of luring Absko out of his country where one or more interested parties will be able to capture him."

He paused for a breath.

She opened her mouth to ask another question.

He cut her off with a hand, resuming. "At the same time, we're stringing Ostrovsky along with the promise of long lost scrolls, maintaining a communication path through which we can a) further the Absko goal, and b) assist Mrs. Absko in her getaway."

She waited a beat, eyebrows perked. He graciously motioned to proceed.

"That was all great. Great summary. So what's the deal in *there?*" indicating the Taria hanging behind his T-shirt.

Matt took a deep breath, an awkward smile scrunching his mouth as he deliberated. He was debating whether to tell her. Apparently it was as big a deal as she'd thought. As seconds passed, she wondered if it'd be best to let him off the hook. In truth, he wasn't obligated to tell her anything. It was simply a courtesy, and his promise of honesty a week ago was so she could trust him, and not question his motivations with her. Trust was no longer an issue, and this was his own thing.

Matt spoke up before she could stop him. "Something did happen with the Taria. On the island ... and since. Something ... unprecedented. It's not that I'm keeping secrets, it's just that I'm still in the process of figuring it out. The imprints are ... um, well, I haven't really explained to you how it normally works, but this thing's different. I have no control over how it plays out. I just have to watch what she's showing me."

"Watch what she's showing you? 'She' as in Patra? The librarian?"

"Yeah. Like I said, I'm still figuring it all out. When I have a better understanding, you'll be the first to know."

He offered Joss an earnest smile, and touched her leg. She liked it too much—the notion that he felt obliged to share his experience, like she was a partner in this adventure, not the leg touching thing ...

well, maybe a little of that, too—and so she reverted to the former topic.

"Back to your uber-complicated scheme real quick. What happens after the whole Absko thing is done? I presume Ostrovsky's not going to up and forget about his coveted scrolls, and I take it there aren't really any out there to be discovered?"

"You're half-right there …"

Over Matt's shoulder, Joss spotted a figure—two figures—exiting the complex gate. The woman, Jo Shelsher, wore wide-legged cargo capris, a long denim shirt, beat-up leather boots, and a wide-brimmed sun hat. Mrs. Shelsher was recognizable from her online photos, but Joss hadn't a clue about the man walking with her. He was a bit below average in height, slim, dark-skinned, with spiky hair, and wore a short-sleeved, plaid button-down, and khakis.

She pointed, interrupting Matt. "Here she comes."

Matt spun around. "Oh … shit."

"What?"

"That's Pete Sharma with her."

Joss looked at the approaching man again, his eyes widening over a beaming mouth.

"So?" she said. "Why oh shit?"

Matt scowled and grabbed the door handle. "So, he's not supposed to know I'm here." He opened the door and stepped out, peering down the street.

Joss got out on her side in time to hear Peter Sharma's jubilant greeting.

"Matty Matty Matt-Matt!"

To Joss's surprise, Matt sent a terse glance his way, said "Hey, Pete," and stepped instead to Jo Shelsher. "Thanks so much for taking the time to help us today, Mrs. Shelsher."

She shook Matt's hand, though visibly distracted by the obvious Peter snub. "Oh, it's no problem at all, Matthew." She set a hand on Matt's shoulder, and motioned sideways. "What a small world, eh? Last night I start telling my neighbor here, Peter, about the unexpected call—"

"Yeah, man," Pete said. "What the heck's going on?"

Matt continued facing Mrs. Shelsher. "We're going to have to catch up later, Pete. I need you to shake my hand as if we're meeting for the first time, and for *nobody* to look around. There's a minivan with dangerous people parked at the end of the block. When we drive away, Pete, and you go back to your apartment, those guys'll follow us, and not give you another thought."

"Excuse me?" Mrs. Shelsher said, and began turning to peer down the street.

"No, ma'am!" Matt insisted, and she snapped her head back to him. "Do *not* look around." Matt turned toward Pete, nodded politely, and shook his hand. "Nice to meet you. Joss, Mrs. Shelsher, let's go ahead and load up, excited to be on our way."

Pete waved and moseyed back toward the complex as Matt walked around to the driver's side.

"Can't say I'm too thrilled with how we're starting off here," Mrs. Shelsher said through a rigid smile as Joss helped her into the van.

Joss climbed in and slid the door shut behind her. "It's going to be fine, Mrs. Shelsher. It's all a mere abundance of caution."

Matt steered the van around the cul-de-sac. "Exactly." As they approached the parked minivan—custard yellow with a peeling black bar down the side—Matt said, "Now everyone keep their eyes forward. Nothing to see here ..."

He turned onto the next street, keeping an eye on the rearview mirror. Joss and their fuming guest remained silent in the second row. Tension thickened the van's air. Matt crept to the main street's red light, chanting quietly to the mirror, "Come on ... Come on, guys ... Don't lose him ..."

Mrs. Shelsher, dismayed: "Are you *waiting* for them?"

"Yes, I am," Matt said slowly. "It'd be verrrry bad if they shift their atten—ah, there they are! Finally." He stepped on the gas, slipping into the main street's morning traffic. "Now, let's get our seatbelts secured and hang on to something."

"You gotta be kidding me," Mrs. Shelsher said as she grappled about for her belt.

Joss helped her strap in. "We're so sorry. This definitely wasn't on the agenda."

"Okay, hanging on now," Matt warned, and then swerved left, cutting off a taxi, and continuing through a tiny gap across two more congested lanes.

A jarring brake, zooming forward, veering around a box truck, skidding tires, and the van spilled out of traffic onto an empty side street. Windowless brick buildings flanked the thin street as Matt gunned it down the block, eyes flashing between the rearview and road. And then, halfway to the next street, he let off the gas and eased back into his seat.

"They just passed," he said, "still in the far lane. Didn't see us turn. We're in the clear."

He turned left, heading against their false escape route. After a few more turns, he pulled the van off the street into a vacant lot, and parked.

Matt turned around with an apologetic smile. "Can we start over, Mrs. Shelsher? Pretend none of that just happened?"

She drew in a deep breath, raspberrying it out. "There's no forgetting *that* lunacy, that's for dang sure, pal. Who were those people? What would they have done if they caught us?"

Matt waved it away, a silly concern. "Nothing at all, really. They're just guys someone hired to follow me." She wasn't convinced. "Because they think I'll lead them to some long-lost treasure. If we find a good spot today, that's where I'll have them follow me next time. My real aim just then was to keep their attention off Pete. Honestly, nothing to worry about."

"Sweetie, that is the exact opposite of what you said not three minutes ago. 'There's a minivan with dangerous people,' you said.

But fine, I'll let that go. You believe we're safe now, I'm gonna give you the benefit of the doubt … God knows why."

Joss thought it a good moment to chime in, reinforcing Matt's confidence in their safety. "Mrs. Shelsher, you're absolutely—"

"Call me Grandma Bubsy, hon. Only telemarketers call me Mrs. Shelsher."

Joss flicked her eyes Matt's way. "Oh, okay, sure. I was just going to echo Matt's sentiment about our safety. Trust me, I wouldn't be here if I had any doubts. I'm a big chicken."

Matt thanked Joss with a quick look, and turned back to Bubsy. "I do appreciate the understanding, Bubsy. We've heard all about your—"

"*Grandma* Bubsy, sweetie. I didn't spend twenty years in grandma school for nothing. Or Meemaw, if you prefer."

"Grandma Bubsy, it is. We've heard all about your projects out here. Very impressive stuff, to say the least."

"Well, thank you." Surprisingly, she blushed. "I've, of course, heard of you, Matthew. My husband and I read your books. We loved the one about the dome people, but you lost us on the Cuba Viking one. So violent."

Matt nodded, avoiding Joss's look. "Yes … thank you. Good feedback."

"Anyhow," Grandma Bubsy went on, "if you put out any more, just try to keep them fun and interesting. Now then, I understand you want to see some of the lesser-known sites outside the city?"

"That's right. At least an hour out of Alexandria, deserted, and not visible from the highway."

"Well, there's plenty of sites with those conditions, but we'd have to head past Cairo for anything truly interesting. Amarna would be the most obvious spot, though we'd be looking at seven-plus hours of driving. And I don't do helicopters, if you're thinking of suggesting it."

"Definitely not Amarna. And it doesn't have to be interesting at all, actually. Ideally, it'd be a structure we could enter, but even that part is optional."

Grandma Bubsy scrunched her face, searching her memory. "If I had my maps or laptop, I could bring up a good list, but ... hm. I assumed you'd want to see one of my pyramids. That's what I get for assuming. And now, I'll assume once more you don't want to drop by my rental so I can pick up some stuff." Matt's expression told her this would be less than desirable. "Well, there are ruins I know off the top of my head, but they might be a little too interesting for your needs, whatever those might be. About three hours east: Sân el-Hagar. Plus, it's a real pretty drive along the Mediterranean, if you appreciate pretty things."

"Sân ..." Matt echoed, the name ringing a bell. His eyes widened. "Wait, is that Tanis?"

Grandma smiled. "Look at you, Matthew. You really *do* know a thing or three, don't you?"

Matt's thoughts scattered then converged, overlapping and shaping an idea within a previously cloudy placeholder. Tanis was inscribed on one of the Tarias. It'd be a perfect diversion for Ostrovsky, validated by his existing research. But Matt would be surprised if archaeologists had fully abandoned all excavations at Egypt's former capital city.

"Wouldn't the site be fairly active?" he asked. "At least with tourists?"

"There're tour groups that come to one little section, but the ruin I'm talking about is a building foundation with no building, out beyond the hills on the east end of the city, and accessed via unpaved road. The French team's digs are a couple miles to the north. No one goes to this spot, hon."

Matt grinned. "Then I want to go to this spot, Grandma Bubsy."

He put the van in gear, driving off toward the International Coastal Road.

* * *

Ancient rubble and modern-day garbage littered the wide tunnel's sandy floor. Joss stepped over a pile of charred wood and crushed, soot-coated beer cans. Behind her, Grandma Bubsy grumbled sporadically. Outside, the plucky archaeologist had said, "There's nothing to see in there but broken glass, graffiti, and heaven knows what else," but Matt insisted on walking the full length. He'd offered to go alone, but Joss suspected their guide felt obligated to stay with him, given that she'd brought them here.

It was unexpectedly cool and humid inside, the sand floor compacted and moist, and the sunny entrance—at least fifty yards behind them—seemed to offer zero illumination this far in.

Joss wondered about the old firewood. Wouldn't the whole tunnel quickly fill with smoke? And then she wondered if they'd stumble upon the remains of some inept hobo.

"Careful," Matt said, pointing his flashlight at glass shards poking up through a patch of loose sand. He continued skimming the opposite wall with his fingertips.

Judging by the fetid air, Joss was more concerned about stepping in a pool of human urine and/or excrement. The chilly, graffiti-lined passageway appeared to have hosted decades of visitors. Hopefully, this wasn't the case today.

Grandma called from behind Joss, "In case you folks were wondering, that smell is none other than the brown and yellow. Sticking to your guns on that 'have to go all the way through' thing, Matthew? *Eesh*, what was that? Like wood, but squishy. No, don't! Don't turn your light on it. If I wanted a light on it, I'd have put my own on it. Just keep moving, for the love of Pip."

"I'm so sorry, Grandma Bubsy," Matt said as they continued on. "I didn't know it'd be a biohazard in here. I should've told you up front that I'd need to inspect any tunnels."

"No, no. No sorries," she replied. "Don't you mind my nattering nonsense. I'm fine. All I'm telling you, hon, is there's nothing to see in here that we didn't see in the first twenty—Oh, sweet cheese and crackers!" Her flashlight whipped about, and she gasped between statements. "That used to be a cat. That right there was once a cat, and too *dod gamn* recently. Darling, we need to about face and march right out of here!"

Matt paused, shining his light past Joss to Grandma Bubsy. "I'm just verifying it still goes all the way through, like you said. You two can turn back and meet me outside. I don't mind. Nobody's come this deep for a few years."

Grandma Bubsy grumbled, "That's 'cause *Nobody* had the wisdom to respect their senses. I'm leaving my pride with this here cat cadaver ... catdaver. Well, that's funny, I suppose." She peered up at Joss. "You coming with me, hot stuff?"

Joss glanced at Matt's dimly lit face. He nodded, motioning for her to go.

She pulled her phone from her back pocket and activated its light. "I'll be right behind you, Grandma."

Grandma called once more to Matt. "You should see the light from the other side after the bend up there. If you're interested, the old slide rails for the sluice gate are still attached on that side." She reached behind her in search of Joss's hand. "Let's go, sweetie. Pray with me we don't find whatever squished earlier."

Joss took her hand, treading carefully at her heels as they crept back toward the dime-sized glow of the tunnel entrance, the bright circle widening like an iris, bit by bit. Behind them, Matt coughed periodically. He sounded close, but each time Joss glanced back, there was no sign of him, not even a distant flashlight.

Finally reaching the warm and untainted air of outside, glorious outside, Grandma Bubsy gasped as if breaking the surface from a deep dive. She leant forward, hands on knees— a lighthearted show of elaborate panting—as if she'd held her breath the entire time.

She peered up, squinting at Joss, and winked. "Well, sweetie, a flood tube isn't quite the same, but I think I can scratch off 'Explore an urban sewer system' from my bucket list."

Joss laughed. "What about rats, and the flowing waterfalls? You might be missing out."

"All that and more was going on in my mind back there. Might as well have been rodents crawling over our feet, for all my imagination had churning about."

"I didn't run into any rodents," Matt said, suddenly right behind them, "but there's a snake here."

The women spun about and, upon seeing no sign of Matt, realized his oddly reverberant voice was carrying through the tunnel.

"I think it's a sand boa," he continued. "Probably who we should thank for the lack of critters in there."

"Feel free to pass on my thanks," Grandma Bubsy yelled into the tunnel.

Joss didn't think they needed to shout. He'd apparently heard them talking about rats.

She said at a normal level, "Are you coming back through, or going to walk around?"

"I'll walk around," said the disembodied voice. "Hey, Grandma Bubsy. There're tire tracks back here, leading off east toward some dunes. Is there another road nearby?"

"Ahh ..." She thought a moment, then called back, "Yeah, yeah there is. A ways out there, but yeah. Though I'm betting those tracks are from dirt bikers. I've seen them all along those dunes—the dirt bike kind and the four-wheel kind. That's probably our friends who're using the ruin as their port-o-john."

"There're definitely more leavings on this side than that. You two were wise turning back." He coughed and spat. "Did you hear me gagging before?"

He received no answer, save for the surreal echo of wild laughter.

* * *

In the van's back row, Matt sat staring at the static No
SERVICE, in Greek, atop his phone screen. He needed to check in
with Iris.

A mild, salt-tinged breeze flowed from the open driver-side
window. Up front, Joss sat in the passenger seat, listening to
Grandma Bubsy behind the wheel.

"Glenn?" she said. "No way, he's all for it! We talk every day,
sometimes twice in a day."

"He ever come out here to visit?" Joss asked.

"Nah." She cracked a sunflower seed between her teeth, and
tossed the shell out the window. "He came with me the first time.
Stayed for a few days. Even though I'd been talking with my sponsor
out here for a few months, neither one of us really knew what to
expect as far as me being American, a woman, Christian, et cetera, et
cetera. By day three, he knew I was in good hands, and that our
trepidations were misplaced. Even though we're mostly retired, he
serves on the boards of a bunch of companies, and he's got at least
one meeting per week, so he flew back. So far, my work visas have
been limited to three-month stints, and I love being home, but I just
adore it out here. This is my third stay." Her blonde hair waved in
the wind as she glanced Joss's way. "*Hoonah yaty thalath merott.*"

"Oooh," Joss said. "Is that Arabic?"

Matt cut in. "*Hatha ho ziyarti althalithuh.* The other way
comes off like 'Three times here come.'"

Grandma Bubsy eyed him through the rearview. "Put a sock in
it, peanut gallery. At my age, that's about as good as it's ever going to
get. You want a language face-off, put your French on the table."

Matt saw Joss raise a warning hand, and then whisper.

Grandma ignored her volume. "He's good at French, too? Oh.
What about Spanish? Okay, fine, I'll be impressed." She peered back
through the mirror again. "I don't suppose, what with your super
power or whatever, that you can do Ancient Egyptian?"

Matt smiled. "I just might."

In his experience, people working on ancient civilizations were left speechless whenever Matt demonstrated an extinct language they'd studied. He knew Grandma's day was about to be made.

His phone suddenly vibrated in his hand. A text message from Iris. Two bars of signal. Three!

> IT: Did you have Pete assassinated or something?
> IT: He's missed his last two hourly calls, voicemails, and emails.
> IT: I'm not complaining, but strangely, his silence is deafening. Weird, right?
> IT: Assuming you don't have signal right now. Get back to me when you do.

Matt was sure Pete was okay—after their brief encounter, it'd make sense for him to halt his unrelenting campaign to get in touch. But now there was a bug in Matt's head. Once he'd lost them, what if Rostik *had* gone back to the condo complex, having no other leads to follow?

"You can't leave it dangling in the air like that, mister," said Grandma Bubsy.

Matt looked up from his phone, blinking. "Leave what? Oh, right. Just a sec. I have to make a call. Are we close to the city? Will this cell signal stay?"

"We're still a ways out, but you should be good the rest of the drive back."

Iris answered on the first ring. "Hey." The sound of furious typing filled the background.

"Hey. We actually ran into Pete earlier today, so it'd make sense for him to lay off, but can you check in with him, just in case? And tell him I'll reach out tonight."

"Okay," Iris said, her keyboard still under attack. "And will you really?"

"Yeah, why?"

"Never mind. What else?"

Matt gazed out the window, past the glimmering sea, toward the horizon, beyond which he imagined Sicily lay. "Any check-ins? Or any word at all?"

"From Palermo? Nada."

"Or any word at all?" he repeated.

"No. No one."

"Well, have you called anyone to check? Or you're just waiting?" He sounded jerkish, he knew, but they should've heard *something* about Tuni by now.

The typing stopped. "Dude, chill! Of course I've called! I've called everyone who might have an update, *and* I'm all over the feeds out of Kenya. The unrest is getting out of control in spots, but the palace is fine. No breaches, and they've got a fricken army guarding the perimeter, so if she's still in there, she's fine."

"I'm sorry. Thank you. I'm sorry … It's just, if she's still in there, she's far from fine."

"No, I know, brother. I meant, she wasn't caught up in the–"

"No, I got it. Thanks for staying on it. I'm going to call someone you haven't."

A twinge of offense from Iris. "How do you know I haven't?"

"I'm calling Markus."

"Oh. Copy. Bye."

Copy.

An unexpected Dad-ism to further muddle his head.

Matt felt eyes on him, glancing up to find a sympathetic Joss face—her brow knit, and chin resting on her seat back. He smiled his thanks and dialed Markus; the first ring lit up his head with a jolt.

Crap. My phone!

He sighed with the second ring, resigned to tossing this phone the instant the call was done.

Damnit, Joss's too.

It'd be a simple matter to track his phone back to the store in Greece, seeing what else was sold.

Or … This could work out perfectly. Yes, yes it does.

"Well now," Markus's words slithered through the tiny speaker. "To where are we driving, Matthew?"

Could he have a GPS trace already?

"Just headed to the drug store for tampons. So ... interesting news out of Kenya, eh?"

"Without a hand on my shoulder, is this the sort of bungling effort to which you're reduced?"

"Pretty much. Or maybe I just miss hearing your voice."

Markus held silent a beat, before replying, "Matthew, in the event of an erred impression, understand this: my attraction to you does not render me some manipulable twit."

Oops. He took it as flirtation.

"No, of course not," Matt said. "Honestly not my intent."

"Of course it was. Sadly, more bungling than the first." Not a trace of playful banter remained. He sounded genuinely hurt. "Mrs. Absko escaped the compound. She's safe from the President, but what happens next, who knows?"

She made it out! Though that last bit was perfectly ambiguous. Intentional? Threatening? Or simply a generic "Anything could happen out there in the world."?

"Well, thanks," Matt said with earnest. "I do hope that information I provided was helpful."

"Little helpful for Mr. Ostrovsky thus far. He waits to see."

"And the body?"

"Bod*ies*," Markus corrected. "All unearthed this morning. Press have already begun their onslaught." Detachment persisted, but at least the information was flowing.

"Man ..." Matt began, then eyed Grandma Bubsy through the rearview. Her gaze was glued to the increasingly busy highway, but the women had been silent since he'd begun his calls.

Intrigued by the sudden silence, Joss glanced back, and Matt perked his head toward Grandma. Joss caught the cue and acted at once.

"Grandma Bubsy, you never mentioned how you found those first pyramids on the internet."

"Truth be told, at first I didn't know they were undiscovered …"

Markus remained silent on the other end.

With Bubsy instantly engrossed, Matt resumed, "I only wish I had Absko's private cell number. The guy's probably a straw light of breaking." No reply. "Maybe a Skype account …"

Markus kept mute for a long while, such that Matt pulled the phone from his ear to verify the call was still active.

Finally, "Amaranth Vineyard. Google Hangout."

Matt snatched up his notepad and wrote down the name. Markus hung up before Matt could thank him.

He checked his signal. Full bars.

Beyond the windshield, Alexandria's first buildings stood silhouetted against the golden hour sun.

He opened the video call app and tapped in the account name. It was there.

A deep inhale.

Odds were, it wouldn't be this simple. Some assistant would have the phone on them, or an answering service screened all incoming communication. Matt knew that the face—a face the thought of which always gave him a headache—realistically, wouldn't just pop up in front of him, filling the phone screen. But Markus would most certainly have contact info that'd get Matt within two degrees of separation, if not one. If Absko wasn't nearby, the message would surely reach him in no time.

Exhale.

CALL

The classic telephone ring jangled from the speaker. Matt's face appeared in one corner, framed in a little square. He held the phone low, facing up at him, limiting the visible background to the van's beige roof, and a sliver of pale blue sky through the rear window.

A quick check up front. The outside world had swapped rural fields for aged suburbs. Bubsy was still talking about satellite photos. Joss *oohed* and *aahed* while her canny eyes greeted Matt's through her sun visor's mirror.

The ringing stopped.

A bouncing camera on the other end of the video call corrected its white balance, adjusting the overexposed glare, and resolved its focus. A suspicion-laden, golden-brown face coalesced. It was him. It was actually Absko, marching through a high-ceilinged hall. A chorus of hard soles clacking on smooth tile. Absko's furrowed brow twitched as his eyes scrutinized the unfamiliar bearded visage.

Matt centered his gaze on the little circular lens above his screen so the image in Absko's hand would stare directly into his eyes. Stressed background voices argued in Swahili. The shaky phone steadied as the President's pace slowed. He appeared on the verge of recollection. Matt's mouth ripened into an insolent smirk.

Abkso halted.

The din of footfalls stuttered to a stop as one of the voices asked, "What is it?"

The flash of shocked recognition had dissolved in an instant to bristling rage. "Leave me."

"Hi!" Matt began. Oozing with chipper cockiness, he spoke swiftly before Absko could interrupt. "It looks like you're super busy rearranging deck chairs on the Titanic, so I'll be quick and just say: first, Tuni is safe. I'll be taking care of her now. As you know, she has no interest in speaking with you ever again. Apparently, you—um—weren't all she'd hoped. You should tend to your own life, what little of it remains. Buh-bye!"

Matt's thumb hovered over the hang-up button, frozen by a burning need to witness a reaction. Plus, he no longer wished to conceal his location—quite the contrary.

Absko fought to exude composure, but even with the video's choked throughput, Matt observed a nostril quiver, neck muscles contracting, and taut lips striving to curl into a defiant smile.

"In a world so small," Absko finally said, "so ... *accessible* ... it's reckless to exchange security for pride."

Matt made a show of laughing and choking. "Pride? Is that the first stone you're casting?" He wiped faux tears from his eyes as he laughed on.

Grandma Bubsy had stopped talking and both women now watched the odd gregarious display through their respective mirrors.

Absko shed the false poise. He growled, "You apparently care nothing for your friends and family! I will swaddle you *both* in sheets of your sister and mothers' flesh! I will feed you your favorite pets' entrails! You, Matthew, may already be dead when this happens, but have no doubt it'll happen, and my whore wife will *certainly* not doubt she'll be very much *alive* and absent the mercy of eyelids when I open up her son in front of her and before I cut off her lips and extract her—"

Eyes widening and brow knit with hyperbolic terror, Matt interrupted, mocking him, "Favorite pet's entrails? Have you used that one before? You have, haven't you? Anyhow, fear not ..." Absko tried to interject again, barking something about Matt thinking this was all a joke, but without pause, Matt repeated, louder, "... *Fear not* about me doubting your ultra-villainous wrath, or whatever. I'm sure once you—or really *anyone* with narcissistic personality disorder— sets their mind to something, they're fully committed to staying the course. But considering how your world is crumbling around you, I *kinda* don't really see you making it another four hours with your head still attached to the rest of you—*maybe* six."

An eerie calm fell upon Absko's face. His eyelids sank to half-mast as he drew his phone closer, focusing on the camera as Matt had, and enunciated, "I've survived unimaginable warzones and—"

"Pffft! You survived *shit*. Save your fictional war stories for someone who hasn't explored every rancid corner of your memory. How about this, Mr. Survivor? I'm so confident of your imminent deadness that I'll save you the time tracking me down! Alexandria. Karmus Hilton. Tower two, room six-thirteen. Now, that's the

Karmus Hilton, not the Cornische over by the sea. I don't want you to get lost, okay? You've got toddlers to murder and skin blankets to wrap me in. No time to dilly-dally."

Absko's callous mug glared silently for a moment, and then disappeared.

Amaranth Vineyard ended the call.

Matt inhaled deep. Exhaling, he felt his neck and shoulders ease out of a rigid tension he'd only just then perceived.

Joss piped up from the front, "Well that sounded like a sensible, well-grounded, not-at-all-suicidal speech."

"I needed him to come here," Matt said flatly as he removed the battery from his phone.

Grandma Bubsy chimed in, "Honey, that didn't sound like a man I'd want in a thousand-mile radius of a thousand-foot pole."

He held up his phone battery, motioning Joss to pull hers, as well.

"One way to achieve complete strategic surprise," he said, "is to commit an act that makes no sense, or is even self-destructive."

Library of Alexandria
O. Von Corven, woodcut, circa 1870

SIXTEEN

Hello Steward,
The voice conveys knowledge.
The scribe preserves a word.

   Alexandria, Aegyptus – 271 CE

In the Governor's atrium yesterday, as Patra concluded her hour-long dialogue with her childhood friend and pseudo-sibling, Cassius, a strange thing had punctuated the increasingly warm exchange.

Shortly before they'd stood to say their farewells, Cassius had finally pledged his ongoing support, referring her to a former senior Centurion named Barbillus, available for hire along with a personal army of highly-trained warriors. He'd told her where to find Barbillus, how much she should expect to pay, and that it'd be best to go alone or with only one other.

Patra had thanked him, and the subsequent minutes exhausted all remaining wine as the conversation digressed to fond memories. Musing over a former city prefect for whom they'd shared contempt. Patra's father feeding an insatiably famished hippopotamus, rolling cabbage after cabbage down an embankment. The debacle before Cassius's wedding ceremony during which the sacrificial pig—only half-sacrificed—tore through the crowd, spraying blood, defiling pristine wool and linen.

"If ever there was a bad omen to be heeded," Cassius lamented.

He set elbows upon knees, casting his gaze floorward to the polished tile. He slid a palm over his smooth head, quietly chuckling.

Patra followed the thick, ring-laden fingers up his scalp, herding a roll of skin from forehead to crown.

"You know," she began, "we've never once acknowledged that time in your father's vineyard."

Cassius sat up. He said nothing, regarding her with only his characteristic vague smile, revealing no perceptible intent to reply.

To fill the air, she went on. "It may be long from your memory, but I've gone back there—in here—from time to time, replacing my young eyes with these, and I feel just so … *absurd*." She lowered her voice. "We two probed and rubbed and squeezed for *ages*, and yet it wasn't until the kiss that I understood what was going on! In my silly mind, it'd all been a fascinating investigation! Looking back, some years later, I supposed that if we'd pubesced alike, or—if I recall my own flowering correctly—had the encounter been just eight months later, we'd have found ourselves splayed and stacked, no doubt."

His placid face held.

Uncertain whether she'd overstayed her welcome, or perhaps failed to emphasize her gratitude for his support, Patra bent forward, reaching out to caress his hand, but he leant back, reclining against the pillows, and began twisting one of his rings around its finger. She touched his knee instead, and noticed him brooding on her hand.

Both had then stood to say their farewells, and Cassius—apprehension saddling his face—added, "Never mind Barbillus and his mercenaries. I'll send a century of my city guards to the Musaeum." And then he stepped forward, wrapped his arms around her middle, and pulled their bodies together, resting his cheek on her shoulder.

The pair hadn't shared a hug since adolescence. So taken aback was she that five seconds may have passed before she allowed her floating arms to drop and return the embrace. Cassius's chest rose and fell against hers. Was that a whiff poached from her palla? The soft, fleeting hum of a lover?

He'd released her and met her eyes, smiling. "I don't want you to be afraid. Get your collection moved to the Serapeum as fast as you can, and leave the Musaeum to me."

Crossing the palace's garden to the rear gate, Patra had mulled those final minutes with Cassius. By the time she'd reached the delivery road's end, she'd deduced what had happened.

Just as she'd suspected, he'd planned to betray her, but only at first. Somewhere along the way—perhaps the more they spoke, the longer those numbed eyes beheld her—he changed his mind.

Initially, this mercenary, Barbillus, and his army would arrive at the Musaeum gates, allowed inside to inspect the walls' strengths and weaknesses, and instead capture or slaughter any member in sight. But then it was *"Never mind Barbillus ..."* Forget he ever mentioned the name. And the embrace: an unspoken apology for an unspeakable plot. To squeeze and absorb the warmth of this being he'd nearly forsaken.

* * *

The city guards arrived late that night, and at an auspicious moment. The Emperor's land attacks thus far had been small, harassing excursions meant to either assess or taunt the city's defenders, while the majority of the armada loomed at sea—a full-force assault possible any second.

In the observatory—the Musaeum's highest point—Patra rested her elbows on the balustrade, stretching her sore back as she surveyed the beleaguered city with Philip. Twilight had nearly surrendered to dusk, and the smoke wafting from a string of fires along the coast cloaked the harbor and much of the sea beyond.

"Have they seized the lighthouse?" Philip asked.

Patra stood up straight, peering out to the dim, gray space in the sky where, for her entire life, at this hour, a brilliant light had unfailingly shone. "It's possible, though that's not why it stands dark. Orestes has kept it unlit these past three nights to dissuade attacks."

"Wise," Philip murmured. He yawned and rubbed his eyes. "Back to it? Kaleb believes we're over halfway there."

Patra sighed and turned to follow him. "You know he hasn't–"

"Hold on," Philip interrupted, and dashed back to the balustrade. "The smoke …" He studied the entire panorama, scrutinizing every faint patch of light outside the Musaeum walls. "Couldn't it be a cunning tactic to conceal the armada's movements?"

He was right, and while the fires had been set seemingly at random throughout the day, the smoke's distribution now appeared spaced ideally to create this veil.

She whispered, "Then the attack comes now."

"There!" Philip said with a jerk.

Patra looked and, indeed, ranks of armored warriors had freshly rounded a corner, marching their way. Tight columns snaked from behind the Caesareum's southeast corner, advancing toward the Street of the Sema.

"We must alert the others!" Philip hushed, as if the approaching legion would hear him over the rolling footfalls and clanking metal.

"Yes," Patra breathed. "Go." But she remained frozen on her high perch, entranced by the parade as it reached the Musaeum wall, and split in two—one half continuing on toward the main gate, the other wrapping around the outer wall.

The complex was surrounded in less than ten minutes.

But as she, and the frantic others in the courtyard below, awaited the crash of a battering ram, a new threat arrived silently from the west: armorless Roman fighters in dark garb, carrying only short swords and bows, spilled from the Temple District onto the adjacent street.

The street, however, had been the closest these stealthy intruders came to the Musaeum, as they hadn't, in fact, come to rejoin a legion of noisier brethren. They'd come alone. So instead of witnessing the new arrivals greet fellow imperial soldiers at the wall, Patra watched them stop in their tracks, and then retreat, cut off by the two hundred city guards sent by Cassius to surround and defend the complex. Not only had the Governor delivered on his pledge, he'd bolstered the donation twofold!

While Patra required no further provocation to hustle, the narrow escape had shaken her, and everyone in her charge. By morning, they'd lost eighteen more dedicated allies, leaving seventeen, including the stewards. With all of their horses, donkeys, and carts dispensed to fleeing members, Kaleb had had to secure replacements from neighbors.

Last night's close call had quashed any lingering questions as to the Emperor's primary target, and all of those kind souls who'd previously declared their eternal support for the Library had now reexamined their priorities—once the Musaeum fell, its wealthy neighbors didn't want the Emperor's men to find they'd lent a single donkey or horse to the offenders, thence greeting an army at their own villa's gate. Of course, none cited this as basis for retrieving their animals. They'd all simply found their palaces suddenly overcome by the need for laborious upkeep.

Regardless, the dedicated few Musaeum members and sympathizers who remained to help, did so with only their limbs and backs, but only until reaching the Serapeum...

* * *

Despite five centuries of invasions, weather, and intentional destruction, the Serapeum remained Alexandria's grandest temple. After the city fell to Rome, the already magnificent precinct was renovated to repair damage, widen the expansive courtyard's surrounding walls, and to reflect modern Roman architecture. But the temple's redesigners had done more than extend perimeter walls.

Following Lucas, a Temple of Serapis priest, through a brisk subterranean corridor, Patra observed the milky skylights embedded in the high-vaulted ceiling. Shafts of sunlight plunged from the small squares, banding the wide passage with diffuse bars of light and dark.

How many weeks had it been since Patra stepped over those anonymous tiles, unaware what hid below, on her way to meet with Zenobia? And now, as half of Alexandria's small fleet lay bubbling beneath the harbor, the other half captured by Emperor Antonius's armada, and the first significant land skirmishes beginning west of the city, did Zenobia reflect on their conversation and regret her negligence?

"They are here, Steward." Lucas motioned to a torch-lit passage off the main corridor. Not much older than her, the warmhearted priest carried himself like a decrepit old dog—hunched back, quaking hands. Even his voice meandered from him atop wheezes.

Patra peeked in, observing long shadows and flickering light from deep within. "No one's entombed in there?"

"No, Steward. The Romans purged all of the catacombs during transition, and these new ones were never put to use. This tunnel …" He hesitated, nodding farther down the main corridor. "… leads to the Temple altar. Its primary use … it's for *enhancing* ceremonies."

"No concern of mine, Lucas. May I?" She gestured to the catacomb entrance.

Lucas bid her forth with a trembling hand: *Please do.*

Just inside, Patra extracted a torch from a rack, lighting it with the wall sconce, and continued into the catacomb. Three or more figures up ahead unloaded carts with promising tempo.

Lucas called behind her, "Two more carts from the Library just entered the main corridor, Steward."

"Thank you again," she replied without turning. "We all appreciate your support."

As Patra neared the Musaeum aides, one of the young men startled, shielding his eyes from the torches to glimpse the intruder. He appeared to recognize her, swatting the leg of another boy behind him—or, moving out of shadow, not a boy but a young man she knew from one of her classes—as he shoved three scrolls into an over-packed recess in the wall.

"It's Steward Supatra," Patra reassured. "And don't trouble about delicacy. Tertius here has the right idea. Haste precedes care. You're almost through with this load?"

"Yes, Steward," said the first boy.

The third boy shoved the last bundle of scrolls into an already full alcove, papyrus crunching in protest. Stepping into Patra's torchlight, he said in a heavy Egyptian accent, "That why I heared this scrolls good only for help fire?"

The first boy, ostensibly the youngest of the three, chided his colleague. "Harwa!"

"No, my friend," Patra quietened. The drone of grating wheels entered the catacomb, signaling the arrival of more carts. "It's warranted. You've all undertaken a perilous responsibility, and deserve to know if you risk your lives with cause."

"I not know all this words," Harwa said with eyes downcast.

Tertius attempted translation, but Patra relieved him, repeating herself in the boy's tongue, and adding, "We would not waste your time or our own on worthless scrolls. Every tomb filled is akin to a century of study. I thank you." She kissed Harwa's head, then returned to Greek, addressing his companions and the new arrivals behind her. "I thank you all. Thank you. Your efforts equal those of the scribes who created these works. To save them now is equivalent to having written them then. Thank you."

As Lucas led her back to the stairs, describing how his workers would later seal and mask the shaft entrance, Patra's thoughts remained with those boys. She'd believed her assurances as they'd left her tongue, but should one or more of the aides be killed, would they have truly died defending the collection?

None of them could read a single word on the papyri they'd dared to transport across the besieged city, and hopefully they'd never know their true contents: Hebrew bills of sale, debt lists in Demotic, Aramaic legal documents, personal letters, marriage and divorce records, shipping manifests, apprenticeship contracts for flute players and harpists—scrolls only good for helping start a fire.

* * *

Wary of watchful eyes on their porters, Kaleb had devised the manner with which the scroll collection would be evacuated. The moment the Emperor's fleet dropped anchor beyond the harbor, Musaeum members commenced gathering thousands of decoy scrolls, mixing the assorted legal and commerce documents with genuine Library scrolls, albeit commonplace pieces with abundant examples elsewhere.

Prior to losing their beasts of burden, a team would leave the Musaeum through one of various known entries, hurriedly guiding their donkey and laden cart straight to the Serapeum's catacombs. Sans the aid of work animals, carts were pushed by hand, but by then the bulk of decoy scrolls had already made it beneath the Temple.

Other members, clad in slave's garb, occasionally steered refuse carts at arbitrary intervals through separate gates. All day and night, still more individuals trickled from the complex, burdened with some form of sack, crate, litter, or anything in which one could conceal two hundred or more scrolls. They, too, ventured out in nondescript attire, and ambled toward locations inconsequent, before zigzagging back around toward the Serapeum, though these couriers—those bearing genuine papyri of value—would never approach the Temple's grand entrance.

Near Alexandria's towering south wall lay a Coptic temple closed for renovation, the large storeroom at its rear gradually filling with precious scrolls. Across the street, Nelpus—one of the Musaeum's wealthiest members and a Library scribe—owned a large villa. Here, too, inside a grand bathhouse, scroll mounds swelled wider and taller with each hour.

Behind Nelpus's bathhouse stood a high, vine-draped wall with a linen-toned access gate that a passer-by must seek out to discern anything but a continuous, plaster-coated wall. Exiting the villa through this gateway, onto the main north-south thoroughfare, one found themselves faced with but a single, all-consuming view: The Serapeum.

Peering left from Nelpus's gate, the road ended at the city's south wall. The wall was a short jaunt from either the Coptic temple or Nelpus's villa, and it was there Kaleb had enlisted a number of his fellow Kushmen to receive bundles of salvaged scrolls inside a dry canal duct, mere steps from the Serapeum's secluded rear embankment.

The Kushmen took the bundles and loaded them onto donkeys outside the wall, and then guided the herd to the nearby Lake Mareotis shore. From there, waiting Musaeum members gathered the bundles into a train of small, tethered riverboats, and then rowed eight or more hours to a granary storehouse at the mouth of the Nile. Every hour or two, they'd pass one of the other crews on their way back to the lake shore for another load.

Of the roughly 700,000 scrolls in the Library's collection, a little more than half had either made it to the granaries, or were already on their way. Included in these were the 43,000 works the stewards considered "imperative" to save, 130,000 deemed "critical," and, thus far, around half of the 415,000 they'd branded "important." The remaining 100,000 were augmented by more worthless old legal documents, and spread throughout the Library's stacks as ill-conceived decoys.

It wouldn't take an extraordinary intellect to seek out and expose this ruse, proceeding on to unearth the scrolls' true hideout: the library at the Serapeum, now brimming with its recent additions (also enlarged with city records in little-known languages).

But wait. The stewards are far craftier than that. They'd be the sorts to create an even deeper ruse! Let us seek out a third *layer to this ploy!*

And from beneath the Serapeum, crammed into catacombs behind painstakingly camouflaged, freshly sealed walls, they'd produce the final cache. In the courtyard above, soldiers would hurl the precious papyri atop a growing pile. Perhaps Emperor Antonius himself would set the mound ablaze.

And no one need bother digging for a still-deeper fourth layer.

While informants from every city quarter confirmed hearing of the Library's clandestine relocation to the Serapeum, none seemed to know of any other covert exploits.

* * *

On her way out the Serapeum, Patra bid Lucas farewell, declined the offer of a chariot to shuttle her home, and began descending the substantial stairway to the street. From her lofty vantage point, the entirety of the city lay before her, from the vast western necropolis, to Pharos Island's broad wing, cradling the West Harbor, its slender talon and the Lighthouse shielding the Great Harbor; the Musaeum perched atop its lush, flowery knoll; the Caesarium and Amphitheatre; all the way past the Jewish Quarter to the Hippodrome beyond the wall … were it visible.

The noonday sun shone bright overhead. Clusters of evacuating citizens trudged southward and eastward—those optimistic few who believed the impending invasion threatened not ordinary citizens, but the insolent elite across the city. The majority of Alexandrians still maintained this outlook, but something had changed the minds of those now littering the streets so many days after the initial exodus. The fires perhaps, or one of the isolated skirmishes meandering too close to home, or vandals, or looters.

Lingering a few steps beneath the stairway's summit, Patra inspected the shrouded scene beyond the Jewish Quarter. A dust storm obscured everything outside the east wall.

But nowhere else?

Still scrutinizing the dust cloud, Patra slowly, became aware of a commotion in the streets below. It began as a vague recognition of increased activity—a persistent child's intensifying tug—but her concentration held.

In an instant, her ears perceived a rising howl, and she finally noticed the chaotic activity in her foreground. Glancing about, she beheld a hastening rush of evacuees. Like a crested and crashed ocean wave, wailing crowds filled in the streets, compressing and advancing in a uniform arc. It was as though herds of rampaging bulls had materialized in the middle of the city, driving the previously dawdling masses outward in every southerly direction.

Patra composed herself and checked the Coptic district roads to her left. Finding them relatively clear and calm, she scuttled down the mountain of steps.

Egyptians eyed her as she dashed past the market, her palla flailing behind her. All appeared oblivious or indifferent to the neighboring goings-on.

Moments later, as Patra turned right onto the busy Canopic Road, clanks and clinks rang out from a troubling direction. A new wave of distraught Alexandrians fled toward her, and she yielded the road, opting instead for the shaded stoa. The atypically few merchants along the columns and walls craned their necks to assess the commotion, gauging whether it warranted abandoning their wares.

Patra crossed the turbulent intersection from the stoa to the adjacent shrine's portico. The streets were near empty now. Creeping between columns, dread bubbled in her throat. Would she soon behold slaughtered city guards littering the Musaeum perimeter?

Nearing the end of the portico, she heard the first shriek: a sudden, guttural yowl, aborted as fast as it'd begun. Shouted orders, rattling armor, pleading voices, more screams, distant swords hacking away at stubborn locks.

Horrified, Patra slid back into the shadows. What could she do? Nothing. There was nothing she could do.

An onrushing scream behind her—obstructed, but growing less so. She slid around to the outside of the column until just a sliver of the Musaeum gate entered view. The screamer stopped, or paused for air.

"Please!" a teenaged boy implored, somewhere just out of sight, inside the complex wall.

"Get around behind him!" snapped a gruff voice.

"Run!" cried a woman from a far off place.

An angry man demanded, "Why are the gates still open?"

A sword's glancing blow against stone.

"I've done nothing!" cried the boy, and an instant later, he appeared from the gateway, stumbling backward with his hands before him.

"You're running away!" From the gate emerged a city guard, spear in hand. "Stop walking, or I'll put this through your eye!"

Patra slipped behind the column once more. Her chest refused a breath—maybe a small sip ... no, no only as deep as her neck. There were no piles of butchered city guards. The guards *were* the butchers.

"I'm not running!" shouted the boy, begging, and then a gravelly skidding, the thud of a body tumbling down stairs.

"Go!" roared a guard. "*Go!*"

Hustling leather soles on sandy stone.

Patra shut her eyes as if they were her ears.

A grisly *squitch* as a spear, no doubt, punctured the boy's abdomen.

"Got him!"

Weak, bewildered cries, as though the young man simply failed to comprehend why this was happening to him—it was the unfairness of it that seared his stomach. But not for long ...

"Move!"

Like a brick to a melon, a broadsword split the wounded youth's skull.

Patra gasped though her nose. Her eyes still shut as if glued, she clawed at the pillar behind her, wishing to clench it in her fists.

Seconds later, a mother's howl buckled Patra's legs. Over and over, "Phorus! Phorus! Phorus! ..." and Patra crumpled onto the hot stone.

"Silence her!"

260

"Phorus! Phorus! Phor—!"

* * *

The chorus of carnage had ended, replaced by more insistent pounding and smashing, and reassuring calls to open doors. *"You won't be harmed!"* How many survivors remained blockaded inside Library or Musaeum walls? And how long until an exasperated commander summoned a battering ram or some other siege weapons? Were Kaleb or Philip among the trapped, dead, or somewhere else entirely? Patra wouldn't wait to find out. There had to be a way to rescue whomever stood defiant behind those doors.

She bolted from her hiding spot, back down the Canopic Road, her mind awash with unviable ideas, all while defying the nagging pinch of this treachery's source.

"I do hope that all you've shared was for the benefit of our audience?" Zenobia had said in Isis's Temple. Patra had confirmed it was so, but her heart still ached ever Wahbi's return.

"Sorry, yes," Patra had replied, shaking the tension from her face. *"Thank you for playing along. It's also why I shared plans with the Governor, though now I believe he may genuinely support us. He's sending city guards to defend the Musaeum."*

Zenobia had raised a skeptical eyebrow. *"I wouldn't rely upon it. One may always have faith in the treachery of their closest friends."*

Patra had cast this aside like any other pessimistic notion with which she disagreed. Nobody understood her relationship with Cassius, or their decades of history. No one would grasp the nuance and depth of the moment they'd shared yesterday.

Leaning slightly into a doorway, she peered into the Trade Office's skylit atrium.

She whispered, "Hello? Is anyone here?"

No answer. She sidled inside.

Upon reflection, Cassius had seemed intent on deceit when she'd first arrived (serpentine words from the wretch, Thomas Egnatius, still twisting inside his ears). She'd gone through it all in her head. She was supposed to contact the mercenary, Barbillus. A dubious pursuit. But after her conversation with Cassius—reminiscing, reconnecting—he'd shown a change of heart.

It'd all made sense before: She commissions a scoundrel to bring his fellow disgraced warriors to "protect" the Library, and just when everyone feels safe, their protector attacks the Library.

But Barbillus didn't.

The city guard did.

Which meant, setting aside the unlikely event the guards had been usurped by Antonius, the city guard had *come* with the intent to massacre. Was Cassius's change of heart, therefore, the *inverse* of what she'd inferred?

That warm embrace—almost sensual—was it goodbye?

Patra eased down a hall and poked her head into a deep, narrow office. At the other end, a thin sliver of sunlight lined the edges of an exterior door, illuminating a band of floating dust. A wide work table sat along one side of the room. With her eyes still adjusting, she could vaguely discern codices stacked on the table, and maybe some loose papyrus sheets.

Stepping inside, she spotted a dark rectangle in the corner nearest her. A closet. Appearing as good a hiding spot as any, she inched in, probing before her with fingers and toes. She felt shelves on one side, and a bundle of leaning sticks in a corner. Brooms, perhaps. She slid down the one open corner, and sat there in absolute darkness, massaging her sore feet.

Cassius had planned to support her. She must have said something to reverse this. Thinking back, visualizing his face in the closing minutes … It was the vineyard! That's when he'd gone mute, staring with that inscrutable smirk.

It meant she'd hurt him, and deeply so.

It meant he loved her.

He condemned her and every person she held dear to a violent death, and venom of that potency could only seethe from a broken heart. Now, her students, colleagues, and maybe even her closest friends either lay slashed and mangled, or barricaded inside structures not built to resist a determined intruder.

Their fear suddenly stabbed her in the chest. What hope could they have at this point? Who could possibly save them?

They'd soon—if not already—succumb to the reality of imminent pain, terror, and death. Best to comfort and hold each other, and share a collective strength, wherein, as individuals, none remained.

Even if she were able to rally every willing sympathizer in the vicinity, courage alone wouldn't transform affluent citizens into the small Army she needed. She'd have to …

Barbillus!

The city guard's deception hardly served as evidence to the mercenary's honor, but if she could find him, and if he didn't slit her throat on sight, he'd surely accept the fortune she planned to offer.

* * *

Vibrant, terraced gardens gave way to sterile dirt patches, aging mudbrick homes and markets, collapsed walls and crowded wells. In Rhakotis, the native Egyptian quarter, Patra asked a Coptic glass blower if Barbillus worked in his shop. Formerly, but not for some time, it seemed. Last he heard, Barbillus was doing masonry in the Temple District.

With much of the Temple District abandoned, it was easy to pinpoint active construction sites. Patra located Barbillus, a bronze colossus of a man—though with more fat in the middle than muscle in the chest—perched atop an ornate new façade, chipping away at the excess mortar between stones.

From the scaffolding high above, he called back to her, "You call Cassius friend? He's a coward and lackey. He sent you to *me?*"

She yelled up at him, "I'd share every detail of all that's brought me to you with this offer, but we may already be too late. Just know that your name was mentioned as a fearless warrior with a strong army for hire."

Barbillus laughed. "Those words were not spoken by Cassius, but I know who *you* are, and I'll take your word you can deliver on your bid. What happens if we get there and everyone's already dead?"

"You'll receive one quarter, and then we'll part ways."

"I'd make more than that on this job over the next month, but they don't take kindly here to a man abandoning waged work. And here they don't thrust javelins at the work force. Tell me, Miss Steward, is your word-stock truly as sparse as you exhibit? You must think me a foolish man, especially here toiling at the goddess's house as war looms but a whisper away?"

"It is not, and I do not. Perhaps you alone, wiser than your fleeing competitors, engage your skills in the most erudite of chores: tending to Venus's shrine as her lover's sword arcs overhead. In truth, I think of you—with guarded-yet-burning optimism—as my quiescent hero."

Barbillus chuckled. "Wiser, perhaps, but for the graces of Plutus, not Venus … *'Quiescent hero'* … If only so scholarly a mind as yours should have plucked the tiny urchin Barbillus from the streets of Ancyra."

"Then said mind likely would have now reached its hundred and twentieth year of scholarship. Now, if I've amply satiated your thirst for lively discourse, those dear to me live or die by our haste. I trust the coin also speaks to you more than parlance?"

Barbillus clapped white powder from his hands, crawled to the scaffolding, and began climbing down. "At present. I've two offspring I'd see made citizens through means other than the Legion. If those dear to you have already died, I'll receive one *half*, and then we part ways." He leapt the last six feet, landing in front of Patra.

"Fine." She shook his dusty hand. "How long to assemble your army? As I said, the Library's doors may have already been breached."

He flashed a wincing smile. "I probably wouldn't use that term to describe the group I can assemble as fast as you want. For some strange reason, city residents have been packing their belongings and hastening south."

"There are two hundred trained city guards in there," she replied, furious he decided to wait until now to share this news. "How many do you think you can amass?"

"If you want an Army, go talk to your beloved Augusta. Hmm, no. I just recalled how she took them all and abandoned the city."

What did this man know of Zenobia? Nothing.

Patra scowled. "She was drawing Antonius away from the city. Successfully, if you hadn't noticed."

"An army gives chase to fleeing enemies, lest they return another day to catch you off-guard. Call it 'drawing away,' call it whatever you wish."

"That's precisely what she—"

Barbillus cut her off. "Every second counts, remember? You want me to embark on your mission, or you seek more lively discourse?" She clenched her jaw and waved him on. With a more kindly manner, he said, "You head back to a safe hiding spot, Steward. If there's anyone in there with a heartbeat, I'll bring them to the racetrack by the Serapeum—east end. And cover up all that …" He motioned to her head. "In most parts of the city today, Musaeum members have more to fear from Alexandrians than legionaries."

MICHAEL SIEMSEN

SEVENTEEN

Vicinity of Ngong Hills, Kenya – Present day

Forty minutes from the Presidential Palace—Tuni's bejeweled prison for the past several years—a remote, derelict farmhouse lay at the end of a rutted, weed-riddled dirt road. Its paintless corrugated roof and exterior walls had long ago surrendered to rust, much like the property's scattered collection of discarded vehicles, appliances, and farming equipment.

Yesterday morning, on their way here, Tuni had done her best to remember each turn her professed rescuers had taken. At the very least, she knew the highway and the overcrowded town they'd passed through before well-kept asphalt became less so, transitioning to wider-spread shanties that matched well the increasingly demoralized concrete roads, followed by the final unpaved stretch. Undeserving of *"road"* designation, it was more of an untamed overgrowth through which someone had once stamped tire tracks. Alexander had giggled for the first few minutes of bouncing, and then complained for most of the remainder.

"S'okay, s'okay." The favorite phrase of the man in the front passenger seat. "Close to here."

Tuni's thoughts focused not on whether these men were trustworthy, or wondering if she might be in danger, but on the *magnitude* of the danger. She had asked twice where they were going, neither time receiving a remotely straight answer.

After that, she'd decided the best strategy would be to avoid appearing a flight risk, ensuring more opportunities for escape. If her marriage had taught her anything, it was how to smile in a nightmare. Though her freedom might have come easier—and without the current snag—God, she hoped it'd turn out only a *snag*—if she'd more convincingly feigned happiness with Jivu.

Now, she sat on a tractor tire "chair" inside a sweltering shack akin to a sauna in the devil's colon. She'd spent the past twenty-four hours happy-facing both her mysterious rescuers/captors, and her confused son, so he wouldn't be afraid.

She hadn't yet gathered much info on the Russian duo. 1) They weren't Russian, but Ukrainian. 2) The younger man—thin, early twenties, curly blond hair, spectacles—was called "Zyana" by his partner, and Zyana didn't like it.

With evening approaching, Yulian—average build, late forties, crewcut silver hair that made his short-trimmed black beard appear unnaturally black—had apparently told Zyana to go fetch dinner. Zyana replied, pointing a thumb to the car parked outside.

Yulian grinned and retorted, pantomiming swinging across tree branches like a monkey, and laughed.

An irritated Zyana snagged the keys from the cardboard box "table," and stomped out.

Yulian spun round on the cushionless barstool, radiant with self-satisfaction. "Ah-bee-ZYAH-nah!" he enunciated to Tuni, then raised an arm to tickle an armpit. "Hoo hoo hoo, hah hah!"

Tuni obliged with a smile.

"Zyana real name Stepan, but we say Zyana for like monkey: *ah-bee-zyana*. He say car petrol low, I say find *trees* to get to store. He hates!" Yulian performed the monkey-swinging motion again. His shoulders shook as he giggled.

"I climb trees good," Alexander said without looking up from his Lego instructions. In the fusty room's corner, primary-colored bricks littered the floor around him.

Weary of the constant questions and complaints, Zyana had run out to buy books and toys this morning, though no broom, as Tuni had requested.

"Why there's no trees anywhere?" Alexander continued.

"Why *aren't* there trees anywhere," Tuni corrected.

"That's what I said."

Tuni inhaled a silent sigh and glanced toward Yulian. He met her eyes with a grandfather's knowing amusement. She seized the chance.

"Do you have children, Yulian?"

An emphatic nod. He held up five fingers.

"Grandchildren?"

"Many many. Some not from mine, but, you know, like with cousin and marriage. *Mpwa.*" Yulian's Swahili was even more limited than his English, but he often used it well filling in gaps.

"Nieces and nephews, yes," Tuni said. "Children are such a blessing, aren't they? I'm just so eager to show this one the world outside of … *there*." She scowled toward where she imagined the Presidential Palace.

"Outside where, Mama?" Alexander said. He was always listening.

"The whole world, bubu. You'll see it all." She turned back to Yulian. "Do you suppose—?"

"We have to go home first," Alexander cut in, "or tell Baba to bring Rafiki and my toys. You say I can have one toy, but I got none."

Yulian clapped his hands onto his knees, averted his eyes as he stood with an achy groan, and moseyed to the front door. Alexander's interruption had blocked Tuni from reaching her point. Frustration overtook her.

"They got you toys, bubu. Many many toys, and books you haven't touched. They were being nice—didn't have to bring you anything at all. And you want *Daddy* to bring you things here, really?"

He glared up at her, pouting, defiant, and nodded yes.

She wrestled herself out of the tire, and onto her feet. "Is that so? Have Daddy come *here*?"

As he watched, she ran fingers over the scabbed gash in her cheek, then probed the wide bruise on the opposite. Bending over, she reached out to touch the bump on Alexander's forehead—the one Daddy gave him. He recoiled, scowling. He knew exactly what she was saying, even if he wished to forget what had happened.

"But you're right, angel. You need your blanket and *those* toys. If Baba wants to hurt Mama some more, I'll just have to deal with it. Your things are more important." She felt like an evil, manipulative witch, but she couldn't help it any more than Alexander could help his own feelings—uprooted from the only world he'd known, now in a strange place with strange men; the trauma of witnessing everything before their escape. As sickening as it made her feel, he probably missed his father already.

Head hung low, Alexander watched his fingers rolling a Lego brick over and over in his lap. He murmured something.

Tuni moved as if to find Yulian out front. "What's that, bubu?"

He mumbled a bit louder.

"I can't understand you, dear. You have to speak—"

"I said he doesn't have to come!"

"No?" Tuni said theatrically. "Are you sure? What about your toys?"

"I'll play with these ones," he grumbled, returning to his Lego building.

"And your blanket? You'll wait for me to buy you a new Rafiki?"

"Yes!" he barked.

We don't yell at Mama, but she'd let it go this time. He'd gotten the point, and hopefully she'd never have to suffer another peep about having Daddy stop by with a few things. Alexander sulked as he continued building, and Tuni went to the window. Through the cracked, yellowed plexiglass she spotted Yulian's face aglow from his cell phone, ambling about the gravel and weeds, smoking a cigarette as he spoke.

She leaned left to check the driveway. No sign of a returning Zyana, and with twilight waning, he'd certainly have the headlamps on. This was their chance! A final glance at Yulian—still on the phone, meandering a few dozen yards in front of the farmhouse.

"Bubu," she whispered as she strode to him. He looked up, about to answer. She shushed him with a finger to her lips, and said near his face, "It's quiet secret adventure time again. Put these down a moment, and come with me. No words now, hm?"

He grasped what she meant—moreso than she'd have expected—and he nodded, wide-eyed, and took her hand. Through the doorway into the house's one bedroom, across the matted carpet, past the coil-spring bedframe, they reached the rear window. It seemed at first the window had been sealed shut, but a second fierce pull jerked it free, and sent it squealing and crunching over the track. Alexander and Tuni both flinched, and she knew Yulian had to have heard it out front.

Wasting no time, she boosted Alexander over the threshold, then climbed up and joined him in the prickly brush. After listening for an instant, she hauled him up and ran.

In the daylight, the house enjoyed an unhampered view of a wide hill, its peak speckled with tall, white wind turbines. Nearing dusk, she could now make out the faint silhouette against a midnight blue sky. The hilltop appeared taller than any building in New York City, but the approach hadn't looked all that steep to her. If it proved too much, they'd walk around it, and see what's on the other side. In her mind, everything in the other direction was far scarier than ending up lost.

As they reached one hundred yards from the house, Yulian's voice called behind them.

"No run, ledi! Come back, ledi!"

Trudging on, she watched the uneven ground before her. The last thing they needed was for her to roll an ankle. Alexander felt to be gaining a couple pounds with each dozen steps. Soon, she'd have to put him down and have him jog with her.

"Please, ledi! Not safe! I can't chase!"

Keep yelling, Yulian, she thought. It was good to hear his voice grow more distant. And each time he called out reassured her that he had no intention of pulling out a gun and shooting into the darkness.

"It has the wild, ledi! Not safe! The baby with ... wild!"

Safer with wild than kidnappers, comrade.

"Please come! Simba waporini, ledi!"

Lions? That can't be true.

"Lions, Mama?"

"Not true, bubu," she panted. "He's kidding."

"He sound scared ... And this hurts. Can I walk?"

She set him down, taking a moment to breathe. The light from the farmhouse was a tiny square. No sign of Yulian, but dusk had now fully set in.

"I'm scared, Mama. How you know there's no lions?"

She wished he'd stop saying it. Each time the word was spoken made it sound a fraction more possible. When was the last time she heard of someone being attacked by a wild cat? Last year? But that was in the Preserve—the National Park.

Oh, bollocks ...

It suddenly struck her what lay on the other side of this hill. The highways they'd taken, the exit, right turn, left, the fork, and then on in that direction for what felt like forever. This hill was the National Park's southern border.

You bonehead. You daft cow. "Mmm, that hill looks familiar!"

Gazing back at the little light, Yulian's faint voice still beckoned, but she was tuning him out.

"I want to go back, Mama."

She looked down at Alexander, his eyes ashine with stars.

She took his hand. "Yes, bubu. Let's go back."

EIGHTEEN

Alexandria, Egypt – Present day

In light of the yellow minivan earlier parked on Grandma Bubsy's street, Matt convinced the spirited archaeologist to let them drop her off somewhere else. After she and Joss swapped seats, Grandma Bubsy opted for her office in the Al-Labban district.

"I've got a poop-ton of Ministry reqs to file, anyway," she said, turning to Joss. "Just follow the signs to the Temple/Rhakotis Village, but you're going to turn right before we get there. I'll tell you when."

Matt perked up from the van's back row. "The Temple? Rhakotis?"

"Yes, sir," she replied, and swigged from her water bottle.

He caught Joss's curious look in the rearview mirror.

"Temple of Serapis," he explained. "The Serapeum."

"Correctamundo, amigo," Grandma Bubsy said. She motioned to the high-rise buildings on the left side of the street. "If these weren't in the way, right now you'd see a great big pillar holding up the sky. Just don't call it 'Pompey's Pillar,' for the love of Chrysler."

"Diocletian's Column," Matt said just as Joss passed through an intersection.

A clear strip of sky flashed by, exposing the towering monument, only a few blocks away.

"Whup, that was it!" Grandma pointed. "Didja see it? We can stop by there, if you like. I mean … I don't have all afternoon, but it's really quite breathtaking."

"Yes, please," Matt said. "That'd be fantastic. Just a quick stop, if you really don't mind."

"Sure don't," she said. "Turn left up here, Ms. Joss."

* * *

Joss peered up at the looming stone pillar—so much taller now that she stood right at its base—and wondered what occasion was so momentous that people decided this thing just had to be made. The nearby bronze plaque pegged its height at eighty-eight feet, and the column alone, carved from a single piece of red granite, weighed 285 tons. But the only history mentioned on the plaque (at least the section in English) said it was made in 297 AD to honor the Roman Emperor, Diocletian, for the successful repression and murders of ancient Alexandrians.

Matt knelt a short distance from her, gazing absently at the shabby apartment buildings that blocked the seaward views, as he plucked little rocks from the dirt and flicked them away.

She called to him, "Hey, you seen this thing when it was brand new?"

He kept on with the pebbles. "Nah. That went up a couple decades later … honoring the Emperor who suppressed a bunch of rebelling Alexandrians, bringing the city back under Rome's control."

"Oh, so is this for *the* dude? I thought his name was Antonius."

"It is … was." He stood up, ambling over to her. "The pillar was put up for Diocletian—a different Emperor than Antonius— who did basically the same horrible stuff as Antonius, except Diocletian was actually trying to quell a rebellion and dethrone a self-appointed Emperor named Domitianus. In Patra's time, Emperor Antonius was only using that whole 'savage Zenobia took over!' thing as an excuse. He did what he did because his ego had been stabbed. Only the agony and blood of his *'attackers'* could satisfy him. I think the Library's destruction had a few different purposes. Punishment, of course, but also a message to other 'uppity' intellectuals around— this is what happens when you try to express yourself. Third, I believe he wanted to take the whole city down a few notches. Alexandria was the wealthiest, most cultured, beautiful city in the world. Nowadays, people say it was the Paris of ancient times. He wanted to put them in their place. 'Everything you have here, everything you think is so much better than everyone else, it can all be taken away.'"

Grandma Bubsy appeared, making her way up the short hill from the visitor's center. "My, oh my. Those facilities are *not* for the faint of heart." Reaching the top of the rise, she paused to catch her breath, pulled off her hat, and wiped her forehead on her sleeve. "Just couldn't wait for the office. You need to use it, Ms. Joss?"

Joss frowned and waved an *I'll pass.*

"Probably wise," Grandma said, and peered around. "Sites like this are always a mix for me. Beautiful and inspiring, gives you a more physical sense of the history. But centuries of souvenir-takers, vandals, and everything? So much more is lost to those who actually appreciate a place than in the wars that ruined it in the first place. Depressing. That's why I prefer my *buried* treasures." She winked. "We ready to scoot?"

"Yeah, Joss said. "Matt was just telling me about this emperor and why they put this up for him."

Grandma Bubsy nodded. "He tell you how the monster ordered all the Manicheans to be burnt alive along with every one of their group's scriptures? Cut tongues out, scourging, decapitations, you name it. A real sweetheart. I'm heading down to the lot. Don't rush on my account ... but don't take your time either." She smiled and started back down the hill toward the parking lot.

Joss turned to Matt. "Is that what happened to Patra and Kaleb and everyone else?"

"She's talking about Diocletian, again, but ... yeah ... I don't know about Patra yet, but it definitely didn't end well for Kaleb. He was crucified, among other things, down by the harbor."

Joss caught herself before *"Jesus"* slipped out.

They began following Grandma Bubsy down the hill.

"Yikes," Joss said. "So ... I guess it's hard for me to grasp the amount of power these people had, or how much fear ruled over those people, or something. I mean, I'd think there's a certain amount of brutality you can get away with where people stay scared and in line, or whatever, but if you go hog wild, burning half the people alive, chopping heads and stuff, it seems like you risk the people rising up."

Matt eyed her. "If they put you in charge, you'd, what, limit public choppings to hands or limbs?"

She laughed, and raised her chin regally. "That's right. And for my leniency, I shall be beloved."

"In truth," Matt said thoughtfully, "most of the texts and philosophies on war miss a vital component. People write about how to achieve victory, but what happens *after* one side has won the war? Some of them say the only way to truly win is by vanquishing the enemy so utterly that they couldn't ever rebuild for a future attack. Less extreme folks might agree you have to break the enemy, but then immediately make peace afterward. Others suggest, 'True victory in war can only be achieved if you never begin in the first place.'"

They passed under the plaster archway to the parking lot.

Joss asked, "And what do *you* say?"

"Me ... I think the most important thing is being able to walk away from a conflict without living the rest of your life looking over your shoulder, or worrying about your friends and family's safety. I'd maybe try to find some way to combine the two extremes."

"Completely vanquish the enemy without ever fighting?"

Grandma Bubsy was already sitting in the van, the sliding door open wide for ventilation. She was clapping them on to rush.

"Sure," Matt said as he walked to the passenger side. "Seems like that'd be the ideal, right?"

Joss climbed into the driver's seat. "Right."

"Hang a left out the driveway," Grandma said from the second row. "Well, Mr. Matt, it's been a privilege. You're every bit as eccentric as I expected, and I love it. When do I get to buy you dinner and pick your brain?"

Matt chuckled. "Whenever you want, Grandma Bubsy, but *I'll* be buying. Well ... after this week, whenever you want."

"Left at the light, then first right. I'm going to take you up on that, sir. Balbaa Village. If you haven't been, then I insist on treating you!"

"We'll see," Matt said calmly, and then placed his hand on Joss's forearm—a gentle-yet-purposeful grip. "I need you to slow down, safely but quickly, and stop up here on the right."

Joss had no clue what he'd suddenly seen, heard, or sensed. She nodded as her fingers tightened on the steering wheel, her foot shifting to the brake. "Hang on to something, Grandma."

"Oh, what now with you two? We're a block away. Just one more block."

The brakes squeaked as Joss brought the van to a full stop by the curb, her eyes darting about in search of danger. Still nothing apparent.

Matt unclipped his seatbelt and grabbed his door handle. "I'm getting out here. Grandma, please take my spot up front. Show Joss where it's safe and legal to park, and hopefully out in the open, then please take her into your office with you. I'm sure this is nothing, but just making sure. Joss?"

She nodded confidently as he stepped out, only realizing as his door shut that her *"confidently"* was wide eyes, a too-fast head nod, and knit brow.

Grandma Bubsy climbed in front, grumbling. "You two. Why does everything have to be a thing? So nice for a bit there ... Got to see the ruins, a little history, some scholarly discourse, making dinner plans, and then *plppb.*"

Joss waited for a truck to pass, then pulled back into traffic, passing Matt on the sidewalk. He walked with one hand in his shorts pocket and the other holding his dead phone at belly height—head down as one engrossed with their device.

Grandma Bubsy directed her around the block to what looked like a big shipping dock's roll-up door. She had Joss enter a code on a keypad post in the driveway, and the door clanged and clattered as it slowly opened.

"Follow the lines to the right for the underground parking," Grandma Bubsy said, but Joss stopped just past the door's threshold, her eyes fixed on the mirror. Grandma gawked. "Well ... what?"

"It goes down automatically?"

Grandma shrugged. "Yes. Of course!"

"Well, then I'm waiting for it to go down."

"Ah, yes ... prudent. *My bad*, as the grandkids say."

Now they both watched the loading bay with edgy eyes, ensuring no one would slip in behind them. Finally, the door touched down on the concrete with an echoing bang and rattle. Joss proceeded down the curving ramp to the parking lot.

* * *

Chin down, but eyes aimed up before him, Matt strolled the sidewalk alongside a deteriorating apartment building. Locals chatted at a small table outside a café in the building's ground floor. The two men glanced up at him as he passed, but didn't skip a beat in their football discussion.

Reaching the intersection, he kept his head down. Across the street, beside another high-rise apartment building with a row of cluttered storefronts, the yellow minivan with the black stripe down the sides sat parked, facing away. Inside sat three men—two in front, and one in the second row. Backseat guy's body seemed to be pressed oddly close to the window on the driver side, hinting toward a fourth passenger recently occupying the space beside him.

Judging only by the backs of heads, the minivan crew's attention appeared split between their respective laps, and the large, nondescript building across the street: the building Grandma Bubsy had pointed out as her office. Rising three stories, and stretching out the full length of the block, its clean, ground-floor walls bore no windows, and only one pair of tinted glass doors stood all the way down the street. Offices on floors two and three enjoyed no shortage of windows, with a few tilted open on the second level. With such a narrow road below, someone would have to stand close to one of the windows to be visible from street level.

The light changed, and Matt proceeded to cross.

Down the intersecting street to Matt's right, a conspicuous glass door lay between a small bicycle shop and another eatery of some sort. The door hung slightly ajar beneath a dozen or more exhaust vents, where telltale cords of lint fluttered against streams of hot air.

Matt pivoted right, losing sight of the minivan within a couple steps, and headed down the side street to the door. Beyond the door he found a long, thin hallway that smelled of cooking onions and spicy food. He stopped at the first door on the left, through which hummed the sounds of agitating washers and tumbling dryers. A doorknob-sized hole occupied the space where a doorknob would normally be found, so he pushed the door open.

A row of dissimilar dryers lined the facing wall. He stepped in to find an equally distinct collection of washing machines along the opposite wall, and between them all, an alarmed, hijabed woman his age. She stood frozen by a half-filled washer, hunched over her laundry basket, and staring up at him.

"*As-salāmu ʿalayk,*" Matt said with a peaceful smile.

She stood up straight, gave a little nod, and muttered, "*Wa-Alaykum.*"

Matt took another step forward, and surveyed the dryers. The second and third to last weren't spinning, and dry clothes crowded against the glass.

The woman frowned and said in Arabic, "You don't live here."

"You are correct," Matt replied, matching her urban dialect. He motioned to the dryers. "May I?"

He opened one and browsed the selection. Trousers, polo shirts, undershirts … nothing of use.

"Those aren't yours," she persisted, now more adamant.

Behind the second dryer door, Matt found what he was looking for. He slid out a long, slate-gray gellabiya, and draped it before him by the shoulders. Perhaps a little short, but it'd make it close to his ankles.

"May I buy this from you?" he asked.

"It isn't mine," she snapped. "You should leave. I can't talk to you, anyway."

Matt hung the garment over one arm, pulled out his wallet, extracted two $100 bills, and repeated, "May I *buy* this from you?"

Her ire shifted back to puzzlement for an instant, and she began to say again that it wasn't hers, but stopped short. She stepped forward, and reached for the bills.

He jerked the cash back, just out of reach.

"Would you happen to have a turban for sale, as well?"

She sighed and rolled her eyes, groaning, "You don't have to wear a turban. Men don't go around like this in the city."

"Men don't go around like *this* in the city." He waved to his wrinkled cargo shorts, and red band T-shirt wrapped from top to bottom with a less-than-muted slogan: FIGHTOFFYOURDEMONSFIGHTOFF…

"Well, I don't have any turbans. And I don't know what they have." She cut her eyes toward the dryers. "I can't talk to you."

Matt handed her the cash, then rifled once more through the open dryer.

"Ah-hah!" he said, producing a small white skullcap.

She wasn't impressed.

"The peace be upon you," he said as he left the laundry room.

"And upon you," she growled.

Matt donned his new outfit in the hallway, slid on his sunglasses, and stepped back outside. Rounding the corner back to the main street, he took a mental snapshot of the men's profiles in the minivan. In front of the first shop, he turned his back to them, and proceeded to browse a spinner rack of women's necklaces, using the thin mirrors between each of the stand's sides to spy on the van.

The driver—late twenties, crewcut, short goatee, Slavic features, pale skin—perused a phone in his lap, while glancing periodically toward the adjacent building's entrance. The passenger was maybe forty, with dark, weathered skin, salt-and-pepper stubble, and a baseball cap worn in a soldier's low-in-front fashion. His intense gaze panned along the adjacent building, from the nearest corner, to the windows above, and main entrance. Nothing seemed to be able to tear backseat guy away from whatever was in his lap. With his cheek mounted upon one hand, elbow planted on an armrest, he might have even been asleep. Matt couldn't see his eyes. He too, appeared thoroughly Slavic, with long, curly, heavy metal hair tied back in a loose ponytail.

The passenger suddenly glanced Matt's way, as if he'd sensed watchful eyes.

Matt held up a string of turquoise beads to the shopkeeper inside, and incorporated the laundry room woman's accent into his Arabic. "I'll give you ten pounds!"

"Read the sign," said the disgruntled owner. "Everything on that rack is seventy-five."

"Seventy-five?" Matt scoffed. He stepped forward beneath the shop's awning. "You think I'm an idiot? Give me the real price, please."

The man stood up from his stool and stomped out from behind the glass display counter. "Seventy-five, you shameless thief! Now put down my jewelry and go shit in someone else's ears!"

"Okay, okay …" Matt grinned sheepishly and raised his hands in surrender. He sidestepped to another rack, watching the ornately framed mirror on the back wall. "How about these chess sets? Let's make a deal!" Another step, and now the minivan passenger was back in his sights. The man had zero interest in the nearby argument. "I give you fifty pounds for this chess set and the necklace. My final offer!"

"Fifty pounds?" The owner's face was about to explode. The temporal artery swelled from his temple. "The cheapest chess set is two hundred and fifty pounds! Get out of my store, you son of a donkey!" He pulled something from behind a stack of cartons, and rushed at Matt. "Screw you, and those who gave birth to you!"

Matt stumbled backward out of the store, hands up for defense. "I'm sorry, I'm sorry! I just want a good deal!"

The owner's rage wasn't going away any time soon, and he followed Matt outside without hesitation, his fist wrapped tight around a short, black club.

Matt continued shuffling backward until he slammed into the parked minivan's front passenger door. With one hand in front of him and the other braced against the van's window, he yelled, "Okay, fine! Two thousand! Two thousand pounds for the chess set and necklace!"

The owner froze with the club cocked behind his shoulder.

Guess that was a little too much. He was actually going to beat the crap out of me!

Stunned, the man said, "Two packs?"

A fist pounded against the window behind Matt. Muffled yelling to get the hell off the vehicle.

"Yes, sir. Two thousand Egyptian Pounds." He opened his hand, revealing the stack of crumpled E£200 bills. "My final offer."

The shopkeeper would've been as crazy to refuse the offer as Matt was to offer it. It amounted to $260 for forty bucks in merchandise. Outrage—doused. He clamped the club in his armpit, gingerly took the money from Matt's hand, and beckoned him to follow.

"Come, I'll wrap them up for you."

Matt pushed himself off the minivan window and trailed the owner back inside the store, allowing the van's occupants—the Russian driver, Padla, and Ukrainians Vanko and Max—to resume their stakeout.

* * *

Grandma Bubsy's office was on the second floor of the Gaston Maspero Egyptology Research Center, or MERC. As she explained to Joss on the elevator ride up, an ever-rotating assortment of small teams and individual foreign researchers shared the space, along with a few bigger outfits with longer-term projects. A scuba diving archaeology org, for example, currently occupied a quarter of the suites.

"But I don't deal much with them," Grandma said, "outside of the occasional 'how do you do' in the restroom."

Once they'd parked, Grandma seemed to feel safe, and Joss had no desire to change that just yet, even though she felt no such confidence. Matt had to have seen something seriously troubling to ditch them like that. She felt she now had a pretty good handle on how he thought in dangerous circumstances. It was like every situation was part of some greater war, and he was the general in charge. Assessing risk, calculations, options, strategy. He often mentioned books like THE ART OF WAR, and SOMETHING ABOUT FIVE RINGS, and HISTORY OF THE SOMETHING-OR-OTHER WAR. And he liked to throw out these sayings from Plutarch, Musashi, and a bunch more names she'd never heard of.

She liked to screw with him whenever he was getting a tad too deep and philosophical on her.

The other day, he'd said to her, "Strength of character doesn't consist solely in having powerful feelings, but in maintaining one's balance in spite of them."

To which she nodded astutely, saying, "Mmm, yes … *Isosceles.* His sagest advice, if you ask me."

And Matt had returned a lighthearted glare (he'd given up correcting her).

Hopefully, he'd get there soon, letting them know there really was nothing to worry about.

Joss followed Grandma Bubsy down a carpeted hallway lined with framed, poster-sized photos of old Egyptian sites and artifacts.

Grandma pulled a jangly key ring from her backpack. "Hm, not locked." She dropped her keys back in the bag. "Some workaholic must already be here."

Stepping into the sun-lit suite, Joss strove for calm. To have faith. Why was it so difficult? Was it some sort of daddy thing? A shrink would answer that by raising their bushy eyebrows, gazing shrewdly over their glasses, *"Is it?"*

It was like there was this *promise* of Matt—of the reliable, superhuman, handle-anything, always-in-control hero, but, in the back of her mind, she was always waiting to be let down.

That had to be a dad thing. She'd always held her father in such high regard. He was very much the superhero, until Mom could no longer hide his bipolar condition. Those ups and downs ... The illusion of everything being all right this time ... No more need to study Daddy's expressions when he'd gone quiet for a bit longer than usual. She learned to not wonder *if* he'd go dark again, but to live uneasily, waiting for the *when*. You know what they say, *"Fool me once, shame on you; fool me 3,722 times, shame on me."*

So that must have been it. She'd put Matt up on a pedestal, and was now waiting for him to fail her.

No, that wasn't fair. Not even accurate. She reminded herself that Matt was far from perfect. He failed left and right. The difference, though, was that when he was wrong about something, or plans didn't work out as he'd anticipated, he always knew how to correct the mistake, change course, or find a quick solution.

Following his sage advice on powerful feelings, she resolved to remain vigilant. To shove aside all of her ineffectual anxieties and nonstop *"but what if…"* doubts. And no more Dad comparisons for Matt.

Ugh.

Grandma pointed to an open doorway off the reception area. "We have our own kitchen through there. Free drinks and snacks up the wazoo, though most of the folks here are crunchy granola types who stock the cupboards with literal crunchy granola."

The common area ended at a floor-to-ceiling glass wall through which a conference room could be seen, with a broad window boasting a sweeping view of rundown apartments. A central hallway stretched out from the conference room in both directions.

Continuing Joss's tour, Grandma Bubsy pointed as she led them down the hallway's right branch. "Meeting room … *big* meeting room … a locked closet I've never seen inside of … and these three offices are my good buddies setting up the Heracleion Museum, one of whom also happens to be your bossman's good buddy."

They reached the third street-facing offices and Grandma halted with a start.

"And here he is, in the flesh!"

Joss leaned to see inside, spotting an excited Pete Sharma seated behind a precisely organized, mahogany desk.

"Always lovely to see you, Mr. Pete, but what're you doing here on a weekend?"

Pete stood and came to the door, noticing Joss along the way. "Meeting with the Thonis team earlier," he replied in an elegant British accent she hadn't noticed that morning, though his energy had tensed upon recognizing her. His attention fixed squarely on Joss, he continued, "Now I'm doing final script revisions for an *event* tomorrow. Is it just the two of you here?" He peered down the hall.

"Er … at the moment," Joss said.

"I'm sorry …" Pete said, and sharply stuck out his hand, "… I don't believe we were formally introduced this morning. I'm Peter Sharma. Are you an associate of Matt Turner?"

Grandma Bubsy answered first. "Indeed she is. She's his executive assistant, occasional driver, and certified apology conveyer. Ms. Joss Lynn Leland."

Joss offered an awkward smile and shook his hand. "Yeah … sorry."

"Not at all," Pete said. "Pleased to meet you, Ms. Leland. Matt and I have been close mates since he was a teenager. I wonder, when Iris Turner tells me she's left a message with his assistant, is she referring to you?"

Oh, great.

"Yeah. Sorry again. I've felt really bad about that. But I swear he's been avoiding you for a good reason! I don't know *precisely* what that reason is, but I know for sure he'll tell you the moment it's safe to, and you two'll have just the greatest laugh together. And beers … or whatever."

Pete gave her a part-amused, part-skeptical, part-intrigued look. "Brilliant." He turned to Grandma Bubsy. "So, Gram, are you staying long … the two of you?"

"Just giving her the nickel tour until Mr. Matt shows up. He's outside somewhere doing who-knows-what."

"Outside here?" Pete said, turning. "Downstairs?"

He went to his window and scanned the street below.

"Yes, sir. Dropped him off by the shawarma café down the block."

Joss wasn't sure if it was a good idea for Pete to be gawking at the window. "I'm sure he'll be right up any second."

"Speaking of people who should be up," Grandma said with a peek at her watch, "I'm going to go call Glenn and tell him all about today's adventure in the ancient tunnel of human fecal matter." She marched off down the hall, leaving Joss in Pete's doorway.

A curious glance from Pete, before surveilling the street once more.

"Hey, Peter," Joss said gently, "it might not be a good idea standing in the window there."

"That's an excellent suggestion," Matt said as he strode toward her from the reception area.

Relief deflated the wad of tension in Joss's chest, despite her denial of its existence. *"Phew!"* must have flashed across her forehead, because Matt frowned at her curiously as he came to a stop just short of Pete's office. He gave her a reassuring *"everything's fine"* face, just as Pete's vertical blinds rustled shut.

"You son of a bitch!" Pete thundered on his way around his desk, then softly appended, "… apologies to Beth. But what the eff, man?!"

He went around Joss, stepping right up to Matt, though was careful not to touch him. His arms fidgeted at his sides—his whole upper body, in fact. Joss recognized the dithering posture. She, too, had done a version of this when meeting Matt again, for the first time, in front of Cam's merch table.

And like at UPenn, Matt allayed the obsolete fear with a warm embrace. "It's really great to see you, Pete. Sorry about everything."

Pete floundered. "Oh hey, ah, your skin—"

"Nah, it's all good now," Matt said as he clapped his friend's back, then pulled away, holding Pete's shoulders for a beat. "Listen, before we get into everything, is there anyone else in the building?"

Pete mulled. "Um, yeah … that is, besides us, Gram down the hall … The undies should still be here. They're in the next suite over. Etienne's supposed to be in later for another meeting."

Matt said, "Undies?"

Pete chuckled. "Ah, apologies. The Euro guys working on Thonis in the bay. I say 'undies' since European Underwater Archaeology Institute is a right mouthful, and *Yoo-aii-ee* makes for a shite acronym. Worse, since I'm managing the new museum, some—"

Matt cut him off. "Sure, sure. Later. What's the most secure area or room in the building?"

"Oh, that'd be the scroll vault, by far. Reinforced doors, plating in the walls, access code lock-out, law enforcement notification—"

Matt, intrigued: "You have a 'scroll vault' here?"

Pete let out a dramatic sigh. "Man, if you would call a brother back some time!"

Matt clutched his forehead. "No … You didn't … Don't tell me—"

Thus far excluded, Joss sidled up to them. "What scrolls are we talking about exactly?"

Matt ignored her. "You said they were on their way to Cairo three weeks ago!"

Exasperated with Matt, Pete turned to Joss. "The Library collection. Well, 78,000 pieces of it." Back to Matt: "She doesn't know about any of this? Do you talk to *anybody* about *anything?*"

Matt groaned with anguish, pacing circles as Pete went on grousing, "One call, man, *one* call and I could've told you what happened! An email—a secure email, encrypted or something! A fax! You said not to say *anything* about them on the phone, or 'any other electronic means,' that you'd get back to me. Not even in code, you said. I followed *your* rules. That sort of system only works if *that* bloody side of it actually gets back to *this* bloody side when *this* side is obviously desperate to reach you! Like, what did you think, man? I was just being a pest?"

Defeated, Matt sank against the wall and closed his eyes. "Why didn't you move them when you said? That Thursday, you said the trucks had already arrived. The first one was inside the shipping bay being loaded. Now I've led Ostrovsky's men straight to them."

Mirroring Matt, Pete slumped against the opposite wall, his head set in an endless no-nod as he rubbed his eyes. "Environment control was absolute rubbish. The company's rep had crowed on about his brilliant system with integrated dehumidifiers and monitoring." Matt raised his eyebrows. "Yeah. Digital thermostat and an off-the-shelf needle hygrometer velcroed to the side of this little box. Monitoring? The driver slides open a wee door by his head, shines a flashlight in, and all's marvelous. I discover all this when I come down to the dock to ask the supervisor for the monitoring URL and how to setup alerts. Laughed in my face … wanker."

Joss took another stab. "So these are the scrolls Patra and everyone were hiding?"

"Who's Patra?" Pete said.

Matt stood up straight and heaved a deep, cleansing breath. "I'll get back to that. Where's this vault?"

* * *

After fetching Grandma Bubsy from her office, the four took the elevator back down to the basement parking level, but instead of exiting the lobby into the garage, Pete swiped an access card through a reader on the wall, and entered a code on the pad. The double doors unlocked with a resounding *thunk*, and he led them into a brightly lit, albeit windowless hallway with a glossy white tile floor.

A hydraulic arm pushed the heavy door closed behind them, and it slammed and rattled.

Matt stopped and grabbed one of the door's push bars, shaking it back and forth. "You call that reinforced? They open *in*. A solid shoulder outside there and this thing'll pop right open."

Pete glanced back and sneered. "Sheesh, man, you aren't going to let up, are you?"

"When the men outside march into this building, they will not let up."

"Well, those aren't the doors anyway. Give me a *little* credit, buddy." He pivoted on the slick floor, continuing down the wide hall.

"Here's an outlandish question," Grandma Bubsy said. "Why in the screaming heck hasn't anyone called the police?"

"The men outside haven't yet committed a crime," Pete said. "They'll simply leave when the officers arrive, and return once they've left."

"And they'll be more careful next time," Matt added. "We have the edge at present. The smallest advantages often decide the victor."

"All right, Sun Tzu," Grandma scoffed. "But calling the cops means your crooks run off, and no more crooks means the good folks in this building all get to go home safe."

Matt didn't answer right away. Only the shuffles and clicks of their shoes filled the hall as they passed unmarked doors on either side. Painfully bright overhead lights. The pleasant aroma of cleaning chemicals.

Walking beside Grandma, Joss leaned close to her and whispered, "Believe it or not, I'd trust him with my life over some random Egypt cops."

"My-my," Grandma murmured. "You carrying a torch, or are you two carrying on?"

A shriek-laugh burst from Joss, choked off the instant it chirped out. Matt and Pete peered behind them with matching, speechless expressions.

"Carrying on" had caught Joss off-guard, and she chortled inside even as she felt her cheeks flushing at both of Grandma Bubsy's inferences—loud enough for all present to consider.

Joss swallowed and cleared her throat, turning to her. "No, Grandma. Neither. I simply know what one is capable of, and not the other."

Pete and Matt mercifully moved on.

Reaching the double doors at the corridor's end, Pete dared, "Now, try and force your way into *this* one."

The doors before them were equally unremarkable.

Matt snatched the card from his friend's hand, swiped it through the slit in the access pad, and punched in a code.

"Hey! Not fair!" Pete protested.

A red light flashed three times in sync with beeps. *Denied.* Pete crossed his arms, smiled, and sniffed with pride.

Matt held the card in front of him a moment, and said, "Oh," before punching in another, longer code. Double beep and a green light, followed by humming, and impressive, deep *shunks,* as if massive beams were sliding out of a big castle door's metal beam-holder things.

All the sounds halted.

Pete's head wobbled from the weight of excessive smug. "Now what, cheater?"

Matt ran his fingers down the right-hand door, stopped at a particular spot, and pushed in. A cylindrical bar popped out a couple inches, and he began spinning it counterclockwise, gloating eyes fixed on Pete's.

"Yeah, yeah," Pete grumbled. "Guess we have to return the bloody vault."

"I'm impressed, actually," Matt said as he tried to pull the door. "You weren't messing arou—what the hell?"

The door wouldn't budge.

"It's the ventilation," Pete said. "Just pull it slow."

A high-pitched whistle grew louder and more sucky as the door inched open. Just before the vacuum released its grip, the widening sliver hissed, deepened, and emit a creepy, final howl. A thick, brushed metal frame was exposed, also revealing the left-hand door to be a useless fake.

"Nice façade," Matt said. "The first step in securing valuables is to hide the fact that there's anything valuable to find. This should work well." He glanced at his watch. "We need to speed this up. If you're security guy up front activates the alarm, will we hear it down here?"

"Of course, man," Pete said. "And the perimeter lights in here all flash red. Don't worry. We'll know if anyone's coming in."

"Regardless," Matt replied, "we don't know how long we have."

Pete motioned inside. "Just give me this one minute, okay? Just one damn minute?"

Matt pressed his lips together tightly, resignedly waving him in.

A dozen or so feet past the vault door's steel frame, Joss spotted their reflections in a glass door. She followed the others inside an enclosed chamber the same width and height of the entryway, but illuminated only with light from the hallway behind her.

Pete struck something on the wall, and cool-toned LEDs brightened above them, but *high* above them. They were essentially standing inside a big transparent shoebox inside a giant warehouse, and all around them, thick columns of ethereal light shone upon individual tables or desks, lined up in neat rows, and on those tables lay thousands of scrolls. *Seventy-eight* thousand, evidently.

Some of the surfaces held divided clusters of rolled papyrus—five here, a space, thirteen there—while others featured a single, contiguous collection from end to end, resembling some giant pan flute or bamboo fence laid on its side. A few tables were littered with little tools and magnifier lights on mounted arms, and unrolled papyri laid out flat. The majority of the scrolls, however, sat atop the desks piled inside big open-top containers with a sort of thread netting for sidewalls.

Joss tried to take it all in—not just the impressive display, but the fact that these scrolls were anywhere from 1,700 to 4,000 years old, and that, for all these days, Matt had pretty much been *living* the story of their escape. "Wow," she breathed.

Grandma was equally staggered. "Ho-ly shit ... excuse my French. How long has ... Peter Sharma, how in dangnation have you kept this secret from me?"

"Just following *orders*, Gram." Scorn flung Matt's way.

Matt motioned to the door separating them from the rest of the warehouse. "I gather you want to keep that closed."

"Yep. None of them have been treated in any way. We've got chemicals circulating to handle any critters, but mold is a bigger concern. We'll have plenty of time for you to peruse them after everything's been certified. All of this is nice, but it's still not a proper environment for them."

"Well, obviously I'm not looking for a tour just yet," Matt said. "I meant for everyone to hide behind your glorious mega-door. The upstairs people, too. Probably wouldn't shove more than eight in your little airlock here, though. How many do you think there are in the whole building?"

Pete counted in his head, mouthing names. "Eight, actually. Oh, plus the security guard. Oh, and *us*. Not sure if anyone's on the third floor today."

"I saw a few cars in the garage I recognized as third-floorers," Grandma said.

Pete shrugged. "Hell, there could be anywhere from twenty to thirty. I mean, honestly, if the vault door is shut behind us, we don't need to wait for the airlock to dehumidify. People can file in, shut the door, next batch of folks. I'd only try to avoid a wide-open airway, and in the grand scheme of things, if lives are at risk, to hell with the climate, right? We do what we have to do."

"Perfect," Matt said, then turned to Grandma Bubsy. "Would you mind staying here to guard the door until we gather everyone up? I have more confidence in your ability to keep the wrong people out than Pete's fancy door." He winked.

"You're sweet. And my knees appreciate you not making them walk all the way up there."

Heading back to the elevator, Pete grinned and said, "Guess what's on the tables in the far back left?"

Stepping into the elevator, Matt shook his head, amused. "You really can't wait for a moment when armed thugs *aren't* a hundred feet away, preparing to raid your office? You wouldn't happen to have a master key to this place, would you?"

Pete slapped a button and the doors slid shut while he dug in his pants pockets. "Multiple full collections of the Epic Cycle. *Multiple*. All one hundred percent complete, and pristine condition. Table next to it? Aristotle's dialogues. Table next to that? Wait for it …" A *ding* signaled their arrival on the second floor. "Socrates!"

Joss observed Matt's sudden inability to resist the thrill. Besides knowing the names, and that they were famous philosophers, she hadn't a clue why they were so excited. As they hustled down the hallway to another suite, Pete answered a few clipped questions from Matt, and Joss surmised there were writings that modern people knew existed once, but that no one had ever found.

Matt swatted Pete's elbow. "... but you haven't had anyone besides Linus inspecting them, right?"

"*Pshh*, of course not, man! But hey, if you're questioning his–"

"No, no, not at all. Just thinking in terms of exposure."

Pete checked a knob and, finding it locked, he rapped on the door. "... 'cause he might be young, but the kid's Greek bona fides are beyond reproach."

"And he believes they're by Socrates' hand?"

Pete knocked again with greater urgency. "If not these, than he thinks they were copied straight from some originals. Let's the try the other door."

They rushed down to the hall's last door.

"I'll keep my fingers crossed they're not copies. Do you remember any titles? Or *are* they titled?"

Pete grinned as he banged on the door. "'Remember.' Heh, you forget who you're talking to, man! Take note ..." He theatrically wiped an invisible marquee in the air. "... ELENCHUS, ATOP RED-DROWNED SOIL, EPITAPHIOS, and DAEMONES."

The door finally swung open, with Matt standing bewildered, as if sprayed with cold water.

A tall, collegiate, twenty-something guy ogled them. "Holy hell, what the f—Oh, hey ... um ... Pete. Sorry, um ..." American. He eyed Matt and Joss as he scratched his shaggy beard. "Etienne's not here yet."

"That's all right, Leo." Pete pushed in past him. "We need to gather everyone together right away. We've got a building emergency."

Pete's voice trailed off while Leo, back in the doorway, scratched his belly through his T-shirt, squinting at Joss and Matt, then Joss, then held on Matt. "Do I ... Have we—?"

Matt composed himself and stuck out his hand to shake. "We haven't met. This is Joss Lynn. I'm Matt. We should be getting in there."

Leo absently shook his hand, shuffling backward. "Leonardo," he said. "Leo."

Matt grabbed Joss's hand, pulling her past the mystified twenty-something, and emphasized, "There really is an emergency, Leo."

Pete had already assembled most of the marine archaeologists, and they gathered the stragglers on the way out. The Leonardo kid was holding the door open, and as Joss approached among the murmuring herd, she watched his eyes hunting through the crowd, swiftly finding and locking on Matt, in front of her. Clearly, Leo was more concerned with a familiar face than the prospect of an armed assault.

Evacuees bunched up at the exit, and Matt slowly advanced to within a couple feet of the captivated American kid.

Joss saw his gears cranking ... more beard scratching ...

Aaaaand ... blam-O! Recognition!

"No ... *way!*" he said.

Matt glanced Leo's way as they rolled by, and said, "Mr. Dunch ... Can we chat?" For some reason Matt had adopted an airy manner.

They stepped outside the door, moving aside to allow others to exit. Joss stuck to Matt's wing, and observed the awestruck Leonardo float through the doorway like a ghost, his face alight as if he'd just witnessed the greatest magic trick in history.

Matt called down the hallway, "Hey there, you two!" A young man and woman slowed and turned, wondering if he was talking to them. "Come here for a second." They shared a glance and hesitantly returned. The woman had a cell phone in her hand. "Does that get signal in the basement?"

"Yeah," she said. "In the garage, at least. Why?"

"May I borrow it?" A pleading smile. She groaned and plopped it in his hand like owed money. "Thanks." He looked at the guy, a stocky surfer type in flip-flops, with a long, sun-bleached-blond ponytail. "Hi there. What's your name?"

"Um, Josh."

"Nice to meet you, Josh." Matt held up the woman's phone and gestured to Josh and Leo. "Either of you have Tiffany's number in your phones?"

They answered "Yeah," in unison.

The woman's brow puckered. "How do you know my name?"

"Ah, someone said it inside," Matt said, and hurried her off. "Go on now, catch up with the group!"

Befuddled, she resumed toward the stairwell.

"Where was I? … Right. Joss, may I have the van keys?" She pulled them out and tossed him the clacky little ring. "Thanks. Hey … where's Pete?" He poked his head into the suite's exit.

Joss guessed, "He's probably doing a final sweep of the offices."

Matt peered over at her. "Probably right. You mind grabbing him?" And didn't wait for her answer before turning back to the two confused, waiting guys.

She snapped a nod anyway, and darted back into the marine group's suite.

"So, Josh, what do you do?" Matt asked casually.

"I'm, um … I'm the cook. On the boat."

"Sweet …" was the last thing Joss heard Matt say before she cut left toward a big open cubicle area.

"Pete? Peter?" She peeked into each office and conference room until reaching the last. No Pete. She shouted, "Pete!" and listened. Nothing. She jogged back to the reception area, catching a glimpse of Matt still talking to the guys outside the suite, and continued her Pete-hunt into the opposite wing. Still Pete-less, she went to tell

Matt. Unless there were secret passageways here, there definitely wasn't anyone else in the office.

She hung a left, hit the final stretch to the lobby, and Matt appeared, heading her way.

"No?"

She threw her hands up.

He stopped and waited for her. "I must've missed him. Probably went up to get the third floorers. Let's get you down to the vault."

"Sure, yeah," she said, looking up at him. "What was that all about with the lads?"

"I sent them to prep for an errand." Matt handed her the borrowed cell phone. "And you'll cue them when the time is right."

"I have a feeling that's all the information you're going to give me."

Earnest confusion.

She gave him *the lids,* as her mom always called the expression. "*How* will I know when the time is right?"

"Right, of course … That's still on the T-B-D list." He walked into the nearest street-facing office.

Joss watched him from the doorway. He crept to the side of a vertical blind-shrouded window, and ever-so-slowly pushed the first hanging panel aside. Careful to keep out of the sunlight, he craned his neck to inspect the street.

"They're still in the minivan at the end of the block. Thing is, there're two other vehicles and six other guys, one of whom is the least predictable factor."

"How do you know? Is it Rostik?"

"Yes it is," Matt said, and moved slowly right to examine the adjacent apartment building. "Unfortunately, his own guys don't know where he went to post watch. He simply radioed them to stay put, and said he was heading to another vantage p—Shit."

"What?"

"Found Rostik." Dropping the ninja sniper act, he whacked the blinds aside and gazed back down the street.

"You saw him?"

"I saw a dark sliver between two mini-blinds slowly close." Before she could ask how mini-blinds plus dark sliver equaled Rostik, he added. "And there's the radio call. They're getting out. We have to move."

As they ran out of the suite and toward the stairwell, Matt said, "You hold onto that phone, okay? There's a text message to Leo already primed on the home screen if you wake it up."

Scuttling behind him, she unlocked the screen to verify there wasn't a passcode. Indeed, an unsent message sat ready on the screen. "It's just a period," she said.

"Yeah, it could be anything. They're just waiting for a text from that phone."

He paused by the stairwell door, opened it a crack, and listened.

She whispered, "So do I send it now? What's the cue?"

He shook his head and put up a hand for silence, held it for an instant, then swung the door open. "Tread lightly," he hushed.

Of course, they were the metallic-type stairs that thrummed and echoed for anyone but cats wearing socks. Matt led them down with modest racket, balancing well the values of both haste and stealth. When they reached the ground level, he switched places with her, taking up the rear for the last flight down to the garage level.

She pushed the latch bar, shouldered the door out of their way, and popped out into the basement lobby. A sudden jerk from a tight grip around her upper arm. She almost fell on her ass, but caught her balance, freezing in place. She scowled silently at Matt. He had one hand holding her still, a finger pressed to his lips, and an elbow impeding the self-closing door.

And then she heard it, too: Russians in the stairwell (or Ukrainians, or whatever). Two or three different voices. They didn't seem to be going up or down—probably listening to determine which.

Time, as it often preferred, decided to crawl. Maybe twenty words were spoken between the unseen intruders, but in Joss's mind it felt like the sun had fallen, risen, and burned out. She moved only her eyes back to Matt, observing his were closed. He seemed to be holding his breath. She followed suit, and a few seconds later, the exchange ended with a metallic stair ringing out—Matt instantly exhaling and easing his death grip on her arm. He'd discerned their direction from the sound of the very first step. Clanging footfalls climbed, quieting as they went, and Matt released her entirely, guiding the door to a muted closure.

Fortunately, Pete (or whomever entered last) had left propped open one of the double doors to the big hallway. No need for Matt to give it that solid—and probably quite loud—shouldering.

They strode past the garage entrance and, just as Joss crossed in front of the elevator, a loud *ding* sounded above. Both heads shot right to see the illuminated P1 above the doors. Without hesitation, they continued inside the white corridor, and Matt maneuvered her around the propped door and into the corner behind it. From the lobby came the sound of heavy rolling, and dim flute music. Matt inched backward into her, setting one hand on her hip.

Now her pulse had really woken up. Now she wished she'd followed the damned crowd into the vault. Matt's martial art stuff meant nothing against a gun. If it had to happen, she hoped it was quick. She'd always been a wuss about pain.

Strangely, though, there was no other sound from around the corner. Either the elevator had come down empty, or an expert slinker was gently making his way to the opening.

What if he shot through the wall? Pete talking about plated walls around the scroll vault made her think about the soft, flimsiness of every other wall in the world. She might as well have her back to one of those Japanese paper screen things. *Shōji?* Is that what they were called? Where the hell had that come from? She couldn't recall

301

ever knowing the name for the things. Her brain's Department of Useless Stored Knowledge had decided to work, for once. Maybe to distract her from paralyzing terror.

Matt's finger tapped harder on her hip. He'd been tapping her hip! She looked up to see him glaring down at her. *Tap tap!* His gaze flashed to the phone in her hand.

The text message!

She unlocked the screen and hit **SEND**. A semicircle swirled around, considering whether to deliver the message, or deliver the finger.

SENT.

The hammering in her ears rising, she turned the phone to show Matt and he nodded, returning his attention to the thin gap between door and frame.

It felt as though a good minute had passed since the elevator opened, but only now did the doors finally slide shut. Matt touched her hip again. The soft *tick* of a button press next door. The elevator rolled open once again. Someone was definitely out there.

A tiny plastic *click* preceded a hushed, bassy voice. "*Ya proveryayu podval … Da.*"

Unclick.

He must have had an earbud for his walkie-talkie. And no beeps before and after. Smart. Smarter if there was a larynxbud to keep others from hearing you talk, Joss supposed.

She closed her eyes. Now she could hear him moving closer to the corridor—the rustle of clothes, a faint wheeze in each exhale. Matt took his hand off her. She opened her eyes and saw him move a thick key from left hand to right. He rolled it in his palm until centered, then thumbed the thin end forward between his middle and ring finger. His fist tightened around the new punch-enhancer.

Wheezy was getting close. His shadow glided into view on the tile. Matt pressed his back into her.

The tinny sound of a voice through a little speaker stopped the man. His shadow arm moved up to his shadow neck. Another *click*, and he spoke at a less cautious volume.

"*Kakaya storona? Kakiye ulitsy? … Nyet, nyet mashin.*"

He turned and dashed away, his hard soles clomping as he went. The door to the garage opened, inviting in the drone of a giant ventilation system. He stopped in the doorway and radioed again, presumably reporting nothing to see in the garage.

Matt spun about, gave her another shush sign, and pulled her out of the corner. He pushed her toward the vault end of the hall, guiding her from behind, sticking to the side. She tread as lightly as she could, but wished he wouldn't shove her along. It wasn't helping her to move any faster or quieter.

She passed the first side door, and was abruptly stopped. Matt had a firm grip on the back of her shirt and, despite what she may have thought, there existed only two types of movement: Go! and Stop! Nothing between. He kept his fist tight in the small of her back while his other hand rested on the door handle, checking something. Beyond him, the elevator lobby remained clear.

Go!

He drove her forward another twenty feet or so to the next door.

Stop!

She watched the hall as he examined the new handle. A few seconds later, he jerked her back to him, slipped in the key, rotated the door handle, and thrust her into a pitch-black room. Her shirt was freed in favor of a perfectly soundless door shut.

The ribbon of fluorescent light tapered until it disappeared, and a twist-lock clicked in the darkness, followed by an exhale from Matt.

"Sorry about the manhandling," he whispered, and his hand found her wrist. "Your ears are keener than mine. Also nice to have a second pair of eyes on lookout."

Oh, hell. He was reading me the entire goddamn time.

"So listen," he went on near her ear, "this is just a big empty room except for some old janitorial supplies that way." He took her index finger and used it to point to the front, right corner. "And there's a bundle of network cable hanging from the ceiling, all the way to the floor, over there." He turned her gently by the hand and opposite elbow, aiming her finger toward the back, right corner. "Whereas the door that exits to the street …" She heard the smile in his voice. "… is around sixty feet *that* way, and we have a *mostly* clear path. Someone set down a spray paint can about fifteen feet in. Kicking it across the room would result in a less-than-smooth escape. I'm going to go first and lead us around it with plenty of buffer space between, so as long as you don't swing out like you're singing in the rain, we'll be good the whole way."

His sweat had mixed with a deodorant or cologne, creating some kind of magically delicious chemical reaction. She stole another whiff, and said, "Okay."

And I don't care if you're in my head. Someone should bottle that shit, because damn.

He slid his hand back to her wrist, and she wondered if he could read her through the wispy little thread bracelet. He led her deeper into the blackness, their arms outstretched between them, providing ample room to walk normally without tripping each other up.

I wonder what it tastes like.

"*Shh,*" he hushed.

Mortified, she whispered, "Oh my God, shit, I'm so sorry, I-"

"*Shhhhh—*"

Matt's shush was cut off by a loud clang at his feet, but it sounded nothing like a spray paint can, and it immediately struck something else, like china or a ceramic pot, and Matt grunted as his hand yanked off her wrist, and there came such a resounding crash— as if a tower of home improvement store shelves had collapsed before her—and invisible objects pelted her shins and knees, shattering glass struck her neck, cheek, and ear, while impulse clenched her body into an ungainly mass, stumbling backward.

The Canopic Road - Alexandria, Egypt circa 270 AD
Artist unknown

NINETEEN

Hello Steward,
The voice conveys knowledge.
The scribe preserves a word.
A token holds the sum.

Alexandria, Aegyptus – 271 CE

Patra was wise to heed Barbillus's advice. As dusk approached, mobs large and small roamed the city. Some sought to loot abandoned homes and businesses—or had already done so, evidenced by arms filled with valuables, or dragging trips of bleating goats—but other gangs carried with them rage and clubs or blades, hunting the streets for affluent garb.

Despite her humble stola and palla, wrapped over all but her eyes, Patra felt she'd be accosted at any moment. She wondered if her unadorned, recognizable face would stand out more than one apparently seeking to not be recognized. Once the last bits of twilight retired, she resolved to let her palla hang free, but to walk as one elderly and infirm.

Bypassing a crowded east-west road, she continued south to the first block of the dense Christian district, spotting a trio of women huddled and veiled as she. A relief to know her guise would be seen as unexceptional.

But as they approached on the opposite side of the street, one of the very women from whom she'd gathered confidence fixed her eyes on Patra. Then, collecting her company's attention, proceeded to stop and discuss the passing stranger. What had struck the woman's senses? Would they call out to the nearest horde of bandits? No, it seemed. Instead, as Patra diverted her eyes and sped her pace, she observed peripherally the trio crossing to intercept her.

Alternatives lacking, Patra hiked her stola and broke into a run.

"Steward!" one of them hushed in Greek. A young girl's voice. "Wait! It's Eugenia!"

Patra spun and allowed the three to catch up. Eugenia was with her mother, Lucia, and … not a woman at all, but one of the young men who'd been helping evacuate scrolls, her student, Tertius. Patra embraced all three, drawing them to her and clutching them tight as if they might float off into the sky at any second. She'd thought all three of them among those killed or trapped in the Musaeum.

"I'm so overjoyed to see you," she said. "How did you escape? Were there others? Where are you going? Do you know where to find safe shelter? We should keep moving … get off the street."

They checked for onlookers, and resumed walking as a single group.

"Steward Kaleb got us out," Lucia said. "He showed us the … how you've been moving your—"

"Yes, I understand," Patra interrupted. "It's fine. The passage has served its purpose. Did he get others out?"

"He went back in, Steward," Tertius said solemnly. "To fetch others."

A jubilant crowd danced by waving torches overhead, singing a Coptic feast song.

"Don't call me that for now," Patra said to Tertius.

"Apologies."

"So did he get more members out?" Patra knew the answer, but wished to know what else they weren't saying.

"No, Stew—No," Eugenia replied.

"Well, we don't know that for certain," Lucia said. "He forbade us from waiting. We saw nothing after leaving the Royal Quarter."

Patra stopped abruptly, and turned to them. "Tertius? Eugenia? One of you needs to tell me now what you saw, heard, suspect, or believe."

"We hid beneath the aqueduct to Pharos," Tertius said. His big, wheat eyes fought to hold in tears. "As was one of the original plans ... And a short while later, Philip came to check for members."

"He told us to take a boat up the canal," Lucia cut in. Patra could see she was pinching the back of Eugenia's neck.

"What else? *Please!* I cannot beg for a single word more today!"

Tertius resumed, "He said the Emperor landed at the Palace Docks, and that Prince Kaleb went there to turn himself in."

"He went—" Patra couldn't breathe or swallow.

"...To get the Emperor to end the siege."

How could he?!

They'd discussed and eliminated this preposterous idea days ago! Kaleb knew as well as any of them that such a gesture would be meaningless and fruitless—a gift to no one but Antonius, so he could drape a mutilated body from the Musaeum gate. Not one life would be saved; however, countless others would be devastated by the sight. A fleeting gift for a vile man, a lifelong curse for those who loved him. And Kaleb had wholeheartedly agreed.

He agreed!

Patra tore through the others, heading back toward the harbor.

"Steward!" Lucia called after her.

With her palla flapping behind her, Patra disregarded the beckoning shouts of looters. Fatal blows may have struck her from behind at any moment, but it seemed the prospects of further plunder outweighed the effort of giving chase.

Heedless to her path, she weaved northeasterly through the city toward the Palace District. Before she knew it, she'd run broadside into the Avenue of Knowledge, and the Musaeum's west wall.

How long had it been since she parted ways with Barbillus? Twenty minutes? Thirty? Would he have yet assembled his group and weapons? Might they be arriving imminently? Were the murderous city guards still about? She retreated back to the side street of affluent villas, and into the cover of lush, vine-covered arbors and pergolas.

Now that she'd stopped, she found it impossible to catch her breath. Her body throbbed from end to end, and her pounding head did its best to remind her of her age. She noticed a small fountain in the dark behind her and went to sit. Splashes of cool water on her head and face eased her pain and fatigue as breaths came in more measured streams. Would she have even made it to the docks, or would she have collapsed in another block?

The pulsing in her head settled, replaced by the din of the city. Far-off cheers—or perhaps jeers—mingled with shattering objects, a constant pounding, and beneath it all, a growing rumble.

Patra raised her chin and pulled her hair behind her ears. A muted tone accompanied the percussive sound—a higher pitch, as if this section of the orchestra was building for their part. And then it grew even more like musical instruments, now discernable as individual beats, overlapping. It was armor, she realized. Armor, shields, galloping hooves, chariots, all approaching the Canopic Gate beyond the Musaeum and Jewish Quarter. Zenobia returning, triumphant? Or Antonius?

Tertius said Antonius himself had just landed at the Palace Docks. This wouldn't be the move of a defeated leader. Quite the contrary. Which meant these were *his* soldiers preparing to enter the city, unopposed. It meant Zenobia had either been captured or killed. It meant there'd soon be nowhere to hide in Alexandria. It meant this was the last moment to accomplish anything in the city, including to escape it.

A voice from beyond the Musaeum wall. "Hurry!"

Feet pattering down steps, little feet among them.

Patra popped up, reinvigorated. She bolted from the small courtyard and out to the road, cutting left toward the Musaeum's front gate. Her course matched that of the unseen others inside the complex, and when she reached the corner, a little girl sprang from the open gate.

"Wait, Cyra!" called another girl just as she too emerged. It was Theophila! Both of Philip's daughters had survived!

Cyra slowed and silently observed the bodies strewn about the stairs, aglow beneath the starlight. Theophila grabbed her little sister, and turned to see Patra climbing the steps. And in that instant, from the Musaeum's wide gateway appeared Barbillus, equipped with sword and shield, followed by another armed man, and another— five in all.

Barbillus's gaze snapped right to Patra as she came, and then he peered back inside the gate.

"Just the two—?" Patra began, but two more stepped out—an adolescent boy, and young woman, followed by a desolate Philip, his head sort of lolling atop his shoulders, as if drunk.

Barbillus stepped down to her, a wall in her path to Philip. "Easiest assault, yet. They'd only left eight guards in front here."

"Poorly trained guards," one of Barbillus's men snickered. "And yet they say we're too old to join."

"Every door was busted in by the time we got here," Barbillus went on, rolling his meaty shoulders and rocking from foot to foot, invigorated. "Nothing pretty inside, but elsewhere, as you can see, these folks were the clever ones to hide, and *stay* hidden." He followed Patra's gaze to Philip, lingering at the top of the steps. Barbillus lowered his voice. "He just found his, ah, wife, I presume."

Oh, no. Julia ...

Barbillus peered down the Canopic Road. The Roman Army was now visible inside the walls a mile away, marching in wide ranks, and double-stomping every third step, broadcasting their victory.

"You shouldn't have come back here, but now that you have, get him and the others out, immediately."

"I can't," she said. "I'm not done."

"You're on your way to the Palace Docks, aren't you? Well, don't bother. They've already got your friend nailed hand over hand to a pole down there. Balthasar saw it with his own eyes. Scourging him, branding—"

"That's not all Romans did," added a grim Balthasar. He was as tall as Barbillus, but fat all over, and with the dark skin of an Aethiopian. "Once stripped to the wind, he tried to pray in the Christian way, but they hauled him up, rugged him over a rail, and at least four different Centurions—"

"Enough," Barbillus barked. "Hey." He snapped Patra out of her horrified daze. "There's nothing more for you down here. Take them, and go. And not just so we can one day have us a scholarly interchange. If you don't live, we don't get paid."

"Patra?" Philip said distantly.

"I can't leave yet," she declared. "*You* take them. Don't worry, Philip will pay you."

Barbillus growled and eyed once more the approaching ranks. He grabbed her arm, his fingers wrapping all the way around. "I'm telling you, dammit, there's nothing you can do for him! He's dead!"

"It's not him. It's the Library. I need to burn it down."

Barbillus gawked at her, speechless.

"You what?" said another of his men.

"I'll do it," Philip said, still in a haze as he descended the stairs to Patra. "I've already prepared the draperies and kindling." He embraced Patra weakly.

Barbillus rubbed his neck, shaking his head. "I think maybe I'm just a bit confused about what stewards do—"

"We need to leave, Barb," Balthasar said.

Patra kissed both of Philip's cheeks, and forced him to look at her eyes. "You saved your daughters. They're standing right there, waiting for you to take them the rest of the way out of the city. These two, as well." She motioned to the other members—the woman and young man near the girls, both wearing anxious, pleading expressions. "Take them out the way you planned. You figured out all of this for us. I'll be along right after you."

Philip returned a wistful nod, gathered his girls and the others, and set off southward down the Avenue of Knowledge. Barbillus's men dispersed as well, sheathing their swords and ambling casually away.

Barbillus stood over her, pointing after Philip. "Right along after is right. You're going now, so that *I* can go now."

"I don't have time for this! What do you care? I told you, you'll get your money!"

"It's a fool's errand, that's why. Let that polished pile of manure come and burn the place down himself. You rob him of that satisfaction, he'll seek it elsewhere."

Patra ducked under his arm, and up the steps toward the gate. "I'm not robbing him of satisfaction. I'm finishing my job."

Barbillus marched up the stairs after her, four steps per stride, and blocked her at the gate. "I get it … I see. You're covering up. Another *performance*. Such irony."

Patra stared up at him, seething, arms locked and fists balled at her sides. She didn't know how far her trust in this man should stretch. A glance to the road—the Army's front line was only one block away.

She sighed. "We've many religions within these walls. For some, to be left unburned or unburied is to be cursed to the dark abyss."

"So you're going to help out all those disciples that happened to die in the Library? You going to drag up all the other bodies lying everywhere else, too?"

He was too smart.

"Please just let me by. The Army will see us any second now."

He picked her up by the waist, set her on the top of the staircase, and pushed her inside the gate. "It's too late for either of us to run off that way now. I'll venture you know where this supposed secret exit is?"

"I do. It's the exit I'll take once I've set the fires."

Barbillus sniffed. "You know what's interesting? Plato said wars are occasioned by the love of money, and that's been true of every real war I've seen or know of. Until now." With one firm hand still clutching her arm, he jabbed the other thumb over his shoulder toward the booming parade outside. "There are safer things than war for a *muse* to inspire, but it's impressive, nonetheless."

Her hands now quaked, unsure if legionaries would at any moment surge through the gate beside them. She stared into Barbillus's eyes. His reservations appeared genuinely rooted in concern for her, but it'd be impossible to make him understand, or care, and so she fumed helplessly and glared.

A soft, rhythmic ticking neared the gate, and a scruffy gray head emerged at knee height. A wandering city dog. It snapped its attention to the pair of unexpected observers. Patra and Barbillus stared at the appraising eyes.

Barbillus stomped a foot. "Hyah!"

The dog balked and retreated a step. It watched a moment and, determining no immediate threat, continued inside and sniffed the closest city guard's bloody face. A couple tentative licks preceded a full face cleaning.

Barbillus scoffed. "No taste for foul meat."

The dog raised its head to look around, and Patra's repulsed expression turned to one of disbelief. "I *know* him ... The guard ..."

"Apologies ... I didn't ... We had to—"

"No need to apologize," she said coldly. "He was not a good man."

The dog tramped across the sheet of blood expanding from the city guard's gashed neck, laid down on a dry patch of pavement. It then set its chin on the ground at the edge of the red pool, and proceeded to lazily lap at the blood. An instant later, two more gangly dogs entered the gate—these less cautious than the first—sniffing about for an instant before slurping desperately at another spreading puddle.

"Thirstier than they are hungry," he finally said, and turned to her. "I don't plan to be here when they're ready for the meat. I'll set your damned fires."

Before she could reply, he pulled her to the east wall's recessed stairway. Practically carrying her by one wrist, they scaled the flights to the Library level.

He sat her down on a secluded landing behind a hedge. "I venture you won't leave with only my word that it'll be done?"

"If we both go, it'll be faster."

"Not so," he said. "Stay here. Don't move. They're gathering in front, preparing for something. Could enter the gate any second now."

Huddling low, he scrambled up one more flight to cut across the green beside the Library. Once she'd lost sight of him, she counted five, and edged up the low wall, peeking beneath the bushes down to the front gate. Indeed, soldiers were amassing on the road at the base of the stairs.

Focusing over the wall to the harbor, Patra observed the Imperial Palace, its facing walls aflicker. At each of the Palace's corners, spiring flames danced high over long-dormant torch pots. Prudently, Zenobia had never taken up residence there, wary of provoking a response from Rome. The Emperor's sensitivity (and reactions) to affronts was legendary long before a farcical performance brought him across the sea.

Kaleb…

Her heavy eyes drifted over the Palace's private marina, past the royal wharf, and froze on another collection of quivering flames. While the bodies were too small to discern at this distance, it was clear from the moving torches and glinting helmets that a cluster of soldiers had assembled where the beach met the main dock. They appeared to be celebrating.

And then a previously dark patch lit up bright with fire, and Patra spotted the pole rising from the sand. They'd set someone on fire. Though she knew it was Kaleb, it couldn't be Kaleb. The torches scattered, and someone doused the fire with a basin of water, and then the torches reassembled beneath the pole. They were still torturing Kaleb. But it wasn't Kaleb. Her heart couldn't allow it to be Kaleb.

Without even the tiniest spark of a plan, Patra dashed up the stairs, past the Library level, past the main level to the arboretum. Ensuring the area was clear, she went to the small grove of plum trees—an orchard set right up against the east wall—and she dropped to her knees, poking her fingers into the soil. She found the hidden door, slid it aside, climbed down into the dark, shallow tube, and slid the hatch back over—but stopped halfway. Barbillus would still need an exit. The side gates had all been barricaded from the inside and out, and he'd never find the other secret exit on the southwest terrace.

She pressed her shoulder to the hatch's underside, and lifted with her legs. Straining to the very end, she raised it until it leant against the wall, then pulled her palla from around her neck, draping it from the corner as a flag.

Sitting down at the bottom of the vertical tube, she slid feet-first through the darkness, reaching the small tunnel's end a moment later. The circular door rolled aside, and she eased out, rolling the camouflaged disk back to its recessed seat. Concealed by a low wall and dense foliage, she rushed to the terrace's high point where the retaining wall met a walking path through the Musaeum's tiered garden.

Now able to view the Canopic Road, the mass of legionaries in front of the Musaeum appeared to be lining up, facing away. Centurions called orders to their units, indeed preparing for a formal event. Patra expected this would be Antonius riding in a chariot to the Musaeum's steps, followed by a delegation of torch-bearing aides.

Reminded of the Library, Patra glanced back and looked to the sky. Her chest welled with prickly relief. She held there a moment, watching the thin stream of smoke billowing from beyond the wall, and then tramped down the path to the empty Street of the Sema, running across to the darkened neighborhood ahead.

The following intersection revealed the Army's apparent tail end, so she continued to the next transversal road, turning left toward the harbor, and sprinting as fast as her knees could bear. What would she do when she reached Kaleb? If his tormenters had bored of their depraved sport, and if air still filled his lungs, she'd find a way to end his suffering. Sickeningly, that'd be the best case. She entertained no more fantasies of rescue. Or perhaps he'd achieved death much earlier, and the fiends had had to relegate their sadistic appetites to desecrating a corpse.

* * *

Patra suddenly realized she'd blindly crossed the hundred-foot-wide Canopic Road, oblivious to the gathered Legionary. She hoped the reverse was true, as well, but if she were honest with herself, by entering the heart of the Palace District, had she not just surrendered any hope of escape? She'd followed Kaleb directly into agony, humiliation, and death, and yet she somehow continued on without hesitation, and with zero expectation of a favorable ending.

Because she didn't love him as she loved Philip, or Wahbi, or Zenobia, or her scribes, students, Unza. She was *in* love with him, and his presence in a room produced the same warmth in her as simply knowing he was nearby, and it felt the same today as it had a decade ago. With her life's work over, and her life's one love stolen, what worth did life now hold?

Gasping, she staggered across the small bridge to the Poseidium's rear wall. Roman soldiers were everywhere—walking about, carrying crates from the docks, guiding horses into the city, and all with a euphoric air. Laughter rose from the torch-lit Palace District as much as it had during Kaleb and Philip's performance.

None seemed particularly mindful of her presence (slaves, too, moved about the area, also bearing a heavy burden of cartons), but with empty hands, this neglect wouldn't last.

She slid along the thin ledge that followed the temple's back wall. Only half a step from the wall flowed the Poseidium's surrounding moat, and though only waist-deep, a clumsy splash, or even the resultant ripples around front, would not go unnoticed. Fortunately, the paths along the temple's west side remained unlit, and therefore untraveled. Patra kept on the ledge—heel to toe—until reaching the open peristyle at the front where the enormous columns had been carved into statues of the Sea God.

No one stood inside the peristyle; however, Patra could see between columns a small group of legionaries kneeling before the reflecting pools in front—gratitude and prayers for this and future safe voyages.

Centurions' urgent calls to join formations grew more insistent, and the divided troops scrambled to their units on the temple's opposite side. Patra overheard garbled questions from legionaries, but fragments of a leader's answer revealed enough: "City Guards already lit the building ... displeased but the ceremony commences shortly."

Unobscured by nearby hand torches, the main dock slowly materialized in the night's blue glow, and with the Lighthouse rekindled beyond, a ghastly silhouette gained focus. It was the thick wooden pole, rising up from the shallows beside the dock, and attached to it a shrunken, crooked figure.

The soldiers' cadence faded behind her and, after a quick scan of the area, Patra bolted through the peristyle, past the towering stone deity surging from the reflecting pool, and down the loading path to the dock.

Just as her first sandal hit the dock—such that she momentarily thought it her own doing—a sudden *pop* preceded an abrupt tearing, like that of fibrous, charred meat, and Kaleb's body fell hard upon the concrete ramp. The sound recalled a taut roll of branches more than human being. He'd been suspended by rope, and his overlapped hands had been nailed to the post. The knot had apparently burned away, placing his full weight on the spike. It'd torn up through both hands.

Unwary of potential ears catching her startled whoop, she resumed to the blackened form ahead.

Her legs buckled as she came upon him, and she crumpled to the unforgiving surface. They had not stripped Kaleb entirely, as Barbillus's man had recounted. Kaleb's distinctive ornate sleeves had bonded to his arms and shoulder, and his frayed Kushmen's tunic clung to his jutting sternum, all begrimed with dark soot.

Though she couldn't bear to look, and her eyes blurred with relentless, stinging tears, she glimpsed his gaping, lipless mouth, where browned teeth held frozen in a pleading wail. With her face in her hands, she moaned and clutched her cheeks, wishing to claw out her own eyes. Kaleb's beaming face flashed in her mind as he gloated about his superbly white teeth, countering someone's suggestion that his grooming time could be better spent, since "... *we'll all be bones or ashes in a few turns of the sphere,*" to which Kaleb quipped, "*But my skull will boast the purest, whitest gnashers around ... The envy of the catacombs.*"

Patra wished to curl into him, or at least to caress him, but her horror acted as a barrier, repulsing her floating hand. She swiped away her tears and rocked with fury, murmuring over and over, "Kaleb ... Kaleb ... Kaleb ..." What purpose had this served? Who would be saved or pardoned by his irrational act?

His chest caught her eye once more, and she noticed the oddly sharp edge of his breast bone.

Not a sternum!

She broke through her dread, wrapped her hands in her stola's draping material, and grabbed it—seared cloth and burnt flesh flaking away as she pried it from him his chest. The flax neck cord resisted two yanks before the scorched end snapped at the key's loophole. Tunic material and thin patches of other matter remained glued to the surface, and she brushed the key wildly between stola folds until most of it was gone.

With his Library key cradled in her lap, she experienced an odd new relief, or perhaps peace, or vision of future peace. With this token that he'd kept on his person as often as she with her own key, she'd take him with her wherever she went. There'd linger only the memory of today's agony that she'd need to overcome—and it would always be there, a flaming shield guarding a lifetime of beautiful memories.

* * *

Across the placid marina, rollicking laughter roared from the Imperial Palace as Patra crept from the beach. She'd plan to escape eastward, through the Jewish Quarter, but didn't realize Romans still occupied the Palace, or any other structures along the curved shore.

She dropped to the grassy sand and peered past the water. A group of highly decorated Romans streamed out onto the flickering veranda, along with apparent non-soldiers in embroidered tunics.

The group—a dozen or more—swigged the remains of their wine as they edged toward the bridge leading down to the path. The very path from which Patra lay an arm's length away. They had to be heading to the Emperor's ceremony, where the entire Army presumably still waited. As if on cue, a grand Centurion helmet rose from the pack, its polished iron and brass gleaming in the torchlight. Spread wide above, a searing red crest of horse hair stood angled front to back. Little helping hands emerged from some unseen servant below raised a molded bronze facemask, and affixed it at the helmet's sides. While Patra couldn't make out the mask's details, it was well known that Antonius fancied himself the embodiment of a fierce wolf, and at such a ceremony as this, with the Emperor in attendance, no one but him would present themselves in such a way.

Patra needed to find quick shelter before they exited the torches' cloaking shroud. She hopped to her feet, crossed the wide walkway, and ran into the floral orchard that lined the path. An array of thorns greeted her upon entrance, slicing one arm at various heights. With the joyous voices growing louder, she stifled a wince, and tiptoed alongside a decorative wall. If her memory and sense of direction were correct, the orchard continued to a subcottage of the Palace, and the wall ended at a gate leading to the Caesarium.

A moment later, she found she was almost right. Both the orchard and wall ended at the guest cottage, but no gate lay in view. The wall wasn't much taller than her, and its blocks provided moderately helpful steps, but she hadn't scaled a wall in decades.

She tossed Kaleb's key over first. It landed with a soft crunch in dead leaves.

Horses' whinnies reverberated between structures somewhere a few buildings over, back toward the road into the city. As she reached the wall's wide top, the horses' clamor was replaced by clopping hooves and the rattles and clanks of one or more chariots, but then abruptly stopped.

She glanced about her in search of onlookers in the darkness, but found none.

Nonetheless, she rolled off the wall, crashing down into the soft leaf pile. With her hands wrapped once more in her stola, she swept around the leaves in search of the buried key.

"Who's there?!" called a gruff, old man's voice, and Patra spotted him on a balcony ahead.

She hadn't entered the Caesarium, but one of the many wealthy estates speckled throughout the area. She guessed he was one of the consuls in the magistracy, and would no doubt recognize him given a closer look. He must have been watching the parade when she crunched into his garden. Leaning over his balustrade, he inspected the courtyard, but even if he saw her, he wouldn't be able to recognize her in the dark. Nevertheless, just one block away, it sounded as though something had stalled the Emperor's chariot ride out to his legions.

"I hear you there," the resident said. "If you've come for spoils, you've come to the wrong quarter. Back to the slums with you before I summon the entire Army!"

Definitely a consul.

Patra searched the courtyard for a gate or other accessible exit away from the house. Her only quick option seemed to be a half-wall dividing the outlying garden from a veranda area. The half-wall intersected the main wall—offering a much easier ascent than her prior effort—leading directly to a shoulder-width gap between two adjacent structures.

Wrapping Kaleb's key back in her stola, she left the noisy leaf bed (after two final crunching steps), scurrying to the low wall.

"I see you there!" She must have appeared as some shadowy creature by the new tremble in his voice. "I see you right there! I see you! Go! Just go!"

Patra vaulted herself up the two wall tiers, threw her legs over the top, and paused. The space between the small structures was as black as the Library's secret tunnels. She was as likely to land on piles of twisted metal as much as discarded blankets.

Unwilling to leave it to fate, she clinched the key under one arm, and pressed her feet and arms against both walls, slowing her descent. Not as bad as she'd feared, but a splintery board had been shoved into the small space, and tore her stola as it scraped up one of her legs. The sting lasted only an instant, however, because some hidden animal bustled about in the blackness, only a step ahead of her.

Was it a city dog? A large cat?

Its head turned to her, and froze—the minutest white glow dotting each eyeball. Reason preempted her instinct to shout it away. If it lunged for her, she could strike it with the key's stone end. Rather than waiting, she thought to thrust a desperate kick to its backside, when a faint aroma curled into her nostrils.

She inhaled … deeper.

A pungent odor she generally associated with Coptic men pervaded the dark gap—stale though, as that of old clothes versus fresh sweat—but it was the unique scent it carried with it that sent her thoughts asunder.

It was the smell of ... "Kaleb?" she whispered.

"By the grace!" he choked. "Patra!"

Each rushed forward, colliding in the tight gap, and their arms became crazed serpents embracing every part of the other, as if each strip of the other's back must be held for validation. He grasped her shoulders and neck. She seized his jaw and cheeks, and fell into him once more, planting her face in his neck. There, she found, his scent dwelt most prominently, and his borrowed peasant's rags could hardly infringe.

"You made it out!" he whispered right beside her ear. His breath warmed her entire body. "Philip? Others?"

She didn't want to begin an exchange just yet, needing to live in this a moment longer. She nuzzled into his neck, stroked his cropped-off hair, caressed his face. A vague observation that his beard was gone.

"Alive, alive, alive ..." she droned, and then desperately needed to say more. She clutched his head beneath the ears, holding his face right before hers. "I love you, Kaleb," she said quietly. "Kaleb, I love you."

"I love you, too, Patra," he whispered, worried they might be heard. He tried to glance back, but she held him fast. His hands wrapped around her wrists. "You know I do."

"No. Beyond that," she said, breathless. "You're everything to me. I can't live without you. You're everything. I love you."

Wind whistled softly into his nostrils as he inhaled. She didn't care if he said something dismissive, or grateful, or generic, or something about his wife. There was no need for promises of some glorious, imaginary future together. In this moment, she'd simply felt compelled to say those words to his face, and to continue holding him. But he was hiding nothing from her as he had in the past. His true feelings surged through her hands and into her head, and he pulled her to his lips.

* * *

Leaning against the opposing walls near the end of the building gap, Patra and Kaleb's arms interlocked beneath each other's sleeves.

Closer to the road, dim starlight shone on Kaleb's face from a patch of open sky. "You're certain Philip got out of the city?"

Patra's thumbs stroked his forearms. "Not absolutely, but fairly."

"And the smoke was from the Library? Not the halls?"

"Fairly certain."

Kaleb sighed and nodded and peered back toward the wall at the end of the space. "I thought that official was calling to *me*. Saying he could see me somehow. I thought the Emperor would hear and send legionaries. His convoy was stopped just beyond the stables there." He nodded to the long building across the road.

"Who was the man at the docks? Everyone thinks you went to the palace to turn yourself in. That you sacrificed yourself—for no real benefit, I'll add. I couldn't believe you would be so stupid. I was utterly lost."

"I see that. I'm so sorry. And no, I could never. I thought you'd know, I'm far too much of a coward. What they did to that man …" He stared off in a haze.

"Who was he?"

"A Kush farmer. His land was seized by the magistracy last month. He'd come to me offering himself into slavery if I'd support his family. *Eleven* children. I sent for him yesterday, offered his family half my wealth and all of my titles. He didn't hesitate a second, even after I explained there'd likely be unimaginable torture. He asked to swap clothing at once, only wishing to know when I'd deliver on my end of the bargain. I told him to spend time with his family, meet me again today. I trimmed his beard to my way, shaved off mine, and I had him do this to my hair." His gaze drifted again, toward the wharf. "I watched it all from this spot."

Patra felt his pain and remorse. She hazily grieved for the dead man and his family, but only Kaleb mattered at this moment. Only his warm skin and beating heart and that face. "You look like Philip now."

Kaleb stared at her like a riddle, then emerged from the fog in his head.

He eyed his rags, smiling weakly. "He'd take offense."

"Your key!" Patra shuffled deeper into the gap and probed the ground with her sandal. She found it near the wall and bent down.

"Don't touch it!" Kaleb whispered behind her.

"I'm not." She picked it up with her stola, and turned back to him.

"I don't want it," he hushed. "I *can't* have it ... And you shouldn't either. Get rid of it."

"I will not." She touched his arm again. "Now ... What's next?"

"I commissioned a porter to meet me here with a large chest, or some sort of crate requiring multiple carriers. He's late."

Patra glanced out to the road. "How late?"

"Hours. He was supposed to arrive at sundown. And no, I didn't pay him first. I provided a small stipend. And yes, he may have recognized me, and yes, he may have sought a larger pay-off by turning me in."

"And perhaps met with laughter and discipline for his attempted fraud. They've already killed Prince Kaleb, have they not?"

He nodded. They stood there a moment, thinking.

Kaleb gripped her arm. "Kiss me again."

"Rich man!" called a hushed voice in rough Greek.

They looked up. No one stood in view outside the space.

"Rich man! You still inside?"

Muted knocking on thick wood.

Kaleb slid past her. "That's him." He poked his head out the gap. He whispered, "What are you doing? Where have you been?"

"Rich man! You said you be in here."

"Not in there. In *here*. It doesn't matter. Where's the load?"

The unseen voice wore a constant smile with many missing teeth. Even having only heard the voice, Patra didn't trust him. "We have around that side … Over there."

"We?" Kaleb whispered, irritated. "Who's 'we'?"

A dramatic singsong—the negotiator's hymn: "Rich maaan … How I bring load for many *people* … with no many *people*?"

"I didn't say multiple—Ah. Forget it. It works, actually. My apologies for doubting you." Kaleb stepped out of the gap, and Patra peeked out behind him, seeing the porter's face for the first time. Kaleb clapped his back warmly. "You tell anyone else about me?"

Astonished innocence. "Anybody *else*? What anybody *else*?"

"Do you know who I am?"

"You rich man!"

Kaleb turned back to Patra and said in Latin, "I'd have never guessed in a hundred years, but he's telling the truth. Let's go."

At the Caesarium's front corner, three other men loitered by a large, sealed crate resting upon two carrying staves.

As they approached, Kaleb said, "We'll only need one of them. The others can go."

The dismissed two complained in Coptic as they shuffled off, demanding to still be paid. The fast-talker told them they'd discuss it later.

Kaleb positioned himself at one of the front ends, motioning Patra to take up the other end of the staff behind him. All four knelt and gripped their respective pole positions.

"What's in the crate?" Patra asked before lifting.

"Heavy thing!" the porter beamed, and then counted down, "Shomunt, sno, wah!" The crate rose with minimal effort—likely only the weight of the crate itself and the staves. The group paused at waist height, then he called, "Eetsweh!" and they brought the poles to their shoulders. "Pah-awtz!"

They commenced walking toward the Canopic Road, followed the two turns before the road widened, and offered a direct view of the amassed Army.

"Turn before the Canopic," Patra said in Coptic.

"Ah, like a true Egyptian!" the porter said with delight. "Like an Egyptian priest, most comparable, I think." As they reached the last east-west road before the Canopic, he ordered, "To the right!"

Two blocks later, the thick smoke from the Library came into view, and the voice of the Emperor or some other official or general broadcasted an impassioned speech.

"Steer clear of them," Kaleb murmured, and Patra stuck her head out to see past him. "Steer wide … and slower."

Files of legionaries extended all the way from the main thoroughfare to this parallel road, their unit's flag and torch-bearing end rank blocking half the intersection. Patra now regretted the arbitrary choice to carry the left staff. If any soldiers glanced back at them, both she and Kaleb would be in full view. Thankfully, at the moment, neither of them stood out as particularly affluent. Her hair was in tangles, and she imagined her face must be thoroughly smudged with assorted filth.

"…and despite strategic setbacks, it was the faith, skill, and perseverance of all of *you* who won not a narrow victory, but a decisive one!" Cheers from the throngs as Kaleb and the porter led them in a wide arc behind the soldiers. "I needn't tell you that this woman, despite the hindrances inherent in the sex, is no woman in the Roman sense. Is she *Warrior Queen*? I leave that to her vanquishers to determine …" Laughter from the crowd. Dismayed, Patra tried to steal a glance to the Musaeum stairs. "But there's no denying her army fought as true warriors, and our fallen …"

Passing the last file, Patra glanced once more, catching a glimpse of not just Zenobia—decrowned and wrists bound, standing on the highest steps, close to the landing—but Wahbi, too, at her side. The speaker in front of them wasn't Antonius, but some general. Antonius, in his wolf mask and helmet, sat upon a gilded throne above them all in the Musaeum's front archway, his wide-spread feet resting upon the heads of two lion skins.

"Your Emperor recognizes the bloodline of this boy, and does not fault him for the acts of his petulant mother..."

"You, porter!" a nearby Centurion called as they left the intersection.

"Rotate right," Patra whispered, and the others complied, bringing the crate around so their Egyptian friend could respond.

"Yes to the soldier, respectfully," the porter said with his usual pleasantness.

"Come back here," the Centurion barked. Someone whistled from up the road, and the Centurion motioned to hold, tilting his spear toward the crate-carrying group. "What's that you're carrying there? And where are you from? All of you."

"Rhakotis is my home, and all of our home," the porter replied, and Patra felt the weight shift as he bowed.

The Centurion sauntered closer, right up to Kaleb, and Patra's gut tangled up all over again. "I want to hear *him* say where he's from."

Kaleb's skin tone was essentially the same as any native Egyptian, so she didn't understand why he was being singled out. She wanted to break out ranting at the Centurion in Coptic as she'd seen from upset women on many occasions, but it could just as easily raise suspicions further, rather than help.

Kaleb didn't speak more than two words of Coptic, but if he answered in Hebrew or Kush, the soldier would know no difference.

"Rhakotis," Kaleb said quietly.

"Rhakotis, huh?" The Centurion leaned close to Kaleb's neck. "Then why do you smell of Cretian iris perfume? You're not from Crete?"

"Keep it down, back here!" the senior Centurion said as he stomped up to them. "The Emperor's about to speak! What's so important?"

"Smell this man."

"Excuse me? Fall in, Naris."

"No, no, listen," the first Centurion insisted. "I know this aroma. Smelled it instantly as they passed. It has Cretian iris oil in it. If you can even locate a purveyor, that's three hundred denarii, minimum."

Now he had his superior's attention. "Three hundred? That's half a year's salary. You, put that down and come here. Let me smell this oil. And hurry up."

In front of Patra, Kaleb's shoulders rose and fell with a deep breath. His head turned subtly toward the Emperor, two hundred feet away.

No, no, no, don't do anything foolish! Please!

"Soldier, sir," the porter attempted.

"Silence!"

They slowly lowered the crate, still acting as though it held a burdensome load, and as soon as Kaleb's fingers released the staff, he lunged at the first Centurion, snatched away his spear, and charged toward the Musaeum.

"Stop him!" cried the senior Centurion.

"He's a thief!" shouted the first.

Patra clapped her hands over her mouth.

Kaleb! They hadn't suspected anything but robbery!

He bypassed the ranks of legionaries caught off-guard, reaching only the middle of the Canopic Road. Shouts and drawn swords. Antonius rose from his throne. Zenobia studied the spear-wielding gatecrasher. Wahbi stood oddly still and confused.

In seconds, Kaleb was surrounded—well before reaching even the base of the stairs. He swung the spear wildly about him, barking at the advancing circle of spears, "Back! Get back! Rape! Fratricide! Incest!"

The evenly filed troops muttered and laughed, breaking ranks and spreading out wide, now blocking all but the view of Antonius, and fleeting glimpses of Zenobia's face. The crowd's calls grew to muddled chaos.

The din rapidly lowered to soft murmurs.

"I'll ask only once more, my audacious friend …" Antonius unfastened his wolf mask, curling it under an arm. "… What's your name?"

Now the whispers fell completely mute. Patra's head spun. Her body tilted. Someone grabbed her at the elbows and held her up. Strange words whispered near her ear.

"… last chance. We go now …"

And then her ears sharpened at the first syllable trumpeted from Kaleb's mouth. "I am Steward Philip Ammonius of Alexandria!"

Patra's legs betrayed her, shuffling below as firm hands on her arms drove her from the scene, and up the deserted side street.

TWENTY

Alexandria, Egypt – Present day

"Matt? … Matt?"

The deafening commotion had finally ended, now reduced to the sporadic clinks and clatter of a settling disaster, stray fragments bouncing outward from the unseen chaos, and most dreadful: the muffled crunch of a buried object when it finally gives in to the burden above.

Matt wasn't answering—or making any sound at all, for that matter. She wanted to rush forward to where she last heard him, but she had nary a clue what she'd be walking into. Perhaps there was a light switch by the door. Where was the door? There wasn't so much as a feeble sliver of light creeping in from the hall.

If she hadn't left her battery-less phone in the—

The phone!

She'd stuffed the phone Matt gave her into her front pocket! She pulled it out and hit the Home button. The lock screen was dim, but in the pitch black of the room, it cast a surprisingly helpful glow. She shined it before her and the outline of a barbed, tangled heap appeared in the blue glow.

"Matt?"

She unlocked the screen and tapped a random icon, hoping for a brighter color. A white background appeared, boosting its radiance many times over. Now, the room materialized in front of her and, with it, answers.

Before Matt and Joss's visit to this storage room, one would've found a hastily arranged space with slapdash rows of dissimilar shelves, wire-style baker's racks and wheeled carts, and repurposed cubicle desks, all jam-packed with seemingly ancient artifacts. What didn't fit on surfaces was clustered in sections on the floor, or stacked up, or leant against other objects. Pottery, spearheads, tools, sculptures, glass jars of coins or rings, disembodied stone limbs and heads, and hundreds of other random fragments that may or may not have been in pieces prior to their arrival.

Joss guessed these relics had been whisked from the scroll vault so it could be made into the scroll vault. Somehow, the door handle must have given Matt an outdated view of the room. Maybe it was a new knob. Maybe it was moved from some other door. Or hell, maybe Pete or whomever moved this stuff in here had worn gloves!

As she tiptoed through the outlying debris, the terrified quake in her chest intensified. Only one of Matt's legs protruded from the mountain of rubble, and it wasn't moving. Threads of blood trickled down his exposed calf and ankle.

The screen shut off and she flinched as though the darkness was a physical thing, enveloping her. Pulling herself together, she reactivated the screen and steeled her nerves. Whatever his condition in there, her trepidation wouldn't help.

Nor, she imagined, would the shouting Russian man in the hall.

"*Vykhodeet! Ya vizhu, vy tam!*" It sounded like he was yelling from the elevator lobby.

Joss touched the screen again to keep it lit, set it face up on a cardboard box, and plowed her way through the crunching wreckage. It appeared Matt had tripped over an object on the floor, blundered forward to discover even less stable footing, and then fell into an open space ahead, arms blindly grasping for a handhold. His hands found waiting on either side two overloaded, unstable wire shelves—probably on wheels—that toppled inward, unleashing a cascade of fragile artifacts, colliding and shattering and raining down on a body with only a T-shirt and cargo shorts for protection. The shelves' bottoms looked to have rolled outward, smashing into yet more racks. Their final state was a sort of overlapped tent roof.

Joss tossed aside some sort of shield, then kicked and burrowed her feet until they found mostly firm ground. She knew she was creating another noticeable commotion, but the guy outside didn't need any more clues to know something was up. Uncovering Matt was her top priority, either way.

No matter how she did this, more stuff was going to fall on Matt. As long as she didn't lose control of a half-raised shelf, she figured matters couldn't be made any worse.

She stretched back to reactivate her inefficient light source, took a breath, and hoisted up the top rack. Debris had settled beneath its former standing spot, so it didn't exactly pop right up. She had to heave and twist and ended up finding more success in pushing it backward rather than sideways. More ancient artifacts crunched and popped, and something big shattered when she powered through the final shove. Out of her hands, the rack continued forward, sliding off the other shelf resting atop Matt, and crashed to the concrete floor.

Joss wrestled her way back to a standing position, trying to ignore the cold, spreading wet on her freshly sliced shin. Back in the dark, she fumbled around in search of the infuriating phone.

There's gotta be a way to keep this damned thing lit ... Does this OS have a flashlight function?

She hadn't wanted to waste time figuring it out, but now she was wasting more time having to turn the thing back on every ten goddamn seconds.

Bam!

A flashlight icon had been sitting on the home screen the whole time. And now the scene shone bright and clear. Matt was even visible between some gaps in the pile.

The man in the hall shouted some demand again, but this time from the other side of the door. He pounded and slapped, and then revealed he knew a word or two of English.

"Open I shoot!"

More pounding as Joss adjusted her footing to tackle the other rack of shelves. This one appeared to be putting the most weight on Matt, and she wouldn't risk sliding it away. She slipped the phone into her breast pocket so the light shone outward, and grasped the top shelf's broad-side edge. It lifted up and away from her as she extended and arched to avoid stepping forward. A good, solid shove sent the rack tumbling all the way over, setting off a fresh series of thunderous pandemonium.

Joss didn't wait for the dust to settle. She rolled away the heavy remains of a vase, a porous stone face, and other larger items before carefully removing the most hazardous fragments like sharp-edged ceramic and glass.

A second Russian-sounding voice joined the hubbub at the door; this one's English enjoyed a much wider vocabulary. "We won't hurt if you say where Matthew Turner gone. Don't say? We get inside there, we take finger and piece like ear until you say. Or you save trouble, save hurt if you say now."

"*A yesli oni vroot?*" the first one said.

"Da. If say lies, we come back ..." he said as Joss continued swatting or throwing aside the smaller intact items and parts. The second guy figured right that she couldn't hear over the racket, and repeated his latest message louder. "... we come back and take finger and piece, kill, and kill familut."

As he waited for a response, Joss found and brushed off Matt's face. Reddish-brown powder coated his beard and face. Around his lips, nostrils, and corner of his eye, the dust had concentrated in the moisture, forming little muddy sections.

She patted his cheek, whispering, "Hey!"

It was probably a good thing that these guys thought Matt had left. She didn't want to risk them hearing his name.

But Matt didn't flinch in the slightest.

Oh God, what if his neck is broken?

She put her fingers under his nose to check for breathing. Nothing.

Come, this can't be happening. With all the shit you've been through, a crazy accident gets you?!

The door erupted once more with furious banging and unintelligible blabber. She wondered if Pete was standing by at his monitor watching all this go down. Would he open the vault to appease them? What about police? Had they been called, despite the notion that it would only delay the inevitable? She imagined these guys had definitely done something to warrant an arrest, or at least—

Ptaff! Ptaff-ptaff-ptaff!

Gun shots rang out.

Joss ducked, but it'd do no good. Nothing lay between them and the door, and she didn't think the door was bulletproof.

Ptaff-ptaff!

More shouts.

"Skolko eekh!"

Ptff-tff-tff-tff-tff-tff!

Machine gun fire. The corridor sounded like a warzone. Without any more sounds coming from the room, the Russians were apparently done waiting. They were going to blast away the entire door or frame and kick it in.

Ptaff-ptaff! Ptff-tff-tff-tff-tff-tff! Ptaff!

Joss smacked Matt's cheek, though if the ear-piercing melee outside the door wouldn't wake him, how the hell could she? And what if he wasn't coming to because—

No, none of that! Just get him outside goddammit!

Slipping her hands under his back, she winced as jagged edges tore at her flesh. Without letting up, she hooked her arms into his armpits and dragged him backward.

Ptʃ-tʃ-tʃ-tʃ! Ptʃ-tʃ-tʃ-tʃ! Ptʃ-tʃ-tʃ-tʃ!

Machine gun bursts, then a pained shriek outside. The gunfire halted. Someone moaning. There'd been others shooting! They were firing at each other, not the door. Police, after all?

Matt's legs cleared the debris, but beneath his legs or shoes, residual bits grinded across the cement like a fork on a chalkboard. She made it in between two more racks where ancient artifacts still lay upright on their shelves. Holding for a moment to catch her breath, she sat down, spread her legs, and let Matt's arms flop over them. She hunched above his slumped head to shine the phone's light on the back of her bloody hand. The cuts didn't bother her as much as the tiny bulge she found. Grimacing, she used her thumb to prod the tormenting shard of glass out from under the skin.

Ptoff!

A single gunshot, just outside the room.

A new voice—not Russian—disgusted: "Piece of shit."

Ptoff!

Joss was reasonably sure these new arrivals weren't Egyptian police.

A woman called from the elevator lobby, but too quiet for Joss to understand.

"How long ago?" the man replied.

Joss plucked the phone from her pocket and directed the light behind her. They had a straight path to the exit door. With their luck, someone had built a brick wall on the other side.

The man's voice—maybe an African accent—drew close to the room, becoming clearer, just as the Russians' had a few moments ago. "If he's certain that's all he has of value, tell him to put him down, and the other one, too—not a single one of them left alive in the country ... Imara, wait. Why were they still here?" The door handle rattled. "The men down here weren't on their way out, or at least they didn't appear primed to go."

Joss turned off the phone's light and closed her eyes, resting her chin on Matt's head.

Shwup ... clack-shink-click ... and then the dull *shunk* of a pistol's top part sliding forward with a fresh supply of bullets.

Joss had seen and heard the operation on TV and movies enough times to feel like she'd done it herself. And the abrupt end to the dialog outside foreshadowed nothing good. In the center of Matt's chest, she slowly curled his T-shirt into her grasp, and then suddenly noticed something. She pressed her hand down flat.

Yes!

She *knew* she'd felt a heartbeat! And a quick one, at that. His chest was rising and falling, too.

Quick, short-stepped footfalls approached the door along with the woman's voice, which definitely sounded like an African accent. "... at the end is electronic lock. All the rest are key."

Without warning, Matt groaned in her lap. It was barely audible, but she cupped her hand over his mouth to keep him from blurting something out.

"Go fetch the keys off that guard," the man said. "Isaiah slid him into the closet behind the desk."

Matt writhed a little and moaned again, louder. Her hand was doing nothing to contain the sound.

His nose!

She pinched it shut with her other hand.

Outside, a woman's boots padded off, just as a cell phone began ringing a short distance from the door.

One of Matt's hands gently pried Joss's fingers off his nose, and he inhaled a slow breath.

"Where are you?" the man outside demanded. "Why exactly are you speaking to me that way? I certainly hope there are others. ... Fine, I understand. How many? ... Fine. Now, rather than asking whether you're certain, tell me your *degree* of certainty ... What?! ...

Out of ten, or out of one hundred?" He sighed and was quiet a moment, then slowly headed toward the lobby. "Don't worry about them. Keep your distance and call me back when they're on a long enough stretch …"

The man's voice faded as he left. Silence finally returned to the basement. Joss only hoped the ordeal was truly over.

Matt's hand returned to delicately remove her palm from his mouth. He whispered, "Let's wait here a couple minutes, okay?"

She couldn't see his face in the dark, but she could hear the shape of his mouth in his words. No doubt the rest of his face, too, wore that soothing, zen expression he used to reassure and calm. An involuntary sniffle escaped her, and her ribs quaked with an odd mania of relieved joy mixed with the escaping stress and dread that'd lay pent-up for too long. She clapped her hands against his fuzzy cheeks and quietly giggle-cried, while Matt emitted a fatherly shush.

"*Sh-sh-sh-sh* …"

TWENTY-ONE

Alexandria, Egypt – Present day

"Usually I can shut it off entirely," Matt said as Joss tweezed from the back of his neck another sliver of white ceramic. "And if not, I can generally filter out the noise of a pretty high number of simultaneous imprints. Mind you, these have tended to be contemporary objects—all the parts of a subway seat, the grab bar, pants of the guy on one side, blouse of the woman on the other—not a hundred different ancient artifacts screaming at me at once."

"And I don't suppose being gouged and crushed by falling stuff helps much, either."

"Physical stimulation can be a factor. Good, now there should be a chunk of green glass somewhere. You see anything obvious?"

She squatted to look at his legs again. He peered down at her through their new hotel bathroom's mirror.

"Mind if I wipe them down again?" She grimaced at the backs of his legs. "I know it stings like hell, but the blood's still making a mess of things."

"Not at all. I'm fine." He dabbed a washcloth on his right forearm where the nastiest wound occurred: a postage-stamp-sized chunk of flesh carved right out, now rotting among the offending shards in the store room.

Joss wrung out her hand towel in the sink and returned to the vanity stool behind him. He inhaled a slow breath as the warm cloth slid down a leg.

"Sorry," she said for the hundredth time. He dismissed it once more, busying his mind applying antibiotic cream. "You know, you never struck me as the macho, *'I don't feel pain'* type."

He chuckled as she began another wipe. "Neither did I ... about myself. My dad was like that. 'No blood, no pain' and that sort of thing. There's something to be said for it, though, in terms of survival. Mind over matter is a real thing. Tell yourself it doesn't hurt, and at the very least, it lessens it. Macho is more about what other people think, and I don't believe it does much to convince the central nervous system."

"So just pretend it doesn't hurt, huh?" she said with a little smirk. "Does that work for emotions, too?"

Kaleb, Wahbi, Zenobia, Phorus, the members, those dogs ... Jon, Rheese, Chuck ... Isis ... Dad.

"Hey, not to change the subject," he said to change the subject, "but can you check if Pete sent those stills from the building surveillance yet? He said he'd email your *j-lynn* account."

She stood up and walked out of the bathroom, half-smug, half-wounded.

It was getting weird with her. And that was dangerous.

He needed to change out of these clothes, too. His T-shirt was practically marinated with her imprints. The compulsion to *"accidentally"* read them was not only distracting, but wrong. Was his ego so deprived after Isis?

Ugh ... Isis. She actually did the test.

He drove Isis's smirking *"told you so"* face from his mind, and lifted his shirt, sticking two fingers into his waistband, and running them along the skin from one side to the other. Nothing in front, however, the same swipe across his lower back yielded the stray shard he sought. It fell past his cheek, dropping from his shorts to the floor. Now, all that remained was from dust that should (hopefully) all wash off in the shower.

"I'm hopping in the shower," he called, and shut the bathroom door. Remembering another thing, he cracked it open and said, "Let me know if you hear from our friends."

Joss acknowledged, and he began his ritual scouring process. His cuts weren't pleased with it.

A numbered and bulleted outline of the next few days expanded in his head. Unlike the previous version, littered with ambiguous gray placeholders, the latest draft retained little haziness. Jivu Absko's fortuitous arrival at the MERC earlier tendered more than a reprieve from Rostik's men and Matt's ridiculous bungle, but also a firmer timeline, and the unexpected gift of insider information. Sadly, Absko must have been wearing gloves, but his phone conversation outside the door yielded invaluable intelligence. Also unfortunate was the fact that Rostik was not among the bodies Absko left behind. Were the men Absko now had following Rostik capable of taking out the Russian mercenary?

From what Matt gathered from the bodies at the MERC, Max and his men were local mercenaries Rostik retained to bolster his numbers. Their orders had been to not kill anyone, but only to capture Matt and Joss. This would have boded well for Leonardo and Josh the cook, but now that Absko was involved, would the guys come out unscathed? Matt had known the pair would be potential casualties, and yet, despite sharing the risks with them (though, perhaps with more optimism than he truly felt at the time), he'd exploited Leo's apparent adoration for the famous Matthew Turner.

He wondered how Joss was doing after witnessing the bloodbath Absko left behind. Her myriad layers of relief had filtered the scene as they walked out with Pete and the others, but a disturbing sight like that could simmer in a person—pools of shiny red on bright white tile; static astonishment from unseeing eyes; the settled dew of aerosolized blood; carmine splatters, drips and streaks, outlying droplets … a charred carcass curling into itself; a beloved one squealing in agony as their insides spilled—

"Nothing from Pete," Joss's voice suddenly came, and from *inside* the bathroom.

"Hey, I'm still showering," Matt said. He'd forgotten to relock the door. Patra's trauma amplified his irritation.

"I know, I'm not coming in. I'm talking through a *weeee* gap, and my eyes are closed."

"Okay, great. I'll be out soon," he said, more graciously. Joss's intrusion had, in fact, come just in time. A welcome distraction.

Was *Joss* a welcome distraction?

"Cool … cool," she said, "… I also have a text from one of your dudes. They finished passing Abu Qir Bay I guess about twenty minutes ago. The silver SUV is still following them."

"Perfect. Please remind them to not be looking back or in the mirrors. Just two guys heading off for field work, you know?" Had he sent them to suffer as Kaleb did, but merely to advance personal revenge?

"I actually replied with pretty much that. And I said if the SUV comes up beside them or something, to stay casual and not look at them all scared, but also not keep staring ahead like robots pretending there's not a big-ass SUV next to them, or worse, to look out the side window and suddenly recoil dramatically like '*What the gosh? Where did* you *come from?*' and then touch their chest all '*Phew! Scared me there, strangers! Teehee!*'"

Was this why he needed her around—perpetual sunlight to match encroaching shadows?

"You texted *all* of that to them?" He felt the last bit of imprinted material leave his body.

"Maybe not *all* of that," she replied. "Anywho, what were you saying before I so rudely interrupted you to go check my email?"

Matt shook his head. "I don't remember. We'll wrap it up when I'm done in here." It wasn't easy being an aloof dick with her.

"Sounds like a plan … So, I've been wondering … Why did you and your girlfriend break up?"

Better than where she'd been trying to go earlier, and did he *really* want her to leave him to his thoughts again? He shut off the water and grabbed a towel from the rack. "She's a cheater."

"Oh, man, I'm sorry … I didn't mean to—"

"No, it's all right. I'm more than over it. She's just wired that way. Always has been."

"Yuck," Joss said, her voice farther from the door now, no longer having to talk over the shower. "Stumbling upon that must have been pretty gut-wrenching. Especially for you."

"Yep, though not in an imprint, if that's what you mean. Isis doesn't leave any."

"What? Like, her skin *never* does the thing? Thoughts just don't … go into stuff?"

He wrapped the towel around his waist, stepped out, and glanced at the door. It was still cracked open, but she'd moved behind it to give him privacy (and to continue talking). "Pretty much, yeah. Hers never have, just like her father, Jon. Something about the Meiers. Her mom imprints, though."

"Uh, that seems like a *really* big deal," Joss said, "but I'm guessing by your reaction that it's sorta common? I'd taken it for granted that everyone just … imprinted on stuff."

Matt slid on fresh underwear, hung the towel over his neck, and went to the counter. "No, you were right. Everyone else does … that I know of. Just the Meiers, so far."

Would the baby?

It'd only just then struck him. Clearly there was heredity involved on the Meier end. But what happened when Matt's blood and Meier blood combined?

Probably nothing.

He went on, "It never occurred to me about Dr. Meier until I got together with Isis after he died. She came to my old house a few years back, said I'd missed the funeral, and gave me a box her dad wanted me to have. I still wasn't ... *at my best*, at that point, and I didn't really know her that well. I think we'd met a couple times at the museum when she was maybe twelve. But I felt like such a selfish jerk for not just getting my shit together and going to the funeral. After my, um—after Cuba—he was sort of a mentor figure for me."

"Yeah ... I wrote that part of Cam's script for the shows. It always resonates with the crowds." Matt held the antibiotic cream in the air. She quickly added, "Please forget I just said that. Jesus H. Mm-hm, go on."

"Right ... so ... I invited her in, and we talked for a while about her father. I opened the box and inside was a bunch of different artifacts, among them this wood block, three-sided, with engraved writing on all sides. You picked it up off my shelf back in Jersey."

"Oh, right, yeah! I remember that. And you snatched it right out of my hands, shoving me along to look at other stuff. I forgot about that."

Matt stepped into clean cargo shorts and snickered. "I wouldn't say I *snatched* or *shoved*, but yes, I did return it to the shelf. Anyway, once I was able, I spent quite a bit of time with that block." He turned on the clippers to trim his beard, raising his voice to talk over the buzz. "It was carved in a city called Tadmur, in the middle of Syria, by a furniture maker named Aviena. Her great-grandfather—supposedly—Prince Kaleb of Kush, had passed down the polished stone version of it, but this original had at some point fallen and broken into multiple pieces. Aviena's medium was wood, so she decided instead of trying to bond it all back together, she'd reproduce the keystone the best way she knew how."

"That's amazing," Joss said. "So Isis's dad gave you the first Taria. Crazy. Wait, but that block on your shelf was *way* bigger than a Taria."

"The head librarian's keystone was much larger than the others, and Patra hated the weight of it. She traded hers for Kaleb's early on."

"So you've known the *whole* Alexandria story, and exactly where all the scrolls were since ... since three *years* ago?!"

"Not exactly. All of my information before we got hold of Ostrovsky's pieces was a hundred years more recent, so obviously not from anyone physically present at any of the major events. Though certainly useful, everything was secondhand. Aviena doesn't ... well, *didn't* even know the names Patra or Philip—only that, besides her ancestor, there'd been two other stewards: a man and a woman, and that the man had been killed around the same time as Kaleb. Aviena's a second-generation Palmyrene sculptor with no real personal affinity for Alexandria or the Library. Every day she sings the song her mother taught her while turning the keystone over in her hand. She knows there are hidden scrolls, and that every six seasons, she's supposed to go to Thonis to meet the others. But more as tradition, versus mission. She often skips it."

Matt rinsed his face and grabbed the can of shaving cream.

Joss was leaning against the doorframe now, watching. "When you were having me jot down all those translated words on the plane ... that was all for Markus's benefit."

"Not entirely, no. There was definitely new information I wasn't expecting on the other keystones. But we'll get back to that. Where was I? Yeah, Aviena ... Not much interest in her family history. See, in the decades after Zenobia and Patra, the Library's shelves were rebuilt and *mostly* restocked. A bunch of scrolls from other libraries were acquired or copied, and scribes had almost immediately set to work recreating what they knew had been lost. In the minds of the stewards' descendants, they were keeping a rather useless secret about some rather commonplace items. They had no idea that a hundred years later, another attack and a huge fire would reduce all of it to ashes. Plus huge cultural changes swept the region over the centuries. Society stopped caring about keeping a giant library full of information, or at least information about cultures or religions other than their own."

"Sad," Joss said. "Probably thought they could just erase competing religions."

"Yup. That exact mission has been more successful than people know, on multiple occasions. There's a legend—I don't know personally if it's true—that a Muslim Caliph, after conquering Alexandria, was told of this great library of knowledge. He supposedly told his general, 'If these books agree with the contents of the Qur'an, then they're redundant and unnecessary—burn them. And, if they don't agree with the Qur'an, then they're heresy—burn them.'"

"Yikes. Society's come so far." He eyed her and she winked. She went on, "Sorry again, um … You said this Aviena didn't know much about the Library and everything, so with only her wood reproduction, how'd you know where the other Tarias were?"

"I knew where Patra's was." He rinsed his razor in the sink, and continued shaving. "One of Philip's daughters came back to Alexandria a decade after the tragedy. She made many of the greatest sculptures you find in Egyptian museums today. She and the other descendants always met beneath one of her most famous works: the statue of Cleopatra the Seventh. And when two of those families joined, they decided it probably wasn't the smartest thing having two keystones in a single household. So the daughter, Philip's daughter, I assume, created a secret compartment in the statue's shoulder, and hid Patra's Taria in it. A few weeks after I called Pete to tell him where to find the scrolls, I saw an underwater photo of that statue on the cover of National Geographic. Scooped my jaw up off the floor and got to work planning."

"*Wow*," Joss said. "So you *are* learning new things from Patra's Taria."

Matt nodded and continued shaving in silence. For some reason, his reticence to share *everything* he'd discovered about the Library's stewards lingered on. Even what he'd earlier witnessed about Kaleb and Philip's true fates. Why keep any of this from Joss, while also telling her so much?

Ever since that first time in the mirror—the startling eye contact. Patra's words *"I hope your objectives are in accord with our society's timeless principles … "* had been gnawing at his brain. Though separated by seventeen centuries, maybe he was, by default, a sort of honorary new member of a defunct society. It'd probably be wise to learn exactly what those *"timeless principles"* were before he considered talking about it.

Joss gleaned that he wasn't going to elaborate. "Backing up a little, you said this Aviena girl was a descendant of Kaleb's, and that *two* of the stewards' families joined. I didn't think Kaleb or Patra had children, and you said both Kaleb and Philip died in that invasion."

Just tell her. No, not yet.

He didn't even know the answer. In Aviena's memory, she's got her mother and father, Sopatrius, and then there's Sopatrius's mother and father, Skyla and Neos, and Neos's father is Kaleb of Kush. Kaleb, Neos, Sopatrius, Aviena.

"Good catch," Matt said, "and nice to know you're paying attention when I blabber on about Patra. The heirs thing is still up in the air. Patra definitely has no kids at the time of the attack, and she's pushing forty. To my knowledge, Kaleb has no biological children, but he does have a wife in another land that he might've impregnated back when they got married. I'm not sure how long it's been, or if they ever saw each other after. But somehow it *was* Kaleb and Patra's families who merged. Maybe siblings or something."

He set down the razor, rinsed himself off in the sink, and then toweled his face and neck.

Joss crossed her arms and smiled. "Ten years younger. And much more Matthew Turnery, I might add. Just need to grow out the top a bit and ..." She mimed tousling her hair.

She moved to allow Matt out of the bathroom. He grabbed a white T-shirt from his bag and pulled it on.

Joss had followed him. "I've been wondering ... Pete said there were seventy-something thousand scrolls in that room. Didn't you say at some point that the Library had like seven *hundred* thousand scrolls?"

"In all, yeah, but let's pick this up again later. I need to call Markus. And you were going to … *ahh* …" He motioned to her dusty, imprint-riddled clothes.

She peered down. "Oh, *yeesh*, you're right. Sorry. Probably contaminating this whole room, too." She spun about and marched to the bathroom, adding as she went, "Grab me some clean clothes when you have a chance, will you? I don't want to transfer anything. I'll leave this unlocked." The door clicked shut.

Matt sighed.

She's incorrigible.

"Another new phone?" Markus said. "I've been trying to reach you."

"For obvious reasons," Matt replied. "Have you heard anything yet?"

"Yes, we have. Listen well, and no backchat. You need to stay out of this now. It's escalated to something far beyond you and hobbies. Mr. O may reengage with you at a later date. If you're able to leave the country, I advise doing so at your earliest convenience, and not under any existing passport."

Muffled jet engines roared in the call's background, trailing off just as a commercial jet soared over Matt's hotel. Markus was in Alexandria.

"Further," Markus went on, "and this is from me, not him— you should consider temporarily relocating known family and associates. Consider our business for the moment closed. This number will be deactivated upon our goodbyes."

"Thank you, Markus."

The line remained open for a moment, and then Markus hung up.

Good advice. He'd already taken most of it. The dojo would remain on break for the week, I.T. and Mom had gone north to visit Aunt Denora and Uncle Andy at their timeshare, and Isis and the baby were staying at some new dipshit's flat in Manhattan. The latter was the least secure, but Paul had a detail of top folks watching the building.

As for fleeing the country to let the two gangsters battle it out? Not so much.

* * *

Ninety-eight hours he'd stayed awake in Afghanistan. A separate stint of eighty hours that same year. Two and three-day-long operations had become the norm for the past decade. And yet this loathsome, monotonous drive was killing him.

In the SUV's passenger seat, Yuri had fallen asleep again. Dima and Andru yammered on in back about asses, guns, tits, cars, and asses, and Rostik couldn't decide if Andru's deep, nasally, moronic voice was actually helping to keep him awake via ever-mounting rage. Along with his grating tone, the punk's big, wide-set eyes, and his long neck saddled with an inexcusably large Adam's apple, conjured such a dopey creature that Rostik found himself beset with visions of that extinct cartoon sloth, and fingers penetrating and twisting and snapping its neck.

"Would you, Rostik?" said a jubilant Andru, spit sluicing between teeth and cheeks. Rostik eyed him in the rearview mirror. "Would you do a sandy girl?"

Rostik's gaze returned to the road, and the white van half a kilometer ahead.

Andru hardly skipped a beat. "I would. I absolutely would. Yuri did an Irani girl."

"She was Uzbek," Dima countered. "That doesn't count. Huh, Yuri? That Uzbek girl … you consider her like a sandy girl?"

The van turned off the highway, and a plume of dust rose behind it.

"Shut your mouths!" Rostik barked, and slapped Yuri's chest. "Wake up. They turned off."

Yuri—supposedly a cousin of Rostik's, somewhere across the tree branches—sat up without blubbering or signs of disorientation. Rostik always liked Yuri for that instant acuity.

"Any road signs back there?"

"No," Rostik said, and veered onto the dirt road. "Look at the map if you still have signal."

"Have signal. Hold." He paused, zoomed, swiped, paused. "I don't see this going anywhere special. It goes a long way."

Rostik slowed as he entered the van's thick cloud. Upside: they wouldn't notice a pursuer. Downside: if they stopped, he might plow right into them.

"Can we just run them off the road now?" Andru whined. "No more other cars to witness."

Rostik had been considering it, should wind or an opportune turn provide the necessary visibility, but now that the little sloth suggested it, Rostik felt an immature compulsion to wait for the van to stop.

Andru leaned forward, draping his hands over the two front seats. "What I'm saying is we ride up on them, scary-like, and—"

"Shut up and sit back, Andru," Yuri said. "Your breath smells like diarrhea."

This brought a genuine chuckle from Rostik, and Yuri—not intending humor—glanced over with surprise, and laughed himself. Dimu joined, as Andru grumbled and pouted in his seat.

After another ten minutes of jouncing pursuit, curving over, around, and between knobby dunes, the road widened and ended at the remnants of an Egyptian structure. The ruin was about the height of a one-story house, but as wide as a 747 jet was long. Turner and the woman had parked in front of the ruin's only opening: a small, dark cave. Rostik guessed the structure had been a bridge across a river that had since dried up.

He promptly stopped and reversed, backing the SUV behind the small dune they'd just passed. The mound only rose as high as the hood, but patchy grasses and desert shrubs offered them sufficient cover, especially with the sun setting behind them. He killed the engine.

When the dust cleared, they were able to see between the hearty bushes' gnarled branches to the van's front half and cave entrance.

Yuri focused his binoculars on the van. "They left the vehicle. Must have gone in."

"What if it goes all the way through?" Dimu said. "A tunnel. They could be getting away."

"Let's go!" Andru said, and a rifle rattled behind Rostik's seat.

"Hold!" Rostik snapped. "My employers say Turner isn't stupid—quite the opposite. Look at that approach. Wide open for a hundred meters in every direction. How do you know there won't be a scope on you the second you pop your idiot head out?"

"I was just saying ..." Andru muttered.

"Look at the map, Yuri. What's on the other side?"

Yuri handed him the binoculars and looked at his phone. Rostik studied the entrance. This was interesting timing with sunset looming. The van had cruised at a static 110 kph the majority of the drive.

"The building's as deep as it is wide, and it looks from this shadow that there's either another cave on the opposite side, or a tunnel goes all the way through. See?" He angled the screen. "Looks like a depression with the sand all funneling toward this spot."

"Good eye," Rostik said, and returned to the binoculars. "What about farther back? Is there another road? And can we drive around this?"

"Nothing paved anywhere near, but a lot of farmland ... Looks like hiking trails in the highland between. Thin trails ... but maybe dirt bikes?"

It'd seem an awful lot of trouble to bring a tail all the way out here, just to pull a vehicle transfer and escape. That could've been done in a thousand better places between here and Alexandria. He didn't think that was Turner's game. Showing up at the office building despite surveillance, then slipping out the back in the same vehicle they'd been driving around in? He wanted to be followed here. But so remote, as if to provide a witness-free environment.

"Zoom out some more," Rostik said. "Where are we? Give me the nearest town names."

"Ahh ... bunch more farmland ... Tall San al-Haja, San al-Hagar, Ezbet Ata Allah, Ezbet Abou Shalaby ... ezbet, ezbet, ezbet."

"San al-Hagar?" Rostik squinted at the phone screen. "Show me San al-Hagar."

Yuri swiped over and zoomed out. Indeed, to the north lay a sprawling, colorless area dotted with thousands of pale lines and squares—the ruins of an ancient city. Specifically, the ancient Egyptian city of *Tanis*. Rostik only knew this city because Ostrovsky had sent him there for photos just a couple weeks ago. Rostik knew then that it'd had something to do with the stone piece he'd pried from the statue under the bay. And here now was Turner, the man who'd stolen the artifact from Ostrovsky, at an isolated ruin only a kilometer from that well-known landmark.

Turner wasn't drawing his pursuers here; he had no idea he was even being followed! Panic had driven him from the office building, and they'd come straight here without a single stop. Whatever Ostrovsky had hired Turner to find, it was here.

"I need to make a call," Rostik said, and turned on his mobile as stepped out of the SUV. He didn't like using a phone, and avoided it as much as possible. That's why his basic old brick of a mobile did one thing: send and receive calls.

He shut the door gently, leaning in and shoving it until the second clunk. As he clicked the arrow-pad downward through the device's only recent calls, the rear passenger window slid down a quarter of the way, revealing Andru's detestable profile, gazing off coolly as his head bobbed to a non-existent beat.

"Close the fucking window!" Yuri snarled, and reached back, swatting at the cringing imbecile until the window rolled shut. Much to Rostik's pleasure, a muffled tirade continued. "How stupid are you? You know the man's making a call ..." as Andru pleaded ignorance.

Ostrovsky's "red" mobile rang thrice before he answered. "What the shit is going on?"

"I followed them for the past three hours," Rostik said. "He's stopped somewhere you'll be very interested to know. Whatever you've been looking for, I guarantee it is here."

"I'm talking about the diver people building—the goddamn massacre! *Your* people being carried out in body bags!" Ostrovsky's shouting voice crackled in the speaker. "But what? Where are you? Why are you only now calling me? Follow who?"

Yuri and the others in the SUV didn't yet know what happened after they'd left the MERC building. At this point, it wouldn't have been useful for them to be informed.

Rostik disregarded the ranting. "I want to know what the stone piece leads to. What's the real value to you?"

The line hung quiet for a moment before Ostrovsky snorted. "You're looking to renegotiate? With what I'm already paying you? Why would so wise and reliable an asset seek to jeopardize what has been such a long-standing, lucrative arrangement?"

"I don't," Rostik said, resigned. "I simply wished to know of any unstated risks."

"Okay, of course you *wished to know*. I'll tell you then, all is as previously discussed. However, if you abandoned your customary discretion at the divers' building, you will understand if *I* must avoid the *risk* of future exposure."

"I had nothing to with anything that occurred there," Rostik said, eyeing his companions in the SUV. "I left behind a sub while we followed the target out of the city."

"Give me the details of your location."

As Rostik organized his thoughts, he shared the location and specifics. Once Ostrovsky confirmed everything and was satisfied, Rostik asked, "Will you be coming here personally?"

"Perhaps. I'm already in the region. Just remember that the target—neither target—is to be harmed in any way."

After hanging up, Rostik shut off his phone and slipped it back in his right pocket, then withdrew the other phone from his left pocket and waited for it to power up. Yuri gave him an inquiring look and thumbs-up/thumbs-down gesture. Rostik motioned to standby one more minute, dialed the number, and turned his back to the windows.

"Status?" the man said in English.

"They arrived at destination. It is place my employer seeked. You say when we make deal, target is one, plus bonus paid for bonus things. I think this qualify as big bonus."

"That's fine. I'll hold up my end."

Rostik appreciated the man's business sense. Not like Ostrovsky, who punctuated each statement with demands. The man saw when talk shifted to negotiation and always spoke with the proper respect due a partner. When a deal is set, a deal is set. He's then calling the shots. This was the arrangement. But at this stage, whenever it should arise, they were equals.

"What if there was *bonus* bonus?" Rostik added.

"Compensation would be scaled accordingly," said the man. "Do tell."

"What if my employer should be arrived in person?"

"Mmm ... yes, by all means, this would indeed call for a significant raise. I believe a double-over would be fair in this instance. One for the target, two for the bonus materials, four for the guest. Seven total. If this is agreeable, I have questions prior to securing a new verbal contract."

"This is agreeable," Rostik replied. This was far more than agreeable. Rostik had expected standard bonus divisions: half a million for first bonus, another half for second, totaling two million. But *seven* million US? He could more-than-comfortably retire on that. "What is your questions?"

"With how many others will he be arriving?" the man asked.

"Not sure," Rostik said. "Assume no less than four, no more than ten. Four or five is most likely. Plus his self."

"And you still have three with you?"

"Yes."

"Fine. Here is what I'll need, and we'll have a new contract …"

* * *

Leonardo entered the tunnel first, pulling on the headlamp and preparing to bolt all the way through to the other side. He heard Josh's footsteps—close behind at first, but then mute. Leo glanced behind him to see Josh kneeling down just inside the archway.

"What are you doing?" Leo whispered. "We gotta move!"

Josh laid flat on the damp, compacted sand. "I think they're backing up. Hang on a second."

"Dude, are you mental? This might be our only chance! Matthew said not to take any stupid chances, or even look back to see if they're following. What do you think we have to gain by seeing what they're doing?"

"They stopped behind that last mound," Josh hushed.

"I'm seriously about to leave you here, dude. If you can see them, they can see you. What if the quads were stolen and we have to boot it out? Our only advantage is a head start, and bullets sort of narrow that gap."

"They can't see me. I'm in the shadow and looking through a super thin sliver under the van … The SUV's just sitting there. Why would they just sit there?"

"Okay, they're sitting there. Your spy skills are friggin mind-blowing, dude. Let's go. Now."

Josh scooted up on an elbow and twisted around to look at him. "What if they're not coming after us because they've got another car on the other side, waiting to head us off? What if we're sandwiched in here?"

Leo rubbed his head and pulled at his beard. "There's literally *zero* reason for us to think that. Can we just stick to the damned plan?

And seriously, if some fantasy other car is on the other side, how does it help us to be over here on *this* side, this close to the friggin car we *do* know is full of killers?"

Josh's head now lay sideways in the sand, inching to the left for another angle on their pursuers. "Personally, I'd rather be close to the vehicle we can jump back into in two seconds if we have to. Oh, hey, one of them got out."

"Screw it, I'm going!" Leo turned to run.

"N'n'n'no!" Josh whispered. "He's getting on the phone."

Despite the cool, feces-tinged air and constant breeze, Leo's back and chest were sweating like he'd run a marathon. He paced and considered ditching Josh. This was *not* what Matthew had said to do. He was so specific, like *"Do all of this exactly as I say, and you've got nothing to worry about."* What the hell made Josh—a goddamn cook—think he had better judgment that Matthew Turner, who's obviously been through so much unbelievable madness?

More importantly, why was Leo even thinking about any of this? Just go! Josh wants to stay and gather friggin *intelligence*, or whatever, fine! "I'm leaving. See you on the other side, dude."

"All right, all right, I'm coming—wait, he's getting back in!"

"So?!"

"So, what if they just leave right now? You wanna ride forty miles through the desert for nothing?"

Two dull *thumps* sounded outside, like hammering underwater at solid rock. An instant later, two more ... another—five in all.

"Holy hell." Josh clambered to his knees, crawled backward, and sprang up. "Holy hell, dude, go!" He shoved Leo forward. "He just shot them!"

"Shot who?!" Leo said as he scurried deeper into the tunnel, fumbling to turn on the headlamp. "Who shot who?!"

"The driver guy! He closed the door, said some stuff, and just shot all of his buddies, like in two seconds!"

The headlamp's beam bounced and swung across the tunnel walls. Keys and coins and footfalls echoed as if amplified ten times.

The man in the car would hear them and come after them. The tunnel smelled of sewer and death, and Leo imagined he knew why. This was where anyone could kill someone and just leave the body to rot. The squishes and crunches beneath their feet were dozens of decomposing carcasses.

Light!

The other side appeared after a bend, and a few strides later, the silhouettes of ATVs sharpened at the tunnel end.

As Matthew had indicated, the ATVs' respective keys sat taped behind the center tail light.

"Hang on," Josh said as Leo mounted the first quad. "Let's push them out and to the side. Might not make much difference, but I know for a fact starting them in here is gonna blare out the other end like a megaphone."

Leo didn't argue. He kicked the transmission into neutral, and rolled the ATV outside. Josh pushed from the back, helping him up the small rise. He set the brake, and the pair retrieved the second quad.

Helmets and goggles on, they started their engines and eased from the clearing, following the northeast trail.

Forty-five minutes later, with the last of twilight's blue glow dimming in the west, they reached the two-lane road and crossed into a private farm's driveway. As Matthew described, the property was surrounded by a tight wall of poplar trees, and just beyond the trees sat a nondescript box truck with ramp rails. Josh raised the truck's roll-up door, and Leo drove the first ATV inside.

Once both quads were fully secured inside, Josh found a small cooler in the cab. He handed an icy water bottle to Leo (who was now lighting a second cigarette with the remnants of his first), and they toasted to "Not being dead yet."

A hollow rhythm began clapping from the low range of hills behind them. As it grew louder and deeper, Leo realized it was only an echo, and that the beat of the helicopter was, in fact, emanating from southwest.

TWENTY-TWO

Alexandria, Aegyptus – 271 CE

Hours passed in a bewildering haze of movement and whispers, strangers and familiar voices, unintelligible questions, a juddering cart, rippling river. Someone had earlier wrapped Patra in a cloak. Another put her in a cart that smelled of goats and old milk, draping a heavy sheet over her. By a river, someone tried to pry Patra's hands from her waist, where Kaleb's key sat in rolled layers of wool, secured under her belt.

"*He longs to be held as well as to hold, Steward,*" insisted a voice.

White beard, gentle eyes.

Dark face, suspicious eyes.

"*My Queen is not knowing of this person.*" Another man—thick, formidable voice attempting Greek. "*Orders they were clear.*"

Patra became aware of arms wrapped around her waist. A knobby knuckle pressed into her hip.

Another man: "*Our Queen knows me, and I know him. In any case, I'm afraid there are no other options. I leave you now.*"

Creaking wood, a stick's crack, hooves, wheels rolling away.

Patra's focus moved from a man waiting in a small boat, to the old man before her. Nelpus ... It was Nelpus. He was speaking to a tall Palmyrene man in a cloak, one of Zenobia's commanders disguised as a Jew. A matching Palmyrene—wide and stocky—stood with him, face recently mauled, though the gash, stretching from one side of the nose past the opposite side of the mouth and jaw, no longer bled.

As more muddled words were spoken, her gaze hung on the ripped flesh around the lips, the missing teeth, the man's intermittent sucking and licking around the hole. He caught her staring, glared, and snappily cut his eyes down to her side.

Puzzled, she followed his look, finding a hooded young man clinging to her waist, head down. She'd been aware of the trembling arms, the knuckle rooting into her bone, but only as some distant, detached phenomena.

"Hello," she said, and the word cracked in her dry throat. She swallowed. "Who is this?"

Nelpus—it was Nelpus who accompanied her here—drew his attention from the boatman and came to her. "Steward, yes, good to see you … *rousea*." He extracted from a satchel a tied bundle of three scrolls, holding it before her. "From the Prince. Protect these as you would the boy. They go with him. The Prince promised his titles and wealth, *eh*, to the boy's father."

Her cramped fingers uncurled from the key, and she took the scrolls from him. "Kaleb?" She peered once more at the cloaked young man's head. "He was captured."

"Capture and *el-yetht*, Lady," the commander said.

Patra once knew this word … Aramaic …

"Please," Nelpus interjected, "the Steward needn't hear of these things now."

El-yet … when butchering an animal … Like the Jews, they hung the beast to drain the blood and empty the viscera. Kaleb …

"Go on," she said in Aramaic, "I understand."

"Yes, my Lady," the commander replied, relieved to speak naturally. "The ruse endures, however. They believe him the other man, so now only seek you."

Kaleb sacrificed himself for Philip. He could've run, though! We all could've run together! Someone will recognize him. Too many people know the stewards.

The sky was brightening beyond the river.

"Was—" The words caught in her throat. She coughed and swallowed. "Was he burned?" The boy hugged her tighter.

"Steward, don't," Nelpus attempted.

"Was he burned?!" she demanded. "If he wasn't, any number of snakes will be all too pleased to expose the deception."

"He was burned," the commander replied, "by my Queen. They strung him from the Library arch, made him suffer for a short time, demanding to know where you were. And my Queen seized a torch to end it and keep the deception."

A mix of horror and relief washed over Patra, but only for an instant. "And what did they do to the Queen for this?"

"The Emperor ..." Agitated, the commander shifted his neck. "The Emperor laughed and applauded her for doing his work for him, but this was only to take away his embarrassment. Then he said to his people that my Queen was renowned for her chastity, that in her life she never took for herself no men but her husband, even so long ago dead. And then he said instead of taking her head, he would take her with him back to Rome ..." He shuddered. "He said the voyage back would be *enjoyable* for them both."

"And Wahbi?" Patra said. "Your King?"

The commander hesitated, eyes wandering about. He cleared his throat. "The Emperor then said that since he wasn't taking my Queen's head, the balance of justice was spoilt. And he went behind my King, rubbed his shoulders in a father's way, and cut his throat open."

A stifled scream burst from Patra, and her knees weakened once more, but before she could collapse, the quaking boy on her side stiffened his grip again. Her heart was withering. She could endure no more of this. She would grab up one of the chests littered about the riverbank, and hurl it, and herself, into the canal.

The monster executed him in front of his mother. Zenobia would've killed Antonius with her bare hands if there were any opportunity whatsoever. So, too, would I.

Swiftly, Nelpus moved close to her, touched her arm, and gently lifted her chin to face him. "Steward, please. You've this boy, *Neos*, to care for now. I had the adoption ratified yesterday. He is now Prince Kaleb's son."

"Adoption?" Patra murmured.

Nelpus nodded purposefully, eyes wide and kindly smile. "Yes … Neos."

He directed her attention downward while raising the boy's chin.

Neos's face came into view, twisted with angst, his weeping eyes clenched shut. He wasn't trembling with fever, but inconsolable grief. He wasn't the son of a perished farmer who masqueraded as Kaleb, he was King Wahb Allat of Palmyra, son of Queen Zenobia, or his Roman name, Augustus Julius Septimius Vabalathus Athenodorus, or as Patra knew him: Wahbi.

"Yes, yes," Nelpus cooed while his warning expression advised discretion. "The rest of the boy's family fled south, so if you don't mind the burden—"

"It's fine, of course," Patra breathed, and gripped Wahbi's shoulder. She could see now where he'd been, and how he came to be here at her side.

He opened his eyes and she smiled for him. His head lowered once again, nestling back into her abdomen.

"Who ratified the adoption?" Patra asked Nelpus. "If Cassius—"

"He's dead, the Governor," the commander interrupted.

"Yes," Nelpus said. "The Governor and Thomas both. From what I understand, they approached the Emperor after the ceremony and revealed the Serapeum as the collection's true refuge."

"Why were they killed? For not revealing it sooner?"

Nelpus shook his head with contempt. "Thomas spoke out of turn. It was wholly unnecessary. He said 'It's just one disgusting mockery of Rome after another,' or something of the sort. The Emperor asked, who was this man speaking to him as a bathhouse chum."

"He made them be speared to tree trunks, through here," the commander drew a circle just beneath his rib cage. He switched back to Aramaic to be clear, "The Emperor said, 'One's hole ceases to be charmed when a tongue extends too far inside.'"

"Very well," Patra said. "Who is this boatman?"

The commander sneered. "My Queen's cousin vouches for him, but I cannot personally."

Patra stepped aside to see past Nelpus. Wahbi shuffled along with her. The seemingly oblivious boatman held the mooring rope coiled around the post. He was a dark, sinewy, younger man with a headful of thin braids.

She assumed he was Egyptian, and so addressed him in Coptic. "Sir, may I ask your name?"

The boatman peered up, uncomprehending.

"Aramaic as well, my Lady," the commander said.

Now she understood why the commander had felt the need to torture her with the tale of Wahbi's supposed execution. He didn't want the boatman knowing this precious secret. She wondered who the poor boy was who died in Wahbi's stead. If only Zenobia had kept doubles of herself in her company ... But she'd never allow another to accept a sentence intended for her. Wahbi, of course, was another matter. The poor boy, whoever he was, so brave. Cold comfort to his family, but at least it sounded as though he didn't know what was coming.

A rattle up her spine as she pulled Wahbi with her to the small berth's edge, leaning on the mooring post with her free hand. In Aramaic, she said, "Good morning, sir. May I ask your name?"

"Tavi, my Lady."

"You'll take me and this boy safely upriver?"

"Yes, my Lady."

"And what will you do after that?"

"I don't know, my Lady. I pray I find travelers seeking passage back down the Nile."

She turned to the commander. "I have a sense for character, and I trust this man. I wish you both safe travels and peace in life." Both men bowed their heads, and she took Nelpus in one arm. "Are *you* safe?"

He smiled. "I'm safe. Worry not, Steward."

"What if someone discovers your bathhouse?"

He shrugged. "It wouldn't shine too positive a light on me, but the magistracy has always enjoyed both my support, and my *support*. I expect I'll be fine."

She kissed his forehead. "I love you, Nelpus. I could never repay you for all you've done."

"You already have," he said, guiding her down to the boat, "as you have for every other thinking soul immortalized by your selfless deeds. Please pass on my well-wishes and gratitude to your colleague."

Patra sat down on a small, cushioned seat at the boat's rear, and Wahbi—Neos—curled into the floor at her feet, wrapping his arms around her leg, and resting his head near her knee. She pulled at his cloak, spreading it over his legs and tucking it in around him.

The second Palmyrene warrior passed her a small chest, and she set it on the floor in front of Neos. The boatman took another two chests and a food crate, filling in the rest of the boat's floor space.

They pushed off from the berth, and the boatman used his long staff to fight the opposing current, hardly moving at first, but then slowly gaining momentum. Patra waved farewell to Nelpus and the Palmyrenes. She lifted Neos's hood a little, sending loving thoughts through her gaze as she thumbed away his tears. He wanted to tell her things—so many things flashing through his mind. Not until they were very far from here, and alone.

He scooted in closer between her legs and rested his arms and head atop her thigh. After a startled wince, he moved his elbow away, and probed around her waist.

Remembering, she lifted the folds of her stola, sucked in her stomach, and unwrapped Kaleb's key behind her belt. Neos accepted it with wonder, rolling it over in his hands.

"This is yours now," she whispered, "and everything that comes with it."

Bibliotheca Alexandrina, Alexandria, Egypt, 2014

TWENTY-THREE

Alexandria, Egypt – Present day

From his balcony on the twenty-third floor of the Royal Harbor Paradise Resort, Matt took in the sunny view of the Bibliotheca Alexandrina and the adjacent Alexandria University campus—the modern day's counterparts to the ancient Library and Musaeum. Though the new library's brochure proudly cited a close proximity to where its long-lost forebear once stood, Matt found the site rather ironic.

The new library—a magnificent facility in its own right—had been designed to evoke a rising sun, though Matt thought it looked more like an enormous stone coin, aloft in mid-flip, or maybe a sharp-edged cheese wheel. In seeking a tiered internal layout to reflect the original Musaeum's terraced levels, the architect had come up with a brilliant design that made the building's exterior appear to tilt on its axis—rising from Earth on the inland side, dipping underground on the opposite—and placed an infinity pool around the perimeter to offer the illusion of dipping into the sea.

Only yesterday he'd roamed the cobbled streets that once partitioned this area. The pool in front of the Bibliotheca sat where a floral belt and wall had snaked eastward toward the Caesarium, and the building's disk now dipped into the ground where a certain Magistracy consul's estate dwelt long ago.

The vast Imperial Palace could be found a stone's throw north of the new pool, though today such a stone would splash into the harbor's gently rippling shoreline. The peninsula below had been on quite the diet for the past millennium, shrinking from a few football fields wide to the width of an average interstate. The Palace District's once-extravagant acreage now hosted parking lots, apartments, barren fields, and a gridlocked coastal motorway. The only remains of Patra-era mansions lay as rubble on the harbor floor.

The glass door behind Matt slid open, and Joss's head popped out. "Phone for you." She mouthed *"Markus"* and grimaced.

The man's resourcefulness wouldn't concern Matt so much if it didn't highlight the fact that Absko could potentially track him just as easily.

He stepped inside and grabbed the receiver from the nightstand. "Please tell me it took you more than a couple minutes to find us."

Markus chuckled. "Hour after hour, day after day of grueling data analysis, private investigators, satellites, you name it. *Endless* labor."

"We've only been here a day."

"Yes, well, I was exaggerating for banter's sake. I thought you'd like to know your friend left the safehouse where she'd been staying." Matt sat up, stiff. Markus continued, "She's now far from inquiring eyes and under the protection of a Kenyan opposition group, the National Unity Party, whose members aided her initial departure—"

"So you've been holding her all this time?" Matt said. "You told me she escaped."

Markus's attitude changed, as if Matt was being ungrateful about them releasing their hostage. "Escape she did. *Also* with repeated help from Mr. O. Now, she and the boy have been kept safe for a week by our people, while her husband's *extremely* motivated agents sought to recapture her. Am I to understand you wished her and her child to roam the slums, unguarded, until you completed your business, swinging by to pick her up on your way back to the U.S.?"

"No, of course not. I'm sorry. I appreciate all that you and Mr. O have done to help with everything, especially in light of our own unresolved matters."

"Marvelous. Next topic: were you aware of our operative's maligned loyalties?"

Rostik? Maligned loyalties?

"Do you mean working for that other guy? The gray gentleman?"

"So you did know," Markus said.

"Well, no, not until you just mentioned it. But I did happen to hear that he *fired* his own team. Makes sense now, I guess. Do you know where he is now?"

"I do," Markus said airily. "He *remains* with his team, where your two young American friends last saw him."

Rostik's dead. That's a relief. One less thing to worry about today.

"I see," Matt replied. "By whose doing? Yours or the gray guy's?"

"It doesn't matter." That meant it was Ostrovsky who had Rostik killed.

"Well, thank you for the update."

An extended silence, and then Markus added, "Is there anything else you need?"

"Oh ... ah ... no, I think we're good."

"Good. Then I'll ask you. Do you happen to know the present location of the *gray gentleman,* as you say? I'm sure you heard as I did of his arrest on the highway to the Tanis site."

Matt smirked. Markus and Ostrovsky had no idea where Jivu Absko was. "Hmm, so your tracking powers *do* have limits. No informants inside the Egyptian Ministry, eh?" No reply. Matt could feel the disgruntlement seeping from the receiver. "Well, that makes two of us. I really wish I knew where they have him."

"Good day, Matthew." Markus hung up.

Matt glanced at the clock: **10:41 AM**. Time to get dressed.

Joss called from the bathroom, "Shouldn't you be getting dressed?"

* * *

"Target exited lobby," Isaac reported on the radio. "Alone ... Heading to fountain ... *Left* at fountain, *left*. Target *not* heading to hotel car park. Heading east, on foot."

Jivu Absko shifted in the Mercedes's back seat, raising his walkie to his mouth. "Hold position, One. Let Two maintain eyes ... Two: copy?"

"Copy," Imara radioed. "Target in sight."

Jivu leaned to the black-out tinted window, peering up at the hotel's top floor, and spotted Imara's subtle dark bump on the roof's edge. "I hope I don't have to remind you, Two—or anyone else for that matter—that fingers are to be kept loose and obtuse."

"No, sir," she replied.

From his van in the hotel's roundabout, Isaac echoed, "No, sir."

"No, sir," said Jivu's driver, Siko, through the Mercedes's open partition.

Jivu was less concerned with his number one, number two, or Siko, than with the others in Isaac's delivery truck. All had been trained well for standard operations, but in such situations, and at any time when being attacked, it's a natural reflex to protect one's life. They didn't yet appreciate that when Jivu's orders were to not shoot under any circumstances, this directive included to save one's own life. The only life they were authorized to save in this case, if it required mortally wounding Turner, was Jivu's—and there'd better be a true, imminent threat—hands around Jivu's neck, or a cocked pistol with quaking trigger finger hovering near his head.

Having developed an incredibly reckless arrogance over the past few years, Turner thought his insolent remarks would goad Jivu into a hasty, impulsive reaction, as if one so volatile could attain this level of prominence and power. Obviously, Jivu's wrath was not immune to ignition, but the key to victory always lay in one's actions directly *after* their passions flared. Analyzing an opponent's motivations, expected outcomes, their capabilities, connections and allies, and, of course, calculating the enemy's assessment of *your* capability.

Surprise was the most powerful weapon in any man's arsenal. Appearing weak when you are strong, rash when you are cunning and calm, defeated when you are poised to strike a final blow.

Once he'd discovered Rostik's communications had been compromised (a disappointment from one so experienced and careful), Jivu had stopped his convoy to Tanis. The local police he'd paid to accompany him had been justifiably confused at first, but they performed their roles as instructed, and word of his arrest spread swiftly across precincts.

Now, Turner's arrogance and inferior tactics would be his downfall, and Jivu would not be robbed of the satisfaction he'd so painstakingly assured. He needed prolonged, uninterrupted time with his quarry, because he was not so short-sighted as to only seek Matthew's suffering, certainly not for the sake of mere revenge. Turner alone offered guaranteed access to the First *Whore* of Kenya. Turner's pain would be Tuni's pain, and even if her mama lioness's instinct wisely kept her from surfacing personally, her guilt and residual affection would incite irrational behaviors—electronic communication with known associates, accessing old email accounts for contact info—some rash act that would expose her location. He need only provide a short video of a ravaged Matthew to someone who would then, unwisely, share it with her.

"Target cut south behind perimeter hedge," reported Imara. "No eyes on target."

Jivu should've split the team in case of easterly travel. He shouldn't have assumed Turner would take his rental car.

"Should I pursue on foot?" Isaac radioed.

Jivu motioned to Siko to start the engine, and pointed to the parking lot's exit. "Negative, One, hold. We're going around the block to cut off that route. Two, what's on the other side of that hedge? Is it still hotel property?"

"Yes," she said. "It's a ramp to a dock … deliveries, garbage bin, recycling compactor."

Siko gunned it from the parking lot, passing Turner's empty rental car on the way out.

"The long way," Jivu directed him. "All the way around back, then up the alley." He pressed his walkie's button. "Two: the other side of that ramp, it's a tall perimeter fence, yes? No exits unless the docking bay is open, correct?"

"Correct," she replied, "and everything's closed back there. Looks like one door into the bay, the big roll-up door, and then two emergency exits. And no path around the building. The fence ends flush with the building corner."

Her attention to detail was a thing to love. She answered all of his other questions before he could ask.

Back to Isaac. "One, do you have eyes on target through that hedge?"

The delivery truck was parked right alongside the high wall of bushes Matthew had turned behind, but Jivu didn't know how dense the foliage was near ground level.

"Negative …" Isaac said slowly as he confirmed. "Small gap near the trunk of this one near—*No, Mabo, I said hold for orders, so hold* … Shall I exit vehicle to check, sir?"

As Siko tapped the steering wheel, awaiting a light change, something occurred to Jivu: Turner's motives. Someone does not simply walk inexplicably down an empty delivery ramp. There's always a motive. If nothing of interest lay within the dock area, one must expand their field of scrutiny to adjacent areas. And just two meters from that ramp, separated only by branches and leaves, sat a delivery truck full of Jivu's men. *That* was something of bloody interest.

The light changed.

"Go, Siku, fast!" Jivu shouted, and then, into his walkie, "One: beware, beware! You might be compromised. Two: status?"

"No eyes on target. Hedge clear in front and back of One, but no eyes on eight meter segment beside—" She cut herself off, and then, with her voice lowered, "Standby. I believe building security approaching. Advise One relocate immediately." Her transmission clicked off.

Siku veered across traffic, bouncing across the driveway into the alley. Loose objects flew about. Jivu braced himself against the roof and the facing seat across from him.

"Show them your badge!" Jivu replied to Imara. "If the five-second excuse doesn't work, handle the situation." He'd give her a minute to deal with the trouble. "One: proceed as advised. Relocate. Not far, though, just move away from those bushes. Block in those hotel vans across the way, if necessary."

Isaac's flustered transmission began mid-sentence, "—to the truck! Standby, standby!"

Siko screeched to a stop on the other side of the hotel's perimeter fence. The ramp and loading dock were empty. They could see the wall of bushes, but not beyond it. Jivu peered up to Imara's position. She had yet to return. Was it all a bloody setup?

"Keep alert," he said to Siko. "I'll watch over there. You watch everywhere else."

"Yes, sir."

Jivu cracked his window open a few centimeters, and listened. Only tweeting birds and the din of the nearby coastal road, but only for an instant before a hollow *bong!* rang out from beyond the hedge—the sound of someone's back hurled against the inside of a delivery truck. And almost in sync with the impact, a single gunshot.

"Damn it!" Jivu roared.

"—arget hit, target hit!" Isaac blurted amongst a jumble of background commotion.

"Hit where?!"

Jivu waited. Beyond the bushes, muted tumult persisted—as, apparently, six goddamn men couldn't subdue a wounded adversary with zero combat experience.

"Shall I drive around?" Siko asked.

Jivu sighed. He wanted to, but the gunshot could bring authorities any second. "No." He brought the radio to his lips. "Isaac: he dies, you die."

"Target on foot," Imara radioed. He could see her back in her position on the roof. "Headed to the road along hedge… wounded … abdomen."

"Are you *clear* up there now, Two?!"

"Yes, sir. Target heading east again, toward Zero position."

"There!" Siko said, and Jivu spotted him, stumbling down the sidewalk a mere twenty meters ahead.

It was Turner, for sure. He'd shaved his beard. White keffiyeh on his head, matching white dishdasha, save for the bright red stain blossoming at his midsection. He passed the perimeter fence and walked along the parking lot, checking for pursuers behind him. Turner straightened his posture as much as he could manage and began bunching together the bloody front of his dishdasha. He twisted the mass of material into a ball, pressing it against the wound to slow the bleeding.

Passing vehicles gawked at him, but no one stopped. No one wants that sort of trouble, now, do they?

"Should I go fetch him?" Siko asked.

Jivu considered as Turner cut diagonally across the empty, little-used lot, toward the mass of vehicles parked up close to the shopping center entrance.

He was out in the wide open, seeking cover and shelter. The fact that he still strove to appear normal, concealing his wound, meant he didn't trust local emergency responders. Jivu had none on the payroll today, but it was a shrewd precaution, nonetheless. What better transport than an ambulance to covertly shuttle a captive from the city? A delivery truck had felt the more discreet option.

"No. He's not seeking medical assistance. If he keeps walking, no matter how much pressure he tries to apply there, he's bleeding out inside. He'll be dead within minutes. We don't need that happening on the floor of this fine machine."

Siko threw an arm over his seat, turning his thick neck to face Jivu, and lowered his sunglasses. His scrunched forehead looked like eel sushi.

Jivu smiled. "No, I don't need you to kill Isaac. Thank you, though. Stay here and watch me. If you lose sight of me, correct it." He picked up the walkie again. "Two: you still have eyes on target?"

"Yes, sir," she replied.

"Zero pursuing on foot. Watch both. One: stay where you are. I don't want to know who was unable to follow orders." That should calm the nerves surely building in the truck. "Two: do you have eyes on Zero?"

He opened the door on the hotel side.

"Eyes on Zero," she replied. "Target now crouched between blue Bug and gold sedan."

Jivu stood up, and found the indicated vehicles around thirty meters across the lot. His spine popped as he twisted his sore back, too long stagnant in the car. He turned the radio down and slid it into his tight jeans' back pocket, ensuring his silk polo shirt's tail covered the little .380 Ruger clipped inside his waistband.

Strolling around the rear of the Mercedes, Jivu kept his eyes fixed on Turner's shadow beneath the rusty old VW Beetle.

What would he say to him now that time was much more limited than planned? Did it matter? Was a more anguished death really his goal for Turner? There was no lesson to be taught here, no *"next time you'll think twice"* nonsense, or *"I warned you what happens when..."* type of movie villain clichés. He was not the villain in this scenario. He was only a businessman and leader willing to do what every other truly successful man in history had done. And he was a husband and father. Turner was no liberator, but an embittered meddler who *lost*. He lost to a worthier suitor, a superior lover, a superior man.

Jivu slowed as he rounded the VW's back end, craning his neck for a vigilant preview. Imara's muffled voice reverberated in his pocket.

The space between the cars was empty.

Turner had strung his bloody dishdasha across the cars' door handles, and left.

Jivu pulled out the walkie. "Where is he?!"

Imara, containing irritation, "Target now *fifteen* vehicles east of Zero. Shall I slow target?"

Jivu skimmed the tops of vehicles. "How fast is target moving?"

"No eyes at present. Alternating between a sliding low crawl and high crawl on last engagement."

"Then no," Jivu said. "Loose and obtuse."

A noisy family of bag-laden shoppers congregated around a vehicle two rows over, oblivious to the nearby goings-on.

Jivu abandoned the complacent saunter, striding purposefully down the row of cars. How moronic it would be to miss Turner's last moment and last breath, all for negligent overconfidence.

"Eyes?" he inquired.

"Negati—affirmative! Target crossing Ali Moustafa toward the library plaza!"

"What?!" Jivu bolted across the parking lot. The street was more than a hundred meters away! Turner had to have stood and ran to get that far. "How could you have missed him?!"

"Sorry, sir. Target must've cut south to the other rows blocked by the hotel's east tower. Repositioning to east tower now."

"No! Go get the girl!"

"Moving," Imara replied.

Jivu fumed as he ran. Everyone needed to stop underestimating this American punk. "Siko, you with me?!"

"Right behind you," Siko replied. "Pick up?"

Jivu reached the sidewalk and halted, waiting for speeding cars to pass. He glanced back at the Mercedes, driving through empty parking spaces and rolling up behind him. "Too slow. Exit the lot and pull into that drop-off area, there." He pointed to the small avenue that divided the Bibliotheca Alexandrina from the University. "I may need you on foot."

"Yes, sir," Siko replied as Jivu dashed across the street. "That's bus and taxi zone, though. If you want me to leave the car, I might …"

He shoved the radio back in his pocket and veered left into the funneling plaza entrance.

Tourists and students ambled aimlessly through the brick-paved strip, likely enjoying the shadow-cast realm between the library's tall, outlying buildings. Not so many as to obstruct his chase, but he slowed so as not to raise alarm. Besides, Turner was hobbling along less than ten meters ahead, and the run had clearly ruined him.

Turner's head was cocked slightly right, his shoulders arched forward, and each step on his right side triggered a little jolt. Now, sans his dishdasha, he had on a pair of bronze-tone slacks and an even whiter dress shirt. Dragging himself along with one hand pinned to his abdomen, some passers-by threw double-takes toward his belly, and though most immediately averted their eyes, a few kind souls actually approached, asking if he needed help.

And like a gift to Jivu, ensuring they'd have their special moment together, Turner cordially waved them all off.

A Spanish man who had offered assistance murmured to his companion as they passed Jivu, "… said he only needs to find a lavatory."

The promenade widened at the buildings' ends, and the Bibliotheca's array of glass doors stood before them, curving off toward a fountain. Only a dozen or so of the center doors appeared to be accessible, and uniformed guards with security wands stood at each.

Jivu paused and glanced right toward the university campus. Siko had parked at the front of the bus stop and had a keen eye on him.

"Shall I come?" blared from the walkie he'd left at max volume.

Jivu fumbled it from his pocket and glared across the sunny courtyard. He pressed his lips to the mic and whispered, "Standby!"

A female guard waved Turner through the door to the busy lobby. Jivu strolled along outside, tracking Turner's deteriorating shamble across the room.

Finally, he radioed Siko, "Come here, fast as you can!"

Jivu meandered to the last open door and held there, thumbs in pockets, pretending to examine the toe of his shoe. He wouldn't risk attempting to get his gun past one of the guards, but plenty of other weapons adorned his person that no metal detector would find. The ceramic dagger dangling from his neck would be sufficient in any unexpected event.

Siko jangled up behind him, wheezing.

Jivu kept his back to him and muttered in Swahili to hold his gear, "*Kuchukua bastola yangu na redio.*" Siko wanted so badly to ask questions or comment, but he'd worked for him long enough to know to hold his tongue. Jivu turned to him and quickly said, "Stay out here. Keep me in sight," and then marched to a door.

The tall, black guard shot a look his way, and Jivu halted in place, digging in his pockets as if he'd forgotten something. But what had really stopped him was doubt. Turner hadn't looked back once since entering the promenade, nor stolen a glimpse outside since entering the Bibliotheca. He was the injured bunny awaiting the lurking wolf's inevitable attack.

What exactly awaited Jivu inside those doors? A hundred soldiers? Why not surround him now? Why wait for him to enter? Just to disarm him and lure him from a single armed associate? It would make no sense. You'd never want to bring the dangerous person *inside* with even more innocent bystanders. And what, had Turner not really been shot in the truck? Some ruse, perfectly timed as Imara was drawn away? But what then? He risked a sniper's shot to the head for that entire walk across the parking lot?

Turner was almost out of sight, staggering at the far end of the lobby. He appeared primed for collapse at any second, tottering head searching the ceiling mounted banners and signs. He crossed behind a column and plowed straight into a stainless steel garbage bin, lurching over the top, and both went crashing to the tile with a harsh clatter.

That was clearly no farce.

Jivu cast aside his debilitating paranoia, only hoping it hadn't once more robbed him of something precious. He offered a pleasant grin to the distracted guard, received a cursory wanding, and entered the lobby.

A crowd of overly compassionate witnesses was gathering around Turner, some righting the waste bin or gathering the strewn garbage, while others tried to talk to him or check his wound.

"I just need a goddamned bathroom!" he shouted, and flew into a coughing fit.

This soured the vast majority, but an especially altruistic pair helped him up, guiding him down the hall until they too were cast away with a belligerent thrash. Jivu passed them on his way down the hall.

He smiled and said in Arabic, "So ungrateful, no?"

The pair nodded and shrugged, one saying, "What can you do?"

Nearing a large, illuminated lavatory sign, Turner lost his balance once more, tripping over himself and veering to the wall opposite the restrooms, disappearing into a recess.

Jivu jogged forward to catch up—this being the perfect, inconspicuous little nook—reaching the corner just in time to see an auditorium door swinging slowly shut. Inside, a flurry of laughter rose from a large audience. He opened the door just as it finished shutting.

A bright spotlight shone on a well-dressed American man standing beside a lectern, addressing the spectators with his microphone. "And that's not even the most exhilarating from the find!"

Applause.

Spread across the stage, and lit dramatically from above, stood four or more black kiosks bearing papyrus scrolls. A large screen behind them displayed live magnified views from a nearby camera, and above the screen stretched a wide banner:

THE LIBRARY OF ALEXANDRIA
ANCIENT KNOWLEDGE OF HUMANITY: RETURNED

An Egyptian man at side-stage translated the speaker into Arabic.

More applause.

The American began pacing the stage. "Many of these ancient intellectuals invented entire *disciplines* like geography, or musical theory, and authenticated scientific facts that wouldn't be discovered again until as recently as the twentieth century!"

Jivu stepped inside and eased the door shut behind him. A man with a large tripod and glowing camera glanced back at him before returning to his monitor. A tripod and various gear bags obstructed the aisle behind the back row of seats, and sticking out just beyond the corner, the legs of another tripod, suggesting the entire aisle was a blocked-off mess. Turner had to have cut left.

"But hey," the emcee went on, "any random person can read a script. How much more thrilling would it be to hear about some of these scrolls straight from the source—the man that brought these invaluable pieces of human history back from obscurity?"

Tentative applause during the translation. Turning heads, searching eyes.

Jivu leaned against the wall and peered around the corner.

"That's right ... All the way from New Jersey, U.S.A.—a gifted, generous man I'm so very honored to call a lifelong friend—Mr. ... Matthew ... Turner!"

A bar of black swung from behind the wall, striking Jivu across the eyes. Hands—dozens of hands, it seemed—grappled at him from head to shoulder to shirt to groin. As wild applause rang out through the theater, his body slammed to the ground. Something that felt like a leather arm rest clapped down over his mouth, and wrapped around-side his head. His nose had been broken, eyes stung, knees on his shoulders as his shirt was torn open, fingers digging through his pockets, shoes ripped off, hands probing every inch of his body. Within twenty seconds, all of his weapons had been found and removed.

"Thank you, Cameron," Turner's entirely healthy voice through the loudspeakers. "That was quite the introduction." The translator began to speak, but Turner stopped him, saying in an elegant Egyptian Arabic, "Oh, thank you sir, thank you so much. It's okay, I'll repeat for everyone."

Applause, as Jivu was pulled to his feet. Behind his back, restraints cinched around his wrists, and then more, pinning his elbows together.

The miracle of a white man speaking their language.

"This man *loves* to be on stages," Turner said in Arabic. The audience cackled.

They had Turner blown up on the big screen. He had on a sport coat to cover his stained shirt, though thinking on it now, Jivu guessed it hadn't had a drop of blood on it—real or fake. Maybe some wrinkles and dirt stains.

Turner's friend was off beside him—no clue what was being said—grinning stupidly as Turner went on. "He and I met once before, for *maybe* two minutes. But he's a fun guy, so when I point to him, let's give him some huge applause ... Cameron Langley!" The astonished friend appeared near to climaxing there on stage.

Jivu glanced around at the faces of his captors. Also, clearly American. It was to be an unsanctioned snatch-n-grab. Brilliant, actually, given that he wasn't an Egyptian citizen, nor was he even officially in the country. The video call, that whole performance from the hotel to the waste bin ... all orchestrated to draw him to this exact spot. Admirable planning and dedication, but Jivu's team would be waiting outside to—Unless ... they, too, had been captured.

The operatives began shuffling him toward the corner doors—the doors out of which Turner must have slipped as Jivu entered the theater.

"Oh, and we also have another special surprise guest," Turner announced, motioning to the back corner. "The beloved President of the Republic of Kenya, Jivu Absko!"

Cameras swung about and Jivu saw his bleeding, gagged face projected above the stage. Awkward applause from a few random seats. The operatives all spun away, ducking their heads and murmuring, "Oh, what a dick," and "You asshole," as they thrust him to the doors.

"Yikes, guess he's in some kind of trouble," Turner said as the doors swung shut.

* * *

Iris walked an erratic path around the cabin's large deck, searching for cell phone signal. As if an elevation change of two feet would make all the difference, she alternated raising her phone overhead, and holding it at eye height. At the farthest back corner, the No Service at her screen's top disappeared ... thought about signal ... thought about signal ... and...

"Two bars!"

"What's that?" called Aunt Denora from the open kitchen window.

"I got signal! Two bars!"

"A miracle, sweetie. You know we have a perfectly good phone inside here, right? Two of them, actually." A boisterous laugh from Aunt Denora.

"Yeah yeah," Iris said as the spinning circle thing spun.

She'd better have a text, voicemail, or email from Matt or Joss. A text message alert appeared, but it was from her carrier, informing her she was approaching her data limit.

She growled and went inside. "I'm taking you up on that phone thing," she said as she passed her aunt, and grabbed the kitchen phone off the hook—one of those 70s-era wall jobs with a wood veneer on the receiver. They just loved wood veneers back then.

The home voicemail line rang and Iris entered the required codes to check for messages. There were many of varying import, from crap to nonsense to ultra-crap, but one message made her freeze in place, wide-eyed.

"Hi there, Turners, this is Tuni …" She sounded relaxed, but exhausted.

Iris jotted down the info on a notepad with more cartoon cats than white space for writing actual notes. The message said she'd only be reachable there for another few hours, but Iris hung up before checking when it was left.

Country code 254. She was still in Kenya, at least when she called. Iris dialed the number.

"Good heavens," Aunt Denora said from the sink. "You calling the space station?"

Iris shushed her lovingly. A woman answered in Swahili, but fortunately also spoke English. She put Iris through to the room number.

"Hello?" Tuni's voice, unmistakable.

"Tuni, it's Iris. I just got your message. Are you okay?"

"Oh, Iris, thank God. I'd cry right now hearing your voice, but I think I've run dry. I'm fine … *we're* fine …" A child in the background, presumably Alexander, asked who Iris was. "She's an old friend, bubu. Let Mama talk a moment, okay? Sorry, Iris."

"No, please, it's just great to hear you're all right. And he sounds adorable." She wanted to say she couldn't wait to meet him, but for some reason that felt too awkward. "So talk to me. What can I do to help? Do you need money, transportation …?"

"Thank you so much," Tuni said, yawning. "Sorry … little sleep the past few days. Actually, the men who were, well … the men we were *with* gave me ten thousand dollars this morning before passing us off to a cab. So I think we're fine in that department, though I'm not at all certain how we'll leave the country without proper papers. I haven't a passport or anything for either of us."

"Well, look, Matt happens to be in Egypt right now, maybe ten hours away. I've zero doubt he'd come to help in a heartbeat."

"No, no, *God* … Thank you so much, again, but no. I can't quite face Matthew just yet."

"I understand," Iris said. "Maybe tell me where you're trying to get?"

"New Haven. My mother's."

"Got it. Can I have twelve hours? You'd said you were leaving in three."

"No … I mean, yes. Twelve hours, of course. I meant no, I'm not leaving. I was going to go to sleep, but *somebody* hasn't seen cartoons in days and just can't bloody settle down. Please, take all the time you need. I feel we're safe here. And again, I can't thank you enough. And please pass that on to Matthew, as well."

TWENTY-FOUR

Heracleion, Aegyptus – 303 CE

Outside the carriage's window, the aging fishing village of Heracleion dissolved into the sea. As with most other Nile estuaries, the coast here had been split into hundreds of little islands, the canals progressively splintering between patches of land, until finally becoming only sea. Long ago—ages before Romans, or even Greeks, had visited Egypt—this place was a bustling harbor like Alexandria. It was called Thonis, and through those docks the old Pharaohs sold Egypt's surplus grain to neighboring kingdoms.

What remained now, Neos observed, were the remnants of both Egyptian temples and Greek, and one of the few remaining places where a person could fish to feed their family without paying an official by the pound.

Neos exited the carriage, took little Sopatrius from Skyla's arms, and peered up at his girls—Afwahlania, eleven, and his eldest, Azeenia, twelve. For the journey's last leg, they'd decided to sit up front and *"help"* Unza drive the horses. Despite her seventy-seven years, Unza needed no help—not with anything.

"Down," Unza commanded the girls, and nudged them toward their respective steps, and then added her version of *be careful:* "No."

Skyla took Sopatrius back from him. "I don't want to take him over those horrible bridges. We'll leave him here with Unza."

"What?" Neos turned to her, and a resolute face awaited him. She looked more like her mother every year, though had *always* had Patra's stubbornness. "Philip hasn't met him yet! Nor have his daughters!"

"No," Unza said, and scooped Sopatrius away from Skyla. The baby cried, and Unza lifted him over her head, spinning him around. "Zuzuzuzuzu …" He gaped, and watched her face and the spinning ground, and he giggled, and drooled.

Unza had always been with them, and helped a lot raising the girls, but ever since Patra died, she'd become the grandmother of the house.

"It's not safe," Skyla said. "Besides, they'll all walk back with us when we leave, anyway. They'll meet then."

Neos conceded, and the four of them left Unza and the baby with the carriage. On their way out to the remains of Cleopatra's Palace—one of the farthest islands in the chain—the girls ran ahead, tiptoeing across the now even-more-untrustworthy foot bridges, and darting in and out of once-magnificent monuments.

Passing the Temple of Heracles—still a spectacular sanctuary—Neos observed a couple of the statues had either been refurbished or replaced. Philip's hand, unmistakably.

"I see the sisters," Skyla said, and Neos gazed across the canal to Cleopatra's island. Philip's eldest daughter, Theophila, was on a makeshift scaffolding, touching up a mural as her sister, Cyra, on the ground, herded their children.

Neos held Patra's keystone in his palm, running his thumb over the etched words. "I don't trust Cyra's husband."

"Neither do I," Skyla said. "But until we know if any of ours can be stewards, we shouldn't have both stones. Logically, *neither* of us should have one—certainly not when there's a legitimate Steward among the group. The sisters are legitimate. And one of them will be inheriting Philip's, when the time comes."

They started across the last bridge just as the girls went gleefully screaming into the crowd of young cousins. Philip's daughters both peered across the canal and waved. Neos and Skyla waved back.

"I know I don't have to remind you the whole point of keeping the keystones apart from each other—"

Skyla interrupted, "It's a true relief you know this," and smirked.

"I'm going to speak with Philip about it. He'll understand. I don't think he's all that enamored with his son-in-law, either. It's really up to him, as the last of them."

Once the reunion cheer had settled, stories old and new shared, and children all reintroduced, Philip took Skyla and Neos with him to the Temple's wide-open front courtyard. In its peak years of activity, this paved area hosted nonpermanent structures where visitors could purchase illustrations or statuettes of Egypt's last pharaoh.

These days, Rome was all too happy to let that likeness fade away. Neos's mother, Zenobia, had evoked Cleopatra during her "uprising," and the most recent failed revolt, just eight years ago, had been led by Coptics seeking Egypt's return to Egyptians.

"Do you like it?" Philip asked. He wore an odd grin.

"Like what?" Skyla asked, glancing about.

Neos observed a lone statue rising from just beyond the courtyard's low balustrade. "Is that new?"

Philip pinched his chin, mocking deep contemplation. "Is it?! I can't … seem … to recall."

Neos snickered and grabbed Skyla's hand, the pair brushing past him to examine the new statue. From the back, it was obviously Isis—the posture, the tunic, the hair—but sculpted of some exquisite black stone he'd never seen.

Philip's chisels and picks lay about the balustrade and pavement blocks along with all of his polishing tools. Neos stepped carefully through them, sat on the balustrade, and spun his legs over top, dropping into fresh, dark soil on the other side. He held out an arm to help Skyla down as he took in the new statue.

"She's beautiful, Philip," Neos said, and then noticed Philip had carved the goddess's face differently than the traditional—He gasped. "Oh! It's ..."

Landing at his side, Skyla looked up and immediately recognized the face. "Mother," she breathed.

"It's Patra," Neos said, awestruck. "It's her. Perfectly her."

"Oh, Philip." Skyla was crying now, her elbows high and hands cupped over her mouth just as her mother often did. "My father has to see this ... We have to bring him here. Neos, how soon can we return with him?"

Neos considered. His father-in-law, Tychon, wasn't fond of traveling anymore, but he would absolutely come for this. He loved Patra as much as his first wife, and had helped to make her last sixteen years enjoyable ones. Neither had thought they'd find love again, nor had Tychon expected another child—his only girl.

"Soon. I'll make it happen. Perhaps just he and I, though."

Skyla climbed back over to the courtyard and embraced Philip. "Thank you so much for this. She was no goddess or ruler, but she deserves this more than many I can think of. I only lament my inability to follow her path."

Neos stepped to them and stroked Philip's back as Philip frowned. "What do you mean? You're more Steward than any of those ambling the Library's stacks today."

"You know what I mean," she said.

Neos held out Patra's keystone. "We wanted to speak with you about this. We've two in our household, and neither of us proper stewards."

Philip took the keystone from him.

Hello Steward.

The voice conveys knowledge
The scribe preserves a word
A token holds the sum

Of wisdom in perpetuum.

"Yes, it does." Chills danced up Philip's body at the sound of Patra's inner voice.

He smiled and rolled it slowly over, examining the words he'd etched in decades ago. It was Kaleb's originally, but only for that first week. This was all Patra's—all *Patra*—a token unlike any other, more valuable than any other. It was a sort of master token. He could get lost in it for years.

He looked at Neos and Skyla, so like her mother. "I think you misjudge the title. You are no less stewards than me."

"Oh?" Skyla said, nodding to his hands. "It doesn't conjure her in mine. In my hands, it only recalls her death."

Philip wished he could show Skyla herself, as a baby, in Patra's hands.

"And the statue?" Philip said.

Skyla and Neos both glanced back at it.

Skyla swallowed and nodded, pensive. "No, it brings her to life. You brought her back to life."

He smiled, grateful, and looked at the statue, wondering. The two surviving steward families had already grown so large, was it necessary to leave three keystones out in the world? Perhaps this master token would better serve their objectives in stasis? People moved, but this place would be the hub of stewards for generations. How fortuitous they should bring him Patra's spirit on the day he completed her body.

He curled his fingers around the keystone and motioned for them to walk with him. "The role of the Steward is to preserve—and grow, when possible—the collection. And as you know, the collection is multifaceted, as is its current home. The three of us— your mother, Kaleb, and I—understood that in the new, less-than-ideal world, there would always be stewards of varying capacity. We prepared the keystones, these *mysteria*, to maintain the least amount of data required to recover all the data. Regardless of capacity, as long as future generations of stewards know that there is *something* to be preserved, those generations of higher capacity will find all they require."

"All well thought," Neos said, "but what if one of these 'lower capacity' idiots accesses the tomb and celebrates the Great Restoration? Casting the then-'useless' *mysteria* to the garbage heap? What if all that's ever recovered are the tomb scrolls, and no one ever bothers to seek out the full collection?"

"You sound just like Kaleb," Philip mused. "To quote Patra, 'Every scroll is also a token.'"

TWENTY-FIVE

Amarna, Egypt – Present Day

Pete plugged in the work lights, but they didn't turn on. A bar of light shone from the small, unfinished room at the tomb's far end, but the main chamber remained dark.

Matt stuck his head around the corner, squinting to the bright end of the entrance shaft. He could hear the generator running. "We plugged in?" he called.

"Yes, sir," Leo called back. "Plugged in."

"He keeps calling me sir," Matt said to Pete. "Make him stop."

"Is the *orange* extension cord plugged in?" Pete shouted. "Not just the green!"

"Call him sir right back," Grandma Bubsy said as she shone her flashlight at the stack of large, laminated photos. "Never fails. 'Need help outside, ma'am?' 'No, ma'am, I do not, thank you.' 'Any cash back, ma'am?' 'No, sir, no cash back, sir.'"

Joss snickered. "Twice in one sentence?"

The main chamber's lights cracked on, temporarily scorching all eyes in the column-filled cavern.

"Oh yeah," Grandma went on. "That's when they look at me sort of pleading, like they don't know what else to call me. Lady?

Miss? Nothing at all? And that's when I bat the lashes and say 'just call me Grandma Bubsy, sweetie.' And they never forget after that. I have five blood grandkids, but you're one of my hundreds of honoraries."

Pete went to the tomb's far end and ran his fingers down the corner. "I'm telling you, man, this was carved out. It's not a seam."

"Same in these photos," Grandma said. "You can see this rusty vein on the wall here continues in the ceiling in this shot. Not one of these is a false wall."

Leo drifted in from the access shaft, and followed the group into the recently discovered subchamber. "Only had the green cord in."

Matt felt him staring again, and glanced his way. "Thanks for the lights, sir."

Leo had shaved his beard, buzzed his hair to Matt's length, and wore cargo shorts and a T-shirt. "No problem, sir. So … what do we have here? The study?"

Pete pointed to the doorway. "Out there, as we all know, is the unfinished tomb of Ay, a New Kingdom Pharaoh from around the time of Akhenaten. They started building it when he was only a high-ranking advisor, and presumably stopped working on it once he took the throne. His final tomb is in the Valley of the Kings. *That* was unearthed back in 1883. Whereas *this*," he flailed a hand, "was accessed mere weeks ago, by yours truly … after *herculean* efforts expediting gobs of permits from the Ministry, I might add."

"You're appreciated, Pete," Matt said.

"*I* appreciate you, Pete," Joss echoed.

Leo chimed in, "You're apprec—"

"Yes, yes, thank you," Pete said. "The condescension in here is suffocating. As I was saying, this is where we recovered the 78,000 scrolls you all saw back at the MERC. Now, the esteemed Mr. Turner here claims I've missed another false wall that leads to some impossibly vast chamber containing … how many was it? A *kajillion* more scrolls?"

"Give or take," Matt said. "But you didn't miss anything in here. It's through there."

He pointed out the door, nonchalant.

Pete squinted at him. "All the other walls have been—"

"Yes, yes, thank you," Matt parroted as they followed him back into the main chamber. He continued forward into the illuminated, unfinished, side room in the opposite corner. "Here," he declared.

The group took in the tiny space. All the stone surfaces were still rough and unfinished. The back wall hadn't even been made a wall yet—thick tiers of bedrock led from the middle of the floor, upwards to the end of the ceiling, like stairs for a giant.

"Is this the bottom corner of some huge, hidden pyramid?" Joss said, possibly serious.

"I wish," Pete replied, "but no. The excavators simply carved out the rock in sections like this. Certainly safer to go from high to low, rather than the reverse, lest one end up chiseling away quite heavy things over their head. So tell me, man, where in here is our mother lode hiding?"

"Now *that* is a seam," Grandma proclaimed, leaning close and shining her flashlight at the back of the first—and biggest—carved-out block.

Pete glanced her way, and then gaped at the beaming Matt. "You've got to be blooming joking ..." He dashed forward. "Hand me a torch, someone."

Leo gave him a flashlight, and Pete examined the rear of the block where it appeared to be still connected to the next tier of granite, all a single slab. "If this is honestly a separate piece, it must weigh close to a ton."

"Well," Leo began. "If it was separated and put back specifically to hide a passage or whatever, they'd probably carve out the underside to make it a bit more manageable."

"But not too manageable," Grandma added. "This room's been wide open to archaeologists for, what, a hundred and fifty years?"

"Oh, hello there, my dodgy little beauty," Pete murmured as his light traced the seam. Giddiness had replaced his skepticism.

"My only question," Matt said, "is whether Pete has at his disposal the balls to move this thing without first procuring *gobs* of permits."

Pete scoffed, "What, this? This is rubble. Someone fetch me a bloody prybar and some rope, and I'll bodge this thing open in no time!"

* * *

For Pete, *"no time"* eventually meant around four hours, but the group had slid the block a full two inches in the first hour, and Leo got the bright idea of sticking the top of his phone in to snap a shot with flash—much to Pete's chagrin.

"You pop a flash at my scrolls one more time and I'll have your goddamn Visa canceled," Pete had warned, and then said in the same growling tone, "Let me see that goddamn picture."

Everyone's heads had bunched up around Leo's phone, and when he zoomed into the dark, grainy shot, there came a mix of gasps and exhales.

By the time the block was finally pulled back enough for human access, they'd already run power cords into the side room and assembled an array of filtered work lights.

Matt insisted Pete be the first down the short flight of steps, and Pete yielded after a full three seconds' resistance. "No, Matt, it should be you okay I'll go."

He brought with him a tripod-mounted pair of lights. His whups and wild laughter reverberated up the compact shaft, and the group filed in after him.

The bedrock ceiling was low, such that Matt and Leo had to stand with their heads cocked slightly to the side, but the secret cavern's excavators had spared no energy on width or depth. Crosswise, the rectangular room was as wide as a city bus was long, while the side walls stretched off beyond the inhibited lights' reach.

Save for a thin walking path that ran the outer perimeter, the room's entire floor was filled with red, cylindrical pottery of varying heights and girth—like cookie jars, buckets, and umbrella stands—all covered with lids.

The group had spread out along the first wall and stared in silence.

"Nobody touch anything," Pete finally whispered. It seemed right to whisper, as though the collection had slept for so long, it'd be harmful to disturb it.

"You're not even going to open *one* of them?!" Grandma hushed.

All eyes landed on Pete.

"There are nearly 400,000 scrolls in here, Pete," Matt said. "You can risk opening one container. Also, they were loaded in order of importance, so those at the far back wall are the ones deemed 'imperative' to preserve. The ones here, near the entrance, were the lowest priority—besides the ones you already recovered."

"Well that should tell you something right there, man!" Pete said, still whispering, letting his arms provide the emphasis. "What was 'critical' or 'important' to them, isn't necessarily the same for us now. "The fact that we have direct writings from Socrates? Those scrolls were in the stewards' *'kind of nice to keep'* category! As were all the Theban papyri! For all I know, that stack of jars there contains the only remaining copies of Q. I could open it and it all disintegrates into dust!"

"What's 'Q'?" Joss said.

"Hypothetical documents," Grandma said with vague umbrage. "Basically all the sayings and proverbs of Jesus, but from a date before he was born. Folks trying to discredit him and bring down the church."

Pete interjected, "Well, that's not really the point ... That is, ascertaining the truth should always be—"

"Now now, kids," Matt interjected. "Since Pete's ongoing status and position here are at risk, we need to accept his qualms about opening any of this."

"Thank you," Pete said.

"You're welcome," Matt said, and kicked over a stack of three jars. They shattered on the floor, revealing among the shards six to ten papyrus rolls each. Pete gawped as if Matt had just punched a baby. "Crazy how after seventeen hundred years, only one stack fell over, right? How lucky is that?"

"You ... you ..." Pete was losing it.

Matt gently nudged him toward the debris. "You being the expert here, I'd be most comfortable if *you* opened these up first—knowing how to handle them and everything."

Pete sighed and knelt in front of Matt's mess, murmuring obscenities. He brushed off the larger pottery fragments, blew away the smaller pieces and dust, and examined the small clay tabs dangling from each.

"Ah ... this one should be interesting." He plucked the topmost scroll from the middle jar's pile.

"Are those labels?" Joss said. "What's it say?"

Pete didn't answer, busy for a few moments flicking, squeezing, poking, and peeling.

Matt replied, "Each papyri was labeled like that so you didn't have to open it up to know what was inside. Sort of the original book spine." He turned to Pete. "C'mon, man. We've got a plane to catch. Let me see *one* scroll, just one, before I fly home. It'd really mean a lot to me."

"Okay, okay!" He carefully set down the one in his hand, picking up another. "That one was Athens. You wouldn't care as much about it. But *this* one ..." He untied the string and carefully unrolled it on a clear patch of floor.

The group huddled close, trying to make it out in the faint light.

"Is that ..." Matt began. "Is it Alexandria?"

"Mm-hmm," Pete replied. "Eighteenth year of Ptolemy XII. That's Cleopatra's father."

"I've never seen so detailed a map of the ancient city," Grandma observed.

"Because there are none," Pete said. "Oldest Alexandria maps in existence were made a thousand years later, and based on a lot of guesswork. This here is the real deal. Contemporary."

"I'm taking it with me," Matt said, then winked at Pete before he could protest. "Not like that." He took his fingers off the corner, and stood up, grinning. "Bit of work ahead of you, eh?"

Wide-eyed, Pete shook his head, dizzy with the unimaginable scope of the find.

Matt wrapped his arms around Pete and clapped his back. "Our agreement from the first batch still stands, yes? Every single piece."

"Yeah, man. You know it. The entire world—those who care, anyway—will be able to access high-res images, the translations, the whole enchilada."

Everyone said their goodbyes up in the main chamber. As Grandma kissed Matt's cheek, Matt observed Leo bypassing Joss's hand, moving in for a hug.

"Oh ... uh, sure," Joss said, and flashed a bemused look Matt's way.

"We've been through so much, you know?" Leo said.

"Mmm, yeah," Joss said as she stepped out of the columns in front of Matt, heading for the sunny entrance.

Pete said, "Don't be a stranger for so long this time, man."

"No way," Matt replied. "And thanks again, everyone. I'll be back, for sure. Soon."

"Hey, could I get your number?" Leo called after them. "Joss, I mean."

Joss pretended she didn't hear, cutting right at the entrance and hustling outside, and Matt heard someone smack Leo's back.

"What's wrong with you, kid?" Grandma Bubsy scolded Leo. "Can't you see they're together?"

* * *

Flight announcements repeated in multiple languages over the terminal speakers. Matt sat alone at a counter on a stationary stool, charging his phone. Across the busy walkway, Joss held up cheesy tourist-bait shirts to him, eyebrows raised: *This one? No? How about this one?* He gave her a thumbs up when she draped a busy, navy-blue shirt over her front—I.T. would appreciate the cartoony Sphinx perched atop the Great Pyramid, swatting away attacking aircraft.

His phone buzzed in his hand. **Unknown Caller**.

Hmm...

"Hello?"

"Well, Matthew," Markus said serenely, "So pleased I caught you before your flight departed."

Matt scanned the area for any watchful eyes.

He played it nonchalant. "Yeah, me too."

"But of course. Two items. First, no questions, please. I thought you'd be comforted to know that your honorable intentions with our gray friend ended as they should."

"Honorable int—"

"Thanks to recent turns of events, Mr. O's connections with the appropriate authorities there now exceed those waning gray connections. While the admirable Americans there made every effort to covertly abscond with their captive, the locals were waiting outside their base, and in great numbers. After a tense-yet-peaceful bit of diplomacy, the captive was transferred into legal local custody."

"And then what?" Matt thought he knew where this was going.

"Well, there was a bit of a mix-up—it happens sometimes in dense bureaucracies—and now no one knows where the prisoner ended up."

"Right. I'm sure not a soul knows."

"Nor will they," Markus said flatly. "Ever." He paused a moment, allowing that to sink in. He wanted Matt to know, in no uncertain terms, that Absko was dead, and no body would ever be found. Markus resumed with his more playful, disappointed-schoolteacher tone, "Now there is only the matter of the Tarias, and your debts to Mr. O."

Matt cleared his throat, setting aside the Absko revelation for the moment. "I just want to say once again that I appreciate all of the help you and Mr. O pro—"

"Not me," Markus interrupted. "I merely serve Mr. O. You may send all gratitude his way. Likewise, your appreciation for any potential clemency bestowed. The rapidity of new contract signings with the Kenyan VP and neighboring leaders may offer a brief window of good will, however, outstanding issues of property—"

"Of course, absolutely," Matt cut in. "And congratulations on all of the new opportunities. If not for the antiquities officials confiscating everything I had, you can bet everything would have been returned. I do hope, though, that the packages I had sent were accepted as a sincere act of contrition."

A brief silence, then Markus's voice, away from the phone receiver. "Sergei, do we have any undelivered packages in receiving?"

A *beep* and radioed reply, "Yes, a few. Apologies."

"Bring them to me, please. I'm in my office. Hold, Matthew." The line was muted.

Joss walked up and plopped a shopping bag on the counter. Matt mouthed *"Markus."*

She whispered, "Did he get the packages yet?"

Matt motioned that it was happening at that moment—the wooden Taria I.T. shipped from his house, the bundle of scrolls he'd cajoled out of Pete, and the last item, something special Matt knew would seal the deal.

The line went active again, but it was not Markus's voice, but Ostrovsky's, and he was beyond giddy. He'd been in the room the whole time. "You kill me, Matthew! One minute I make plan to have your balls ripped off, and the next I feel I must blow you!"

Matt held up the OK sign for Joss. "That's … great."

"Speaking of," Ostrovsky went on, "is Ms. Leland there with you?"

Matt hung up.

"What'd he say?" Joss said.

Matt adopted an Ostrovsky voice. "He sends his love."

TWENTY-SIX

New York City, New York – Present Day

Jack's Coffee Bean in Manhattan's West Village neighborhood was as busy as Tuni remembered. Though it felt like a decade since she'd last ordered a mocha (and her favorite cinnamon apple mega-muffin), little had changed. There was free Wi-Fi now, and USB power outlets embedded in every table's center, but everything else seemed like she'd only been gone a week.

Seated beside the front window, she found her surreal enjoyment tainted with anxiety. Matthew would be here any moment. They hadn't actually spoken yet—just checking in with her, Iris had mentioned he'd be in the city this weekend, and asked if she'd like to meet up. Crippling fear had made Tuni hesitate, but she'd choked it back and said "Sure, how about some coffee?" And Iris took it from there. And now here she was, terrified of what he'd say, or wouldn't say, or just a look that said enough.

She peered out the window. Many passers-by, but no Matthew.

Perhaps he'd think she brought Alexander not to have the two finally meet, but as a shield from any *real* conversation.

And then she had questions—genuine questions about Jivu's fate since, according to the media, he hadn't been seen in a month.

Was it even safe for her and Alexander to be out in the world? Was it safe for her mother to go about her daily routines?

Another glance outside.

As if she wasn't nervous enough, Alexander was being an intolerable brat this morning.

Only a moment ago, he'd said in Swahili, "I hate this bread."

She was still taking the discipline slow. The adjustment for him was far more strenuous than her. "It's called a bagel, and we're speaking English, my angel."

"I hate bagel," he'd said. "I hate English."

"Hate all you want. We're speaking English. Eat the rest of my muffin if you want." He'd eyed the muffin scornfully, preparing to express his even greater hatred of this thing he'd never eaten, but Tuni cut him off. "Say you hate muffins and it's no TV when we get home. See, sometimes they show muffins on American TV."

He'd been silently grumpy since then, playing with his Ninja Turtles in his lap.

And there was Matthew, ambling carefree up the sidewalk in cargo shorts and a striped white polo shirt. He had on sunglasses and a beard was growing in.

He was also exceptionally *fit*.

She suddenly wanted to pull out her compact for a final face check, as if she'd been instantly demoted to a frumpy old mum. It was bloody silly. She wasn't here to attempt reconciliation, and she doubted Matthew had any such thing on his mind. This was a long-overdue reunion, a chance to close open wounds, and for her to express her gratitude directly.

The door chimed and he stepped inside, skirting past an exiting couple, and scanned across the narrow café.

Should she stand? To stand would necessitate a hug, and he appeared dangerously underdressed. A hug could set them on an awkward start. And where was Iris? She was supposed to come as a sort of buffer.

"This chair is hard," Alexander said in Swahili. "I hate it."

Tuni leaned down to him and adopted the rarely used scary mum voice. "You'd rather I put you outside? No hard chairs outside." His eyes bugged, looking out the window to the busy street, and returned a slow no-nod. "No more 'hate.' No more Swahili."

Yes-nod.

When Tuni looked up, a smiling Matthew had already spotted her, and was veering around the rubbish bin just a few feet away.

"Hey there!" he said cheerily, and she smiled too, scooting her chair back. He strode right past the two chairs on the table's other side and rounded the corner to the Tuni's space by the wall, his arms already spreading. "So glad you could make it out here."

He enveloped her warmly—as an old friend—and though she thought her relief sprang from the release of tension, an unexpected fountain of emotions swelled from her gut: deep, rising, irresistible, crushing. His arms slackened, the standard easing to end a friendly embrace, but she stiffened, squeezed, not letting him go.

"Hey, hey, it's all good," he said in her ear, and stroked her back and head, like a father. "You're safe. It's over. You'll never see him again, and never be in that situation again. Trust me, okay?"

She wanted to wail unrestrained into his chest, releasing everything she hadn't even realized sat burning inside her. His kindness only made her guilt worse, but it also made her want to stay inside this protective shroud. She'd never felt it from him before. She hadn't felt it like this from anyone in her life. *"Like a father"* was right, or perhaps priest. *She* had always been the protector in their relationship—the maternal figure.

His shirt was wet with her tears, and she imagined the entire place staring at them, and so she emit a blubbering laugh and pushed him away.

"I'm so sorry," she said, grabbing up napkins as she sat down. "I'm fine, really, I'm fine … and thoroughly daft."

Matthew maintained the warm smile as he shuffled back around the table, grabbing one of the chairs and sliding it around the corner to sit at the end, near Alexander.

"Hey, buddy. You must be Alexander."

Alexander just sat there and stared up at him.

It was just as she feared. She tried to laugh it off. "We're having some trouble getting used to only English, aren't we, my love?"

His gaze didn't move. Matthew was being patient and great, hunching down to Alexander's level.

Matthew tapped his bare finger twice on the table in front of him, then pulled at his polo shirt's buttons. "*Ni aina gani ya kifungo si wazi?*"

What kind of button won't open? A joke.

"Oh, it's okay, Matthew," she said. "He doesn't quite understand jokes yet."

After a moment's consideration, Alexander demanded to know what kind. "*Ni aina gani?*"

Matthew's hand lurched forward under the table, tickling him. "The belly button!"

Alexander squealed laughing, flailing in his seat.

"Thank you," Tuni said. "That's very sweet." Matthew brushed it off and sat up. "I don't think I'd ever seen you with children. You're good … getting down to their level and all that."

"Probably a bit too easily," he said. "*Now*, that is. Before was … *yeesh*." He motioned as if some sludge monster was about to slather its cooties on him.

"Gloveless and shorts, eh? Are you … *off*, or in control?"

"In control. Finally."

She nodded, sighing, dabbing the napkin beneath her eyes once more, just in case. She glanced outside again. "Iris?"

"She's outside. I asked her to give us a few minutes before coming in. Otherwise, it's like she's the safety third."

Tuni grinned, and probably blushed. "I haven't heard this term, but it's brilliant. Safety third, indeed."

"Actually, safety *fourth*! My man Alexander here's already the third." He poked him in the side and Alexander giggled and grabbed his bagel, now eating it.

Matthew set his elbows on the table and looked in her eyes. His smile slowly relaxed. It was *serious* talk time, and Tuni's chest began tightening once more.

"You heard the news about that Cuban general? Went missing, unseen for the past month?"

A different serious talk than expected ...

"Yes," she said, wriggling in her seat. "I'd wondered what happened there."

"Another country had covertly arrested him when he was in Brazil, looking to bring him back home for trial. Their vehicle was ambushed, though—no one hurt, fortunately, no weapons used— but the general was rushed away." A great stone dropped into Tuni's stomach. Matthew saw it, and quickly continued. "From what I understand, it wasn't the general's loyal soldiers who got him, but a competing general. They say ... they *unambiguously* said the body will never be found."

Tuni forced back a gulp, inhaling a quivering breath. She wanted to accept it as fact. "And you believe this?"

"I do. Zero doubt." He sat back, eyes intense and assuring.

His gaze held, and it made her cry again.

She dabbed the tears with a napkin and mouthed, *"Thank you. Thank you so much."*

She wanted to use that connected moment to say sorry as well, but he stretched out his arms and went on, "Sad, but anyone who feared the general can rest easy."

A bell chimed vaguely in the background, and Matthew looked to the door.

Tuni wasn't sure how he interpreted these fresh tears, whether they were borne of mourning or relief.

Her hand floated to Alexander's head. He sat there unaware, enthralled with an epic battle between two ninja turtles.

Matthew stood. Tuni's ears unmuddled.

"... there's a sale next door on these little overalls. Fricken adorable." It was Iris Turner, and not a hint of the college student air

Tuni had known. She was grown up, beautiful, powerful. If not for the loose flannel shirt and torn jeans, Tuni would've thought her some executive or politician … cop, even. That's what it was. She was like her father, Roger Turner.

But wait, what was this? Iris was pushing a stroller. A stroller with a very small, very Turnerish baby.

Tuni stood and went around Alexander. She and Iris hugged and kissed cheeks.

"You look great!" Iris said.

"*You* look great!" Tuni replied, and bent over the baby. "And who is this adorable young man? *Iris* … I had no idea—May I?"

Iris gave her a *"by all means"* wave.

Tuni wedged her fingers beneath the pudgy arms and lifted the drooly, wide-eyed boy to her chest.

"This is Horus," Iris said. "And, as much as I love him, he ain't mine."

"*Horus?* So whose—"

"I'm gonna head back next door," Iris blurted. "Great to see you, Tuni! We'll catch up again some time." And she scurried out the door.

"His mother's pick, not mine," Matthew said, reaching up to wipe the drool on the baby's bib. "You know, Horus? Son of *Isis* and Osiris?"

It came together quickly in Tuni's head as she carried Horus back with her to her seat. "Isis *Meier?* Jon's daughter? But, how old— I'm so sorry. I sound like an absolute arse."

"Arse, arse, arse!" Alexander was always paying attention at the right time.

Outside the window, Tuni saw Iris meet back up with an attractive blonde woman. "Oh, is that … Is that her outside?"

Matthew glanced back. "Oh, no. Don't scare me like that." He smiled, shook his head. "No, that's Joss Lynn. She's my, *ah* … She was the little girl that got kidnapped when I was around nine, if you recall. Anyway, about Isis Meier, she's twenty-seven. And was a mistake. Just found out about that little gentleman a few months ago." He nodded to Horus. "But now that everything's all, *ah … clear* about my, eh, *role …* I'm oddly finding myself enjoying it. Enjoying *him*." Matt was blushing, cheeks now advancing from red to purple.

"So you and Isis are …" Tuni *clicked* and swiped her fingers before her neck.

"Yeah. Thank God. She's torturing some other guy a few blocks over. Next month, she's off to Cambodia for six months, so this is sort of a trial run. Our first overnighter. I'm going to have my hands full when she's gone, and—knowing her—probably for another seventeen years after that."

"Like a one hundred percent thing?" Tuni said as she made faces at the giggling Horus, bouncing him on her knee.

"Oh, no … gosh … no way. Isis could never stand that. More like ninety-nine." He winked. "Oh, before I forget …" He searched his shorts' pockets and produced a business card, handing it to Tuni. "I told her I was on my way to see you after the pick-up and she asked if you were working. Said to say 'hi,' and that she could hook you up back at the museum, if you were interested."

Tuni felt another surge of tears approaching, but was able to hold them back this time. She continued bouncing little Horus, looked at the card's NYMM dinosaur logo, and said, "I'd be extremely interested."

*

EPILOGUE

Alexandria, Egypt – El Zaytoun Trainyard – Five months later

Along a line exactly parallel to Alexandria's coastline, precisely one mile (as the bird flies) southwest of Diocletian's Column at the ruined site of the Serapeum, lay an array of expansive warehouses situated at the end of an immense train yard. Ostensibly, the yard's placement here, aligned with the current branch of the Nile, and in some respects replacing one of the river's historical functions as a shipping conduit, makes perfect sense.

The city's great harbor no longer served as the country's import/export hub, instead hosting an array of luxurious sailboats and mega-yachts, while the clamor of container ships and tugboats carried on in the less picturesque harbor to the west. It seemed logical to lay tracks leading to this busy port.

What remained odd, however, was the fact that the yard had been built a stone's throw from the Nile, in an area that city planners knew would sell at top dollar as the metropolis grew. And it wasn't as though they were simply bringing transportation where it was needed. The current piers and infrastructure were built at the *same time* as the train yard.

Three more miles west, another port extended from the shoreline—the old port—and cut through a low-income, industrial suburb where near-future residential growth was highly unlikely. Half a century ago, here was where most officials wished to expand the area's shipping foundation, but somehow this proposal was defeated, and now over a dozen acres of prime land lay below tons of unsightly industrial clutter and rust.

Accusations had flown about back rooms and bribes, but most now believed the decision was superstition-based, as the vast majority of acreage had once been known as the Great Necropolis, or City of the Dead. What few tombs had actually been found in the Necropolis had been cleared of remains, and a century of searches for additional tombs had come up empty-handed. Of course, over 2,500 years, it wasn't easy for a hidden tomb to remain so. Nothing was found, perhaps, because there was nothing left to find.

Building 112-E, situated atop the one-mile mark from Diocletian's Column, sat in a secluded corner of the train yard, behind the rest of the much-used, matching warehouses. A curious observer—an observer who'd made it past multiple high fences, barbed wire, and security cameras—might at first find it odd that 112-E had no doors or windows, but would then logically assume it was simply an expansion from the neighboring structures, and therefore needed no entrances of its own.

A few days ago, in the dark of a moonless night, another observer decided to scale the wall, crawl to the peak of the slippery metal roof, unscrew the sole spinning ventilation dome, and rappel inside for a closer look.

His headlamp had swept across the empty warehouse, discerning only splintered concrete pavement full of long-dead grass and weeds. Cracked white paint marked an old borderline or where a road had once passed. It looked like someone had simply dropped the building atop a parking lot.

He'd gone to the innermost wall and walked the full hundred feet from end to end, shifting over several paces, and walking back.

On the third such march, he'd come upon a lumpy, rectangular patch of asphalt, seemingly laid by hand.

Tonight, Matt returned in cargo pants, long sleeves, and gloves, along with a backpack full of noisy tools, and set to work excavating the asphalt. It took a lot less time and effort than he'd expected. The thin layer of asphalt had been spread on top of a steel plate—the sort used to temporarily cover road work. Once he severed the loose bond between asphalt and concrete, raising and sliding the plate out of the way was a simple matter of leverage and a long pry bar.

A short, dingy, aluminum ladder (made of quality materials in Oshkosh, Wisconsin, USA) led down to a claustrophobic crawlspace that smelled of old wood. The horizontal shaft was only about two feet tall by two feet wide, making the journey through it slow and onerous.

Matt followed the shaft through a sharp left turn, and stopped. Before him, the level ground suddenly dropped four feet, and a contorted mummy lay at the bottom, with frayed, almost entirely deteriorated wrappings.

Confused, he backed up, edged around the corner, and examined the walls at the corner. All solid.

He crawled back to the leathery cadaver and shone his headlamp around the area. Beyond the depression, the shaft resumed, but only for another couple feet before ending at a sloped pile of fist-sized rocks. He smiled.

Interesting how the scrolls' hiding spots were so much more complex than this.

He inched forward, braced himself against the side walls, and carefully lowered his feet into the depression. Stepping around the mummy as much as he could, Matt made his way to the rubble on the other side, and began scooping the rocks back, dropping them on poor Mr. Whoever-this-was. Once he'd cleared a suitable path, he climbed up, and continued forward into the chamber ahead.

It was strange not knowing what to expect. A cursory check with a gloveless hand revealed that neither the floor nor walls contained useful imprints. All he knew was that this was where the stewards had hidden what they considered to be the true collection: the *tokens*.

And when he reached the widened chamber, peering down into another depression—this one of unknown depth due to being completely filled from wall to wall—he finally understood. It was the most obvious thing he couldn't believe hadn't occurred to him. And Patra, Philip, and Kaleb had all somehow manipulated their imprints to conceal this utterly pervasive aspect of their lives.

With his boots anchored to the tight shaft's wall and ceiling, one hand twisted backward to hold the ledge, he slid forward and bent over the chamber, hanging precariously above the thousands of strewn tokens. To fall into this quagmire probably wouldn't be as bad as his incident in that basement store room, especially with his body this covered up, but there was a whole lot of pointy and stabby down there.

Stretching … stretching … fingers grazing a peak of tokens …
Got you!

He curled three tokens into his fist, and edged his way back up into the shaft. A moment of breath, tokens secured in a breast pocket, and he began the painstaking journey backwards to the mummy.

Fatigue and dizziness borne of thin air almost convinced him he didn't need to replace the wall of rocks, but he forced himself on, finding every little pebble around, beneath, or on top of the mummy, whom he decided to dub "Jerky Face."

Over an hour later, Matt was finally outside in the cool, fresh air. With the dome vent replaced, he stole across the warehouse roofs to the access ladder, slid down to the ground, and followed his well-practiced path around the surveillance systems, to the isolated corner where he'd scaled the barbed wire fence.

His boots squished down into the strip of succulent groundcover.

A deep, cleansing breath.

Clear.

He brushed from his shirt the dust, cobwebs, and assorted debris, pocketed his gloves, and turned to head up the alley to his car.

"Hello, Steward."

The voice spoke just as Matt's eyes landed on the figure standing only six feet away. Matt startled and his hand reflexively shot to the tactical pen in his belt.

"A fitting tool for the modern Steward, no?"

Matt side-stepped out of the plants for better footing, and to turn the unexpected visitor toward the street light. The voice had been androgynous, the accent indistinct—like a mix of Mediterranean cultures, but using standard American English inflections.

The figure rotated as Matt turned, allowing the light to shine on them. Matt assumed this was a woman by the shape of the hips, and locations of fat deposits. She was only a few inches shorter than him, with a manly haircut vaguely parted to one side, wearing loose khaki slacks, and a baggy shirt that stretched over her neutral chest, round belly, and love handles. Her hands remained in her pockets, and she slouched like a chubby high school kid with low self-esteem. But as the shadows rescinded, her face came into sharp focus, revealing a tranquil, cherubic appearance. She had crow's feet and deep lines, but with big round eyes—pale green and all-seeing—and a latent smile's tiny curl on puckery lips.

"Quite visual," she said. "We're pleased to see you've recovered, Matthew. Displeased to see this fact littering the headlines."

"And who are you?" Matt finally said.

"Anzar. A Steward. May we invite you to tea?"

A Steward! A real-life, modern-day Patra.

"Like Supatra in title and mission," she said, "but certainly not in eminence. We're *particularly* interested in your direct experience with the Steward."

"You're a telepath."

"As are you. It's all in sensitivity and practice, isn't it? Each of us begins with the physical—object-aided is always most potent. And quite the blessing, that is. We couldn't imagine a childhood spent free of limitations."

"'We' ... 'all' ... There're more than one of you?" She nodded and took a step closer. So many questions filled Matt's head. And she could read it all, couldn't she? This was what it felt like to be around him. For nothing to be private. "How, in all my years, have I never found a single imprint from one of us until Patra?"

"For one, we're obviously an exceedingly rare breed, but also because we only imprint when we choose to. Come. Tea."

Anzar strolled on ahead toward the small, dilapidated house on the corner. It was the only residence in the industrial area. With the windows boarded up, Matt had thought it abandoned—condemned, just no one had gotten around to bulldozing it.

He had the three tokens in his pocket. She had to know he'd taken them. He dipped a finger into his breast pocket and extracted an ink-stained cane pen—one of the ancient scribes' writing tools. Every document ever written or copied at the Library—the imprints not only a visual preservation of a scroll, but also capturing the scribe's *intent*. With the thousands of pens and brushes in that chamber, no one need ever *interpret* an ancient document again.

Anzar stopped and glanced back at him. "Yes, your souvenirs. They'll need to be returned, of course ... but not right away." She smiled. "We use it like a library, too. Return a scribe, check out another ... But come, please. Tea. It's nearly four a.m. We'll discuss your ... *ambitious* ideas about the collection. And you'll share Steward Supatra with us."

Matt followed hesitantly, staring at the back of her head.
You have me at a disadvantage.

Not really, Matthew. Let us educate each other.

The Pharos, or Lighthouse of Alexandria
Engraved for the New Geographical Dictionary, 1790
(erroneously depicted with European architecture of the day)

Acknowledgements

Editing services provided by the extremely skilled and generous (of her time) Kristina Circelli from Red Road Editing. As always, these stories would be nothing without my growing list of amazing beta readers: Alyssa W, Angela P, Bill H, Bill R, DeeDee B, Donna R-J, Jennifer S, Jessica B, Joe S, Julie T-M, Karen L, Kristin D-H, Laura B, Laura F, Pascal B, Rachel B, Scott K, Stacey L, and Vicky W— thank you all! Master Scuba Instructor Scott Kehoe for his keen, expert consultancy for Chapter One; Josh Cook for paying attention; my patient, insightful, and patient wife, Ana, (intentional redundancy for patience em*pha*sis) for her ongoing and essential collaborative editing of all my books; and finally, my Ancient Near East consultant, Leah Laird, for sharing her vast knowledge, time, research, and creativity to make the Library and Patra's story as truthful to real history as fiction allows. I also thank everyone else who took the time to answer one or more of my silly questions over the past two years of this book's creation, and, of course, any poor soul who had to deal with me over said two years.

And to you, the readers, who, more than anyone else, have made my dreams of a writing career come true.

About the Author

Michael Siemsen came from Sothern California, moved to Northern California, and now lives at a keyboard. He enjoys his family, pets, travel, rewriting history, imagining the future, and he occasionally wears pants.

Connect with the author:
*facebook.com/mcsiemsen * michaelsiemsen.com*
*twitter: @michaelsiemsen * mail@michaelsiemsen.com*

ALSO BY MICHAEL SIEMSEN

MATT TURNER SERIES
The Dig (Book One)
The Opal (Book Two)
Matty (short)

A DEMON S STORY SERIES
A Warm Place to Call Home (Book One)
The Many Lives of Samuel Beauchamp (Book Two)
A Demon's Story Omnibus (Books 1-2)

Exigency

The Smiths (short)